Anti HERO

C.W. FARNSWORTH

The Kensingtons

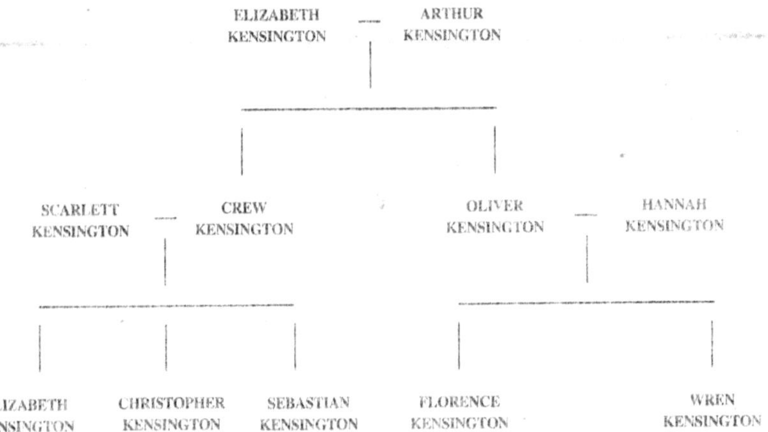

Playlist

Nothing's Gonna Hurt You Baby | Cigarettes After Sex
Old Money | Lana del Ray
Look After You | The Fray
Welcome To New York | Taylor Swift
American Money | BØRNS
Over | Honors
Dark Matter | Andrew Belle
I Dare You | The xx
Now & Then | Sjowgren
Mount Everest | Labrinth
Don't Take The Money | Bleachers
Pillowtalk | Zayn

CHAPTER 1

Kit

I don't have many problems.

My biggest one? She's standing forty feet away, wearing a silk dress that's either blue or gray. I've spent the past ten minutes deliberating which color the flawless fabric is, and I still haven't chosen one.

I'm not an indecisive person.

Except around Collins Tate.

I talk to—fine, flirt with—her; she rolls her eyes and walks away. I say nothing; she walks away. I'm trying to avoid the *walking away* part,

so my dilemma on how to act around her is obvious.

What is she doing here? Last I heard from Lili, her former college roommate was living in Chicago with a boyfriend. But my sister sniffed out my interest in Collins a long time ago, so she's stingy with details about her friend when she's annoyed with me about something. Since Lili's annoyed with me a lot, I haven't gotten an update in a while.

"Don't you think so, Christopher?"

"Mmhmm," I murmur, then swallow a sip of scotch so Joseph Thorne knows not to expect a more verbose response. Expensive alcohol soaks my tongue and burns a smoky trail down my throat, but I barely register the rich taste.

Who knows what I'm agreeing to? And I don't really care. This conversation doesn't matter. Joseph simply wants to be seen with me so he can brag we have a close association later.

My gaze returns to the redhead in the blue-gray dress. Collins's hair isn't really red though. It's more of an auburn—a warm brown, russet, or mahogany—that changes color depending on the light. Copper, in direct sunshine.

If I *ever* confessed I'd spent a single second contemplating the shade of her hair, I'm certain the woman in question would laugh in my face. Collins categorized me as Lili's irritating little brother the first time we met, and nothing I've done or said since to change that perception seems to have made any difference. Not for lack of effort either.

I drain the remains of my scotch and clap Thorne on the shoulder, cutting him off mid-sentence. "I need another round. Can I borrow some cash?"

Joseph blinks at me. His mouth is open, stuck on whatever he was in the middle of saying. Another slow blink. His eyes are flat brown, a similar shade to the ancient wood paneling the walls of the hotel ballroom.

"Oh, uh … um …" Thorne flounders for a few seconds before he glances around, hastily flagging down a waiter. Joseph sets his tumbler on the silver tray and digs through his pockets for his wallet. Very carefully, he slides out a crisp hundred.

I keep a polite smile fixed on my face for the entire excruciatingly long process.

"It's, er, I believe it's an open bar?" Sweat shimmers on Joseph's forehead as he tentatively offers the bill to me, the wealthiest person in the room.

"I know," I confirm cheerfully. "Nice talking to you."

Joseph blinks again, the motion reminding me of a sleepy owl, before I spin and stride toward the bar set up in the opposite corner of the ballroom. With a little luck, I'll be able to avoid him the rest of the night.

"Talk later, Chris!" Joseph calls before I'm out of earshot, shouting the last word the loudest. No doubt an attempt to advertise our false chumminess.

My fist clenches, crumpling the brand-new bill in my grip.

Joke's on him really. I *despise* being called Chris. Anyone who knows me at all is aware of that and calls me Kit instead.

"Macallan. Neat," I request from the bartender—the same floppy-haired guy who served me and Joseph earlier—stuffing the wrinkled hundred into the tip jar, which only contained a ten, when he turns away to pour my drink from one of the assorted bottles behind the makeshift bar.

"What'd you do to Thorne?" Flynn Parks—my best friend—appears beside me. He glances toward the spot where I left Joseph, amusement written across his face. "He looks more … confused than usual."

"I asked him for a favor."

"That'll do it. What the hell for?" Flynn questions.

I rest my elbow on the counter, narrowly missing a stack of cocktail napkins, so I can look to the left less obviously. "To play Robin Hood."

Flynn shakes his head once. "Thank fuck you came. I was worried this party might be dull."

"It *is* dull," I reply.

Flynn talked me into coming tonight because he wanted a final romp with a summer fling who worked at the reception desk here. Up until I spotted Collins, I was thoroughly regretting agreeing.

This isn't just the end of summer; it's my final weekend of freedom. On Monday, I start working at Kensington Consolidated. I'm the company's newest employee … and its future CEO. Not to be dramatic, but life as I know it—light on the responsibility and heavy on the fun—is about to be over.

"Your drink, sir."

I thank the bartender before he moves on to serve the blonde woman who appeared on my other side. She orders an Aperol spritz, then blatantly begins eye-fucking me.

I'm good at sex. I've slept with a lot of women, and every single one sang—screamed, more precisely—my praises. And lately, it's felt stale. Empty and predictable. We flirt. I buy her a drink. We flirt more. I say I'm not looking for anything serious, and she agrees. We fuck. She asks for my number. I reiterate I'm not looking for anything serious. The end. Happily never after.

And it's not because I don't believe in love.

It's because I *do*.

My elbow drops from the counter. "Did I see Perry?" I ask Flynn casually.

He sighs. "Shit. Yeah. I should say hi. Wanna come with? Make it bearably awkward?"

"You're needier than a girlfriend," I say, then push away from the bar.

Flynn snorts as we angle left, toward the high-top table where Perry is standing. They're scattered throughout the room so people have a spot to set drinks and eat the finger food being circulated.

"How the fuck would you know, Kensington?"

"I don't need to jump off the Empire State Building to know that Kensington Consolidated would have to look for a new protégé."

Not that they'd have to look very hard. Half the board would prefer my brother, Sebastian, anyway.

My best friend chuckles. "Don't let the ladies hear you comparing commitment to a death sentence, man. Might kill the mood."

"You have a lot to learn about women."

Some of them set their sights on me *because* I've never been in a serious relationship. They want to be the one who can claim to have changed me—tamed me. And I get plenty out of letting them try.

Flynn grins. "That's not what your sister said."

I snort. Most of my friends have hit on my sister at some point, but I've never interceded. I know the definition of *hypocrisy*. And now …

"Her duke could get you beheaded, Parks. Historically, they take punishment pretty seriously across the pond."

"She's really with that Marlborough guy?"

"I think so."

It's hard to tell what Lili is really thinking most of the time. She learned, same as me and Bash, that privacy isn't a privilege naturally extended to Kensingtons. It's a boundary line you have to patrol and protect. And when it comes to my sister's love life, I'm not in the habit of asking for details. But there's *something* going on between her and Charlie Marlborough. She asked for him, after her accident at the company's annual gala, looking so devastated that I would have told the Brit to fuck off, title or no title, if he hadn't appeared equally gutted. And Lili's supposed to be in Ireland for work, but she posted a photo in London yesterday. Charlie lives in England, and I doubt that's a coincidence.

"What's Perry doing here?" I ask as we continue crossing the room.

"He moved to New York," Flynn replies. "He clerked for a year after law school and is starting at a firm downtown next week."

"What firm?"

"Dunno. Ask him. He'll probably try to sign you as a client."

"I have a lawyer."

Lawyers actually. Public fascination with my family doesn't prevent people from trying to sue, extort, or blackmail us.

Perry spots us heading in his direction and waves.

I raise my glass in a silent cheers.

Flynn groans under his breath. "Don't you dare ditch me once we get over there! I hang out with your cousins."

"You *beg* me to hang out with Wren."

"No shit. She's—"

"Off-fucking-limits," I finish for him.

Flynn rolls his eyes. "Uh-huh. Good luck scaring off every dude in New York."

We reach Perry before I can reply.

I won't have to scare off anyone. Wren can take care of herself. But since she and Rory don't have a brother, I feel some responsibility to warn away anyone I know is bad news. Flynn might be a fantastic best friend, but he has as little experience with commitment as I do.

"Flynn!" Perry greets his cousin cheerfully. "Christopher!"

But I note how his knuckles have whitened around his glass. The contents are completely clear, suggesting he's drinking straight vodka or water. Based on our prior interactions, I'd bet heavily on the latter.

"Nice to see you, man." I set my tumbler down on a customized coaster and shake Perry's hand.

As soon as the pleasantries are complete, I glance around, tuning out Flynn's stilted small talk with his cousin. Flynn will probably grumble about my lack of support later, but his dislike of Perry has little to do with Perry himself. It's fueled by Flynn's resentment toward his dad's side of the family.

Really, I'm doing my best friend a favor, urging him to move past old grievances and form his own conclusions about his cousin.

Finally.

My jaw flexes as I focus on the opening that leads to the restrooms. I force the taut muscles to relax. Make my eyes wander rather than allowing them to remain fixed where they want to be.

As soon as I've completed a lazy perusal of the room, my attention snaps back to her. This time, she's looking back at me.

Collins considers changing direction when our gazes collide. I watch the urge flit across her face before determination replaces the initial impulse for avoidance.

That's my girl.

Well, not *my* girl. But my … something.

Anticipation accelerates my heart rate into an uneven staccato as her steps continue straight this way.

I don't have many problems.

But Collins Tate would be my favorite quandary even if I had hundreds to contend with.

There's no surprise on her face when she reaches the table—only resignation—which means she spotted me earlier and our lack of interaction so far was purposeful on her part.

"Sorry that took so long," Collins says, smiling apologetically at Perry. "There was a line."

"No problem. Your champagne didn't try to run off while you were gone." He grins at his own lame joke.

I glance at Flynn, who's wearing a reluctantly impressed look on his face. Perry is a decent-looking guy, I guess, but I've never seen him flirt with a woman before. I doubt Flynn has either.

My jaw tightens again. I'm entirely still, outwardly calm yet fully tensed. Like a sprinter poised on the block, waiting for the starting gun to fire off. My bloodstream hums with pure adrenaline.

"Hey. I'm Flynn."

I say nothing as Flynn introduces himself to Collins. They've met before—Lili invited Collins to my grandmother's famous Fourth of July party the year they graduated—but I'm unsurprised Flynn doesn't remember. I usually throw my own less stuffy party during my grandmother's annual bash that isn't conducive to a clear recollection of the holiday.

"Collins. Nice to meet you."

They shake hands right in front of me, but Flynn is the only one who glances my way afterward. He's waiting for me to introduce myself.

I'm waiting, too, but not for him.

Her dress is blue, I decide.

"Next time, use the restrooms by the spa," Flynn advises, filling the brief pause. "Not many people know about those. Local secret." He winks conspiratorially.

Flynn—like me—has been to many events here before. The Hamptons' most exclusive parties are held at this hotel or at Atlantic Crest Country Club.

"Good to know. Thanks." Collins picks up her champagne flute with long, delicate fingers.

I've never seen her play before, but I can picture her sitting at a piano so easily. Can practically hear the notes she'd press echo in my head.

Then, my thoughts swerve. I imagine those hands sliding off ivory keys. Running down my chest, fisting my cock. A sudden bolt of heat sizzles down my spine, which I attempt to douse with a long sip of scotch. The effect is more like tossing gasoline on smoldering embers since she's still intentionally ignoring me.

"Is this your first visit to the Hamptons?"

Flynn was the one who asked the question, but Collins looks at me, not him, as she answers, "No. I've been here before."

I hold her gaze, waiting. For a few seconds, it feels like the global population has dwindled down to two.

She swallows once before adding, "Hi, Kit."

Satisfaction swirls with adrenaline as I smirk at her. "Hey. Nice ball gown, Monty."

Collins purses her lips. She's never taken a single compliment I've given her as anything other than a veiled insult. Or maybe she's mad about the nickname. "Thank you. That suit *almost* makes you look like an adult."

My smile widens. "Perfect. I told my tailor tonight's dress code was *overgrown teenager.*"

The last time I saw Collins Tate was the same time Flynn did. A little over two years ago and approximately five miles from here, at my grandparents' Hamptons estate.

When Collins arrived at the party, I picked a stupid argument that ended with her calling me an overgrown teenager and stalking off. Not an inaccurate description or even an unwarranted one, but unpleasant, coming from the one woman I *really* wanted to view me as a man.

Unfortunately, I *do* revert to a teenager around her. Or worse. A juvenile, teasing a pretty girl on the playground because he doesn't know how else to hold her attention.

"How do you two know each other?" Flynn wonders, brow crinkling with obvious confusion.

Our social circles overlap so much that they're essentially the same sphere. Side effect of being best friends since you were in diapers.

"I'm friends with his *older* sister," Collins replies before I can.

The emphasis she places on *older* is impossible to miss. Also unnecessary. I only have one sister. But I'm unsurprised she chose that particular adjective. Collins loves acting like the eighteen months that separate our birthdays are an eon of maturity. To be fair, she's rarely seen me act like a responsible adult.

Most women find my nonchalance charming.

Flynn snaps his fingers, then exclaims, "Oh, that's *right*! You're the hot-dog girl!"

"I'm what?" Collins smiles indulgently, but the way her fingers pinch the stem of her champagne flute betrays her annoyance. The thin glass looks liable to snap, so anger might be more accurate.

I haven't forgotten the topic I argued with Collins about the last time we spoke, but I wish Flynn's alcohol amnesia had lasted longer.

"You're the girl who got into the argument with Kit about hot dogs," my best friend continues, grinning. "Pretty impressive actually. For Kensington's *many* faults, he's one hell of a debater."

"I appreciate the compliment." Collins is still smiling, and it's still her fake one. "But I don't remember that." She smooths her hair, even though there's not a single strand out of place.

Liar, sits ready at the tip of my tongue. I'm certain she remembers, and I'm equally positive we could stand here all night and she'd never admit it. *Stubborn* is the third word I'd use to describe her, right after *devastatingly gorgeous*.

I swish the amber contents in my glass, watching the scotch splash up the sides and drip back down. "Did windy Chicago blow you all the way back to the East Coast, Collins?"

"Something like that." She glances away after that vague reply to my raging curiosity, likely looking for an escape route from continued conversation with me.

Collins Tate is hell on a man's confidence. Good thing I've got plenty to spare.

"I didn't know you lived in Chicago!"

I basically forgot about Perry's presence, but he clearly hasn't forgotten about Collins's.

He's beaming at her as he adds, "I went to Northwestern for law school. *Great* city, Chicago."

Collins nods. "It is."

Her agreement is more matter-of-fact than containing any real conviction.

"And yet you're both in New York right now," I say. "So, Chicago must not be *that* great."

Collins glares.

I grin, holding eye contact as I slowly lift my glass to take another sip.

"Kit! How are you?"

I turn to see Fran, one of Lili's childhood friends, approaching. "Hey, Fran," I greet easily, giving her a quick hug.

Fran's like family. Lili has had the same core group of friends forever, so I grew up seeing some combination of them at every event my family attended. They're all part of the opulent, glittering world people are desperate to gain access to.

She squeezes my biceps. "Damn. Someone's been working out. I bet you look even better in a swimsuit than wearing a *suit*, suit. Now I'm extra mad I missed the Red, White, and Blue party this year."

I chuckle. "Yeah, you missed out."

"*Really* missed out," Flynn adds. "Kit outdid himself this year."

Multiple pairs of eyes are on me, but I can still feel the extra weight of hers.

Fran hugs Flynn, too, then glances at Collins. "Hi! You look *so* familiar. Have we met before?"

Collins nods. "A couple of years ago, I think. Lili invited me to her graduation party. We were at Yale together before she transferred to Columbia."

Fran nods enthusiastically. "That must be it! I'm Fran. Lili and I have been friends since …" She glances at me. "Since before you were born, I think?"

I shrug. "You're asking me if *I* remember my pre-existence?"

"Good point." Fran giggles before refocusing on Collins. "Anyway, it's nice to see you again."

"Nice to see you again," Collins echoes. She smiles, but it doesn't reach her eyes.

She's uncomfortable in this room. Collins didn't grow up in this world. She's not angling to join it either, which makes her presence tonight especially strange.

Fran introduces herself to Perry, then spins back toward me. "Tripp and Jasper are over here. Come say hi." She grabs my hand and tows me toward the center of the room, where more of Lili's friends are standing, without waiting for a response.

I let Fran pull me away from the table. Flynn can fend for himself. And it can't hurt to show Collins that *someone* finds my company enjoyable. The fact that it happens to be one of my *older* sister's friends is simply a bonus.

Collins Tate's opinion of me clearly hasn't changed in the two years since we last saw each other. Chances are high that it never will. I should probably grow the hell up and accept that. The two boyfriends of hers I've met were dull bores. Her type seems to be straitlaced guys who are earnest and unmemorable and agreeable.

Me? I'm more of an antihero.

CHAPTER 2
Collins

Murphy's Law should be renamed Collins's Law, I decide. Tonight, everything that could have gone wrong *has* gone wrong. The evening has been an utter failure from start to finish.

Each step forward exacerbates the painful blister forming on my pinkie toe.

Small talk with several well-connected guests resulted in zero job opportunities, so I'm facing an expensive trip back into the city with no income stream in sight.

The silk dress I splurged on to look like I belonged here is likely ruined. A blonde woman spilled her Aperol spritz on me, resulting in a sticky, noticeable stain just below my boobs. Blondie offered a haughty apology with a pointed undertone of *watch where you're going* before tottering away on her stilettos. *She* had run into *me*.

Me a year ago—me a month ago—would have demanded she pay for dry-cleaning. The red soles of her six-inch heels suggested she could afford it.

But the me tonight, exhausted with sore cheeks from fake smiling, simply took it as a sign to leave before another catastrophe struck.

And the damn cherry on top of a shitty sundae? I'm going to have to find a new neighborhood bar. The bartender at the one two blocks down from my Brooklyn apartment, where I went to see if they were hiring—spoiler alert: they're fully staffed—is who recommended I come to this event. She said Hamptons parties are filled with the bored, the well connected, and the wealthy. Just not the *hiring*, apparently.

"Monty! Monty!"

My shoulders stiffen when I instantly recognize his voice. I would know it was him even if he didn't insist on calling me by that absurd nickname.

I continue walking-slash-hobbling along. Kit Kensington is the last person I feel like facing right now. His presence here tops the list of tonight's calamities.

It's shocking he spotted my departure through his crowd of admirers.

Footfalls sound behind me, drawing closer.

"Go away, Chris," I say without turning around.

Kit *hates* being called Chris.

He doesn't call out again, so I think I've successfully escaped.

But then, as soon as I'm clear of the ballroom doors and inside the lobby, a warm hand closes around my upper arm and tugs me to the left.

Kit's calloused palm and fingers wrap around the entirety of my bicep. Rougher skin than I'd expect from someone born with billions in their bank account. He's never *had* to work for anything.

I whirl on him, more peeved than I've felt since … my last conversation with Kit probably. He possesses this infuriating ability to wriggle beneath my skin like a relentless splinter. Not painful, but annoying. Impossible to ignore.

Three separate conversations I struck up earlier were interrupted by someone realizing Kit was in attendance tonight, so I know he's not chasing me down because he has no one to talk to.

"Let go of me," I state when his hand doesn't drop.

In a humiliating turn of events, my voice wobbles on the last syllable. That crack—hysterical female incoming!—paired with the venom in my tone, would be enough to make most men take a step back.

Kit Kensington is not most men.

And he *is* a man, I acknowledge reluctantly. He's Lili's *little* brother, and I try to treat him like a kid, but he doesn't look like an overgrown teenager. He looks like a fantasy wearing a custom-tailored suit. And he doesn't sound like a boy either. His deep baritone is as attractive as the rest of him, compelling and commanding. Like crisp velvet.

Thanks to the heels pinching my toes, I'm directly at eye level with his shoulders. They didn't look so broad two years ago. Lili's friend was right about him being in impressive shape. Kit loves to sail and probably sails shirtless and—

Crap. I think I'm *possibly* checking him out.

"Why do you smell like—oh."

Kit's focused on the blemish on my dress, not the direction of my gaze, which is a relief. The stain is hard to miss—several inches wide and several shades darker than the fabric it splashed on. Next time I buy a gown that makes a sizable dent in my savings account, it'll be black. Classic *and* durable.

I yank my arm free from his grip since he still hasn't let go. "Goodbye, Kit."

He keeps pace with me easily—damn blister—as I hustle across the lobby toward the revolving door. "Where are you going?"

"Home," I reply curtly.

"Chicago?"

"No. I moved to New York a couple of weeks ago."

Instantly, I regret the hasty admission of details he doesn't need to know.

It never occurred to me that Kit might be here tonight, and knowing he was attending would have kept me from showing up. I haven't told Lili I'm in town. Asking Kit not to mention seeing me to his sister will only pique his misplaced interest.

He surprises me by not pressing for more of an explanation about my change of address. "You should rinse that stain before you go unless you want that dress ruined."

No shit, I think.

"Know a lot about women's clothing, do you?" I say.

"About removing it? Yeah."

I scoff and hobble faster.

Kit doesn't fall a single inch behind as he continues talking. "My mother designs clothes, Monty. And you know Lili. Despite my best efforts, I've absorbed some knowledge. Like that the longer a stain sits on fabric, especially *silk*, the harder it is to get out."

"What am I supposed to do?" I snap. "Go strip in the women's restroom? I don't have anything else to change into, and even if I did—"

I stop talking. Stare at the plastic rectangle Kit just pressed into my palm. His fingers curl around mine, closing my fist, and it feels like a pair of electric paddles were just pressed against my chest.

"I have a suite upstairs," he tells me, oblivious to the cardiac event I'm experiencing. "You can use it to clean up."

For the second time tonight, I pull away. Why does he keep touching me? Hasn't he heard of personal space?

"*Of course* you do," I drawl.

We're at the Hamptons' most exclusive hotel, located right on the shoreline, with enviable amenities. His parents and grandparents both own mansions nearby, yet he has a *suite* upstairs. Probably reserved for tonight's paramour.

Kit grins as he walks backward, not wasting any time returning to the ongoing party. "Top floor. Last door on the left. It's called the Seashore Suite, or something ridiculous like that. You're welcome."

One final smirk, and he disappears back into the ballroom.

I stand, conflicted for a few seconds. My dress is likely ruined regardless. But I'm not really in a rush to return to my apartment and submit more résumés.

I sigh, then start toward the elevator. Kit is probably busy with a socialite—or several—by now and will never know I accepted his help. I'll be long gone by the time he brings someone upstairs.

A silver-haired woman steps off when the shiny doors part. She spots the stain and gives me a sympathetic look. "I hope you packed an extra dress, dear."

"I did." The lie comes out as bright as the gleaming marble floor.

I'm sick of being pitied. The unanswered messages on my phone are mostly filled with sympathies. And most of that concern was fueled by guilt. Which shouldn't make *me* feel more pathetic, but it does.

When the elevator doors open again, I'm on the top floor. The hallway is even more luxurious than the lobby. A pristine white rug runs the length, so plush that I forget about my blister while walking. Each room has a nautical name.

The key card Kit handed me opens the door to the *Seaside* Suite with a soft click.

I kick my heels off as soon as I'm inside, breathing a sigh of relief when my soles sit flat on the floor again. My pinkie toe is bright red, but at least it's not bleeding. The last thing I need is to ruin my shoes too.

I toss my clutch on the neatly made king-size bed and continue into the attached bathroom. The cold tiles aren't as comforting against my sore feet as the carpet was.

Wrestling the zipper down my back takes a couple of minutes of contortions. Finally, my stained dress pools on the white-and-black hexagon in a silken heap, leaving me naked, aside from the tiny thong I wore to avoid panty lines.

As soon as I wet the stain on my dress under the tap, the damp spot spreads to cover most of the bodice. It also makes it impossible to tell whether the stain is still showing or not, although I'm guessing *still there* is the safer bet.

I huff a frustrated breath and drop the dress next to the sink with a wet slap, cursing tonight's events all over again. Then lean a hip against the counter, contemplating my next move.

A firm knock raps against the suite door while I'm still deliberating, followed by, "Collins?"

I snatch up my damp dress and clutch it to my chest like Kit might be able to see through the wooden door and around the corner into the bathroom. "What?" I call back.

"Can I come in?"

No, is my first instinct. It's embarrassing enough he knows I came up here. But this is technically *his* room, so I can't leave Kit standing out in the hallway.

"One sec," I shout, dropping my dress back on the counter. The whoosh of air raises goose bumps on my skin. Which is when I remember that I'm a scrap of lace away from being fully naked. I can't open the door like *this*, and putting my dripping dress back on isn't a great option.

The robe hanging on the back of the bathroom door solves my dilemma. Hastily, I pull it on, tempted to groan aloud when the luxurious fabric slides across my skin. It's *so* soft. Even comfier than the hallway carpet.

I knot the belt and stride over to the door. When I open it, Kit is leaning a shoulder against the doorframe. His tie's been loosened. His hair looks like a hand ran through it roughly and recently.

I wish I could say the slightly disheveled look made him a little less gorgeous.

Kit strolls past me without saying a word, invading my temporary refuge.

It's no longer relaxed and peaceful inside the suite. The quiet is charged. Vibrating with an invisible awareness that's not new, but *is* a lot more noticeable now that we're alone.

"Are you naked under that?" he asks without glancing my way.

I tighten the knot on the robe before shutting the door. "*No.*"

He doesn't argue, but I can hear him calling me a liar in his head.

I follow Kit into the bedroom silently, watching him shrug out of his suit jacket and toss it carelessly before strolling over toward the windows that overlook the ocean. He stares at the sea for a few seconds before yanking the linen curtains closed.

I clear my throat. "The party must still be going on."

"It is," Kit confirms, retracing his steps back to me. "I left my wallet up here."

I blurt the first thought that pops into my head. A snarky, "Trying to max out your credit card before midnight?"

I'm often irritated around Kit Kensington, and it messes with my normal filter for polite comments.

The left corner of his mouth lifts. "Monty, I could buy everything in this hotel tonight—*including* this hotel—and it wouldn't max out my credit card."

I scoff at his typical arrogance, even though I know he's technically right.

"If you *must* know my financial intentions, I wanted some cash to tip the servers." He plucks a leather wallet off the dresser and slips it into his pants pocket.

This is the *infuriating* thing about Kit.

Ninety-five percent of the time, he's ridiculous and reckless and self-serving. But then, when I think it's safe to always assume the worst about him, I get a glimpse of the remaining five percent. He told me Lili was the one who arranged a private car to drive me home after the Fourth of July party. Except, the following day, Lili texted me to make sure I'd made it home okay. I guess it was Kit's way of apologizing for the dumb hot-dog argument we had gotten into.

Most of the guests downstairs are incredibly wealthy. But when I ordered my champagne earlier, the bartender's tip jar was empty. I stuffed a ten in—the sad total of emergency cash shoved in my clutch.

I dislike Considerate Kit a lot more than Obnoxious Kit. Because I've never noticed how thick Obnoxious Kit's hair was or how blue his eyes were. Or when I have, the awareness was easier to ignore.

"What color was your dress?"

I blink rapidly at the sudden and random subject change. It's almost like he's … offering me an out for misjudging him rather than expecting an apology.

"Uh, it was called pewter."

"Damn it. I'd decided on blue."

What?

I frown. "Are you drunk?"

"No, but good idea." He walks over to the armoire that takes up most of the wall next to the mounted flat screen, rolling his sleeves up. "What do you want?"

"Solitude."

Kit cracks a grin as he crouches and opens the mini fridge. "You'd kick me out of my own hotel room?"

"No." I sigh. "I'm the one leaving."

Except … my only outfit is a soggy heap. Rinsing it was a mistake. I can't wear it anywhere now, and I can't walk through the lobby of this fancy hotel in one of its fluffy robes.

"C'mon, Collins." Kit is pulling out an assortment of bottles. "Have a drink with me. I don't bartend for just anyone."

"I'm not having sex with you," I state.

He shakes his head once. "If I had a dollar for every time you said that to me, I'd be rich."

"You *are* rich," I remind him.

He unscrews the lid off one of the bottles. "Never asked you to have sex with me, Collins."

"Ri-ght," I drawl. "I'm sure you only offer drinks to women in your hotel room who you *don't* want to sleep with."

"We both know I want to fuck you. Doesn't mean I expect it'll happen."

I want to fuck you. Those five words leap out in Technicolor, everything else remaining black and white.

I *did* know that.

So, I really resent the frisson of heat surging through me, as if that blunt confession contained new or interesting information. I blame the fact that we're alone and there's a bed in the room.

"Great. Glad we're on the same page," I say. "No sex and no drinks."

Kit splashes some alcohol into a glass. "I'll pay you five thousand dollars to have a drink with me."

I snort and head back into the bathroom. Obnoxious Kit is back.

"Tequila it is," Kit says cheerfully, like my departure was an enthusiastic agreement. A minute later, I hear, "Hi. Yes. I'd like some limes and salt delivered to the Seashore Suite, please."

He called the front desk for *limes and salt.* Unbelievable. Hopefully, they'll get lost, looking for the wrong room.

I start searching through the drawers beneath the sink for a hair dryer. This suite has everything else, so there must be one located somewhere.

"You'd really make me drink alone, Monty?"

I continue upending tiny bottles of shampoo. "There are two hundred people downstairs who would *love* to do tequila shots with you, Kit!"

"None of those two hundred people are *you*," he calls back.

I grind my molars.

That's Kit's allure. In the years I've known him, I've never seen him denied anything.

He's a lethal combination of rich and handsome and—fine—*charming* that people admire instead of resent. Rather than receive less because of all those advantages, he's handed more. He gets bored by it. So, since I'm the rare exception who *doesn't* seek out his approval, he's fixated on me as a personal challenge. Seeking the thrill of the chase.

A couple of minutes later, there's a knock on the door. I listen to Kit joke and laugh with the hotel employee delivering the drink ingredients, shaking my head the entire time.

If there's *one* thing I admire—maybe even envy—about Kit Kensington, it's his unerring ability to put people at ease. He makes friends effortlessly, anywhere he goes, whereas I have a small social circle that keeps shrinking.

Kit would be an excellent person to ask for assistance with employment. There's not a person who wouldn't fall over themselves to do him a favor. But I can't stomach asking for his help. I'd never hear the end of it, and who knows what he'd ask for in exchange?

"What the hell are you doing?"

I startle, nearly banging my head on the edge of the counter as my chin jerks up violently.

"Looking for the hair dryer," I say in as dignified of a tone as I can muster while crouched on tiles in a fluffy robe.

"Come do a shot with me, and then I'll help you look for it."

Kit disappears without waiting for a reply.

I sigh, stand, and leave the bathroom. I've searched everywhere else. The hair dryer must be in the armoire.

Kit grins wide when he realizes I followed. And unfortunately, it's the smile of his that I appreciate. The boyish, genuine one that appears when he's teasing Lili about her shoe obsession or calling his brother, Bash, a nerd for getting straight As. Not the slick billionaire smirk that's used as currency to receive whatever he wants.

He holds out a glass, containing an inch of liquid with a lime wedge perched on the salted rim. "Cheers."

"Cheers," I echo as I take it. "And … thanks."

I'm being ungrateful, I know. He didn't have to offer up his room or make me a drink. Beneath the shameless flirting and outlandish actions, he's a decent guy.

"Gratitude from Monty?" Kit claps his hand to his heart in mock shock. "Is the end of the world tomorrow or not until next week?"

A decent, often *annoying* guy.

I scoff and take a seat, cross-legged, on the edge of the mattress. It's the most comfortable surface my butt has ever touched. As soon as I can afford indulgences, I'll be buying whatever brand this bed is.

Kit settles next to me, lounging back on one palm and balancing his drink on his knee with the other. I'm uncomfortably aware of each inch separating us. Of how low that total number is.

Of how removed the world outside this room feels.

Of how *alone* we are.

He sips his drink, then asks, "Where's your boyfriend?"

"Chicago." I swallow a smoky sip too. "And he's not my boyfriend anymore."

I'm not sure why I admitted that to him. I should have just said, *None of your business.*

Kit was already an incorrigible playboy at sixteen. By the time he left Montgomery Hall after dropping Lili off with his family, every girl in the freshman dorm—excluding me—was in love with him.

Each time I've seen him since, he's hit on me, regardless of whether or not I was in a relationship. Meaning my single status doesn't really matter, I suppose, but it's definitely not going to *discourage* him.

"So, you're single?"

"Yes."

"Same."

I down more drink.

"Aren't you going to ask me why? Since I'm so attractive and charismatic and—"

"No, I get it. Women appreciate modesty, so you're immediately disqualified."

Kit chuckles. "What happened with your ex?"

I flip through possible replies. And for some reason, I settle on the truth. "He cheated on me. With my boss and with who knows how many others. All of his—who I thought were *our*—friends knew. So, he did the shitty thing, but I'm the one who wound up without a relationship, an apartment, or a job. All I got were a lot of pitying texts."

"What an asshole."

"Yep."

That might be the first thing Kit Kensington and I have ever agreed on.

"I knew you had terrible taste in guys," he tells me.

I scowl. "I do not."

"Yeah, you do. Exhibit A: your cheating ex. Exhibit B: you always turn me down. Exhibit C: that Remi idiot you brought to Lili's graduation party."

Remi *was* underwhelming, but I'm not going to inflate Kit's ego by agreeing with him again. I'm surprised he remembered Remi's name; Lili's graduation party was a couple of summers ago.

"This isn't a court of law. And one of those examples is not like the others."

Kit nods. "Exactly. *I'm* not an asshole or an idiot."

"You can be," I counter.

"Maybe I grew up, Monty."

At first, I thought Kit referred to me by my freshman dorm, Montgomery, because he'd forgotten my real name. But he persists on using it, even though he sometimes calls me Collins, simply shortening the moniker to Monty over the years. My younger sister, Jane, calls me Linny, but Kit's the only other person who's ever given me a nickname.

"Didn't seem like it earlier," I reply.

Rather than continue to boast about his personal growth, Kit asks, "What were you doing with Perry Parks?"

"A drug deal," I deadpan.

Kit raises one eyebrow.

I raise one right back. "You don't believe me?"

"Nope." He pops the *P*. "You're way too uptight to do drugs."

"Surprise, surprise. Look who's still an asshole."

"Telling the truth makes me an asshole?"

"Calling me *uptight* makes you an asshole."

"It's not an insult," he insists.

"Please, find me one person who considers uptight a *compliment*."

"I didn't say it was a compliment. Just that it wasn't an insult."

I down more tequila. "You should have been a lawyer."

"Like Perry?"

"What's your issue with Perry? I thought he was cousins with your buddy Flynn."

"I don't have an issue with him. I didn't know you knew him, is all."

"Well, isn't that what parties are for? Meeting people?"

I found out Perry was a lawyer during our conversation earlier. I worked as a paralegal in Chicago, so the legal field seemed like my best bet at a job in New York. But Perry's firm—like every other one I've attempted applying to—isn't hiring.

"Not when all the same people are at every party you go to."

I knew I wasn't imagining that everyone else seemed to know each other. Well, except for Perry. That's the other reason why I lingered at his table after our initial introduction.

"That's one thing I miss about college," Kit continues. "But there's a lot more I don't."

"Congrats on graduating." Something I should have said earlier.

"I saw your dad after the ceremony," Kit comments. "He was supposed to say hi to you."

I rub my finger along the glass's rim, brushing most of the salt off. "Oh. I haven't, uh, talked to my dad recently."

"Recently? Or since May?"

Another thing I dislike about Kit: he's perceptive.

I deflect. "Did he remember you?"

"Of course he did."

I shake my head at his arrogance. They talked for ten minutes six years ago.

"He was my professor for a couple of major requirements," Kit continues. "Inorganic Chemistry and Biochem."

"What?" I let out a startled laugh. "You *majored* in chemistry? *Why?*"

According to Lili, Kit is expected to succeed his uncle as CEO of Kensington Consolidated. A science degree is an odd choice for a corporate career.

"I *double majored* in chemistry and business because of that shocked look on your face," he replies.

"Surprising people can be fun," I concede.

My parents are both professors at Yale. My dad teaches chemistry, and my mom is part of the English department. I wanted nothing to do with either discipline, so I can appreciate choosing a contrarian path.

Kit shakes his head once. "Sort of sucks too. Usually means they didn't expect much."

I stare at him, unsure and a little contrite.

I've never hid my disdain for his partying or his playboy ways. And I was plenty disapproving during the memorable time he called Lili from a Monaco police station and I had to break out my high school French to talk to one of the officers. But why would my opinion matter to him?

I drop eye contact first, raising my glass and draining it. "Does this bar offer refills?"

Rather than replying, Kit takes my glass and walks over to the makeshift bar. I wasn't expecting him to serve me again.

I open my clutch and pull out my phone just to look busy. I have one new text from my sister.

JANE: *You're coming home for my bday, right?*

I gnaw on the inside of my cheek as I deliberate answering. Jane is about to start her senior year at Yale. Her birthday is next month, and she's expecting me to come home for the occasion. My mom asked the same question when we talked yesterday, and she clearly mentioned my vague *we'll see* to Jane.

"Here."

I toss my phone aside and accept the refill Kit's offering. "Thanks."

"Yep." A folded piece of paper drops onto my lap before he returns to his seat beside me. "That's for you too."

I frown as I unfold it. Stare, forehead frozen in a furrow, at a check for ten thousand dollars. It's an actual check, dated today. He *signed* it and everything. I could deposit this, and I'm certain it would clear.

I'm not envious of his money. But I do covet Kit's cavalier attitude. The luxury of acting first and worrying about consequences later. Of *never* worrying about consequences because money solves most problems.

I rip the check into tiny squares, then toss them in his face.

One lands in his drink. The rest scatter on the comforter like confetti.

Kit smiles as he fishes the shred out of his glass. That was the reaction he expected, I realize. I'm not sure how he knows me so well.

"You know what I like most about you, Collins?"

"My excellent aim?"

"You do what you want."

"Wow. *What* a compliment."

"It is," he insists. "Most people aren't that brave."

I'm a better actress than I realized. Because I haven't felt *brave* lately. I've felt like I was lying on a trampoline and life was jumping all over me.

"*You* do whatever you want," I say. "And that's *not* a compliment, by the way."

"I do, huh?" His tone is wry.

"Name one thing you want to do, but can't."

His reply is immediate. "Make you come."

My lips part, but no words leave my mouth.

I should have expected some variation of that answer.

Kit thrives acting on—and saying—the outrageous. He's pushy and obnoxious. Yet there's something oddly compelling about it. Like a reckless riptide that seizes control and sweeps you away.

I'm a strong swimmer, even though I avoid the ocean.

I drain the rest of my drink and use setting the glass down as an excuse to hide my flushed face for a few seconds. He might be a playboy billionaire and Lili's brother, but he also happens to be an extremely hot guy. Willpower has its limits.

"At least you're honest," I state. "My ex didn't have that self-awareness of his skills."

Kit's chuckle is dark and dangerous. Goading him wasn't my most brilliant idea.

"It has nothing to do with my *skills*, Collins, and everything to do with how you won't let me touch you."

"And if I did?"

His slick billionaire smirk appears. It might not be genuine, but it's damn effective. And it reeks of smug superiority that I can't help but want to challenge. "Then I could make you come in one minute."

One minute? I'm a chronic overthinker. *If* I come, it's never a quick process.

"I don't believe you," I say truthfully.

"Too bad there's no easy way to prove it."

The simple statement lands like a grenade. A challenge poised to explode.

He doesn't think I'll agree. I'm certain about that, the same way he predicted I'd rip up the check. And it's suddenly of the utmost importance that I surprise Kit Kensington. That I stand up on the trampoline.

"Then prove it."

I *do* surprise him. Startled blue eyes meet mine as my impulsive reply registers.

The worst, unlikely outcome? I enjoy an orgasm that doesn't involve a battery-operated toy for the first time in months. Best-case scenario? I get to wipe that cocky smirk off Kit's face before resuming my search for a hair dryer.

There's no smirk now. Kit's head tilts as he studies me, his expression surprisingly serious for a childish bet.

Butterflies riot in my stomach. Beneath the plush fabric of the robe, goose bumps rise on my skin, waiting for his reaction.

I've just given Kit permission to touch me. And if I had known saying those words would incite the most thrilling sensation I'd ever experienced, I would have done it years ago—or never dared to. I've never been addicted to anything, but I could become attached to this feeling. It's how I imagine skydiving would feel. Weightless and reckless and *oh shit, I already jumped, so there's no escape route.*

Kit bends forward to set his glass on the floor, then lounges back on his palms. "Straddle me."

A request he issues in the same tone you might request a refill. Rote.

He does this all the time, I remind myself. This is an ordinary evening for him.

I scoff to conceal my growing apprehension. "*Straddle you*? So, I'm going to do all the work? Why even bother—"

Kit's huff cuts me off. "Yeah, that's what I thought would happen. The hair dryer is—"

It's hard to say who's more shocked when I climb onto his lap—Kit or me.

I think it's Kit actually. Because *I've* always known that I harbored a secret fascination with him. That under the irritation, there was some giddiness associated with our interactions. That on the rare occasions I saw him on campus and he acknowledged me, it'd be the highlight of my day. He's fun to look at and talk to and be around. A presence impossible to ignore, so the contrarian in me always took some satisfaction in pretending to.

Right now, straddling his lap and staring at his stunned expression, I can't hide my reactions the way I'm accustomed to. Kit notices my rapid inhales. I'm breathing far too fast to make any claim of unaffected, the ragged rhythm filling my head with the scent of his cologne. Something woodsy and citrusy and intoxicating.

His hands land on my hips, their heat burning through the layer of luxurious robe, before moving to deftly untie the knot. The front gapes open, the brush of soft fabric against sensitized skin almost unbearable. I need it *off* all of a sudden, but Kit doesn't seem to be in any hurry. My breasts feel tight and heavy. My inner muscles clench tight with anticipation.

"Set a timer."

I blink rapidly, drugged by the exhilarating sensation of his fingers skimming over my skin. "Huh?"

The left corner of Kit's mouth lifts. "Set a timer, Monty. One minute, remember?"

I'm alarmed by how fast I forgot this was all part of a bet. By how badly I suddenly want to lose.

Wordlessly, I reach for my phone. Kit's thumb traces the hem of my thong while my shaky fingers fumble through setting a timer.

I flash him the screen as sixty seconds drop to fifty-nine.

At fifty-eight, the lacy barrier of my underwear loses all effectiveness. My phone falls to the mattress as I gasp loudly, my hands grasping the broad shoulders I was admiring earlier. He feels strong and capable and solid, and I suddenly wish I weren't the only one losing clothes. That I could see him naked too.

His thumb is circling my clit now, heat gathering deep in my pelvis as nerve endings spark alive in response to his touch. Forget the paddles to my heart. This feels like a constant flow of electricity. I'm embarrassed by how slick I am, but it's rapidly replaced by satisfaction when he fills me with two fingers. And still, I want—*need*—more.

The pleasure escalates, but I'm still racing toward the peak at the same speed. He's doing all the work, yet my body wants to participate. Is desperate to chase the high even if the destination is inevitable.

Nothing's ever felt *this* inevitable. Maybe that's why I keep choosing wrong.

My eyes flutter closed, and I bite my bottom lip hard, silencing the moan that's struggling to escape.

The thumb of the hand that's not busy making my thighs tremble tugs my lip free.

My eyes fly open, meeting his intense gaze. Kit's eyes are a fathomless, focused blue. The same shade as the hottest point of a flame.

"None of that, Monty. I want to hear how much you love having my hands on you. *In* you."

He sounds *so* arrogant.

I wait for the familiar urge to argue, but it never appears. I'm finished fighting him. In response, I bear down on his fingers as hard as I can.

"You're so fucking wet," Kit continues conversationally. "Already dripping for me. Have you been sitting here with dirty thoughts in that pretty head? Because mine are filthy around you. Earlier, when you went to the restroom, I thought about following you. About locking the door and pulling that *pewter* dress up and fucking you while you held the sink. You came so hard, and you screamed my name. Are you going to scream my name, Monty?"

I don't know what to focus on—where he's touching me or what he's saying. It all swirls around me like a maelstrom of pleasure, building and colliding and enveloping me entirely.

I don't *scream* his name when I come, but I do say it really loud.

My curled toes and numb fingers are still tingling with the aftershocks of pleasure when my phone alarm goes off a few seconds later.

And I breathe out the one word I swore I'd never say to Kit Kensington.

"More."

CHAPTER 3
Kit

From the fifty-fifth floor, New York looks tiny.

Well, on the street below—the people walking, the yellow cabs honking, the pigeons flocking—*they* all appear miniature from this distance. Nothing else appears small. The skyscraper that houses Kensington Consolidated's corporate headquarters is surrounded by buildings of similar heights, the backdrop an endless stretch of bright blue, dotted with fluffy blobs of white. Castles in the clouds, surrounded by sentries.

Morning sunlight reflects off the windows opposite mine, making me squint. My grip tightens on the mug I'm holding, the ceramic burning my palm while my retinas are seared by the brightness.

There's a soft *snick* as the door to my office opens.

I turn, expecting Indy. Asher's assistant has been helping me until I hire my own.

Instead, my sister waltzes in. Her heels click against the hardwood as she lifts her phone in my direction.

I'm positive she's taking photos.

"You look so grown up!" Lili props a hand on her hip as she surveys me. She's wearing a colorful sundress that stands out amid the dark, muted shades decorating my office and a smirk that suggests she's here to make fun of me.

"Lili," I grind out between gritted teeth, "you can't just barge in. I could have had a meeting happening in here."

She waves away the possibility with a flick of her wrist, then walks over to the towering bookcase to run a finger along the leather spines. "You *didn't* though. Where's your assistant? It was either 'barge in' or stand out in the hallway."

I walk over to my desk and set my steaming coffee cup on the coaster next to the keyboard. "*Knocking* was a third option."

Lili flings her Birkin onto one of the armchairs facing my desk, then dramatically sprawls in the other.

Great. She's staying.

"Why don't you have an assistant?" Lili asks, twirling the end of her ponytail around one finger.

"I haven't gotten around to it yet." My eyes flick toward the stack of résumés piled at the far end of my desk, right next to the earning statements I'm supposed to review in advance of the board's monthly meeting.

A personal assistant—just like a corner office on the executive floor—is a luxury I inherited. I might have been born with the pedigree to be a big deal in the business world, but a few months ago, I was attending frat parties and playing pranks on my housemates. I feel like a fraud. A kid playing at being important.

Plus, I've been so busy that I literally haven't had *time* to look at the résumés.

I take a sip of my Americano, then glance at my email. The number of unread messages has doubled since I arrived at the office an hour ago, suggesting it's going to be another long day and late night.

My attention refocuses on my sister. "How was London?"

Lili half smiles. "You mean Dublin?"

"Nope." I pop the *P* for dramatic effect. "I meant *London*."

She rolls her eyes but is still smiling. And it's not the snarky one I'm used to seeing. It's softer. A tiny bit tentative even. "Fine, yeah. It was a good trip."

"Good? So, I don't need to show up at his house and kick his ass?"

"House?" Lili laughs. "It's really more of a castle. And, no, you don't. I'd be pissed if you did actually."

"Are you"—I grimace—"dating him?"

I can't believe she's making me dig for details like a tabloid reporter.

My sister taps her chin. "You're *such* a gossip, Kit."

"I'm simply curious how you decided he wasn't too *pretentious* for you."

Lili yanks a Post-it Note off my desk, crunches it into a neon ball, and tosses it my way. It lands three feet to my left.

I grin. "You missed."

She huffs. "I was wrong about Charlie. And I *am* dating him, and he's coming to visit before I leave for Dublin. Grandpa wants to meet him properly, so he's hosting a dinner. I'll send you the details."

The smile promptly slides off my face.

Lili has a warm—loving—relationship with our father's father. I don't. Neither does Bash. I don't know if it's because Lili's the oldest or a girl, but Grandfather coddles her and mostly ignores us.

Arthur Kensington has a ruthless reputation. He's a hard man to read and an even harder person to please. I consider any conversation we have that doesn't include a chastisement of my behavior to be a smashing success. I haven't seen him since I started working at the company he used to helm, and it's a meeting I'd like to put off for as long as possible.

"I could meet you guys for drinks *after* the dinner," I suggest.

Lili shakes her head, then sticks out her bottom lip. "*Please*, Kit. This is important to me. I need you to be there."

Poor duke didn't stand a chance. Lili's accustomed to getting her way, and acquiescing is always the easiest outcome.

Even if I hold my ground against Lili, it'll escalate to our parents. Mom will highlight the importance of family time, and Dad will chide me for not supporting my sister.

I fold under the force of Lili's pleading gaze, rationalizing it'll save me more of a headache later. At least our grandfather has the same appreciation when it comes to expensive scotch. A few glasses always take the edge off any criticism.

"Fine. I will be there."

She beams. "Great. Now that that's settled, we can focus on you."

"Me?" I say blankly.

"Yeah. How is—oh, this is a better angle." Lili's phone appears again. This time, she's close enough that I can hear the distinctive *click* that tells me she's *definitely* taking photos. She fiddles with the settings for a few seconds, and then a flash goes off, temporarily blinding me.

I cross my arms and scowl at my sister. "Seriously?"

"I promised Bash I'd send some pics of you 'working.' "

"I *am* working," I state, ignoring the air quotes she used.

"It's fun, annoying you. Plus, we're worried."

I'm shaking my head, focused on the first sentence, so the second one takes an extra second to sink in. "Wait, what? Worried? Why?"

Lili lowers her phone and leans forward. "Do you want to work here?"

"I *do* work here," I reply, stating the obvious again.

"I know. But do you *want* to?"

I sigh, realizing where she's headed with this.

"It's a simple question, Kit."

"It's a complicated answer, Lili."

She sinks back in the chair with a matching, knowing sigh. "Yeah, I know."

We each have plenty of friends who grew up with wealth. But being a *Kensington* is more than money. It's expectations and intrigue and legacy.

I never questioned if this job was the right fit because it was always more than a career. It's my name. My family. Parts of myself I can't extricate from the whole. And I'm determined to not just *be* here. To *succeed* here, even if it's been hard to summon much enthusiasm about the inevitable. Walking into this building on Monday, pretending not to see the stares or hear the whispers, wasn't my *made it* moment. I still need to earn that. Getting this job might not have been an accomplishment, but I'm going to *accomplish* while doing it.

"It's an adjustment period," I say. "I'll figure things out."

"Ah, yes. This"—Lili waves an arm around my large office—"must be a change from your former career, doing whatever the fuck you wanted."

I roll my eyes. "Speaking of hard work, there must be a shoe store nearby. You only have a million pairs. Better get shopping so you can fill up Charlie's castle."

She tries to glare, but her twitching lips ruin the full effect. "Fine. I am late to meet Bridget and Fran. But before I go, I need a favor."

"No," I say immediately.

Lili manipulates her mouth into an exaggerated pout. "You haven't even heard what it is yet."

"I *already* did you a favor. I'm going to the damn dinner, okay? Whatever it is, figure it out your—"

"It has to do with Collins …" she lilts, cutting me off.

I reach for my coffee, buying a few seconds of response time as I swallow a large sip, scalding my tongue. Lili tracks the movement, and I worry I'm acting *too* nonchalant.

"What does?" I ask.

"Well, you remember Collins. She was my—"

My eyes narrow. She's messing with me.

"I remember," I clip.

"I had dinner with her last night."

My knee bounces beneath my desk.

"She moved to New York a few weeks ago. And she's looking for a job, so I said I'd check here. But now that I know you need an assistant … hire her!"

I stiffen with shock, but Lili doesn't appear to notice. She's busy spouting more information I already know—Collins is smart and talented, and I'd be lucky to have her.

Monty said she left her job in Chicago, I recall, but I was too distracted by the high of having her in my hotel room to think through what that meant. To ask if she'd found a new job.

Collins is proud. If she admitted to Lili she's unemployed, she must be struggling to find a job. Must need money.

And I handed her a check for having a drink with me like a total dick. Also bragged about my high credit card limit, if I'm recalling correctly.

"Kit!"

I refocus on Lili. "What? I'm listening."

"No, you're not. Plan out where you're partying this weekend after I leave. I thought *Collins* would keep your attention. You used to have the biggest crush on her. Although, if she's working for you, you'd have to treat her like any employee." She wags a finger at me like I'm one of Dad and Mom's misbehaving beagles. "*No* flirting. Keep it professional."

I don't ask my sister how *professional* me fucking Collins in a hotel room was. I just gulp down more coffee, barely feeling the burn as the hot liquid scorches my throat.

"So? You'll hire her?" Lili presses.

I've never appreciated her persistence, but I'm especially resentful of it right now.

Monty didn't tell Lili we'd slept together last weekend. I'm certain, and I'm not surprised.

When I woke up in the Seashore Suite on Sunday morning, the other side of the bed was empty, the robe was hanging on the back of the door, and the dress was gone. The only evidence that the entire evening wasn't a vivid dream was the second used glass and the ripped remnants of a check mixed with the condom wrappers on the floor.

It happened, but I doubt it will happen again. Collins was using me as a distraction from the mess she'd left behind in Chicago. And, I'm realizing, from the stress of job-searching.

"She won't want to work here, Lili," I state.

Wouldn't have wanted to *before* Saturday night, and I'm positive my ability to make her orgasm in less than a minute isn't going to esteem me as an employer in Collins's opinion.

"That's not what she told me."

My eyebrows rise, betraying my surprise. There's an accompanying pang of concern. Collins must be near desperate, then, and she didn't say a damn word to me. I could have gotten her a job—*not here*—anywhere in this city in a matter of minutes.

"You won't find a better assistant in there." Lili gives the stack of résumés on my desk a dismissive glance.

"I wasn't questioning her qualifications."

My sister perks up, sensing victory. "Meaning the job is hers?"

"If she wants it."

She won't.

CHAPTER 4
Collins

I flop back down on my mattress in a sprawled, starfish position. It's lumpy in two spots, but I'm too tired and hungover to care.

On the way home from yesterday's interview, I celebrated possible employment by picking up sushi and buying a cheap bottle of wine. One—or both—disagreed with my stomach. I vomited twice overnight and still feel nauseous.

My phone begins buzzing on the wooden wine crate I found for free at a liquor store in Dumbo and repurposed as my bedside table. I groan, strongly consider not answering, then lift my head just high

enough to read who's calling.

It's Lili.

We met up for dinner a couple of nights ago. I'd texted her on Monday, finally letting her know I was in New York. It turned out, she was in London—something Kit had *not* mentioned for some reason—but about to return home. We'd made plans to get together once she was back in the city. During our dinner, I copped to my current unemployment, so I texted her on my way home yesterday, letting her know my interview went well. She's probably calling for more details.

I grab my phone, roll over in bed, and answer. "Hey," I rasp.

"Hi!" Unlike mine, Lili's voice is cheery and clear. "Fun night?"

"Not exactly." I rub at my gritty eyes with my free hand. "I think I have food poisoning."

"Oh no!" Her bright tone instantly transforms to sympathetic. "Do you need anything?"

"I'm good. Thanks. Starting to feel a little better."

"Well, this should cheer you up even more—you're employed!"

"Wait, what? It was just an interview, Lili, not—"

She laughs. "I know. I'm talking about another job—at Kensington Consolidated. You start on Monday! Assuming you're feeling up to it, of course. If you're still sick, I'm sure you can start a few days later."

When Lili found out I was job-hunting, she said she'd check if her family's company was hiring. I didn't dissuade her. Because it seemed rude to turn down her help and because I was in no position to. But I figured she'd pass along an email address for me to send my résumé to, not get me hired in under forty-eight hours.

"*Wow.* Uh, Monday? That's ... soon."

"I know. I know. But Kit really needs an assistant immediately."

My brain zooms in on the second three-letter word at a speed that results in immediate motion sickness. And that wreaks havoc on my unsettled stomach.

It feels like the lumpy mattress beneath me has been replaced by sand. Like I'm sinking slowly with nothing to grasp on to except for grains.

"The job is with Kit?" My voice sounds tinny, like I'm hearing it echo through a distant speaker.

"Yes, as his personal assistant. Between that and his fancy corner office, his ego will barely fit in the building soon." Lili giggles. "I know it's not your dream job, but it'll open up other opportunities. My uncle is always complaining about how other companies love poaching from Kensington Consolidated. Stick it out for a year or even just six months, and you'll have your pick of working at tons of places. And it pays well."

I swallow hard, still stuck on that one word. "Lili, I *really* appreciate you setting this up and the opportunity, but I'm just not sure if … you know, Kit and I have never … I'm not sure me working for him is the best idea."

"I talked to Kit," she replies. "He's good with it. And he's taking his job seriously. He's grown up. I know his little crush on you was annoying, but he's totally over it."

I don't even know where to begin processing that response.

Lili talked to Kit about *me*?

He's "good with" me *working* for him?

And he's *over* his crush on me?

Maybe he is. Maybe one night together was all it took. I'm no longer a challenge; I'm a successful conquest. He's probably had dozens of one-night stands. Maybe even hundreds. They must all blur together into one big orgy at some point.

But I can't work for *Kit Kensington*. It would have been a recipe for disaster before we had sex. Now? It's unthinkable.

Except … Kit doesn't seem to think so.

He's one of the few people I've seen successfully tell Lili no. Lili doesn't work at Kensington Consolidated. She has no say in their hiring. Kit approved this—either because he doesn't care if I work for him or because he doesn't think I will accept the offer.

It took me three weeks to get an interview anywhere. And that interview was no guarantee of an actual offer, like I just reminded Lili.

Kensington Consolidated doesn't have a single New York opening listed on their website. I checked when I first moved and was compiling a list of places to apply to. I doubt I could get an interview there on my own. But connections are how the real world works, right? And I could really use a win right now. Lili's right; it can be a temporary stepping stone.

I know *I* can be professional.

And Kit's the future face of the company. For all his faults, I can't picture him risking his reputation to flirt with a woman he's already fucked. Maybe it's for the *best* that we slept together. Maybe it defused the strange awareness that'd always existed when we were in the same space. Most likely, I haven't crossed his mind since Saturday night. My pride has already cost me plenty. This is Lili, my friend, doing me a favor. Not Kit.

"Collins? You still there?"

I suck in a deep breath and send up a silent prayer this won't be another wrong choice. "Okay," I agree. "I'll take the job. Thanks."

There's a brief burst of relief. The weight of failure lightens a little because I'll at least have a regular paycheck to rely on again.

And it's almost enough to bury the apprehension about facing Kit in a few days.

Almost.

CHAPTER 5
Kit

"For the sake of my dick, you need to get up."

I don't so much as blink, unfazed and noncompliant. "You're going to have to clarify what *you* getting laid has to do with *my* location, Parks," I tell my half-full glass.

Flynn sighs dramatically. "We've been friends for long enough that people see me in Proof and expect you to be here too. And if you're hiding in a back-corner booth, for example, women ask me *why* you're hiding in a back-corner booth instead of asking me to take them home. See the issue now?"

"Yep. Your game is pitiful, and you're looking for a scapegoat. Keep searching because I'm staying put."

Another heavy exhale from my best friend. "Worth a try," Flynn grumbles, then snags the complimentary champagne that was starting to swim in the ice bucket and takes a swig straight from the bottle. "What's wrong?"

"Nothing's wrong. I'm just tired. Exhausted actually." I drag a palm down my face. "Long fucking week."

It's past midnight on a Friday night. So technically Saturday. Prime partying hour. I'm sitting in the VIP section of one of Manhattan's most exclusive clubs. And all I can think about is how badly I'd rather be in bed, fast asleep. How being home suddenly seems like a luxury after a week of meetings and conference calls and presentations and pitches.

"It'll get easier, man," Flynn tells me. "Your new assistant is starting on Monday, right?"

"Right." The reminder results in me swallowing the rest of my scotch.

When Flynn stopped by the office earlier to talk me into coming here, someone from IT was setting up a new computer at the desk outside my office. At the desk that now belongs to Collins.

I already knew she'd accepted the offer—Lili texted to tell me what she termed "amazing news." And as her direct supervisor, I was cc'd on the emails human resources sent her about direct deposit and health insurance and 401(k) contributions.

But it didn't feel real until I left the building earlier and realized she'd be there the next time I walked in.

I can't believe she took the job.

I can't believe the first time I'm going to see Collins since being inside of her is as my fucking *assistant*.

A former relationship—if you could even call a one-night stand that—with a current employee isn't a violation of any company policies. I checked. But it's certainly not encouraged. Hiring a woman you've fucked is a poor professional decision by any standard.

It wasn't just my decision though. Collins knows our history as well as I do, and she *chose* to take the job.

She'd also snuck out while I was sleeping.

For as long as I've known Collins, she's controlled the narrative between us. I've been the one begging for her attention. She's been the one who walks away.

Last week, that shifted. *She* begged. *She* stayed.

And it's about to change again. We were finally on equal footing, and now I'm technically her superior. Her *boss*.

"At least your family thinks you're capable of responsibility," Flynn tells me. He swallows more champagne, then adds, "Not sure *why*, but they clearly do."

I muster a smile, appreciating his attempt to cheer me up.

Our entire lives, Flynn and I have been on symmetrical paths. That's just changed. He's studying for the LSATs and then will possibly attend law school, depending on when—or if—he decides to defy his father. My dad respected my decision to not go to business school after graduating undergrad *and* stopped by my office on Monday to tell me how proud he was.

I feel shitty, complaining about my supportive parents and important job, but at least Flynn doesn't have to worry about disappointing everyone.

"I'm grabbing another drink," I tell Flynn.

He whoops as I stand. "Attaboy!"

Everyone in a fifty-foot radius glances in this direction as I start walking. There's a private bar located in the VIP section, but I head toward the main one instead. I *was* hiding, and it didn't help. Might as well search out a distraction. This club is crawling with people who want my attention. Who expect me to be entertaining and exciting and *fun*. I spent a large portion of the summer as Proof's main attraction, making the most of my dwindling days of limited responsibility. The whispers and stares around me make me feel like a celebrity. They set the stage for the part I'm supposed to play.

Tonight, I'm too distracted to fully register the attention, much less appreciate it.

I could still call this off. As persistent as she is, Lili doesn't have any *actual* power at the company. No matter how much she protests and complains, she can't pick my assistant for me. Not unless I let her.

But … I can't do that to Collins. She had a choice, too, and she decided to take the job.

I prop my elbow on the edge of the bar top and drag a palm down my face, releasing a frustrated groan that gets lost in the steady bass pumping through invisible speakers.

As soon as the nearest bartender spots me, he hurries over.

Lili and I have been coming to Proof since high school. Surprisingly, I don't think Bash has ever stepped foot inside this bar. He's always been the most measured of the three of us. Part of it's his personality. Also, after he spent years of watching Lili and me push boundaries, I guess him doing the same lost some appeal.

"What can I get for you, Kit?" the bartender asks.

"Tequila soda, Scott."

He nods and bustles down the bar to make my drink.

"Tequila, huh? Must have been a long week."

I glance to my left, toward the voice. And then down when I realize it belongs to a woman whose head is level with my shoulder. Standing, not perched on one of the stools.

"Never-ending," I answer.

She smiles. "I'm more of a gin-and-tonic girl under stressful circumstances."

My eyes dart to her drink. "Gin and tonic?"

"Ding, ding, ding!" She pairs the sound effects with a series of ridiculous hand gestures, and I can't help but grin in response.

"What are the stressful circumstances?" I wonder.

She shrugs a shoulder. "I just moved here. I'm searching for a job, a reasonably priced coffee shop, and a guy who doesn't consider talking about the stock market scintillating conversation."

I'm still grinning when Scott delivers my drink and asks if I'd like anything else. I shake my head and thank him, swallowing a long sip of the smoky, fizzy drink.

"I'm Cleo, by the way," the woman tells me.

"Christopher," I reply automatically.

Which is strange because I usually introduce myself to women as Kit.

"What are your thoughts on the stock market, Christopher?" Cleo asks cheekily.

"Good reminder. I haven't checked my returns in at least twenty minutes." I pull my phone out.

Cleo sighs heavily. "Damn, you're funny. But you still haven't looked lower than my shoulder. So, you're either gay or taken, right?"

"Or I don't want to strain my neck."

She reaches for her gin and tonic. "Funny *and* tall. For the sake of my ego, can we pretend you're gay?"

I chuckle. "Sure."

"It was nice to meet you, Christopher," she says, grabbing her drink and spinning around.

"You too," I call after her.

It's not until Cleo's walking away that it occurs to me that I never considered hooking up with her. That I introduced myself by my full name because I figured I'd never see her again.

She was pretty. Clearly interested. And the thought of having sex with her didn't cross my mind when she introduced herself. I try to picture what Cleo looked like, and Collins scowling at me in a blue-gray dress is the image that I conjure instead. Followed by a rapid succession of memories of what she looked like with that dress *off*. My formerly flaccid dick twitches.

That bodes fucking poorly for Monday.

Lili and her damn meddling. If she hadn't interfered with my assistant search, I'd have been free to remind Collins what a night in my bed was like the next time we saw each other.

I scowl at the floor before swallowing more of my drink. When Collins accepted the job offer, she rejected any possibility of us hooking up again. Everyone in the building already thinks I only got to where I am because of my last name. A fling with my assistant would sustain the office gossip mill for months. Would disappoint my entire family. Would erase any respect I've earned.

I was worried we wouldn't happen again.

The reality that we won't leaves a bitter aftertaste I wash away with the remainder of my cocktail. I should have ordered scotch. I don't drink tequila very often, and I'm not sure why I ordered it tonight. Maybe some subconscious attempt to erase any special association with the alcohol following last weekend.

I text Camden, my driver, letting him know I'm leaving. Then Flynn, reminding him to close out the tab before he heads home. My phone begins buzzing as soon as I slide it back into my pocket, probably with Flynn's protests. This is the earliest I've left a club in … ever. And one of the rare times I've departed solo.

Maybe I *am* growing up.

Several people recognize me and call out to me as I stride toward the exit, but my steps don't slow. It's loud enough in here that I can pretend I don't hear them. I don't feel like talking, and it turns out my dick is only interested in the one woman who's completely off-limits.

Camden is waiting outside, as efficient as always. I ignore the commotion from the hopefuls in line to enter Proof and climb straight into the back seat, relaxing against the plush seat and covering a yawn.

"Where to, Mr. Kensington?" Camden asks.

"Home, please."

"Yes, sir."

I stare out the window mindlessly as the car travels uptown. City lights flash past, the soundtrack of honks and sirens fading into background noise. It rained sometime recently because drops of water blur the glass.

I yawn again. Fuck, I'm tired. And drunk. It's a good thing I never asked Lili for Collins's number or else I'd probably be using it right now.

Camden pulls into the underground garage beneath my building twenty minutes later. Before climbing out of the car, I instruct him to take the weekend off. If I decide to go out, I'll drive myself.

Three attempts are required to correctly punch in the code for the elevator, thanks to my bleary eyes and the alcohol swimming in my bloodstream. I yawn for a third time as I wait for the doors to open.

When they finally do, the elevator is empty, which is a relief.

My penthouse, however, is *not* empty. I hear the voices and rock music as soon as I exit the elevator and approach the door.

I curse Bash under my breath as I fish my keys out of my pocket and fit one into the lock. He got home from an Alaskan fishing trip last week, and he's supposed to be packing before leaving tomorrow. His fall term at Dartmouth starts on Monday.

I kick my shoes off in the entryway and head straight into the kitchen, avoiding the commotion coming from the living room. I should drink some water. And the steak Flynn and I had for dinner feels like a lifetime ago.

"You're home early."

I glance over one shoulder to see Bash approaching. He's balancing two pizza boxes that he drops on the marble counter in a clatter of cardboard.

"Yeah." I grab a water, shut the door, and flip the lid of a box open. It's empty. So's the second one.

"We can order another pizza," my brother offers.

"Nah, it's fine." I uncap the water and guzzle most of it down. "What time are you leaving tomorrow?"

"Dunno yet. Mom and Dad are coming over at noon."

"Okay." I scrub a palm along my stubbled jaw. "I'm headed to bed."

"Seriously? It's not even one."

"Seriously. I'm exhausted."

"From work?" Bash asks dubiously.

"Among other things. Thanks a fuck ton for making me Lili's photography project, by the way. I think I have permanent vision damage."

"I don't see how that's possible. Your eyes were closed, and you were scowling in every single one."

I shake my head and finish off my water.

"I didn't ask Lili to take photos, for the record. Just to send me the ones she took. She sent them to Mom and Dad too. Mom might use one on this year's Christmas card."

"Wonderful," I drawl.

"I *did* suggest she check on you though. You've barely been home this week. I was worried."

"I'm good," I assure him. "I've just been busy."

Bash nods. Glances at the stove, rubbing the back of his neck. "How-how is it? Really?"

He's not just asking as a concerned brother. He's asking because his last name is Kensington too.

I blow out a long breath and admit, "I love it."

Bash's startled eyes meet mine. "What?"

"I love it," I repeat. "I thought I'd be bored or basically just a figurehead. But it's exciting. Interesting. Exhausting, yeah, but in a good way."

"So, you think I should …"

"Enjoy the rest of college," I finish. "And then decide if you want to challenge me for CEO."

Bash smirks. *Competitive* might as well be a synonym for Kensington. But I know my brother well enough to see the relief in his expression too.

Lili picked a different path. He—like me—was waiting to see what the expected one was like.

"Yeah, sounds good," he tells me.

I yawn yet again and decide I'm too tired to hunt for food. I just want sleep. "I'll see you tomorrow. Make sure you're packed."

"We'll turn down the music," Bash calls after me as I head down the hallway.

CHAPTER 6
Collins

I'm concerned I'm going to throw up. Not because my stomach hasn't fully recovered from the food poisoning last week, but because this suddenly seems like an insane idea.

I'm going to *work* for *Kit Kensington*. And I have no one to blame but myself and my damn pride. And Isaac. I blame Isaac too.

Cheating on me was bad enough. But the *sleeping with my boss* bit? That's the sin that resulted in this particular predicament. For a few seconds, I contemplate unblocking my ex, simply to cuss him out again. We haven't spoken since I walked in on evidence of his infidelity,

and the shocked swears I spit at him then no longer feel like enough of a punishment.

A shoulder knocks against my left arm, making me stumble. I'm wearing my nicest heels—my nicest *everything*. I woke up at six a.m. to ensure I had time to straighten my hair and apply a full face of makeup before walking to the subway stop two blocks away.

Watching people walk into the skyscraper that houses Kensington Consolidated's corporate offices, I still feel underdressed. I'm in a sea of suits that cost four figures. Maybe even five.

A wayward elbow hits my bag, and I finally move forward. Standing stock-still on a New York sidewalk is asking to get knocked over like a bowling pin. Especially during commuter hour.

I focus on single steps—one foot in front of the other—as I approach the revolving doors. I pick the center one, which winds up spinning the slowest.

It feels about twenty degrees cooler inside of the lobby. August's heat has bled into September, blanketing the city in a sticky layer of humidity that the vents are working overtime to counteract. They blast the sweat on my skin. I suppress a shiver as I stride toward the front desk as surely as I can manage in four-inch heels with dwindling confidence and increasing anxiety.

"Name?" the receptionist asks when I reach her. She doesn't glance up, busy stamping a form and then typing on the keyboard in front of her.

"Collins." I clear my throat. "Collins Tate. For Kensington Consolidated?"

The woman looks up, a flash of interest breaking through her practiced expression. Her manicured fingers keep up their rhythmic tapping on the keyboard as she appraises me. My unpolished ones drum against the pristine counter as I take note of her sleek bun (professionally styled) and winged eyeliner (sharper than a knife's edge). Part of my first paycheck might need to go toward a new wardrobe. Staying in my pajamas most days was the best part of unemployment.

"One moment, please," she tells me, continuing to type.

I nod, pasting a polite smile on my face as I pull my water bottle out of my bag and swallow a large sip. Cold liquid hits my empty stomach, prompting a loud gurgle. I was too nervous to do more than nibble on a granola bar this morning. Now, I'm nauseous *and* hungry.

"This guest badge will allow you to access the elevators." The receptionist slides a laminated rectangle toward me. "You want the fifty-fifth floor. Someone will direct you from there."

"Thank you," I say, grabbing the badge and joining the crowd funneling through the turnstiles.

A swipe of the barcode at the bottom allows me through, and then I hurry into the nearest elevator. When I press *55*, the six other people in the elevator all stare at me with open curiosity.

I have a better idea as to why when the doors part on floor fifty-five.

The waiting area looks different from the other floors the elevator stopped at. Modern and expensive and *prestigious*. The floor gleams like it was freshly polished. The walls boast artwork that looks intricate and expensive. The front desk is larger than the one in the lobby. Imposing. And, front and center, metal letters affixed to the wall spell out *Kensington Consolidated*.

The law firm I worked at in Chicago handled a lot of corporate business. So, I guess I expected these offices to look similar to theirs. But Carter Thomas LLP didn't radiate importance the way this space does.

The blonde woman sitting at the front desk is on the phone. She holds up a finger, mouthing, *One sec*, as I approach.

I nod, nervously smoothing the skirt of my dress as I wait for her call to end. I stood on the subway, but it still appears wrinkled. One thing the humidity could have helped with.

Two gray-haired men step off the elevator and continue past the desk and down the hallway. They're deep in conversation, neither so much as glancing my way.

A fresh flare of panic appears. What if Kit shows up next while I'm standing here, waiting for direction? What would he say? What would *I* say?

I debated asking Lili for her brother's number all weekend. Who knows how that conversation would have gone? But at least Kit and I would have communicated since I'd snuck out of his hotel room.

I couldn't do it though. I was too worried Lili would read into it, that she would somehow realize what had happened between us.

And I was—am—a coward who wasn't sure what to say. One night managed to erase years of ease in dealing with him. My playbook was simple—ignore, avoid, or argue. Leave the adoration to everyone else. But none of those reactions are realistic as his employee.

I've been exasperated by seeing Kit before. Irritated, often. But never *nervous*, and it's messing with my head.

"Good morning."

The greeting startles me from my thoughts. "Oh. Hi. Good morning."

The receptionist smiles kindly. She's older than me. Late thirties maybe. She looks wise and worldly, and I'm betting she never slept with her future boss.

"I'm Maya. You must be Collins Tate."

"Uh, yes. I am."

My surprise that she knows my name must show on my face because Maya shoots me a conspiratorial look.

"A new Kensington in the office causes a bit of a stir around here. Because of, you know …" She glances over her shoulder at the letters attached to the wall.

I focus on the first word, my gaze drifting over each letter individually. *Kensington*. It looks as important as it sounds.

"Right," I reply.

I *do* know. Lili's graduation party was the most lavish event I'd ever attended. Filled with politicians and actors and all manner of famous, influential people, in the most stunning house I'd ever set foot in. A *summer* home. I had known long before then that Lili came from a very different world than I did, but that was the most drastic example. The moment I'd met my freshman roommate, I had been aware of our different backgrounds, and it's been reiterated every time I've met a Kensington.

It's unsurprising that Kit would be paid more attention than other employees. It is, however, far from ideal. I'm anxious enough without the glare of a spotlight following me around by association.

"Take a seat. I'll let Laura know you're here," Maya tells me. "She'll be the one to show you around, help you get settled."

"Great. Thank you."

I take a seat on one of the couches, fighting the urge to tap my foot as I wait. I settle for playing with the clip on my badge and staring at the large clock on the wall instead.

Ten minutes later, another woman appears. She's wearing an elegant wrap dress. Her dark hair, pulled back in a low ponytail, is threaded with a few streaks of gray. Her posture is perfect, steps purposeful.

She adjusts the tortoiseshell glasses perched on the bridge of her nose before holding a hand out to me. "Laura Skadden. Nice to meet you, Ms. Tate."

I stand in a rush, gripping her palm and hoping mine isn't damp. "Nice to meet you too. And it's just Collins, please."

Laura nods once in swift acknowledgment. Briefly, I wonder if anyone who works here *doesn't* thrive on brisk efficiency. I can't picture Kit working amid such somber organization. Usually, if he's not grinning or joking, he's about to grin or joke.

"Right this way," Laura instructs, spinning in her sensible short heels and striding down the hallway.

I follow, my stomach twisting with a new batch of nerves.

CHAPTER 7

Kit

My dad's studying the sailboat painting displayed on the wall when I approach my office, holding my morning cup of coffee.

It's strange, seeing him silhouetted by skyscrapers instead of palm trees. As a kid, I visited my father in a building that overlooked the Hollywood sign.

When he and Mom announced they were moving back to New York full-time—rather than splitting time between coasts, like they'd done for decades—I had no clue what to expect. I thought I'd be one of two Kensingtons, not three, working in this building.

I've always preferred the East Coast to the West, so it's nice, having my parents' permanent address be in the same city.

But working with my dad? I have yet to decide how to feel about that.

We've always been close. Always been similar. Dad was the one stifling laughter when Mom was disciplining me after my latest escapade. And despite all the trouble I've participated in—or caused—over the years, he's never expressed anything except total confidence in my ability to work here. He's always encouraged Lili's chosen career as a landscape architect, and I know he would have supported me if I'd pursued chemistry beyond earning a degree in the discipline.

Everyone would have paid attention to my arrival at the company regardless. But me starting and Crew Kensington returning? It's made the usual comparisons to my father endless.

I stare at him for a few more seconds, then rap my knuckles on the door to announce my arrival.

Dad startles, glancing over his shoulder and smiling once he sees me. "Morning, Kit."

"Hey, Dad," I reply, heading for my desk.

"I was just …" He chuckles, running a hand through hair that's starting to gray at the temples. "Just looking around. Reminiscing a little."

This was my father's office before he left the company. Something I've been reminded of often and repeatedly since inhabiting it.

"You can have it back," I offer, setting my coffee down in its usual spot on my desk and gesturing around the room.

Despite its prime location, this corner office has sat empty ever since my dad swapped boardrooms for movie sets. Out of respect or regret or some ruling, it was reserved for a future Kensington. A shrine to the speculation concerning my father's departure—sensitive history I've never been told in its entirety.

My dad's new office is at the opposite end of this floor, right by my uncle Oliver's.

"No, it's yours now." Dad nods toward the piece of art he gifted me for my eighteenth birthday. "I like what you've done with the place."

"Thanks." I lean back against my desk, tucking my hands into my pockets.

Since I started work, I've only seen my dad in the office twice. He stopped by on my first day with Oliver, and then he attended the presentation for a newspaper in Phoenix we're considering acquiring. I'm assuming this visit has a purpose beyond a simple social call.

"Good weekend?" he inquires.

"You mean, aside from helping Bash schlep his boxes?"

Predictably, my brother did *not* pack after the party he threw in my penthouse.

I woke up on Saturday morning to a stranger fast asleep under the piano and my favorite scotch atop it, the bottle almost empty. It took me ten minutes to drag Bash out of bed, then another twenty to toss everything he'd stored at my place over the summer into cardboard boxes left over from my move before our parents showed up to accompany him back to New Hampshire.

Dad smiles. "Aside from that."

"Are you asking as my dad or as my boss?"

I'm mostly kidding. I slept, went for a run in Central Park, and got dinner with a few college buddies who also ended up with jobs in the city. All legal activities.

"I'm still figuring out how to be both," Dad admits.

Nice to know I'm not the only one struggling to redefine our relationship forty—actually, more like sixty—hours a week.

"I answered emails, then," I state.

Dad shakes his head. I catch the flash of a grin that appears before he schools his expression to seriousness.

Everyone who knows my parents says Lili's exactly like my mom while I'm a copy of my dad. And they're rarely *only* referring to appearance.

My dad tosses the manila folder he's holding onto my desk. "I really came to give you this. Take a look when you have a minute. Possible acquisition."

I pick the folder up and scan the first page. "A makeup company?"

"Beauty is a billion-dollar business, Kit. Take a look at their earning potential. They're small now, but there's a lot of growth in the market. The founders are coming in this afternoon for a meeting. I'd like you to take point on it."

I glance up at *take point*. A big endorsement for my second week. "This afternoon?"

He lifts a brow. "Is that a problem with your schedule?"

Yes. I've already got a packed agenda. Not only will I have to find time to review this information, but I'll have to reschedule all my afternoon meetings. I'm talking to Kensington Consolidated's COO right now though, not my dad. *Yes* isn't the right answer. Or a possible answer.

"Not at all. What time is the meeting?"

"Three p.m."

I nod. "I'll have my assistant add it to the calendar."

"Your assistant?" He glances at the empty desk outside my office.

I clear my throat. "Yes. She's starting today."

My dad nods. "Good. I'm glad you hired someone." He heads for the door. "I'll see you at the meeting—"

"It's Collins Tate," I blurt.

He pauses. Inclines his chin. "What?"

"My new assistant. My new assistant is Collins Tate. Lili's freshman roommate at Yale? She came to Lili's graduation party? Her parents are both professors—"

"I remember." My dad finally cuts off what was *far* too much information.

"The assistant position was only posted internally," he continues. "How did she … ah. Lili?"

"Lili," I confirm. I have no qualms about tossing the blame on my sister. She *is* the reason Collins was hired. "She found out I didn't have an assistant and knew Collins needed a job. She'd just moved to New York from Chicago."

"Was she an assistant in Chicago?"

"She …" Honestly, I have no idea what Collins did in Chicago. "She's smart, Dad. She'll be fine."

He appears unconvinced. "It's an important role with a lot of responsibility. She'll be managing your calendar, taking your calls, assisting with any projects—"

"She'll be fine," I repeat.

"I know your sister is … willful—"

I snort at the understatement.

A quick smile crosses my dad's face. Lili's a wrecking ball of willful.

"But she chose not to be involved with the company. The decisions you make here are *your* decisions, Kit, understood?"

I'm plenty capable of telling my sister no. Pretty much have a lifetime record of it. But if I say that, I'm worried my dad will wonder why I didn't say no to her about Collins working for me.

And even though I spent the weekend second-guessing my choice to hire her, I'm also oddly panicked by the thought of her *not* working for me. I know Collins thinks pestering her for years was nothing but a game to me, but she's wrong. It wasn't entertainment, and it wasn't simply about sex. Collins has never treated me like a blank check or stepping stone. I *like* her, and that means I'd rather have her as my off-limits assistant than go another two years without seeing her.

"Hiring Collins *was* my decision," I say firmly. "She's competent and qualified, and she needed a job. And I'd prefer to work with someone I know than a complete stranger."

He nods slowly. "Just be careful. Mixing the personal and the professional can get messy."

I lift an eyebrow. "Which is why you work with your brother and hired your son?"

Dad grins. "Touché." He starts toward the door again, only to stop and snap his fingers. "Before I forget, I'm supposed to tell you to be at your grandfather's at seven sharp on Saturday."

I sigh. I almost successfully forgot about that dinner. "Yeah. Okay."

"*Seven*, Kit," he reminds me sternly. "Don't be late."

"I won't be."

Dad looks dubious, but nods. "Good."

"She's really serious about this guy," I comment. "We never had solo dinners with Cal."

"Well, Cal was already familiar with the family."

I don't think that's why, and I doubt Dad does either.

"What do you think of Charlie?" I ask.

"I like him." He gives me a sidelong glance. "But don't mention that to your sister. She's too young to get serious about a guy."

"She's twenty-five. Isn't that how old you and Mom were when you got *married*?"

Dad shakes his head. "That was different."

"Uh-huh, sure. How?"

"Because I had to marry your mother in order to date her."

I laugh. "Sounds like you had some serious game, Dad."

"We've been together for over two decades, son. Obviously, I did something right. See you this afternoon." He leaves, shutting the door behind him.

I take a seat at my desk and start tackling the outrageous number of emails that piled up over the past two days. I should have answered some over the weekend.

But I haven't changed *that* much.

CHAPTER 8
Collins

"And this is your desk." Laura leads me over to a station that looks the same as the ones lining the outside of every office we've passed.

The raised counter around it offers some privacy, almost like a cubicle, but is low enough to see over if you're standing near enough. Aside from a desktop, keyboard, mouse, and phone, the desk is empty. Maybe I should buy a plant to decorate it.

Kit has a corner office. And his door is solid wood, not frosted glass, like the other offices lining this hallway, which is especially

intimidating. I'm relieved by the barrier too. Focusing on tasks would be a lot harder if I knew his eyes might be on me at any point.

Christopher Kensington is engraved on the shiny nameplate left of the knob.

I don't know much about Kensington Consolidated as a company. Just the little Lili has mentioned over the years, plus general knowledge. They're very successful, and they own a lot of subsidiaries—that's the gist of the information I've retained. A lot of the tasks I'll be responsible for—filing, phone-answering, note-taking—are familiar from my job at Carter Thomas. But same as the offices, they feel elevated here. I wasn't working on million—or billion?—dollar deals in Chicago.

"Let's see if Mr. Kensington is available," Laura says, continuing past my new desk and straight toward the imposing door.

I manage a nod she misses, my stomach somersaulting in a way that makes me glad I skipped breakfast this morning.

He's not Lili's little brother here. He's not even Kit. He's *Mr. Kensington*, which sounds stuffy and formidable and prestigious, especially coming from a woman who's roughly the age of his mother.

Laura knocks once on the dark wood. "Mr. Kensington? It's Laura. Do you have a minute to meet your new assistant?"

My mind fixates on *meet* and *new*. I don't know what magic Lili worked behind the scenes, but no one I've encountered so far has had any clue I've met members of the Kensington family before.

It's a relief, honestly, to feel like a regular employee, making a fresh start she desperately needed.

For the first time *ever*, I feel some sympathy for Kit. That's one luxury he *doesn't* have. He couldn't pretend he had no connection to this company on his first day.

"Yes, come in."

I've heard Kit talk many times before. Usually while wishing he'd stop.

Yet, somehow, those three words sound like the first time I've heard his rich baritone.

I swallow hard as Laura turns the door handle and gestures for me to go ahead. I hesitate for a couple of seconds, swiping my palms against the skirt of my navy dress, then enter.

Kit's rising, now standing, behind the massive desk that should dwarf the large space, but doesn't. *He* does, gaze fixated on my every step.

I swallow hard, resenting the warmth seeping into my cheeks despite the cool air.

This is *Kit.* There's no reason I should be blushing right now. No reason … except the highlight reel of filthy words and sensual touches that is burned into my memory. Our night together was supposed to be easy to forget. But the harder I try to, the more stubbornly it's stuck in my brain.

I shouldn't have slept with him.

I shouldn't have accepted a job here *after* I slept with him.

Two decisions I can no longer change.

"This is Ms. Tate, your new assistant."

Laura, thankfully, is oblivious to my wayward thoughts. I hope that means they're not stamped on my face, that Kit is unaware too.

I clear my throat and hold out my right hand, attempting to quickly train my brain into viewing the man in front of me as nothing except an employer.

Boss. Boss. Boss, I chant silently.

"Nice to meet you, Mr. Kensington," I say politely.

Kit quirks a brow, and I think he's going to call me out for the formality. Or start laughing. His blue eyes are dancing in that boyish, mischievous way I've *sometimes* found endearing.

Pretending not to know him at all might be excessive, but it also seems necessary. Our relationship being the definition of professional from here on out feels paramount.

I've seen Kit wearing a suit before. He's *usually* wearing a suit when I see him. But I've never seen Kit in a suit, knowing what was *under* his suit before.

Unfortunately, there's a difference.

He's moving, approaching, lifting his arm to meet my handshake. Each inch that shrinks between us, my heart beats a little faster in response.

Boss. Boss. Boss, I remind it.

"Call me Kit, please."

My heart rate stutters when our palms connect, a spark of electricity racing up my arm and jolting it into a rapider rhythm.

We shake hands, me shoving all memories of the last time we touched into the farthest recesses of my mind. "I'm Collins."

"Unique name." Kit's expression is carefully neutral, but his eyes are still shining with repressed amusement.

Déjà vu hits in full force. For a few seconds, I'm eighteen, standing in a dorm room, watching a stylish stranger unpack Louis Vuitton luggage.

That's what Kit said when we *did* meet for the first time. I'm not sure he remembers. I'm not sure why *I* remember, how that's subconsciously stuck in my head.

"Thank you," I state.

We stare at each other.

Kit is a better actor than I am. I'm not sure I'm being convincingly poised at all.

"I'm looking forward to working with you," I add.

Working *for* you would have been more accurate, but despite taking this job, I still have plenty of pride left. Our job titles define a certain hierarchy, but I have no intention of treating Kit as superior to me. And if he expects that, he can find a new assistant.

One corner of Kit's mouth curves up for a second. A flicker I would have missed if I hadn't been studying his expression so closely.

"Likewise."

"We'll let you get back to work, Mr. Kensington," Laura says. "I'll get Ms. Tate set up at her desk."

Kit doesn't look away from me as he replies, "Sounds good."

I nod in agreement.

I'm sweating. I'm *sweating*, and it's probably fifty-five degrees in this building.

What the hell is wrong with me? *This is Kit*, I remind myself again. He's young and immature and obnoxious and … hot.

Kit is hot. An attractiveness I've always been aware of but have—with one glaring exception—successfully ignored. Kit, in a perfectly tailored suit, with the Manhattan skyline outlined behind him? *Hard* to ignore.

We're still shaking—holding—hands, I realize belatedly. My grip relaxes, and his does the same. My fingers fall, brushing against the stiff fabric of my dress, and I restrain the urge to wipe my palm again.

I give the office a cursory glance, breaking eye contact with Kit for the first time since I entered the room. It doesn't have the generic feel I'm accustomed to, like it's a duplicate of the entire floor. This office contains character.

The walls are paneled with dark wood that matches the door. The effect reminds me of a library, enhanced by a large bookcase. A pair of leather armchairs is angled toward his desk, and an oil painting of a sailboat hangs on the wall opposite it. A matching couch sits on the corner, forming a small seating area. Floor-to-ceiling windows enclose the corner of the building, boasting a staggering view of the city and flooding the space with light. There's a photo frame sitting on the desk, but it's facing away, so I can't see its contents. The one item in the room not on obvious display.

"Ms. Tate?" Laura is smiling at me indulgently as she holds the door open.

Waiting for me to walk out first, I realize.

"Oh, right. Of course." I step back hastily, wincing when the back of my calf collides with the coffee table situated in front of the leather couch.

The glass bowl on the coffee table wobbles, the rattle echoing ominously. I lose my equilibrium for a few seconds, arms windmilling and pulse pounding in my ears.

Kit reaches out and grabs my arm, steadying me. Sparks skitter along my nerve endings as his calluses scrape my skin.

He doesn't spare a glance for the glass bowl, but I do. Thankfully, it's righted itself. Same as I would have if Kit hadn't intervened.

"Thanks," I say, tucking a strand of loose hair behind my ear so I have an excuse to pull my arm away. "I—I haven't worn heels in a while."

Kit arches one eyebrow, and I'm positive we're thinking the same thing—I wore heels *that* night.

"To *work*," I clarify. "I haven't worn heels to work in a while."

My former office in Chicago was more of a flats vibe than corporate runway chic. We were even allowed to wear jeans on Fridays.

"You don't have to wear heels," Kit tells me.

My nod is more of an awkward head bob. "Got it."

I give the coffee table a wide berth as I follow Laura out of Kit's office. I'd love to sink into the swivel chair and bury my face in my hands in silent mortification, but that's going to have to wait until I'm back in Brooklyn.

I hoped my clumsiness in front of Kit was an unfortunate coincidence. Now, I'm concerned it's simple cause and effect.

The next hour passes quickly. Laura already reviewed a bunch of paperwork with me and got me a permanent badge. After I "meet" Kit, she helps me set up voicemail, log in to the company system, and run through the regular tasks I'm supposed to perform.

I pay close attention to every detail, determined not to miss or mess up anything. Laura also shows me around the break room—lunch is catered daily, and there's a fridge of drinks and snacks—and this floor's copy room, which is fully stocked with every category of office supplies imaginable. I run a fingertip along the edge of a shelf stacked with brand-new binders, and there's not a single speck of dust on it.

By the time Laura deposits me back at my new desk with a straightforward, "Let me know if you need anything!" I'm not *positive* she truly means it.

It's 11:02 a.m.

Thirteen minutes later, I catch a flash of pink out of the corner of my eye.

I have a sinking suspicion the woman wearing a full face of makeup and designer spandex is headed this way, even before she stops directly in front of my desk.

"Good morning. Can I help you?" I ask politely.

She glances at the shiny nameplate affixed to the wall behind me, then twirls a piece of hair around a finger. The shade of her nail polish matches her outfit *exactly*. "Hi! I'm here to see Kit."

I stare at her.

Unexpected visitors were not covered in Laura's tutorial, and I didn't think to ask. I'm not sure how this woman made it this far into the building. She's not wearing a visitor badge, and her athletic attire makes me doubt she's a fellow employee.

Is this a *thing*? Does Kit invite random women to his office for …

My expression stays carefully neutral as I ask, "Is he expecting you?"

She giggles. "No. I wanted it to be a surprise."

I attempt a smile, but my facial muscles aren't cooperating. Not only am I uncertain how to properly proceed, but I'm annoyingly bothered by her presence here.

And I'm irritated that I'm annoyed. Kit can do whatever he wants. Here. Wherever. But I'd really rather it not be here.

I glance at the calendar open on my screen. According to it, Kit's schedule is free until a conference call at noon.

I pick up the phone. "I'll check if he's available. What's your name?"

"Sadie Carmichael," she chirps.

I nod an acknowledgment before hitting the button that connects to Kit's direct line.

He answers on the second ring. "Kensington."

"Hi, K—" I falter on calling him Kit in front of his … something. It sounds too casual. "Hi. There's a Sadie Carmichael here to see you. Should I send her in?"

Kit hesitates. And I have no idea what *that* means. "Sure," he finally responds.

I clear my throat. "Okay. I'll send her in."

Sadie beams, then beelines for the door before I can address her directly.

I get a brief glimpse of the sailboat painting on the wall before the door shuts again. A few seconds later, I hear the low rumble of Kit's voice on the other side of the wood, followed by a high-pitched giggle.

I answer two emails, vacillating between desperately trying to decipher the murmuring and adamantly blocking out any surrounding noise.

Five minutes later, I lose the battle with curiosity. I dig my phone out of my purse, duck under my desk, tap record, and whisper, "Does Kit have a girlfriend?"

Once I've sent the voice message, I straighten.

My spine hasn't even hit the back of the seat before my phone's vibrating in my hand. After a furtive look around—no one seems to be paying me any attention—I answer. "Hey."

Lili's laughing. "Kit? A girlfriend? What the hell gave you that crazy idea? He's firmly anti-commitment."

I relax. Kit's close with his siblings. If he was seeing anyone, Lili would know.

And he said he was single—*that night*. Apparently, I *do* have some faith in men remaining because I believed—believe—him.

Yet I'm still bothered by the faint voices I can hear through the door.

"Some woman just showed up at the office and asked to see him. Clearly not work-related."

"Really? Who?"

"Sadie Carmichael."

Lili laughs again in response to my distasteful tone. I didn't *mean* to say her name that way. It just sort of slipped out.

"Wow, you *really* don't like her. Was she rude?"

"No. I just wasn't expecting … I mean, I wasn't sure what to do about her showing up. I didn't know if I should … know her."

Job security is my only concern, I tell myself. If Kit gets admonished for having a random woman in his office, it could affect my role.

"What are they saying?"

"I don't know. I can't make it out." I cringe at the admission, realizing I just admitted I have, in fact, been trying to eavesdrop.

"Aside from Kit's fan club showing up, how's the job?"

"Uh, it's—" I catch sight of two women headed this way. They're dressed in business attire, so hopefully, they're not additional members of Kit's fan club. "I've gotta go. I'll talk to you later. Bye!"

I hang up before Lili can reply, straightening in my seat and dropping my cell back in my bag.

"Hi! We just wanted to say, well, hi," one of the women says, smiling.

"And offer you a sweater," the other states, holding up a navy cardigan. "We think whoever is in charge of cooling the building grew up in Antarctica and has some superhuman tolerance for the cold."

I smile as I stand. "I thought it was just me."

"Definitely not just you," the first woman who spoke replies. "Layers are key all summer long. Dress for summer on the commute, but for winter once you're inside. I'm Stella, by the way."

"And I'm Margot." She offers the sweater she's holding. "Here you go."

"Thank you so much," I say, draping it over one arm. "I'm Collins."

"We know." Stella grins. "The company sends out a welcome email for any new hires. You were the only one today."

"Oh. I haven't seen that yet."

I get cc'd on most of Kit's emails. And Kit gets *a lot* of emails.

Margot's expression is sympathetic. "It's overwhelming at first. You'll figure everything out; don't worry."

I nod. "Thanks."

"Have you worked as an assistant before?" Stella asks.

"Not exactly. But I was a paralegal in Chicago after college, so I have some office experience."

"Everyone thought they were going to hire internally for this position."

There's curiosity in Stella's statement. *Friendly* curiosity, but still curiosity. Interest I don't want aimed my way.

I lift one shoulder and let it drop in what I hope is a casual maneuver. "Yeah, I lucked out. A college friend knows someone high up here. She put in a good word for me."

Margot nods. "Good for you. I swear, connections are the only way to get a job *anywhere* these days. My college adviser was sorority sisters with Sanborn's wife. That's how I ended up here."

The door behind me opens.

"... appreciate it *so* much," Sadie gushes. "You're the *best*, Kit."

My lips press tight together. It's an involuntary reaction, some impulse to school my reaction before I can scowl or snort or do anything else. I'm not sure *why* Sadie irks me, but she does.

Stella's and Margot's attention has jumped behind my desk. Reluctantly, my head turns in that direction too.

Sadie is smiling at Kit as he escorts her out of his office.

Kit's eyes are on me, casually posed with my hip propped against the side of my desk. I straighten, my grip tightening on the folded cardigan.

It's just Kit, I tell myself for what feels like the hundredth time today.

Years of disregard have suddenly snuck up on me, coalescing into this blistering awareness.

"See you later," Sadie trills, wiggling a few manicured fingers before she saunters down the hallway.

Stella and Margot exchange a look. I grab a few papers off my desk and shuffle them, trying to appear busy until Kit disappears again.

"I need to talk to you in my office for a minute, Collins," Kit says, then heads inside. He leaves the door open, that crisp, commanding sentence lingering in the cold air.

I still, papers clutched in my hands.

Why does he sound so curt? He wouldn't *fire* me for letting Sadie in, right?

I asked him first.

He could have said no. I *wanted* him to say no.

"We'll swing by and grab you at lunch," Stella whispers before she and Margot scurry down the hallway.

Neither of them struck me as shy, but both seem intimidated by Kit. Honestly, I'm a little intimidated too.

I start toward the door, then pivot back to my desk to deposit the papers. I also pull on the cardigan from Margot and suck in a deep breath before stepping inside Kit's office for the second time.

It looks the same as it did earlier, but I make a show of looking around rather than immediately focusing on him.

When my eyes do land behind his desk, he's reclined in his chair. I should feel powerful, standing while he's sitting, but I don't. I remember how eagerly he got on his knees and pulled me to the edge of that bed, and it makes mine weak.

"Close the door," he instructs.

I swallow as I comply, then turn to face him again.

"Unless it's my father, uncle, or they have an appointment, say I'm unavailable," Kit states.

"Understood."

"And I need you to reschedule my afternoon." He nods toward papers spread on his desk. "I have to review these by three, then attend a presentation, so everything else has to wait. Make sure the Viridian Ventures meeting that was at two p.m. takes place by Wednesday morning. Everything else, by the end of the week."

I nod, rapidly repeating *Viridian Ventures* in my head to ensure I don't forget to prioritize it. "Got it."

"Laura showed you how to use the calendar system?"

I nod again. "Yes."

Kit leans forward, resting his elbows on his desk. His suit jacket is off, slung over the back of his chair, which makes it too easy to notice the definition of his shoulders and biceps under the stiff cotton of his button-down. "You could have asked *me* about a job, you know."

I tense, although I was already braced for this moment. It was one thing in front of Laura. But I wasn't expecting Kit to keep up the farce of us being total strangers when we're alone.

"When?"

I watch that word land. I know it does because Kit doesn't even blink. He doesn't tease or joke or feign confusion. He was anticipating this moment, same as I was. He was waiting to see how we'd move past that night, same as I am.

"You want to pretend it never happened?"

The question is matter-of-fact, his typical joking demeanor still noticeably absent.

"I want to pretend it never happened," I confirm.

"Okay."

"Okay," I echo. "If, uh, if Sadie comes back, should I—"

"She won't be back." Kit flips open one of the binders on his desk. "Let me know if you have any issues rescheduling."

"Will do."

"Thanks."

He doesn't look up again before I leave the room, and I tell myself I'm not disappointed.

CHAPTER 9
Kit

"Top left."

Collins's head snaps in my direction, ponytail swishing against her shoulder as she hastily stands. "What?"

I leave the doorway and walk deeper into the supply room. "You're looking for the hanging folders, right? Top shelf, on the left."

She lifts an eyebrow. "How do *you* know that?"

"You brought one to match it to." I nod toward the single folder tucked under her left arm.

"No, I mean, how do you know where the files are stored?"

I walk over to the pen section and open a box of my favorites, sliding two out and slipping them into my pocket.

"Because I was my own assistant for a week. Who do you think did the filing until you started?"

"I figured you had a temp or something."

"Well, you figured wrong." I smirk. "I'm very picky about who I work with."

"Uh-huh. You're known for your … discerning taste."

My grin grows as I close the box.

"You came in here to get pens?" She sounds highly suspicious of that fact.

Maybe because I barricaded myself in my office all day. I didn't even leave for lunch; I had it delivered.

"My favorite kind ran dry, and my assistant wasn't at her desk. So, yeah, I came in here to get pens. How many do you need?" I ask, approaching the folder section.

"You don't need to do that," Collins says quickly.

"I know I don't. I do whatever I want, remember?"

"Remember what?" She tilts her head, a serene smile fixed on her face.

Damn, do I like this girl. I like that it's late, and we're alone, and she's *still* determined to act like an encounter I know for a fact she enjoyed never happened.

I've been the definition of *respectable* since she started working here. And fuck do I miss riling her. I'm so sick of that patient, practiced expression on her face.

"My grandfather knows the chief of neurology at Manhattan General," I tell her, "if you want that selective amnesia looked at. How many folders?"

Collins blinks rapidly. My guess? She's trying to decide if chastising me will encourage me.

"Your memory issues are getting increasingly worse, huh?"

She glances at the ceiling. Probably praying for patience. "Twenty," she grits out.

"Coming right up," I reply cheerfully.

I count the numbers aloud until I have the right amount, then head for the door.

She hurries after me. "I can take those."

"You sure are possessive of your folders," I state, slowing my strides so she can catch up.

I hear a huff. Thankfully, the smile's off my face by the time she draws even with me.

Automatic lights flicker on as we walk. Every desk we pass is empty.

Acquiring an office on this floor is equivalent to making partner at a law firm. It's the goal you work toward, an achievement you can rest after. After years of long hours, most other employees are trying to make it home in time for dinner with their families.

"It's quiet," Collins comments, glancing around. "Is it always like this?"

"I've only been here a week longer than you, Mo—" I clear my throat, hoping that syllable got lost in the sound. "Everyone's trying to enjoy the end of summer. Or they've got kids headed back to school. It'll pick up more later into the fall. Everyone on this floor worked hard to get here. They're enjoying the benefits."

Almost everyone, I add under my breath.

"You don't think you deserve to be here?"

My eyes jump to Collins.

She smirks. "My memory might be going, but my hearing's excellent."

I smile reluctantly. Her joking would thrill me under other circumstances. But I'm embarrassed she heard what was meant to be an inside thought.

"I don't think I *don't* deserve to be here. But I … I wish I'd started in an office a couple of floors down. That I wasn't the boss of employees who had worked here since before I was born. But I also know people would treat me differently no matter what. Not a single person used my dad's old office after he left. It was being saved for the next Kensington. Could have been Lili. Ended up me."

We've reached Collins's desk. I set the folders down in a neat stack, pulling one of the new pens out of my pocket and spinning it around a finger.

"Unless I ask for your help with something, you don't need to stay past five."

"I work faster when it's quiet," Collins says. "Just wanted to get ahead of a few things before tomorrow."

I nod. "Okay. Night, Collins."

"Night," she replies.

Back in my office, I loosen my tie before sinking back into my swivel chair. I stare at the legal pad covered with scribbles and a depressing number of strikethroughs that made a new pen necessary.

Tomorrow's the second meeting with Beauté—the makeup company my father is interested in acquiring. I had a meeting yesterday with the team I'm helming to discuss strategies, but ultimately, it's my call how we try to acquire them.

There's a knock on my door when I'm halfway through a fresh page of ideas.

"Come in," I call out, attempting and failing to ignore the burst of adrenaline. It has to be Collins.

Sure enough, she appears a second later.

"I thought you were leaving."

She nods. "I am. I just wanted to finish the notes from the Viridian Ventures meeting first."

Collins adds the notes to the proper stack on my desk without any coaching from me. She's picked up my sorting system—picked up *everything*—with impressive alacrity.

"You're working on the pitch for tomorrow?" she asks, nodding toward the legal pad.

I sigh. "Yep."

"They're a big deal?"

"Honestly? No. There's potential. But little capital and barely any distribution. They need money to increase inventory and circulation. And advertising. But mostly, they need an overhaul. Time and dedication to cultivate a unique brand, which can be a more valuable investment. And a riskier one."

"Why'd you pick them, then?"

"I didn't," I admit. "My dad did. So, if we acquire them and they succeed, it'll be thanks to him. If they don't accept our offer or they do and then sink, it'll be nepotism's fault I failed."

"You're more cynical than you used to be," Collins comments, reaching toward the pad. She sinks down into one of the chairs opposite my desk and starts scanning my handwriting.

"Than *last week*, when we met for the first time?"

Collins manages to roll her eyes while reading, which is actually quite impressive. "This is for the makeup company? Beauté?"

"Yeah," I respond, surprised. She wasn't at the initial meeting with them.

She hears the question in my voice. "They emailed you a copy of the presentation and included me on it. I was curious, so I looked through it." She flips back to the first page. "If you want them to sell you their company, which they've presumably invested a lot into, you need to offer them something they can't find somewhere else. And avoid phrases like 'not a big deal' and 'risky investment.' You're good at making outlandish ideas enticing. Focus on that. Tell them to dream big and then explain how you can make it a reality."

"Did you just *compliment* me?"

She reaches for my pen and circles something. "You should start here. Suggesting specific improvements to their current marketing strategies. It shows you've done your research—you're flattering them by praising decisions they've made—and also allows you to share concrete examples for what Kensington Consolidated has to offer. Constructive criticism. Do you have the numbers for what they paid for advertising last quarter?"

"Yeah, I do." I flip through some papers, then hand her the spreadsheet. "You're good at this."

She tilts her head as she scans the numbers. "You're not the only one in this office with a business degree, Kensington."

I stare at her. "You majored in music."

Too late, I consider it's strange that I know that.

Collins doesn't appear to notice. Or care. "*And* business. As you know, it's possible to double major. My parents didn't think playing the piano was a practical career choice. And they were right. I lasted six months as an accompanist at a local school, giving home lessons once a week, and played at the bar of a fancy hotel a few evenings a week, barely scraping together enough to pay rent, before I started applying for office jobs in Chicago."

"You did it though. For six months, you did it."

She runs the tip of the pen along her lower lip. I decide not to tell her I was doing the same thing ten minutes ago, so we're essentially making out right now.

"I guess," she finally says in a contemplative tone that makes it clear she's never considered that perspective. That she saw it as a simple failure.

"What was the office job?"

"Good to know you looked at my résumé before hiring me."

I smile. "You came highly recommended. I didn't need to look at your résumé."

"Uh-huh. Well, I was a paralegal at a law firm."

I resist the urge to ask if she preferred it to her current job and question, "Why Chicago?" instead.

"I went to college fifteen minutes from the house I grew up in—a free ride to an Ivy was too good to turn down. After graduating, I wanted somewhere different. Boston and New York both felt too close. So, Chicago made the most sense. Same city feel, more distance."

"Did you like Chicago? Aside from your ex?"

"It was … okay."

I lift one eyebrow. "Not the rave review you gave Perry."

Collins raises one back. "*What* is your issue with Perry?"

"He and Flynn don't get along."

"Because of something Perry did?" She asks the question like she already knows the answer, and it chafes. It means Perry told her the full story.

"No."

She nods and looks back down at the legal pad. "We're, uh, getting drinks on Friday night."

The hits you don't expect always land the hardest.

I've been jealous every single time I've seen Collins Tate with another man. But this packs an extra punch. Because I've had her—*I had her*—and now she's going out with someone else. And unless I fire her or quit, there's not a thing I can do about it.

So, I shove the jealousy deep down and cover it with my usual flippancy. "Better caffeinate beforehand so you don't fall asleep during the date."

Collins flips her ponytail over her shoulder. "The fact that you sign my paychecks now does *not* mean you get a say in my choice of company."

It's fucked up, but it feels damn good to hear her haughty tone aimed my way again.

I missed goading her. But more than that, I missed her firing back. Arguing with Collins is like swallowing a straight shot of whiskey after drinking a watered-down version. An immediate, shocking difference.

"Signing your paycheck is *way* below my pay grade," I drawl.

Her eyes flash as she tosses the pad on my desk, ruffling every neat stack. "And advising you on pitches is above mine. I'm only your *assistant* after all. Good night."

Her farewell sounds like more of a *fuck you*. And honestly, I deserve one.

I blow out a long breath as Collins stands and stalks out of my office. Wince when the door slams shut. According to the clock on my computer, it's just after seven.

She stayed two hours late, helped me with my pitch, and I behaved like an asshole because I'm frustrated, immature, and jealous.

I shrug on my suit jacket, jam the legal pad in my briefcase, and rush toward the door.

Collins is still at her desk when I approach it, attempting to shove a water bottle into what's already an overstuffed tote. Predictably, she's careful not to look up as I walk closer. The cold shoulder is a classic for a reason.

"I'm sorry, Collins."

"About what?" she wonders in a detached, disinterested tone.

"About acting like a jerk just now."

"You were acting?"

A reluctant grin tugs at my mouth. I'm pissed—genuinely angry—that she's going on a date with Perry. Emotions aren't logical, so knowing I have no right to be mad doesn't help at all. But she still makes me smile.

"Thank you for staying late to finish the notes. And for your advice about the pitch."

Collins glances at me. She stares for a few seconds, and I can't get any read on what she's thinking.

Eventually, she nods. "Apology accepted. I'll see you tomorrow."

She gives up on the water bottle, tucking it under one arm as she hikes her heavy bag off her desk and onto her shoulder.

"Let me drive you home," I offer impulsively.

"You mean, let your driver drive me home?"

And to think, most women love the town car.

"No. I mean, *I* will drive you home. And forget the *let*. It's happening. Come on."

I start toward the elevators. Collins follows, but I'm not entirely convinced it's not because they're the easier exit.

At least she's not mad enough to tackle fifty-five flights of stairs.

As soon as we step inside the elevator, she says, "I'm taking the subway home."

"Great. I haven't taken public transportation in … ever. Been meaning to try it."

Collins crosses her arms. Her gaze is focused straight ahead, watching the doors slide shut. "What about your car?"

"I'll come back here and get it after."

"That's ridiculous. And wasteful."

"Eh, you've called me worse."

The part of Collins's lips that I can see press tightly together. But I'm pretty sure it's because she's restraining a smile, not increasingly incensed. It could be a little of both though.

"I don't want special treatment, Kit. That's the only way this is going to work."

"You're my only assistant, Collins. Of course I'm going to treat you differently from every other damn employee. None of them stayed late to help me."

"I said I liked an idea you'd already come up with. I hardly played a pivotal role."

"Don't do that."

"Don't do what?" She turns to face me, one eyebrow raised in challenge.

"Don't diminish yourself. You're Collins fucking Tate. Act like it."

"Wow. If this whole future-CEO thing doesn't pan out, consider a future in motivational thinking."

I roll my eyes. "I'm serious."

"I know you are." After a beat, she adds, "Thanks."

"A compliment *and* a thank-you in the same day? Today might be the best day of my life."

Collins exhales, but this time, I do catch the flash of a smile. "I live in Brooklyn."

"So?"

"*So*, that's way out of your—"

"I don't care, Collins."

I really don't. I'm greedy when it comes to her company. She could be commuting from Connecticut, and I wouldn't be deterred.

Collins seems to sense my certainty. Or maybe she's just too tired to keep arguing with me. "Fine."

I grin.

And the elevator stops. Which is normal. But the doors not opening and the number being stuck at *13*? That's not normal.

Collins's eyes widen when she realizes the same thing. "Is this a joke?" she asks, each syllable an octave higher as the elevator continues to not move. She turns to me. "Did you do this?"

I laugh. "You seriously think I'd—"

"*Kit.*"

Okay, yeah. Trapping Collins in an elevator with me would have been a funny prank. *If* I hadn't been working on extra professionalism lately.

"I did not set this up," I assure her. "Kinda flattered you think I'd be able to pull it off though."

She huffs, muttering, "You would be," under her breath.

"I'm sure it's just a temporary … issue."

Truthfully, I have no clue what the hell is going on. I ride the elevator in this office building multiple times a day and the one up to my penthouse at least twice. Neither has ever malfunctioned. If we were on a sailboat, I'd have some clue how to troubleshoot. But mechanical or electrical problems aren't my area of expertise.

"I can't *believe* this," Collins states, dropping her bag to the floor. It lands with a hearty *thump*.

I side-eye it. "What the hell do you have in there that weighs so much?"

"Drugs," she says sweetly.

"Still trying to convince me you're not uptight, huh?"

"Once again, I have no idea what you're talking about." She steps closer to the panel of buttons, squinting at the symbols. "I'm going to hit the alarm button."

"Wait a sec," I reply, pulling my phone out of my pocket.

"Wait for *what*? We're supposed to call for help. Maybe one of the cables snapped, and we're about to plummet to our deaths, and every second counts—"

"Stop talking so much," I tell her. "We should conserve our oxygen."

Collins blanches. "Are you serious?"

I nod somberly as I scroll through my Contacts. Tap a name and listen to it ring.

"Hello?" a man's voice answers.

"Terry, it's Kit Kensington. How are you?"

"Kit! Wow! I wasn't—I'm good. You?"

"Been better," I state, glancing at a pale, scowling Collins. Without allowing myself to think about it, I reach out and grab her hand. Her fingers stay rigid, but she doesn't pull away. "The elevators appear to have stopped working. Electricity in here is still on, but nothing's moving."

"Oh shit," Terry says. "One sec."

There's some garbled background noise, and then a different man's voice comes through the line.

"Mr. Kensington? I'm Steve Damascus, head of building management. My sincere apologies. We were preparing for some scheduled maintenance and testing operations. Signage was supposed to be posted on each floor, alerting that certain units weren't supposed to be used tonight. I can't apologize enough for the inconvenience. Just give us a couple of minutes, and you should be on your way again. If not, please call back."

"Great. Thank you," I tell Steve, then hang up and glance at Collins. "Great news. We'll live."

She rolls her eyes, but there's still no color in her cheeks. "Because your buddy told you so?"

"Because the head of building management told me so," I clarify.

"And you have his number because ..."

I fake a cough to buy a little time.

We're not moving yet, so not replying is going to be fairly obvious. "I was a little ... nervous about my first day here. So, I stopped by the week before, later at night, when I didn't think anyone would be around. But I didn't have my badge yet, so I couldn't get up to the right floor. Terry was working the night shift, helped me out. He gave me his number in case I ever needed anything. And he handed me over to the head of building management when I called just now."

With a whir, we start descending again.

Collins releases an audible sigh. Of relief, I'm guessing.

"Good thing it's not winter," I muse. "We might have needed to huddle for body heat."

She snorts. "You're kidding, right?"

"Still serious," I reply.

"They keep the temperature hovering right around freezing. You haven't noticed how most of the assistants wear sweaters?"

The only assistant I notice is my own, but I keep that thought to myself. "Nope," I say truthfully. "Does that mean you *do* want to huddle for warmth?"

"*No,*" she replies emphatically as the doors open to the underground garage. Collins gives me a disbelieving look. Guess she didn't notice I'd hit the *G* button instead of *L* for lobby. "What if I'd said no?"

"You didn't," I remind her, giving her palm a quick squeeze.

She jerks, clearly having forgotten we were—are—holding hands. "No special treatment," she reminds me, pulling free from my grip and grabbing her bag off the ground.

"No special treatment," I promise, following her off the elevator.

Collins

K it's a good driver.

I wasn't sure he *could* drive. I assumed he'd been ferried around by a horde of private drivers and pilots and sea captains for his entire existence and never bothered to get his license. I can't picture him standing in line at the DMV like a normal sixteen-year-old.

Not only is he a good driver, but he *looks* good driving.

In the enclosed space, all I can smell is the mandarin-and-cedar scent of his cologne. It's even more noticeable than it was in the

elevator. At least trapped in there, I had the fear of imminent death to distract me. As we inch across the Brooklyn Bridge, my distractions are much more limited.

Smell is the sense most closely connected to memory, which is extremely unfortunate right now. The last time I was this close to Kit for this long, we were both wearing a lot fewer clothes.

I shouldn't have agreed to let him drive me home. I said *fine* before our elevator mishap, so I don't even have the excuse of that harrowing experience muddling my decision-making. The subway might be crowded and smelly, but it's a lot safer than being alone with Kit Kensington.

I believed he'd take public transit with me just to prove a ridiculous point, and then I'd end up feeling guilty for inconveniencing him. Which was how I wound up in the passenger seat of his fancy sports car, providing block-by-block directions rather than give him my exact address to punch into the fancy navigation system.

Why? I don't really know.

Half the shit I say or do around Kit, I look back on and can't believe I said or did it. He's worse for my impulse control than anything else in existence. Telling him to turn left or right or stay straight at the end of each block allows me to retain a little control, I guess.

Except for right now, when we're barely moving.

He's my boss, but we're not in the office. That shouldn't make any difference, but it does. The rigid politeness that's stood erected between us since I started working for him is barely standing.

It's a relief. And a cause for concern.

"Was your dress okay?"

My head jerks in Kit's direction. He's focused on the traffic ahead, profile backlit by the bridge lights.

I debate playing dumb again. Instead, I sigh. "What happened to pretending it never happened?"

"I didn't ask if you wanted the thong you'd left back. We can't discuss the party?"

I silently pray it's dim enough inside the car that he can't tell I'm blushing. I realized I'd forgotten my underwear halfway down the hallway, and I had no way to reenter the suite without involving hotel staff or knocking to wake him up.

Does *back* mean he kept it?

"The dress is ruined," I answer.

And whenever I look at it, I think about you.

Two excellent reasons to get rid of the gray dress, but it's still taking up space in my tiny closet.

He makes a humming sound in the back of his throat. "Too bad."

"Tragic," I drone, then look out the window.

Traffic's let up a little. We're nearly off the bridge.

I can't see Kit's smirk, but I *feel* its presence.

"Was that true earlier? You worked with your ex?"

My head jerks back toward him. He's still smirking.

I scowl. "Eavesdrop on private conversations much?"

Kit doesn't look the least bit abashed. "Don't have your 'private conversations' outside of my office, and I won't listen to them."

"Technically, I was having a private conversation in *my* office. It just happens to lack the walls you have. *Thin* walls, apparently."

I had to call IT this morning because of a software problem. The mid-thirties guy who showed up to solve it was friendly. *Very* friendly. He asked if I wanted to get a drink sometime while fixing my computer, so I told him I don't date coworkers after a bad experience with an ex. Which was true. Also a convenient excuse since I didn't feel a spark of attraction toward the employee whose name I've already forgotten.

He brakes at a stoplight. "So, you worked together when he cheated?"

I exhale. "No. I wouldn't go out with him while we worked at the same firm, so he changed jobs."

"How romantic," Kit drawls.

"I thought so," I say, ignoring his sarcasm. "Or I *wanted* to think so. I should have known better. Men love the chase, not the catch, right?"

He worked hard to date me. But as soon as he had me, Isaac got bored. Became sloppy and selfish.

"You're expecting me to agree with that?"

"Well, you're an example."

The red glow from the stoplight gives Kit's expression an ominous appearance. So does his glower. "How the fuck am *I* an example?"

"You chased me for years. Then we had sex, and you lost interest."

"*I* lost interest? You snuck out while I was still sleeping!"

"I thought that'd be easier," I tell him. "It's not like you reached out after."

I hate—*hate*—that the second sentence slipped out. We both knew it was a one-night stand.

A muscle in Kit's jaw jumps. But his eyes are on the road, hiding the rest of his expression.

"Sounds like you *like* being chased, Collins. I thought you leaving meant you had gotten what you wanted and were done."

I did. I am.

The words won't come out because there was a small part of me—

before he became my boss—that was disappointed I'd never heard from him. That wondered what he would have said if I'd stayed until he woke up.

I exhale. "I should have taken the subway, Kit. You're my boss, and this is inappro—"

He interrupts, "Lili told me you wanted the job."

"I wanted *a* job, yeah. But you didn't have to hire me."

"What was I supposed to say to my *sister? Sorry, I can't hire your friend because we had sex last weekend?* If you'd wanted Lili to know about us, you would have told her yourself. You didn't, so neither did I."

"You could have made up some other excuse," I state.

"Yeah? Like what?"

"Like *no! No* is a complete sentence. Or you could have told her you'd already hired someone."

"Lie, you mean?"

"Seriously? Where was this moral superiority when you got arrested in Monaco for stealing someone's yacht?"

Kit scowls. "For the last time, I didn't *steal* it. We had permission to be aboard. There was a … miscommunication with the staff. Am I still going straight?"

"A *miscommunication*, sure." I scoff. "Take the next right."

We've already overshot my street by two blocks, but I won't be admitting that. Kit will figure it out anyway. And it's his fault for bringing up my dress and distracting me.

Kit flicks on his blinker. "It *was* a miscommunication. The police didn't charge us with anything."

"I know. I talked them out of it."

He scoffs. "*You* talked them out of it? Bullshit. Jacques called and explained the situation."

"Yeah, well, *you're welcome*. I had a date that night."

"Oh, yeah? With who?"

I could make up an answer, but I decide not to bother. "I don't remember his name. Take the next right again."

"My sincere apologies for standing in the way of that special love connection."

I shake my head and shift my gaze out the window. We're only a block away from my apartment. "You can let me out here."

"What number are you?"

"Eighty-three."

"That's not on this block."

"The subway station is two blocks away. I can walk one …"

He keeps driving.

I sigh.

"I'm having dinner with Lili on Saturday night," Kit tells me. "Charlie's coming to meet the fam."

At this point, I've resigned myself to the fact that nothing about this ride home is going to be properly classified as *professional*. And since I'm curious to know more about Lili's new boyfriend, I ask, "Have you met Charlie before?"

"Yeah. A couple of times. He's a decent guy. And my dad already did the *bad cop* routine, so I'm good to just shoot the shit with him. Worst part is, the dinner's happening at my grandfather's." Kit pulls his car over in front of my apartment building.

I frown, confused. Lili's always gushed about her grandfather. "Why's that the worst part?"

"Arthur and I don't have much of a relationship." Kit drums his fingers on the bottom of the steering wheel. "And … I expect he'll have some thoughts about my new role at the company. *Good job* isn't really in his vocabulary."

"He must be proud of you." I state that sentence like a fact.

Because Kit's the type of person everyone wants to be associated with. He possesses this invisible draw I—mostly—pretend I'm immune to. And it's not tied to his looks or his money or his personality. It's just *him.*

"Proud, huh?" Kit's tone is wry.

"That you're working at the company, I mean."

"Well, he wouldn't have been happy if I hadn't. But I doubt he's thrilled I'm there either. He and my dad have a complicated relationship. Lili's the only member of the family the old man seems to like. Maybe he sympathizes with her shoe-shopping addiction."

My lips quirk. "Are you close with your other grandparents?"

"Not really. My dad's mom died a long time ago. And my mom's folks aren't exactly the warm-and-cuddly sort either."

I nod. That assessment tracks with my observations at the Red, White, and Blue party I attended at Lili's grandparents' mansion. They were regal, not friendly.

"You talk to your dad lately?"

I'm not sure how Kit, of all people, picked up on the dysfunction that everyone else in my life is—or acts—oblivious to.

"Yeah," I reply, twirling the end of my ponytail.

I talked to my mom last weekend, updating her on my new job, so close enough.

"Is he teaching Biochem this fall?"

It's an innocent question, but I can't help but feel like it's a test too. A quiz to determine if I'm lying.

"I don't know. We didn't discuss his current classes." That's true at least. We didn't discuss *anything*. I clear my throat and glance at the exterior of my building. "I should, uh, go. Thanks for the ride. Say hi to Lili for me."

Kit doesn't reply right away. He's busy peering past me at the building. "You don't have a doorman?"

"That costs extra."

I was apartment-hunting without knowing my salary or when I'd have one again. The only person I knew in New York was Lili, and I was too proud to take her charity. And too cautious to move in with strangers. I was lucky to find this studio.

He's frowning now. "You should really have a doorman. Otherwise, anyone could walk in—"

"Anyone who's not a resident has to buzz in." I don't mention that the door sometimes gets propped open with a rock to make deliveries easier. "This place is way nicer than where I lived in Chicago."

"Is that supposed to make me feel *better?*"

At first, I figured Kit was simply scandalized by how the bottom ninety-nine percent lived. The realization that he's worried about *me* shouldn't make my chest warm, but it does.

My voice is soft as I say, "I'll see you tomorrow, okay?"

Kit's still frowning when he glances at me, but he gives me a reluctant nod. "Okay."

I nod back, unbuckling my seat belt and reaching for the door handle.

"I *am* sorry about what I said earlier. You're not just an assistant, Collins. Selfishly, I'm so damn glad you didn't move to New York to play at Carnegie Hall or do something else to do with music because I love working with you."

I want to cry. Or laugh. Or scream.

There's no way he could have known that I'd dreamed about performing at Carnegie Hall when I was younger. My mom had taken me to a performance there for my tenth birthday, and I was transfixed.

He's apologized—twice.

And the kicker? He said working *with* me, like we're a true team.

I can handle Professional Kit. And I'm an expert at managing Obnoxious Kit. But I'm defenseless against Considerate Kit, it turns out.

I need to get out of this car—*now.*

Why am I still in this car? We've been parked for ten minutes.

"You too. I mean, me too." I fumble with the handle out of sheer self-preservation, sucking in a deep breath when fresh air invades the car. I climb out, then reach down to retrieve my bag from the footwell. "Thanks for the ride."

I can't remember if I said that already. My entire head's a jumble.

"You're welcome." His tone is casual, his elbow propped on the door.

Unaffected.

I wish I were too.

I hurry toward the entrance of my building, discreetly kicking the stone out of the doorframe and making a show of retrieving my keys from my bag in case Kit is waiting. It'll get colder soon, putting an end to that practice.

There's a credit card statement and a postcard from Jane in my mailbox. I smile at the postcard and tuck the bill in my bag to deal with later. Before I head up the stairs, I glance out the glass door.

The curb isn't empty yet.

I swallow hard, then start up the steps to my apartment.

CHAPTER 11
Kit

"What do you think, Kit?"

I glance up from the doodles I was drawing in the margins of the outline at Glenn—my least favorite member of the team my father assembled for the Beauté acquisition. The team I'm supposed to lead, not zone out on. I think most of Glenn's unpleasantness is rooted in his resentment that I'm a year younger and his superior, and I'm essentially proving his point by not paying attention.

I look back down at the outline, pretending to contemplate an

answer. Out of the corner of my eye, I catch Levi Jenkins's pen tapping the fifth bullet point—*long-term outlook.*

My eyes dart back to Glenn. He's sitting right beneath the clock, and I fight a grimace when I see it's already ten past five.

"I think that discussing Beauté's long-term outlook can wait until Monday," I state. "Enjoy the weekend, everyone."

Everyone—with the exception of Glenn—smiles and stands, relieved the long meeting is finally ending. Glenn closes his binder with a disgruntled frown before exiting the conference room. Guess he doesn't have any fun Friday night plans.

"Thanks," I tell Levi, who's draining the remnants of a coffee.

He lowers the cup and grins. "No problem. Have a good one, Kit."

"You too," I reply, tucking my leather portfolio under one arm and heading in the opposite direction from everyone else. None of them have offices on this floor.

I can't decide if I want Collins to still be at her desk or not. It's Friday—her date with Perry. If she's so eager to see him that she left on time for once, that'll suck. If she's still here, I'll have opportunities to say shit I shouldn't.

Her desk is empty, but she isn't gone for the day. Her water bottle is still on her desk, and the computer screen is unlocked.

I open the portfolio on the counter that surrounds her desk and pull out the materials from today's meeting. Rather than leave them there the way I normally would, I round the side of the counter and yank the filing cabinet open. Everything's neatly labeled, so it only takes me a few seconds to find the correct folder and add today's packet.

"Taking over for your assistant, Kit?" Andy Sanborn—one of the board members and the occupant of the office a couple down from mine—pauses in the hallway. He's headed out for the day, briefcase in hand.

I chuckle, shutting the cabinet. "Not exactly."

"Your father was the same way. No job too small for Crew. You're a chip off the old block."

I force a smile and a nod.

Andy's a nice guy, and he's trying to pay me a compliment. But I'm not sure why it rarely occurs to anyone that constant comparisons to my father get old. They have dwindled since I started at least. No one has mentioned how my office belonged to my dad this week.

"Thanks, Andy," I say. "Have a nice weekend."

"You too," he replies, then continues down the hallway.

I head into my office, ignoring the constant buzzing in my pocket.

I'm sure it's Flynn. I promised I'd be on time. And I *would* have been on time if not for Glenn's follow-up points on every single topic during the meeting.

I shut down my computer and am adding a few papers to my briefcase when there's a knock on my office door.

"Come in," I call out distractedly.

"I just printed the report on—" Collins starts, then pauses. "Oh. You're leaving?"

She sounds surprised. She's noticed the irregular hours I keep, and I hope that means she's also noticed how hard I work. I was too cowardly to turn the question around when she asked if I thought I deserved to be here the other night.

"I'm leaving," I confirm. "You should too. Everything else can wait until Monday."

"Right. Okay." She's still standing in the same spot, arms folded over the report she came to deliver, and for some reason, I think she's debating asking me where I'm going.

The longer she's in my office, the faster my willpower is fraying. The more likely I am to mention her date tonight.

So, my tone is brusque as I ask, "Anything else?"

Her chin lifts defensively.

Fuck, that was too dismissive. I should have mentioned I'm in a rush.

"Nope, nothing else," she says coolly. "I'll just leave these here." Collins strides toward my desk and drops the papers.

I'm a jerk, and she's annoyed with me. What else is new?

I don't know how to do this—be friendly and keep firm boundaries in place. Being around her, but not *being* with her feels like settling for pieces when I want every part.

So, since driving her home, I've swallowed jokes and tamped down smiles. Done anything and everything I can think of to make the short distance between our desks a wider gulf. An effort I thought Collins would appreciate, not act offended by.

"It's organized by financial quarter," she tells me. "With the annual overview on top."

Exactly how I like to review reports. Broad, then specific.

"Great. Thanks." I clear my throat and pick the stack of papers up. I can review it on the plane. "Have a nice week—"

"You'd better be ready, Kensington!" Flynn's exclamation precedes his arrival in my office by approximately two seconds. He saunters in, grinning when he sees me standing with my briefcase in hand. "Sweet! Vegas, here we—" He spots Collins and immediately stops talking.

Flynn glances between me and her, eyebrows raised.

I don't think he drank enough in the Hamptons to not remember her again.

Sure enough, the next words out of my best friend's mouth are, "It's Collins, right?"

"Right." She smiles at him. "Nice to see you, Flynn."

Flynn and I haven't discussed the state of his relationship with his cousin recently. But I'm suddenly, irrationally irritated, picturing Collins laughing with her new boyfriend and my best friend. It might make me a terrible person, but I'm hoping Flynn's still firmly anti-Perry.

"You're working here?" Again, Flynn glances between me and Collins.

I'm not sure why he's acting so surprised. He's met Collins once—that he remembers—and he's never asked for details about my job. Why would I have told him she's my assistant?

"Now I get why Kit's so hard to drag out of the office these days," he adds.

"Flynn," I growl.

He just grins. "Are you two still working? I can wait out in the hallway while you finish up."

The comment is for Collins's benefit, not mine. Flynn has never worried about interrupting me a day in his life.

"Oh, no. We're all set." Collins smiles sweetly. "I wouldn't want to keep Kit from *Vegas*."

My jaw's clenched so tight that it aches. I was hoping she'd missed that mention.

"Exactly right," Flynn says, entirely missing the edge to her tone. "It's going to be an epic weekend. I'd invite you to join us, but the plane's full."

"No worries. I've got plans this weekend."

A muscle in my jaw actually pops, sending a stab of pain down my neck. I glare at Flynn, and he finally gets the message.

He hooks a thumb over his shoulder. "I'll be in the hallway. Nice to see you again, Collins."

"You too," she replies, chipper as could be.

I stand stock-still, waiting for the door to shut.

"So, you're going to Vegas for the weekend," she states.

Only part of the weekend. I'm flying back in time for Lili's dinner tomorrow. But I doubt that's a clarification Collins cares about, so I don't mention it. "Yeah, I am."

"Fun." She nods toward the report I'm holding. "Don't lose that at a strip club, okay? It took me an hour to arrange all the sections."

I lift an eyebrow. She almost sounds … jealous?

"There are other things to do in Vegas than go to strip clubs," I say.

"Uh-huh. It's really known for its *respectable* establishments."

I shake my head, letting a smile slip through. "Does it bother you that I'm going to Vegas?"

Collins scoffs. "Of course not." She tucks a strand of hair behind her ear.

"You play with your hair when you lie," I say softly. But loudly enough that she hears.

I watch her shoulders stiffen as the comment registers.

"If that's all, Mr. Kensington—"

"Wow. We've backslid straight to *Mr. Kensington*? You're not even going to try calling me Christopher first?"

Collins scowls. "Have a safe flight. I should go. I have plans tonight."

"Yeah, I know you have plans tonight."

And those plans are a large part of why I agreed when Flynn suggested this guys' trip, honestly. I wanted a distraction.

She stares at me for a few more seconds, then turns to leave.

Panic swells in my chest, making it impossible to breathe and forcing forbidden words out. "Don't sleep with him, okay? Just … don't."

Collins glances over her shoulder. I'm expecting anger, but her expression is serious as she tells me, "You don't get a say in that either, Kit."

Then she's gone.

"To Vegas!" Flynn cheers.

I suck the shot down without saying a word, fighting the urge to glance at my watch again and see what time it is. Drinks are usually early, right?

The entire drive to the airport, I squashed the urge to suggest to Flynn that he invite his cousin to join us. Whether he'd accepted or not, it'd have given me a better sense of Perry's intentions. I barely know the guy. I hardly paid attention to him the last time I saw him.

I didn't think Collins was seriously interested in him.

Is she?

I break away from the clump of my friends, taking a seat near the rear of the plane.

Maybe it's for the best, the rational part of my brain tries to argue. If Collins is no longer single, if she's even *more* off-limits than she currently is, maybe I'll finally get over my obsession with her.

"I heard you have a hot assistant," Pierce Archibald states, flopping down in the seat opposite mine. He went to Dalton Academy with me and Flynn.

I scowl in Flynn's direction. He's too busy pouring another round to notice.

"She's just a random friend of Lili's," I reply.

"Is she single? 'Cause I—"

"She's not single," I clip.

"Bummer." He slouches in his seat, pulling out his phone.

I glance out the window at the tarmac. We should be taking off at any minute.

And I've never felt so conflicted about leaving New York.

Collins

The bar Perry suggested we meet at reminds me of the hotel in Chicago where I'd perform, back before I relegated piano to a hobby. It's upscale and refined and elegant, filled with professionals, wearing suits and sipping on drinks.

How *normal* people unwind at the end of a long workweek rather than jetting off twenty-five hundred miles to gamble and party.

Choosing to do exactly that was a devil-may-care decision that's *precisely* the sort of behavior I should expect from Kit Kensington.

So, I can't figure out why I was surprised by it. Disappointed even.

I skirt around a few tables, tucking my bag under my arm so it doesn't bang into anyone.

There's an upright in the far corner opposite the bar, but the bench sits empty. I study the instrument for several seconds, trying to remember the last time I played a piano.

I have an old keyboard that I hauled from New Haven to Chicago, then from Chicago to New York, but I haven't unwrapped the protective cover since my latest move. There's not much space to leave it assembled in my current apartment, but I'm not sure that's why I haven't set it up.

Since I switched jobs in Chicago, I've rarely played. I didn't *have* to once it was no longer my source of income. And when I chose to play, it was a reminder it was no longer my job. Maybe that was a necessary lesson to learn about practicality. Or maybe I gave up too easily. I was so focused on all the ways I was failing; I never considered the way Kit framed things.

I was never thriving as a professional pianist, but at least I was one.

"Would you like a table, miss?" a uniformed waiter stops to ask me. "We fill up fast on Fridays."

"Uh, in a minute. I'm going to use the restroom first."

I'm a half hour early. I told Perry six, expecting Kit to stay late, like he normally does. Sitting alone for thirty minutes doesn't sound very appealing. I'd rather stand all night.

The waiter nods. "Restrooms are down the hall, to the left."

"Thanks."

I follow his instructions, continuing down the hallway and entering the women's room. It smells faintly of lavender and lemon, which should be a calming scent. But my palms are damp and my heart rate rapid as I pause in front of the mirror to dig a lipstick out of my purse.

I'm not sure I should be here.

Talking to Perry in the Hamptons was pleasant. He was friendly and polite, and when he asked for my number—in case any positions opened at his firm—sharing it seemed harmless enough. So did agreeing to meet him for a drink tonight after he texted, suggesting a Chicagoan-to-New Yorker support group meeting.

He's attractive, respectful, and kind, yet I haven't been able to summon any excitement about tonight.

I'd claim the lack of interest as a side effect of Isaac's betrayal … except I don't have any issues with feeling excited around Kit.

I knew Kit before *everything happened with Isaac*, I rationalize.

I just need time to get comfortable around Perry. And then, hopefully, I'll experience some attraction. I haven't slept with anyone since Kit, and although I'm concerned it'll be an inevitably disappointing experience, it might make working together more tolerable. Should make the temporary bout of insanity that resulted in me in his bed feel farther in the past.

I slick my lips with a fresh layer of pink, then rip off a piece of paper towel to dab at the corners of my mouth. The bathroom door swings open, revealing a woman close to my age.

She glances around the restroom, then focuses on me. "I'm so sorry to bother you, but could I borrow a tampon?" She grimaces. "Unexpected appearance, and I'm in the middle of a work happy hour."

"Of course. One sec." I set my purse on the counter and start digging for the striped bag I keep an emergency stash of pads and tampons in.

I can't find it. I took it out to refill … when? I can picture the striped bag sitting on the bathroom counter, but I can't remember putting it back in my purse.

I can't remember … I can't remember the last time I had my period.

Dread slithers down my spine, landing in the pit of my stomach with an uncomfortable lurch. My chest and neck feel hot, like a heater is being blasted my way. My hands and feet feel numb. The tips of my fingers tingle.

Numbers blur as I frantically try to count backward. I saw today's date dozens of times at work, yet I can't recall it right now for the life of me.

The woman's staring at me, waiting expectantly.

I have to wet my lips and clear my throat before I can manage speaking.

"I-I'm *so* sorry. I don't have any with me." I force those two sentences out, my voice sounding distant to my own ears. The numbness is spreading too fast for me to keep up.

"No worries. I'll make do. Thanks for looking." The woman continues walking, heading into one of the bathroom stalls.

I remain frozen.

There's no way that I'm …

I haven't had sex since—

The tiled floor tilts, rapidly enough that I have to slap a palm against the cool counter to remain upright. My head spins, traveling back in time to another bathroom with a wet dress and a fluffy robe.

A fluffy robe Kit untied.

He wore a condom. We had sex three times that night, and he wore a condom each time.

Dates might be blurry, but I can clearly recall stepping over the wrappers when I snuck out that morning. Underwear-less.

But a condom is a flimsy piece of latex, not a solid guarantee to prevent pregnancy. I've known that since Mrs. Miller's PowerPoint presentation in middle school. But I've never *known* it. Not until—possibly—right now.

I cling to that *possibly* like a life raft.

Possibly is the only way I'm going to make it out of this restroom without having a panic attack.

I drop the lipstick back into my bag and hobble toward the door. The floor feels unsteady, but I know it's really me. *I'm* unsteady.

I walk through the bar and into the lobby like I'm in a trance. It's louder and busier than it was when I first arrived, but all the commotion whooshes around me like a wind tunnel.

I'm desperate to get out of here and also terrified to leave. Once I'm outside, I could go to a pharmacy. I could find out for sure. Could convert *possibly* to a yes or a no.

My phone's fallen to the very bottom of my bag. I dig for it as I walk. I finally locate the device and pull it out, right as I collide with a wall.

A wall that turns out to be the guy I'm supposed to be on a date with tonight.

Perry's face stretches in a broad smile when he recognizes me. It dims when he registers which direction I'm headed in.

"I'm so sorry." The apology spills out in a torrent of words. "I'm not feeling well. Can we reschedule?"

Perry blinks a couple of times, clearly taken aback. "Oh. Of course." His hands drop from my biceps, where he steadied me. "Are you okay? Can I help you get home?"

"I'm okay, thanks. I think—I think it was … something I ate."

Perry nods sympathetically. "Food poisoning?"

The remaining blood drains from my face as I recall the recent times I've felt nauseous and chalked it up to stress or nerves or … food poisoning.

Keep it together, Collins.

"Probably. I'll text you, okay?"

Perry's, "Okay," trails behind as I rush out the door.

Probably to throw up.

CHAPTER 13
Kit

B ash is the one who opens the front door of my grandfather's house. "Hey. How was Vegas?"

I yawn. "It was—wait, what are you doing here?"

My brother rolls his eyes before stepping to the side so I can enter. "Nice to see you too, bro."

"I mean, why aren't you at school?"

Bash hasn't even been gone a month. Normally, he doesn't come home until Thanksgiving.

He cocks his head. "Why do you think?"

"Lili," we say in unison.

I shake my head as I step inside the entryway of my grandfather's mansion. The soaring ceilings and sparse furnishing have always reminded me more of a mausoleum than a home.

"Classes going okay?" I ask.

Bash shrugs. "Yeah, they're easy."

"Right."

Bash is the brainiac in the family. Lili struggled in school because of her dyslexia, and I was always more interested in socializing than studying. Bash doesn't seem to spend much more time studying than I did, yet he's never brought home anything except an A.

A massive gilded mirror hangs directly across from the staircase. I check my reflection in it as we pass and straighten my tie. I changed on the plane back from Vegas, during landing because I had fallen asleep as soon as I was on board.

Above the staircase hangs the one sentimental decoration. A family portrait of my father, uncle Oliver, grandfather, and late grandmother. Everything else—the rugs, the vases, the furniture—is swapped out on a regular basis. But that painting has never moved. Not during my lifetime at least.

"I don't get why we all had to meet this guy *here*," I complain to Bash as we continue toward the sitting room, where drinks get served before dinner. "Not to mention, we've all *already* met him."

"He wasn't dating Lili when we met him," Bash replies.

"What difference does that make?"

"What difference does meeting a *random guy* or *Lili's boyfriend* make? C'mon, Kit. She's our sister. We need to check this guy out."

I snort. "You gonna threaten him to a duel or something? Because that *would* make this dinner worth attending."

"I know it's a foreign concept to you, but this is what people in relationships do. They spend time with each other's families."

"I'm twenty-three. Since when is that the time to settle down?"

"You'd understand this dinner more if you'd ever been in a relationship, is all."

"Because you're an expert?"

Bash dated one girl in high school and hasn't gotten serious with anyone since. He's always refused to talk about it, so I have no clue what went down between them.

"More of an expert than you," Bash retorts, then strides ahead into the sitting room.

I sigh and follow.

The beagles my parents adopted after becoming empty nesters are the first to greet me. Ben drools on my left shoe while Jerry leaves a noticeable tuft of white fur on my navy slacks as he rubs against my shin.

Mom reaches me third, pulling me into a tight hug. Since she's wearing her usual heels, the top of her head fits right under my chin. "You look tired, honey," she says when she releases me, straightening my even tie.

I grin. "Been working hard."

"He just got back from Vegas," Bash comments, sprawling out in one of the armchairs angled in front of the fireplace.

I flip him off behind Mom's back.

"He *has* been working hard," Dad states proudly from his spot on the couch.

He's transferring some caviar—the only hors d'oeuvre my grandfather serves—onto a plate. Ben and Jerry have abandoned their welcoming-committee roles in favor of begging at his feet.

"Thanks for the support, Pops." I clap him on the shoulder as I pass the couch and continue toward the armchair beside Bash. "Where's everyone else?"

Belatedly, I'm realizing there's no sign of Lili or Charlie. I swear, if she made me come to this, only to not show up, I'll—

"They're on their way," Mom says. "Arthur invited them for seven thirty."

I check my watch. It's seven fifteen. "Then why the hell did Dad tell me to show up at seven?"

I shoot him an accusing look, and he avoids my gaze.

"Because Mom knew you'd be late," Bash supplies.

I scowl. "Turns out, I'm *early*."

"What a refreshing change, Christopher."

Bash sits up straight when our grandfather enters the room. So do I. Arthur Kensington has a presence that's impossible to ignore.

"The butler is dealing with an … incident." Grandpa casts a disapproving look at the dogs, which makes me think they were somehow involved. "So, I'll be serving drinks. Scarlett, what can I get you?"

"Some white wine would be lovely, Arthur."

Grandpa nods. "Crew?"

"Usual scotch, Dad, thanks."

"Christopher?"

"I'll take a Sex on the Beach."

Bash makes an awful attempt at covering his laugh with a cough.

"I don't know, nor do I want to know, what that is. Would you prefer scotch or cognac, Christopher?"

I stretch my legs out and cross my ankles. "Scotch."

"Sebastian?"

"Same. *Please*." Bash shoots me a superior grin.

He's always been a suck-up.

Grandpa delivers our drinks, then takes a seat on the empty couch opposite Mom and Dad. Unfortunately, his keen eyes focus on me first. "How is it going at Kensington Consolidated, Christopher?"

I down a healthy amount of my scotch, hoping refills are self-serve. "All right. Company should break even this month."

Bash quickly raises his glass to cover his smile.

Grandpa doesn't appear amused. "I hope you manage to act more professional at the office," he states.

"Stop by sometime and see."

A few beats longer than his usual response time pass before Grandpa responds, "Perhaps I will."

Dad casts a startled look in Grandpa's direction. As far as I know, my grandfather hasn't been to Kensington Consolidated's headquarters since stepping down as CEO of the company decades ago. He'll attend various events, and he's always present at the annual company gala, but he's totally removed from daily operations. I assume that's by choice because my grandfather is relentless when it comes to getting what he wants.

Ben and Jerry, who just settled on the rug, suddenly leap to attention and dash out of the room.

"I doubt the butler will be thrilled about that," Grandpa states.

But *he* doesn't sound all that peeved by the dogs' behavior. This is an awfully big house to live in alone. Must be quiet when it's just him and the staff.

Lili and Charlie appear in the doorway. My sister crouches down to rub Ben's belly while Charlie's watching Jerry sniff his shoes.

"You're late," I drawl.

Lili straightens and props a hand on her hip. "Did Mom tell you six thirty instead of seven thirty? That's the only explanation for why *you're* here on time."

Bash chuckles.

I roll my eyes, but I'm tempted to smile. I missed my siblings. It's been strange, returning to an empty penthouse after having Bash crash with me for most of the summer. And it feels like Lili just returned to New York, and she's about to leave for Ireland to redesign a college campus in Dublin. After tonight, I probably won't see Lili or Bash until Thanksgiving.

"We're just glad you made it," Mom says, going over to greet them. "It's so good to see you, Charlie." She gives him a hug, then embraces Lili.

I study Charlie as he shakes hands with Dad. And I get, a little more, what Bash was talking about earlier. I've met plenty of guys Lili has dated. But this feels more symbolic than a simple dinner, like he's joining our family for more than just tonight.

Bash and I are up next.

"Nice to see you again, Kit," Charlie tells me as we shake hands.

"Hullo, Your Highness," I say. "Blimey, am I chuffed to see you."

Bash groans. "*Kit.*"

"What?" I reply in my normal voice. "That was my best British accent." I glance at Charlie. "Pretty good, right?"

Charlie gains some points in my book for keeping his expression serious. Then again, he's British. Don't they usually look stoic?

"Very impressive," he compliments.

I shoot Bash a *ha* look. He scoffs in response, then starts telling Charlie about his recent trip to Alaska. I mainly tune the story out since I've heard it several times before.

Grandfather's engrossed in conversation with Lili, sporting the first smile I've seen all night.

Mom catches my eye, nodding toward the dogs and then pointing toward the back of the house. *Take them out?* she mouths.

I nod, heading for the doorway. En route, I pause at the bar cart to top off my tumbler.

A low whistle draws Ben's and Jerry's attention. The beagles trot after me eagerly, claws clicking on the marble floor as we pass the twin curved staircases. Glass doors line the far wall, overlooking the pool and the manicured backyard. I open one, letting the dogs out onto the grounds.

Ben—at least, I *think* it's Ben; they're hard to tell apart—releases a joyful bark and beelines toward a hydrangea. Jerry hustles after him, tail wagging at full tilt, and they start wrestling on the grass.

Those beagles went from being next on the list for euthanasia to playing in paradise. Talk about a lucky break.

The patio furniture hasn't been brought in yet, so I take a seat on one of the loungers. It's long enough that only my shoes hang off. I recline, folding my hands behind my head.

The sun's just starting to set, spreading pastels across the sky that reflect off the calm surface of the pool.

"Mr. Social sitting alone? That's a rare sight."

I reach for my scotch, sipping some before relaxing deeper into the cushions as I watch Lili approach. "You left Charlie to fend for himself?"

I've never met a significant other's parents, but I imagine it'd be a rather stressful experience to face alone.

"He'll be fine," Lili says casually. "I was headed to the bathroom and saw you sitting out here."

I yawn. I might have to limit my scotch intake to stay awake during dinner. "Mom asked me to take the dogs out."

Lili glances toward the beagles. "They're probably going to ask you to pet-sit when they visit me in Dublin."

"Hard pass."

Lili smirks as she slips her shoes off and lies down on the lounger opposite me. "Keeping your schedule open for another Vegas trip?"

I shake my head. "Do you think there's anyone in Manhattan that Bash *hasn't* mentioned that to?"

Lili laughs. "C'mon, Kit. He's just trying to be like you. Bash worships the ground you walk on."

I laugh too. "No, he doesn't."

He usually acts more like my older brother than a younger one. If anything, I've provided him a blueprint of what *not* to do.

"Of course he does," Lili insists. "Why do you think he did that trip to Alaska? Because you're always returning from some crazy adventure or sharing some wild story. He admires you. He's trying to act like you. People pay attention to me and Bash because we're Kensingtons. They pay attention to you because you're *you*."

"You're good at making outlandish ideas enticing."

When Collins said that, I was taken aback. Not only because it was vaguely complimentary, but because I'd never thought about my choices in those terms. I've pursued what appealed to me, knowing other people often got entertainment out of it. But never thinking it was an ability or something anyone would admire about me.

"Is this humbleness Charlie's influence?" I ask. "Because we both know you could change your last name and still draw plenty of attention."

"Maybe," Lili says seriously. "He makes me see the world

differently. Does that sound dumb?"

"Nah. That doesn't sound dumb."

"How's it going with Collins?"

I was expecting that question from Lili at some point this evening, so it's easy not to react. "Good. Fine."

"Really? You downgraded from *good* to *fine* in the span of two seconds."

I huff a laugh. "I didn't mean to downgrade."

"Did something happen?"

"Don't sleep with him."

I tap my finger against the side of my glass. "We … argued on Friday."

"I'm pretty sure you and Collins have argued every time you were in the same room together."

"Yeah, well, we haven't been arguing lately, so I … feel badly. I was stressed about some other stuff, and I took it out on her. I'll apologize on Monday."

"You'd better. What was the argument about?"

"Just a work thing."

"Huh."

"She wanted me to say hi to you, by the way."

"If she's talking to you on Monday, tell her hi back."

"Ha," I reply, but unease twists in my chest.

Her *strip club* comment couldn't be categorized as *professional*, but I definitely didn't de-escalate things by interfering in her sex life.

"There you two are! I've been looking everywhere." Mom walks out on the patio.

"You told me to come out here," I point out.

"Twenty minutes ago. I figured you'd been back inside for a

while—oh no." Mom's fixated on a spot by the pool.

I twist to look, too, spotting the hole that's been dug in the pristine grass immediately. It stands out, unfortunately.

"You can explain how *that* got there to your grandfather's gardeners," Mom states before heading inside with the dogs. They trot after her in tandem, the picture of perfect obedience.

I sigh. "I'm never dog-sitting again."

Lili sits up and slips her heels back on. "C'mon, Kit. A little responsibility won't kill you."

"You weren't exactly keeping a close eye on things yourself," I call after her.

Lili just laughs as she heads inside.

I drain my glass, stand, and follow.

CHAPTER 14
Collins

There's a loud thud overhead. Another. Then a third.

I lie perfectly still on my lumpy mattress, silently praying that the ceiling will collapse and bury me in a cave of plaster. Unfortunately, it holds, even as the sounds overhead increase in frequency *and* volume.

Moaning joins the thudding, and I realize exactly what I'm listening to.

You've got *to be kidding me.*

I roll over onto my side, pulling a pillow atop my head in an

attempt to block out the noise from my neighbors. The down doesn't muffle much. Worse, the movement makes my stomach heave.

I slide out of bed and stumble into the bathroom, hovering over the porcelain rim I've spent far too much time staring at in the past twenty-four hours.

Nothing comes out. There's nothing *to* come out at this point.

Rather than return to bed, I sink down onto the tiled floor and glance at the counter next to the sink.

I bought two pregnancy tests. They were on sale—buy one, get one fifty percent off—and I thought, *Hey, if I'm ever late again, I won't have to skulk down the pharmacy aisles.* It felt like a preventative step, the way you convince yourself it's less likely to pour if you bring an umbrella versus going outside unprepared.

My plan was, take one test, rule out the possibility, then save the other for a rainy day.

Except the first test was *positive.*

And one positive result could be a faulty fluke.

But two? That sounds a lot more like a clear consensus.

Another wave of anxiety hits, constricting my chest and chilling my blood. No matter how many times I adjust position, a permanent weight has settled in the pit of my stomach. Like an anchor I can't shake and am stuck dragging around.

I rest my forehead on my knees, forcing my lungs to pull in deep, even breaths. My vision blurs with a mixture of tears and dizziness as my kneecaps press against my eyeballs.

I've never felt more alone. More terrified.

There are people I could tell, but then I will have *told* someone. The words will be out in the world, real in a way I'm unprepared to deal with.

Now.

Maybe ever.

I've never given having kids any real consideration. It was always a choice in the hazy future. Isaac and I were never serious enough to discuss the possibility of marriage, let alone starting a family.

No part of me has ever pondered what this moment might be like. But I assumed—hoped—it'd be planned. That apprehension would be mixed with joy and excitement, not raw panic. That my sole companion wouldn't be this paralyzing feeling of isolation.

I push upward on shaky legs. My feet fell asleep a few minutes ago, and my limbs were already heavy with dread.

My fumbling fingers take a full minute to unbox the second test.

I pee on another stick, then clutch the edge of the bathroom counter as I wait for the allotted seconds to tick by. Busy my brain by teetering between a warm flicker of hope and a cold torrent of terror.

If it's negative, nothing will change. This will be a distant, unpleasant memory that turns into a cautionary tale about staying on birth control after a bad breakup. I'll continue with my normal routine at work, find a gym like I've been meaning to, reschedule with Perry, and—

I glance down, terror dousing hope as I stare at the word *Pregnant* for the second time. Two for two. I should have bought a third test, not that there's any need for a tiebreaker.

My grip tightens on the cold stone of my bathroom counter, clutching it so tightly that my knuckles ache.

Pregnant.

There aren't many singular words that can change your entire life. I'm looking at one of them.

Slow, shocked steps carry me out of the bathroom and into my tiny kitchen. My upstairs neighbors have shut up at least. I begin the process of brewing a cup of tea on autopilot and open a box of cereal, making myself swallow a few bites that I hope won't upset my uneasy stomach.

My appetite might be nonexistent, but my body needs fuel.

I'll be fine, I attempt to assure myself.

I'm pregnant, not dying. Thousands of other women are pregnant at this precise moment. Women take the same test I just did, *hoping* for this result.

The tight knot in my chest eases a little. Perspective is important. And … I have options that don't end with me becoming a mother. Arrogantly—absurdly—I never thought abortion or adoption were choices *I'd* have to contemplate on a personal level.

I have a job, which means money and health insurance. Security, if I stay pregnant.

Except … I can't keep my job. I can't continue working at Kensington Consolidated.

My brain's been shielding me—or maybe it's just too shocked to process—that there's a second half to this equation. This wasn't an immaculate conception, and I've only been with one guy since Isaac and I broke up back in the spring.

I'm not just pregnant. I'm pregnant with *Kit Kensington*'s baby.

Kit, the billionaire playboy.

Kit, Lili's brother.

Kit, my new *boss*.

The electric kettle shuts off, the low *click* barely registering.

I'm too busy retracing all the decisions that led here. I shouldn't have taken the job at Kensington Consolidated. I shouldn't have gone up to Kit's room. I shouldn't have gone to that party in the Hamptons. I shouldn't have worn a light-colored dress that night.

If I'd just kept my legs closed around him, like I'd *sworn* to myself I would, this never would have happened.

But I can't change any of those past choices.

I'm pregnant with Kit Kensington's kid.

No matter how many times I repeat that insane sentence in my head, the shock value refuses to wear off. It's the most insane statement I've ever heard, and it's my new reality.

And I *need* the shock value to wear off because I need to figure out what the fuck to do about it. I have to face Kit at work tomorrow, which I was already nervous about, thanks to our most recent conversation. Him becoming my boss after our summer tryst was bad enough. But I'm *currently* pregnant. I'm carrying around the evidence it happened, and if I stay pregnant, it'll become obvious.

Saying the words seems impossible. I try, in the relative quiet of my apartment. They come out in an intelligible whisper. I can't imagine saying them to someone. And I *really* can't fathom telling *Kit.*

The knot in my chest draws tight again.

I don't have to tell anyone, I remind myself. This could stay a secret—my secret—forever.

But that doesn't seem like a solution. No relief hits when I consider ending this pregnancy. Not to mention the prick of guilt about making that decision without consulting Kit.

I finally pour the boiling water over a bag of chamomile before carrying a mug of tea over to the couch. The steam coats my face with a fragrant mist, making me feel sleepy. Or maybe my body has simply burned through all the adrenaline it's capable of producing for the time being. Worrying is exhausting.

I curl up on the couch, hands cupped around hot ceramic. One drops, my warm palm pressing against my flat stomach.

I'm not ready to have a baby. Eight months doesn't sound like nearly enough time to prepare for the rest of my life to change.

And I seriously doubt the billionaire who knocked me up during a one-night stand and who's spending his weekend partying in Vegas wants to tackle parenthood.

Which leaves me ... where?

Kit

Today, she's wearing a dark green blazer. Yesterday, it was a lilac blouse. Monday, a navy cardigan.

I don't know when I started cataloging Collins's outfits. I never consciously decided to. But every morning, when I walk past her desk, I take a mental snapshot. Throughout the day, I think about her sitting outside my office. And by the end of the day, I've memorized her appearance.

"Morning, Collins," I greet.

She glances up from the computer screen as I pause beside her

desk. "Morning, Kit."

"Feels like fall out," I state.

The weather. I'm bringing up the *weather*, like an unoriginal idiot.

Collins nods. "It does. Nice to not have to add more layers when I get here anymore."

I frown. "You're cold?"

She mentioned the building's cool temperature when we were stuck in the elevator, and they do blast the air-conditioning in here over the summer. But I tend to run warm, and cold air is bliss when you're wearing two layers of starched fabric.

"I'm fine," Collins replies, which isn't really an answer.

I glance at my watch. "You're here early."

It's barely past eight. The company's workday "officially" begins at nine a.m.

"So are you," she points out.

I showed up at eight on the dot on Monday, wanting to clear the air with Collins as early as possible. She arrived ten minutes later, and I didn't ask why. I simply apologized for my behavior on Friday, and she did the same. I didn't ask about her date; she didn't mention Vegas.

We've reverted to the same civility as when she first started, and I keep telling myself it's for the best.

I like Collins. I've *always* liked Collins, and I also happen to be insanely attracted to her. That was true long before she started at Kensington Consolidated, and spending a minimum of forty hours a week in close proximity to her hasn't solved the problem.

But she *works* for me. And not only is she a fantastic assistant, but she's settled in well at the company. I've seen her smiling and chatting with some of the other assistants on this floor. Eating lunch and grabbing coffee.

An affair with my assistant is what some people would probably expect from me. They'd gossip and whisper and point, but plenty of them would wink and laugh and joke. *All* of them would gossip and whisper and point at Collins. I'd be called irresponsible; she'd be labeled a slut. My world is especially vicious to outsiders.

I've already lingered at her desk longer than I should've. We're not alone on this floor, although it's a lot quieter than it'll be in an hour.

I tap the wood counter once. "Hold any calls this morning. I've got to review all the latest *Phoenix Gazette* documents and don't want any distractions."

Collins nods. "Will do."

I nod back, then continue walking.

"Kit?"

I halt and turn around. "Yeah?"

"I, uh …" Collins taps a pen against her keyboard. "I was wondering if it would be okay if I left a little early this afternoon. Around three? I have a, um, doctor's appointment."

My forehead furrows as I take a step closer to scrutinize her appearance more closely. "Are you okay?"

She *looks* healthy. She's wearing some makeup, but not a lot. Maybe she's a little pale?

"I'm fine," Collins says quickly. "It's just a regular checkup." She bites her bottom lip. Nervously almost.

Does she seriously think I'm going to tell her she can't go to the doctor?

"Of course," I reply. "Take all the time you need. The whole afternoon if you want."

Collins smiles. "That's not necessary. But thanks."

"Don't worry about clearing that stuff with me, by the way."

"I'm supposed to. You're my boss."

She grimaces a little on that last word, which makes me grin.

"I trust you. If you need to leave early or come in late, you don't need to ask my permission. Just put it on my calendar so I don't wor— wonder where you are."

"This won't be a regular thing. No *special treatment*, remember?"

I won't be touching the edge in her tone. I know why it's there.

"I told you, it's not special treatment, Monty."

She breaks eye contact when the nickname slips out—practically proving her point—and I curse internally.

I clear my throat. "I'm treating you the same I would any assistant, okay?"

Is that true? I'm not entirely sure. She's the *only* assistant I've ever had, and I can't imagine having a similar rapport with a random woman, no matter how competent she was. I've never had a similar rapport with *any* woman, colleague or not.

"Okay," Collins says, but the word lacks any real conviction.

"You've arrived early or worked late every day since you started," I remind her. "So, I owe you about twenty hours of vacation time. The least I can do is let you leave early once."

"I'll add it to the calendar."

I continue studying her, valiantly attempting to avoid the view of her cleavage that me standing and her sitting offers. "You sure you're okay?"

She's been acting off this whole week, but I assumed it was lingering awkwardness from Friday. Now I'm worried something else is going on. Did something happen on her date? If so, I'm probably the last person she'd confide in.

Her lips press into a tight, straight line. "Do I not look okay?"

Talk about a loaded question.

I attempt a diplomatic answer. "You look … a little tired."

"Gee, thanks." Her eyes roll above the dark circles shadowed beneath them.

"You look beautiful, Collins."

She breaks eye contact when I compliment her. The tally of things I shouldn't have said during this conversation is rapidly rising.

"I haven't been sleeping well. My upstairs neighbor is a sex fiend. It's like living in the dorms again."

I smirk at that. "I didn't realize Montgomery Hall was such a den of depravity. It seemed respectable when we dropped Lili off."

"You mean, *until* you dropped Lili off."

I laugh. "She raised hell from day one?"

I don't remember much of Lili's behavior on the day we dropped her off. I was distracted by her roommate.

"I'm talking about *you*, Christopher Kensington."

My focus sharpens. "What?"

"You swaggered in, all gorgeous and—"

"You thought I was gorgeous?"

Collins presses her lips tight together again. "That was the general consensus."

I guess we can both be diplomatic.

I rest my elbows on the edge of her desk and lean forward. "And did you *agree* with the general consensus?"

She deliberately breaks eye contact to look at her computer screen. "Glenn just sent an email about the Beauté pitch. He's suggesting setting up a follow-up meeting."

I sigh. Of course he is.

"I'll see you later," I say, catching her nod before I step into my office.

No wonder I avoided it for so long. Being responsible sucks.

From: ckensington@kensingtonconsolidated.com

To: imichaels@kensingtonconsolidated.com

Subject: A/C

Hey Indy,

Who controls the A/C on this floor? My office is cold.

—Kit

Christopher Kensington

Vice President

From: imichaels@kensingtonconsolidated.com

To: ckensington@kensingtonconsolidated.com

Subject: Re: A/C

Hi Kit,

Rumor is, you now have your own assistant, who you could ask.

—Indy

P.S. How was Vegas?

Indy Michaels

Assistant to Asher Cotes

From: ckensington@kensingtonconsolidated.com

To: imichaels@kensingtonconsolidated.com

Subject: Re: Re: A/C

Please? I'll send you a *really* nice wedding gift.

Vegas was fine.

—Kit

Christopher Kensington

Vice President

From: imichaels@kensingtonconsolidated.com

To: ckensington@kensingtonconsolidated.com

Subject: Re: Re: Re: A/C

You'll be toasty by noon.

Tony said this was too expensive to include on our registry. *link attached*

—Indy

Indy Michaels

Assistant to Asher Cotes

CHAPTER 16

Collins

<p>aper crinkles as my heels bang against the bottom of the exam table.

Crinkle. Bang. Crinkle. Bang. Crinkle. Bang. A symphony of stress.

I've been sitting here, alone, ever since the nurse left, waiting for Dr. Bailey to come back in and confirm what two tests—not to mention a temperamental stomach, sore boobs, and no period—already told me.

I got through the invasive questions and the internal exam. And

the peeing in a cup. The hard part of this visit is over with, right?

Not according to the nerves tumbling around in my stomach like clothes during a spin cycle. I've been stuck in a permanent state of anxiety since last weekend, walking around with this invisible weight. Cursing my shitty luck.

New York was supposed to be a fresh start after Isaac's cheating. Job-searching the first time was miserable enough. Doing so again, this time having to explain the blip on my résumé at Kensington Consolidated? And possibly considering each company's maternity leave policy? Feels like a really high mountain I have no desire to climb.

The door finally opens, revealing Dr. Bailey. She gives me an apologetic smile. "Hello again. Sorry for the wait."

I push a, "No problem," past stiff lips as she takes a seat in the swivel chair next to the exam table. My palms are so damp that they're sticking to the paper I'm sitting on.

Dr. Bailey extracts a sheet of paper from the folder she's holding. "The bloodwork and urine test both confirm that you're pregnant."

The news I was expecting, but it still feels like the air was knocked out of my lungs. I nod, blinking rapidly. I haven't said *I'm pregnant* aloud to anyone except myself, but hearing Dr. Bailey say it feels very real.

This is real.

This is happening.

The last shred of hope has shriveled up. We're no longer discussing a hypothetical.

Dr. Bailey's expression is sympathetic. "I take it, this pregnancy was unplanned?"

My laugh is thin and watery. "Yes. *Very* unplanned."

"Based on the date of your last period, you're six weeks along."

Six weeks. Based on the date of my last period.

I didn't even know that was how due dates were calculated. I figured you just added nine months to the day you had sex. *That's* how unprepared I am for motherhood.

"Okay," I whisper because I think Dr. Bailey is expecting some acknowledgment.

"That puts your due date at May 18."

"Okay," I repeat.

Dr. Bailey pats my knee. "I know this is all very overwhelming, Collins. If it's any consolation, I've had patients who were actively trying to conceive sit here, shocked."

That does make me feel a little better. But the primary emotion is still panic.

"Would you like to discuss different options?"

I shake my head. "No. I know—I know what my options are. I just … I need to think. Decide if I'm going to … stay pregnant."

That phrasing sounds better than any mention of the B-word. I'm *already* pregnant. *Staying* pregnant sounds manageable. Way less terrifying than saying the words *I'm having a baby* out loud. But one is on repeat in my head. *Baby, baby, baby, baby, baby.* Such a small, short, *scary* word.

"All right. Here's some literature, in case you want to take a look at it later." She pulls out a pile of prepared pamphlets, setting them on the exam table.

"Thank you."

"And we'll go ahead and schedule your first ultrasound. Those appointments fill up fast, but we can always cancel if need be."

I nod.

"Is the father in the picture?"

"I-I don't know," I admit.

I *almost* told Kit. He was staring at me this morning, confident and *concerned*, when I told him about this appointment, and I almost blurted it out. In that moment, it felt like telling him would be a relief. I wouldn't be alone in this any longer.

But I couldn't get the words out.

I wasn't *positive* I was pregnant yet, and I wasn't sure what I'd do if I was. It's not as if Kit is a guy I can easily never see again. Setting aside the work situation, he's Lili's brother. Unless I end my friendship with her and leave New York, there will always be a chance our paths will cross. What if I tell him, decide not to keep it, but he wants me to? What if I tell him, decide to keep it, and he thinks I shouldn't?

This is a big—maybe the *biggest*—decision you can make with someone. And that someone is usually a spouse or some sort of significant other.

I like Kit. I'm starting to respect him. But telling him this will be a lot more vulnerable than him seeing me naked. A risk, and I'm someone who prefers to play it safe.

And setting aside the emotional aspect, he's a Kensington. After living with Lili for a year and working at Kensington Consolidated for several weeks, I have a strong sense of what that means. They're widely considered to be the most important, prestigious family in the country. Unfortunate circumstances—like an accidental pregnancy—don't happen to people like that. If they do, they're dealt with.

Dr. Bailey is waiting patiently. I'm sure she has other patients to visit, but she's not projecting any sense of urgency. There's no judgment on her face.

I didn't want to discuss my options because I'd already decided.

I think it's why I've been panicking so much—because the hard part isn't over. The hard part is the next eight months to eighteen years.

I swallow hard. "How soon can you do a paternity test?"

CHAPTER 17

Kit

I'm halfway down the hallway when I hear my name being called.

I glance back to see Levi striding toward me with a wide smile on his face. "They're in."

I grin back. "Great. The whole team's on board?"

"And Glenn is striding around like a peacock," Levi tells me.

I chuckle at the apt description. "He should save some smugness for after papers have been signed."

But I agree Beauté agreeing to this dinner is a good sign. I know

they've met with other companies. If they're willing to go to dinner with us, we're still in the running, if not their top choice, for a deal.

And Glenn made a good call, suggesting we push for another meeting before the end of the week.

Levi and I confirm the details, and then I resume walking toward my office.

Collins isn't at her desk, but she hasn't left yet. The small suitcase she wheeled into work this morning is tucked behind her desk. She's headed home to New Haven this weekend for her sister's birthday.

I continue into my office and catch up on as many emails as possible before I have to leave.

At five fifteen, there's a knock on my door.

"Come in," I call, expecting Levi.

Collins walks in instead. "Hey."

"Hey," I reply. "Figured you'd left by now."

"Not yet."

My inbox chimes with a reply to the email I *just* sent, stealing my attention. I grind my molars as I mentally uncross it off my to-do list. I likely won't have time to respond before I need to leave for the dinner.

"Can I—can I talk to you?"

I close out of a few open windows on the screen. "Can it wait until Monday? I've got dinner with Beauté's board at six."

"Oh. That isn't on your calendar for tonight."

"I forgot to add it. Levi just let me know. Glenn is gloating, of course, but if this deal goes through, it'll be worth it."

When I glance up, Collins is still hovering halfway between me and the door. She normally strides over to my desk, and she rarely *asks* if she can talk to me. She says whatever she needs to tell me and then returns to her desk.

My fingers slide off the keyboard. Now, I'm confused and curious. "It's fine. I have a few minutes. What's up?"

"Oh, um … well …" She doesn't move, and she stops speaking, gnawing on her lower lip nervously.

I stand. "What—"

"No. Sit." She finally walks deeper into my office. "You should, um, sit."

I frown at the waver in her voice. But I do sit since Collins follows her own advice and perches on the edge of one of the armchairs opposite my desk. *Perches*, like she's prepared to flee at any second. She smooths the skirt of her dress repeatedly, avoiding eye contact.

I've never seen her like this. Fidgeting and pale and uncertain. It's such a contrast from the woman who constantly challenges me.

My mind races with possible explanations. Is she having problems with another employee? Maybe one of them found out she knows Lili and is spreading rumors about how she got the job. Something with Perry? She hasn't mentioned him since their date. Or maybe there's an issue with a project that's going to cause problems for me? Did something happen with her family? Is that why she's going home this weekend? Is she *not* going home this weekend anymore?

"You're seriously freaking me out, Collins," I finally state when she continues to say nothing.

She whispers something under her breath. I have to strain to hear, but I'm almost certain she says, "Just you wait."

My frown deepens. Wait for *what*?

"Okay. Here it is." Collins's shoulders square like she's stepping into a boxing ring to face an opponent. "I'm pregnant. And you're the only person I've had sex with in the past five months, so …"

I've been surprised before. Or I *thought* I had been surprised before.

Surprise suddenly seems like a very small word to describe my brother showing up on my new penthouse's doorstep with a request to stay with me for the summer. Or my sister dating a damn duke who allegedly lives in a castle. Or even my parents announcing they were moving to New York full-time. My dad deciding to work at Kensington Consolidated again.

This is a surprise. A cataclysmic shock that shakes me to my core.

All those theories swirling in my head? Gone.

All my plans for the rest of the day? Vanished.

I can't feel the chair beneath me. I can't move or think or breathe. I can only stare at Collins.

Collins, who's pregnant. Pregnant with my kid.

Her lips are moving again, and I can't hear a single word of what she's saying. There's a dull roar in my ears, like my head is being held underwater or I'm standing in a wind tunnel.

Everything's muffled, all the emotions and thoughts I should be experiencing being held back by an invisible barrier.

I'm floating, with nothing to tether me.

I manage a blink, and my eyes burn like it's been too long since they closed. How long has it been since she appeared in my office? Minutes? Years? I've lost all sense of time.

Collins stands, and the abrupt movement is the first thing to permeate the haze.

Sounds start to trickle in, starting with the buzz of my phone on my desk. Levi is calling.

There's too much happening—a merry-go-round of activity around me—while I'm busy relearning how to blink. Absorbing the impact of this massive boulder that was just dropped on me. A billion tries, and I don't think I would have correctly guessed what Collins came in here to tell me. The possibility simply never occurred to me.

The familiar surroundings of my office spin, making my stomach heave.

I manage to focus on Collins's expression. Her face is impassive, but her eyes are sharp and assessing. Reading my reaction carefully.

I'm not taking the news well, I know.

I should be asking questions, offering reassurances. But I'm just so *stunned*. I'm standing on a stage, under a spotlight, knowing there are lines to say, but unable to recall a single word of the script.

My brain is a blank void, stuck on a loop of Collins's voice saying, *I'm pregnant. I'm pregnant. I'm pregnant.*

"It's almost six. You'll be late for your dinner."

She turns toward the door. She's leaving.

Collins Tate just altered the trajectory of the rest of my life, and she's leaving with a casual reminder of my calendar like I'm not in a catatonic state.

I open my mouth to speak, to tell her to stay, but, "Fuck," is the first word that spills out.

Her shoulders tense, so I know she heard.

She pauses halfway across my office and glances back.

My relief that she's lingering is short-lived.

"Don't worry, Kit. I don't expect anything from you. Have a *great* weekend."

She's gone before I can muster a single syllable in response.

And I'm only certain of one thing.

It's not going to be a great weekend.

CHAPTER 18
Collins

The silver station wagon is waiting alongside the curb when I walk out of the automatic doors. My train ran ten minutes behind, so it's less surprising that he's on time for once.

It's chillier in New Haven than I was expecting, fall's crispness creeping into the evening air. I shove my hands deeper into my hoodie pocket as I start toward the Volvo.

I was dreading this trip home *before* I knew the news I'd need to share. After my awful conversation with Kit earlier, Jane is the only reason I didn't cancel this visit to curl up in bed all weekend.

I open the trunk at the same moment the driver's door creaks open. I dump my duffel bag next to the milk crate, where my dad stores the papers that won't fit in his briefcase, and shut the trunk a little harder than necessary. The entire frame of the ancient station wagon shakes from the impact.

"Hello, Collins."

"Hi, Dad." I shove my hands back into my pocket before turning to face him.

My father isn't a big man. He's tall, over six feet, but slender instead of stocky. He wears tweed suits that evoke his Irish ancestry and horn-rimmed glasses, which are constantly at risk of slipping down his nose.

I watch him appraise the firm set of my shoulders; he looks like he deliberates giving me a hug and decides against an embrace.

Inside my pockets, my hands curl into fists. Fingernails dig into my palms, prompting a sharp burst of pain.

What he did is bad enough. But the way he's never questioned the distance between us, never made any attempt to bridge the gap I initiated? That betrayal cuts even deeper.

"Good trip?" My father's voice is the one thing that doesn't match his unassuming appearance. It's rich and deep and booming, and it commands attention. A tone you'd expect from an army captain, not a chemistry professor.

"It was fine," I answer.

Two hours I spent staring out the window, wondering if I should move to Boston or Philadelphia. I like living in a city, and Chicago's out for obvious reasons.

He nods once, then folds his tall frame back into the driver's seat. Symphony No. 5 is trickling out of the speakers, courtesy of the cassette player. The familiar melody and the familiar ripped seat relax me some despite the awkwardness humming in the air.

We used to talk. About music and books and what was happening in my life—school or friends or boys. Outside of a lecture hall, my father is more of a listener than a speaker. But he was always an excellent sounding board when I needed to vent. And then that awful day happened, and I haven't known what to say to him since.

"I bought some grapefruit juice yesterday," is his attempt at conversation.

Mom and Jane prefer orange juice, so my dad only buys grapefruit juice when I'm visiting.

I open my mouth to say, *Thanks*, but, "I'm pregnant," spills out instead.

To my dad's credit, the car only lurches a little. He hits the brakes too hard, a good foot from the white line that signals the Stop sign. He clears his throat and coasts a few more inches before stopping in the correct spot.

"Wow. That's ... that's big."

My, "Yeah," is flat.

At least he said *something*. I was half expecting him to go mute, same as Kit.

Under any other circumstances—circumstances that didn't point at me becoming a single parent—I would have felt proud of shocking Kit Kensington into silence. I'd never seen him speechless before.

The car behind us honks. We've been at the Stop sign for a lot longer than the requisite three seconds, holding up traffic.

My dad glances in the rearview mirror and sighs like he's disappointed by their impatience before he starts driving again.

Or more likely, he's disappointed in *me*.

Aside from the Beethoven playing, the station wagon is silent. My dad seems to have given up on conversation after my announcement. He could have taken the confirmation that I wasn't a virgin worse, I suppose.

A few blocks later, he breaks the silence again. "Have you been feeling okay? Your mom got pretty sick with you girls."

"I've felt better," I answer honestly. "But I'm fine."

More silence follows.

The first time I got my period, my mom was out of town at a conference. I thought coaching me through that experience, while Jane fretted that I was dying in the background, was the most uncomfortable I'd ever see my father. He tends to freeze under pressure, like a startled deer in headlights. His brain is brilliant when it comes to anything scientific, but emotions seem to require a longer processing time.

So, when we reach the end of the street, he surprises me by continuing the conversation. "I didn't realize you were … seeing anyone."

"I'm not."

My father clears his throat again. Simply, I suspect, to cut through the uncomfortable silence that lingers after that admission. I've just confirmed the worst-case scenario—not only am I knocked up, but I'm knocked up with no support system in sight.

"So, Isaac …"

"It's not his."

I hear my dad's relieved exhale loud and clear between strains of the symphony. He didn't like Isaac. Mom and Jane weren't crazy about him either, but my dad *really* didn't like him. At least us barely speaking never allowed him an opportunity to say *I told you so* after we broke up.

"How is everything else going?"

"Fine."

Another soft sigh. This time, I think it signifies a quiet exasperation with the number of times I've used that four-letter word during this conversation.

But it's the best I can do. Summoning a *great* sounds exhausting. And *terrible* isn't an option. I'm not trying to alarm anyone. Me turning up single and pregnant is going to cause enough concern. My parents aren't religious, but they *are* traditional. I'm sure they expected marriage would predate procreation.

"Jane mentioned you're working for Kit Kensington now."

I glance over at my father for the first time since we started driving. It's strange, hearing Kit's name come out of my dad's mouth in the car I learned to drive in. All of a sudden, he's infiltrating every aspect of my life.

"Yeah, I am."

My dad nods. "I had him in a couple of classes."

"He mentioned that."

"Smart kid."

High praise, coming from my father.

"He has his moments," I mutter.

It caught me off guard when Kit acted like he knew my dad, and I assumed he was exaggerating. Apparently not. Even more strange, my dad seems to like him. I wonder if their bromance will survive when—if—I do a paternity reveal.

A few minutes later, my dad pulls into the driveway of the split-level I grew up in.

I cover a yawn as I step out of the car. It's not even nine, but I feel like I haven't slept in years. This baby is sucking all the energy out of me.

"I've got it," my dad says when I start toward the trunk.

I nod and change course, heading up the brick path that leads to the yellow front door. It opens before I can reach it, my mom shuffling outside in her pink slippers with a wide smile on her face.

"Hi, honey."

"Hi, Mom."

I inhale deeply as she hugs me tight. She smells like lavender; the familiar scent is comforting.

I haven't seen my parents in person since March. My parents visited me in Chicago over Yale's spring break, shortly before everything imploded with Isaac. Once it did, I stuck it out in Illinois for a couple more months before deciding to move to New York. I didn't tell them about the move—let alone the breakup—until after I was already settled in Brooklyn. Accepting assistance isn't a strength of mine.

"Come in, come in," Mom beckons me inside. "I made your favorite."

I glance at my dad, who's headed up the walk with my suitcase in hand. "Great."

My favorite meal—fish tacos—doesn't sound the least bit appetizing right now. I nibbled on saltines during the trip here—the one food I can reliably keep down.

There's a long list of foods I'm no longer allowed to eat. If I'm remembering correctly, cooked fish is fine. Raw is what I have to avoid. Bye-bye, sushi.

"Do you want a glass of wine?" my mom asks as I follow her into the kitchen.

I glance at the doorway trim, where eighteen years of my and Jane's heights are marked with dated lines. "No, thanks."

Newton stands from his favorite spot on the linoleum in front of the stove, stretches, sniffs my foot, and then wanders into the living room to flop down on his bed.

"If you change your mind, I picked up that sauvignon blanc that you liked last time. The one from that vineyard out on Cape Cod, where—"

"I'm pregnant, Mom."

The only reply is a clatter from the fork, which she was using to check the fish's flakiness, falling to the counter.

"So, I can't drink," I continue. "And unfortunately, I'm pretty sure eating cod is not going to end well. Lately, all I can keep down is crackers."

"You're ... you're *pregnant?*" My mom's voice sounds faint, fading, like she's running out of breath.

I nod once and confirm, "Yes."

"I—since when?"

"Uh ..." I suck my bottom lip into my mouth. "I'm six weeks along. So, not long. I went to the doctor on Wednesday. Found out for sure."

My mom's shaking her head. Tugging the strings on her apron loose, like she needs more air. "This is ... I'm just—" She fumbles for her wine and swallows a healthy sip once her fingers close around the glass. Her ability to string together full sentences seems to have flagged for the time being. That, or she's hoping the less she says, the more I will.

I shrug out of my hoodie and drape it over the back of a chair. She left the oven door open, and it's rapidly raising the kitchen temperature.

My mom's gaze immediately falls to my stomach. "Who's ... are you dating someone?"

I break eye contact, sinking into the chair. No sign of Dad. I assume he's taking his time delivering my suitcase, anticipating the bomb that was about to be dropped again. Maybe I should have told my parents together. Maybe I shouldn't have told Kit at work. I have no clue what I'm doing when it comes to any of this, and I'm afraid I'm failing left and right.

"No," I answer. "I'm not dating anyone. He's just a guy I had a … connection with."

Alluding to sex is less awkward with my mom than it was with my dad, but not by much. We're close, but not *that* close.

"Collins, honey …" She's being careful to keep the concern off her face, but I can *feel* it in the fish-scented air as she sighs. "Does the father know about the … situation?"

"No."

I didn't hesitate before lying, and it's not because I'm used to sharing selective truths with my parents.

I was disappointed by Kit's reaction, but I also sympathize with it. I've had some time and a doctor's visit for this baby's existence to be real. I dumped the news on him. And if Kit gets over his shock and chooses to be involved, I want him and my parents to have a clean slate.

"I'm going to tell him," I add. "I just have to decide … how."

"Honesty is always the best policy."

My mom's favorite adage.

"Uh-huh," I agree, standing. Tried that, and all I got was a, "Fuck."

"Can we talk more tomorrow, Mom? I just want to shower and go to bed. I'm exhausted."

I'm also worried she'll have a lot more questions for me once the shock starts to fade, and I'd rather face those in the morning, following a full night of sleep.

She studies me for a few seconds. "You're sure you don't want anything to eat?"

"I'm sure."

"Okay. Let me just grab a couple of things out of your room."

A couple of things turns out to be a nightgown, a robe, slippers, a change of clothes, hand cream, three books, reading glasses, and her laptop.

My parents sleep in separate bedrooms. A suspicion I've had since Jane moved into the dorms three years ago, but they've never been this blatant about it before.

I stand, silent, in the hallway, watching my mom gather up her necessities.

She pauses in the doorway, her belongings stashed in one of the canvas tote bags she hauls around everywhere. She buys the embroidered ones people order and then return because they're always on sale. *Seas the day* is stitched on the side of this one in navy thread.

"You told your father."

It's more of a statement than a question, but I nod. He's still absent, which is a dead giveaway. Probably processing in his office or the garage.

She nods back. "Okay. Sweet dreams, honey."

"Night, Mom," I reply, then head inside my childhood bedroom.

I'm lying wide awake in bed when the door creaks open an inch.

"Linny?"

I smile at the darkness before sitting up. "Hey, Janey."

"I am *so* sorry. I tried to leave earlier." The crack of light from the hallway expands, illuminating the room enough for me to see the silhouette of my sister approaching the bed. She flings her arms around me exuberantly, stinking strongly of spirits.

My nose wrinkles. "Smells like it was a fun night."

Jane laughs as she flops down on the comforter beside me. "It was. We'll go out tomorrow night. There's this really cute bar that opened on Spring Street."

"That sounds fun." I attempt enthusiasm, but Jane sees right through it.

"What's wrong?"

I exhale. I wasn't planning to tell her in the middle of the night, but I don't want to lie either. "I'm pregnant."

There's an accompanying relief when I say it this time. I've told everyone who *needs* to know. Kit, my parents, my sister.

An ear-splitting screech shatters the stillness in the room.

"Jane!" My left arm fumbles wildly for my sister in an attempt to silence her. "Shut up! You're going to wake Mom and Dad."

"Oh my God. Oh my God. Oh my God," Jane chants. "You're *pregnant? Knocked up and growing a baby* pregnant? I'm going to be an aunt! This is so exciting!"

I'm glad one of us is thrilled about the news.

"It gets better," I say dryly. "Remember Kit Kensington?"

"Duh. *Of course* I do."

Jane was one of the unfortunate many who fell in love with Kit during his brief visit to Montgomery Hall.

"Well, he's the father."

"Holy shit." Jane's whispering now at least. "You slept with him? When? And isn't he, like, uh, *your boss*?"

I sigh. "He sure is."

"Holy shit," Jane repeats.

"Yep. It happened *before* he was my boss, which was one of the many reasons I never should have taken the job, but I really wasn't anticipating *this*."

"He's super rich, right?"

"Right," I confirm.

"So, just quit your job. You can live off the child support and finally start playing again."

"It's *child* support, Janey. For the kid, not me. And I don't want his money."

I don't doubt Kit will offer to provide financially. Once his lawyers review the paternity test results, I think he'll set up a trust fund with a lot of zeroes. And, yeah, it's comforting to have that safety net. I don't know much about babies, but I do know they're expensive.

Money doesn't hold your hair while you're throwing up your breakfast though. It doesn't run to the store and buy your cravings. Doesn't help assemble a crib or attend ultrasound appointments.

"Just his dick, apparently." I hear the repressed laughter in Jane's voice.

I groan. "It was a lapse in judgment."

"Was it good? I bet it was good."

"I'm not discussing my child's conception with you."

Jane shifts so she can rest a hand on my cheek. "You're blushing. It was hot, filthy sex, wasn't it?"

Yes.

She giggles. "Did he talk you through it?"

Yes.

"I'm going to sleep."

"Nuh-uh. Not yet. Have you told him?"

"Yeah." I blow out a breath. "I told him."

Jane nudges my arm with the sharp point of her elbow. "And?"

"*Ow.* Stay on your side."

"What did he say, Linny?" she asks softly.

I sigh. "Not much. He was … shocked."

Which I get. I have regular flashes of, *Is this* really *happening?*

The only evidence of this pregnancy so far are the positive tests still sitting next to my bathroom sink and the prenatal vitamins on the kitchen counter. Sometimes, it's easy to forget my life is about to change forever, and when I remember, I'm surprised all over again.

But *Kit* isn't the one who has to grow a human. He isn't the one who has to give birth. I feel entitled to a little more freaking out than him.

"I can't really picture that," Jane muses.

"Well, you met him once when you were twelve, Janey. He's changed."

I thought he had at least.

"I'll get to meet him again," she tells me.

"Maybe," I whisper.

Based on his reaction earlier, probably not.

CHAPTER 19

Kit

*C*ollins is pregnant.

I'm having a kid.

I used to think about normal shit when I ran. School, now work. Upcoming parties or trips. Sports scores.

Now, as I run, those two sentences cycle on an endless loop in my head.

I haven't told anyone. I just tell myself, over and over again, like a motivational mantra. A motivational mantra that makes me want to vomit.

The girl I've been obsessed with since I was a teenager told me she was pregnant with my baby, and my reply was, "Fuck."

Fuck. Fuck. Fuck.

I was shocked. I *am* shocked.

After I brushed my teeth this morning, I stood at the sink for fifteen minutes, watching the toothpaste slide down the drain and listening to, *Collins is pregnant. I'm having a kid,* on endless repeat. Like it was a necessary reminder, not an impossible fact to forget.

I up the pace and sprint faster, even though I'm already dripping with sweat.

I fucked up.

Shock is a shitty excuse for my reaction. I knew I'd messed up before Collins left my office. I acted like a zombie throughout dinner, making up a hasty excuse to leave early, which undoubtedly annoyed the team I was meant to lead and likely meant Beauté would go in another direction.

As soon as I got home, I looked up Collins's number in the employee database and called her. She didn't answer—the first time I called or the three subsequent ones.

Maybe she knew it was me.

Maybe she doesn't answer calls from unknown numbers. I debated leaving a message or texting her, but I didn't know what to say.

Hey, it's Kit. Just wanted to say sorry about my sperm. Call me so we can talk!

If I hadn't known she was out of town, I would have simply shown up at her apartment. But that wasn't an option this weekend.

I grit my teeth and sprint faster.

"I don't expect anything from you."

That sentence stung. Expect is worse than want or need. She

doesn't *expect* anything from me.

Collins thinks I'll—what? Ignore her like an inconvenient truth? Pretend she never said a word? Be a deadbeat dad?

I feel guilty about my initial reaction. Ashamed even. But I'm also pissed. I thought she'd *finally* stopped seeing me as a stupid sixteen-year-old. Since she started working for me, we've acted as a team. Interacted like equals.

I might have a reputation as a partying playboy, one that's not entirely unjustified, but that's not *all* I am. I work hard, and I take responsibilities seriously. She *should* have expectations of me.

The timer on my phone starts chiming merrily. A cheerful sound that only darkens my mood.

I need to shower and change and head into the office. I set my morning alarm an hour earlier than usual to ensure I'm in the office extra early and that there's plenty of time to talk to Collins as soon as she arrives.

Banging the red button on the treadmill doesn't do much to expel my frustration, but it's something. As soon as the belt halts, I grab my water bottle and a clean towel and head for the elevator.

The shiny doors part as I approach, revealing Sadie Carmichael. Her eyes light up when she sees me, her smile only dimming when she registers which direction I'm headed in.

"You already worked out?" She pouts.

"Early meeting. See you around." I step around her and into the elevator, but Sadie sticks a hand out, preventing the doors from closing.

My jaw works as irritation simmers in my bloodstream. My interest in small talk is currently nonexistent.

"Does an early meeting mean you'll get to leave work early? I'm supposed to go to a happy hour tonight with some friends, but I'd rather drink with you." She winks.

I could—and maybe should—simply tell Sadie I'm busy tonight and remind her I'm in a rush. A polite dismissal, like I did when she showed up at my office. Instead, I ask, "You ever have a crush on someone, Sadie?"

"I—of course." She smooths her ponytail, confusion creasing her forehead.

"Well, I've had a crush on the same girl since I was in high school. And every time, I fuck it up with her in some way. I say too much, or I don't say enough, or I—" I shake my head. "I'm trying to stop fucking it up. So, I can't get a drink with you tonight. Or any other night."

The disappointment on Sadie's face fades, little by little, until she's smirking at me. "Aw. That's so cute!"

I grimace. *Cute* can usually be replaced by *pathetic*. "Yeah, thanks. Hopefully, she'll start thinking the same one of these days."

"Pffft." Sadie's gaze traces the length of my body, the appreciation in her gaze not quite extinguished. "How could she resist *you*?"

I laugh as I run a hand through my sweaty hair. A sticky residue coats my palm when it falls back to my side. "She's actually quite good at it."

"Have you told her how you feel? Just straight-up asked her out?"

"Uh … it's complicated."

Sadie rolls her eyes. "Guys *always* say that. Just tell her you like her. How complicated can it be?"

"Well …"

She's my sister's friend.

She works for me.

She's having my baby.

"It's complicated," I repeat.

"Okay. Whatever. If you need advice, you know where to find me."

I smile. "Thanks, Sadie."

"And if you get over this mystery girl, you know where to find me." She winks again.

I huff a laugh and shake my head. Sadie's flirted with me at every opportunity since she moved into this building at the start of the summer. But it never progressed beyond banter. I just bought this penthouse, and I don't want to move anytime soon.

"Bye, Sadie."

"Bye, Kit." She drops her hand, and the doors slide shut.

I got ready for work in record time and step inside the building at seven forty-five. The lobby is empty. So is the first elevator that arrives.

Maya, who sits at the front desk, shoots me a bright smile as I approach. "Good morning, Mr. Kensington."

I smile back, shoving the niggling nerves down as far as I can. I spent all weekend dying to talk to Collins, and now that the moment is almost here, I'm racked with anxiety and terrified I'll fuck this conversation up.

"Good morning, Maya."

I continue down the hallway, passing empty offices and desks, running through the list of questions I prepared about doctor's appointments and custody arrangements and—

She's not here.

I check my watch and curse under my breath. It's five of eight.

After depositing my briefcase by my desk, I head into the break room. I'm halfway through making Collins a coffee when I remember one of the pregnancy sites I browsed this weekend mentioned limiting caffeine intake.

I dump the coffee, brew her an herbal tea instead, and leave it on her desk before returning to mine.

My attempts to answer emails are pathetic. My gaze veers to the clock at the top of the computer repeatedly, literally watching the minutes tick by. I left my door open so I can see when she arrives.

Eight fifteen.

Eight thirty.

At eight forty-five, I accept she's not showing up early.

At eight fifty-nine, I finally hear her voice.

I stand, banging my knee on the bottom of my desk in my haste, and stride toward the door.

She's wearing all blue today. A sky-blue blouse, neatly tucked into a navy pencil skirt.

And she's not alone. She's walking with a blonde woman who is smiling and nodding and looks vaguely familiar. I've seen her around the office before, but I can't come up with her name.

It doesn't escape my notice that Collins normally shows up to work early and alone, but today, she's appearing on time and accompanied. She's also pointedly not looking in my direction. The blonde spots me first, her eyes widening when she notices I'm standing right where they're headed.

"Good morning, Collins," I greet.

Collins's expression is impassive as she nods in acknowledgment. "Good morning." She glances at her companion. "Margot, you know Kit Kensington? My, uh … our boss?"

"I don't think we've ever been formally introduced." Margot holds out a hand for me to shake, smiling brightly. "Nice to meet you, Mr. Kensington."

"Kit, please. And nice to meet you too." My gaze leaps back to Collins. "I need to speak to you in my office."

She sets her bag on the wooden counter that runs around the perimeter of her desk. "I need to check the messages first so I can flag anything urgent."

I rap my knuckles on the wood. "*This* is urgent."

Margot's eyebrows lift an inch. Collins doesn't react at all.

I know I'm acting like an overbearing tyrant. An unreasonable boss. But the past hour spent staring at the clock has frayed my limited patience down to nothing.

I sigh. "Five minutes?"

Collins's spine is stiff as she agrees, "Five minutes."

When I sit back down at my desk, I have eight hundred forty-three unread emails.

I chug half my coffee before clicking on the most recent one. The worst part is, I worked over the weekend. Not very efficiently since I was distracted by Friday night's events, but enough that the number would have been a lot higher if I hadn't.

I still have eight hundred forty emails to go when my office door opens and Collins steps inside.

I sit up straight and adjust my cuff links. Debate standing and decide that's more awkward.

"Take a seat," I suggest, gesturing to the two leather armchairs across from my desk.

"I'm good standing, thanks."

I frown and lean forward, resting my forearms on the edge of my desk. Collins is holding a piece of paper against her pencil skirt, but I can't read what it says from here.

"I called you over the weekend."

As soon as the words are out, I regret them. That's not how I meant to start this conversation—with accusations. But I do want her to know that I *tried* to have this conversation sooner. That I didn't have a *great* weekend, that I had a torturous one.

She doesn't scowl. She doesn't smile either. "I only answer personal calls on the weekend."

"It *was* a personal call, Collins."

"From my boss, who must have gotten my cell number from the company directory."

I clear my throat. "Well, I wasn't *calling* about work. I was calling about …" The word *baby* won't come out. "Will you please sit down?"

I don't want to talk about this at work. In my office, which used to be my dad's office, feeling like a slimeball who's hiding an affair from his wife or something. But I can't act normal all day while she's sitting a dozen feet away. Can't leave things like this for a second longer.

She doesn't look thrilled about it, but Collins sits. Perches on the very edge of the cushion again, but she sits.

I exhale. "I just wanted to say—"

My phone starts ringing, the shrill sound cutting me off.

I wait for it to go to voicemail. It does, then immediately rings again.

"You should get that," Collins comments. "It's probably important."

"So is *this*," I growl, frustration rearing its ugly head again.

I don't mean to snap at her. I'm trying to *apologize*, and it's going terribly. Not only have all my carefully prepared questions fled my head, but it's feeling impossible to have an uninterrupted conversation. Which is why I wanted to do this somewhere else, over the weekend.

My phone falls silent. Then promptly begins ringing for a third time.

I drag a palm down my face, tempted to toss the damn thing in a corner.

"It's probably about the board meeting."

My gaze snaps to Collins. "What board meeting?"

"The one at nine fifteen. It's on your calendar."

Goddamn it.

Board meetings only happen once a month, and they're a big deal. This is my first one since joining the company. I should have been prepping for it over the weekend. Yet another thing I fucked up recently.

I glance at the clock. It's 9:08.

This is going to have to wait. Not showing up to a board meeting isn't an option.

"Are you free for lunch?" I ask.

"I just made plans with Margot."

I clench my jaw, praying for patience. She couldn't have known I was going to ask her, but it feels like Collins is being deliberately difficult. She's certainly not making this any easier.

I deserve it. But I can't fix anything if we don't communicate.

"What about tomorrow?"

"You have a lunch meeting with the Boeing executives."

For fuck's sake.

My phone starts ringing for a fourth time. I answer it, worried there's an actual emergency. Not that many people have my direct line.

"Kensington. What is it?"

"What a pleasant greeting."

My mom. And I know why she's calling—because I avoided her two calls over the weekend.

I pinch the bridge of my nose, already regretting answering. "I'm sorry. But now *really* isn't a good time—"

"You didn't answer your cell, so I was worried. I just …"

I'm distracted from the rest of my mom's sentence as Collins stands, sets the piece of paper she was holding on my desk, and then walks out of my office.

And I tune my mom out entirely as I stare at my pregnant assistant's two weeks' notice.

This awful morning just got a lot worse.

CHAPTER 20
Collins

The swivel chair behind my desk is occupied when I return from lunch. Margot and Stella don't notice Kit right away. They continue chatting about the sample sale in SoHo we're planning to head to after work.

But I can't *not* notice Kit. He commands attention. And it's nothing specific I can pinpoint; it's just *him*.

I notice how similar the blue shade of his shirt is to his eyes. I notice that a piece of hair has fallen across his forehead. I notice the straight line of his jaw, steeled for a fight.

I stiffen, too, squaring my shoulders and lifting my chin like I'm preparing for a war.

It feels like Kit and I are locked in some sort of battle. And honestly, I don't know *why*. I told him about the pregnancy because I felt like I had to. Not because I wanted to. And not because I wanted anything from him.

Was I hoping he'd offer? Yeah. But I'm prepared to do this on my own. I'll follow the plan my mom and I hashed out over the weekend, and I'll—we'll—be fine.

I told him I expected nothing. I'm offering him an easy out, and he's suddenly hell-bent on *talking*.

"Damn," Margot mutters to my left, spotting Kit sprawled in my swivel chair like a king on a throne.

Stella giggles, noticing the same. "Yeah. I'd quit to hit that."

A fresh burst of irritation appears in response to their appreciative tones. What is Kit doing outside of his office, at *my* desk, making a *spectacle* of himself?

"I'll see you guys at five," I tell Margot and Stella, then peel away from them and stride toward my desk solo.

According to the clock on the wall, it's 12:57. Kit has a meeting at one, which is technically when my lunch hour ends. I suggested to Margot and Stella we stop for a coffee to cut it as close as possible, but I didn't delay long enough.

I set my decaf cinnamon latte on the counter of my cubicle, then rummage through my purse for my ChapStick. "You have a meeting at—"

"At one with Benjamin Chase. Yeah, I know." Kit leans forward, resting his elbows on his knees. "How was your lunch?"

"Fine." I can't get the cap of my lip balm off. My hands are too unsteady, shaking with the tension that's tangible in the air between us.

Why is he being so … cordial? I thought he'd be badgering me to talk again. Or angry about the resignation letter I dropped on his desk a few hours ago.

I know he'll have no problem finding a replacement—Margot or Stella would happily volunteer—but I figured me leaving so soon would prick his ego a little bit. Not that I *want* him to be mad, but at least it would be an understandable reaction. Just like I wanted him to say *something* on Friday, not sit silently with a horrified look on his face.

Kit reaches out and tugs the ChapStick from my grip. "What did you get to eat?"

"Uh, soup." I'm preoccupied by how tiny the yellow tube looks in his hands as he wiggles the top off.

He frowns as he hands the ChapStick back to me. "That's it?"

"I wasn't very hungry. My stomach has been …" I let my voice trail as I smear balm on my lips. Glance at the clock—12:59. "You'll be late."

Kit looks at his fancy watch. Stands.

I exhale a sigh of relief. He's leaving.

"I'm taking you out to dinner. Be ready at five."

"I can't tonight. I have plans after work."

"Cancel them."

Those two words are infused with an iron I've never heard from Kit before.

Normally, I consider him too cavalier. He has this ease that's not quite laziness, but close, as if he's always certain he'll get exactly what he wants. Born from a lifetime record of *getting* exactly what he wants.

I wouldn't call Kit spoiled—not unless I was really pissed at him at least—but he's certainly entitled.

His eyes narrow when I say nothing. "That wasn't a request, Collins. Cancel them, or I'll come along as a third wheel."

I almost laugh. Does he think I have a *date* tonight? I don't know whether to be flattered or offended by that assumption. I haven't had the energy to talk to a man who isn't him since I found out I was pregnant, let alone line up a date. Perry has texted twice about rescheduling drinks, and I made up an excuse both times.

I wonder if Kit would drop this if he knew my plans were shopping with Margot and Stella, then decide it's not worth it. If he's going to insist on having this conversation, I'd rather get it over with sooner rather than later.

"Fine," I state. "I'll meet you in the lobby at five."

There's still a chance someone could see us leaving together, but Kensington Consolidated isn't the only company with offices in this building. There's less of a chance.

It's 1:01 now.

I shouldn't like that Kit is prioritizing me over an important client, but I kind of do. I've never witnessed him *fight* for anything before. Yet he's fighting to talk to me, and I'm less immune to that than I want to be.

"Okay. I'll see you then. I mean, I'll see you before, but also—" Kit stops talking, shakes his head once, and then rounds the side of my desk. It's the closest to flustered I've ever seen him. "I hope that's decaf," he adds before continuing down the hallway toward the conference rooms.

I stare after him, stunned.

One, that he has the audacity to imply I'm endangering our— my—baby by consuming coffee.

Two, because in order for Kit to know that pregnant women are supposed to limit their caffeine intake, I'm pretty sure he would have had to do some research.

Which makes me feel a little guilty for dumping the mug of tea that was left on my desk before heading into his office this morning.

CHAPTER 21
Kit

Collins is waiting, arms tightly crossed, when I step out of the elevator.

I don't bother hiding my smile as I approach, even knowing my cheerful expression will only irritate her more.

Because I'm happy to see her.

Collins frowns when I stop a foot in front of her. "You're late."

It's 5:03, not 5:30. But I'll pick my battles tonight, and technically, she's right.

"I'm sorry," I say sincerely.

I catch the flash of surprise. She wasn't expecting me to apologize.

"Let's go," I add, and she nods.

We both know loitering in the lobby together is a dumb idea.

Collins is even more eager to leave than I am. She slips on the marble floor in her haste to spin toward the exit, so I grab her arm to steady her.

The heat of her skin singes mine like an open flame, the silky fabric of her blue blouse so sheer that it's barely a barrier at all.

She tugs free from my hold as quickly as possible, her, "Thank you," clipped.

My, "You're welcome," is equally formal.

Camden is waiting along the curb. I texted him while walking to the elevator upstairs.

"Mr. Kensington," he greets, opening the car door with a polite nod.

I catch Collins's pursed lips out of the corner of my eye.

I could tell her that I've asked Camden to call me Kit dozens of times before letting the matter drop, that he's worked for my family for decades, that he is extremely well compensated for his dedication and discretion, but I don't mention any of it.

She can judge my world all she wants, but she's stuck with an inseverable connection to it—me.

I nod at Collins to climb in first. Once she does, I shut the door.

"Where to, sir?" Camden inquires.

"Maple & Ash, please," I reply before rounding the trunk and climbing in on the other side of the town car.

Maple & Ash is a popular steak house in Midtown, but I doubt it'll be very busy this early on a Monday evening.

Collins stays as close to the door as possible, keeping the maximum distance between us. I shrug out of my suit jacket and loosen my tie before snapping my seat belt into place. My jacket drapes on the center seat between us, one of the cuffs brushing her leg. She stiffens, but doesn't shove it away.

Camden pulls away from the curb, into the steady stream of rush-hour traffic.

"Where are we going?" Collins questions.

"Dinner," I answer as my phone buzzes with a text.

I pull it out and read the new message from Flynn, asking if I want to meet him for drinks at Proof later.

I reply, saying I need to stay late at the office tonight.

Flynn's response is, *Get a life, you workaholic cockblocker, formerly known as my best friend.*

"I'm not hungry," Collins states.

"I am." I ignore Flynn's latest text, drop my phone in my lap, and lean my head back against the headrest.

In the ten minutes since I left my computer, I already have twenty new emails. Fucking West Coast companies. I'm going to have to head back to the office after dinner.

Collins says nothing else for the rest of the drive.

Neither do I.

I trust Camden, but the coming conversation isn't one I want to have in front of him.

When we arrive at the restaurant, I climb out first. Collins slides across the seat instead of waiting for me or Camden to open the door on her side, standing and surveying the glass exterior of the restaurant.

I share a short exchange with Camden, clarifying my plans for the rest of the evening, then start toward the entrance.

Collins doesn't move. She stands so still on the sidewalk that she could be a statue, a few strands starting to fall from the neat bun her auburn hair was pulled back in.

I sigh before spinning and backtracking, positive I won't like the reason for the holdup.

"What is it?"

"I can't afford to eat here," Collins replies.

I stare at her, genuinely stunned by the statement.

I'm not just rich; I'm a fucking Kensington. Everyone— acquaintances, friends, women—knows they have less money than I do. Some expect me to pay; some accept any generosity because they know I can easily afford it.

No one has ever thought I *wouldn't* pay their way.

And, as shocked as I am, I'm unsurprised Collins would be the one to break that streak.

Also offended that she's still assuming the worst about me. I'd pay for her meal simply because I'd invited her out, setting aside the fact that she's Lili's friend or my assistant or the mother of my child.

"My treat," I tell her.

Collins shakes her head. "This isn't a business meeting, Kit. Or a date. I want to pay for my own food, so can we please eat someplace that won't max out my monthly food allowance on one meal?" She exhales. "I'm not trying to be difficult, I swear. I just—I don't want to feel like a charity case either. This situation is complicated enough."

A *charity case*? I've spent *years* begging for a shred of Collins's attention.

I'm the one who's always felt inferior and desperate. I wanted one thing from her—*her*—and Collins wanted nothing from me.

"Me wanting to eat at my favorite steak house has nothing to do with charity, Collins. I chose this restaurant because I'd skipped lunch to sit at your desk and suggested we get dinner tonight, so I'm starving."

Her eyes widen at the impulsive confession.

"I have money. A lot of it. One dinner isn't going to dent my net worth. And I know that's not the reality for most people. That it's not your reality. But it's *my* reality. So … live in my world? Just for one night?"

I know Collins is proud. It's one of the reasons I was so taken aback by her choice to come work for me. But this is more than overcoming her stubbornness. I want to offer something. I want to take care of her. I want her to *let* me take care of her.

"Fine," she says.

I relax. "Thank—"

"I'll eat later," she finishes.

I scowl. For fuck's sake. I'm not going to order and eat a meal while she sits there, staring at an empty plate.

I blow out a long breath that makes my stomach grumble. It feels like we've been standing out here, arguing, for hours. And we haven't even touched the entire reason we're here.

I decide to broach it now.

"You know why I've been trying to talk to you all day, right?"

She hesitates, then nods stiffly.

"You're pregnant with my baby, Monty. What you eat, they eat. By buying you dinner, I'm essentially feeding my kid. You're seriously going to tell me I can't do that?"

Collins says nothing, her expression impassive.

I sigh, then pull my phone out of my pocket to call Camden. "Fine. Where do you want to go?"

She sighs, too, then strides toward the door with a muttered, "The food here had better be the best damn meal I've ever had."

I release a relieved exhale before hurrying after her. When Collins *wants* to move, she's fast. She made all-state in cross-country in high school. I have to jog a few steps to reach the door ahead of her and hold it open.

Surprise crosses her face before she mutters a, "Thanks."

Did her asshole of an ex seriously decide cheating was acceptable *and* not open doors for her?

A smartly dressed maître d' is ready behind the stand. He smiles when he sees me. "Kit! How are you?"

I smile back. "Good, thanks. Do you have a table for us?"

"Of course, of course."

I glance at Collins, who's fiddling with a bracelet on her wrist as she studies the wall display of lit wine bottles.

"Somewhere private, please?" I request.

Collins continues playing with her jewelry. She's nervous, I think. That makes two of us.

"Absolutely. I have just the table. Right this way, please."

I gesture for Collins to follow the maître d' first.

"You must come here a lot?" she surmises once we're seated at a table tucked in the back corner, partially obscured by some potted plants that serve as a green privacy screen.

"Not really. I'm just memorable. Generous tipper."

"Right." She flips her menu open, lips pursing as she surveys the options. Or the prices maybe.

Our waiter delivers two glasses of water and a bread basket. I decline when he asks about other drinks. Collins does the same. I open my mouth to urge her to get something, thinking she's trying to save me money, then remember that she *can't* drink.

It's a sobering—pun intended—realization.

My gaze falls to her flat stomach as the waiter excuses himself, promising to return soon to take our food orders.

I can't picture her with a bump. With a baby. I can't picture *me* with a baby. Until Friday, I hadn't ever thought about having kids.

I take a deep breath. "I'm really sorry about Friday, Collins. I was—it was a shock."

"Yeah. Took me by surprise too." She reaches for a slice of sourdough following that dry statement, slathering the bread with honey butter and avoiding my gaze.

I clear my throat and lean forward, ignoring proper etiquette by resting my elbows on the table. "You've been to the doctor?"

"Yes." She takes a bite.

"That was the appointment you asked about?"

She chews, swallows, then finally makes eye contact. "Yeah."

"You could have told me *why* you were going."

"Kit …" She leans forward, too, mirroring my pose. "We don't have to do this, okay? I *did* tell you once I was sure because you had a right to know. But it can end there. I'm taking care of things."

A tight band suddenly constricts my chest. I figured she was telling me because she'd decided to stay pregnant. I assumed she was *quitting* because she'd decided to stay pregnant.

I feel like a fool. A presumptuous fool. A presumptuous, *disappointed* fool. I wasn't sure if I wanted kids, but I got attached to the idea of this one.

I slam the door on my disappointment, forcing a neutral expression on my face. "Sorry. I shouldn't have assumed that you were … can I go with you to the, uh, procedure?"

Collins looks momentarily startled. Then she shakes her head rapidly. "Oh. No. That's not what I—I'm keeping it. I meant, I have a plan. I'm going to move back to New Haven. I already applied to some admin jobs at Yale, and I'm touring apartments with my sister next weekend. My mom offered to watch the … baby over the summer and then a couple of days a week once the fall semester starts, and there's a day care on campus. I'll figure it out."

At first, I'm relieved. So, *so* relieved.

And then? I'm pissed.

"Your plan is to *move*? Two hours away? When were you going to run that terrible idea past me, Collins?"

She glares. "Terrible idea? I'm doing you a *favor.*"

"What kind of *favor* is taking my kid away from me?"

"Come on, Kit. Your life is practically an endless party. You take weekend trips to Vegas. You go to fancy galas with champagne and caviar. You sleep with socialites and probably live in a penthouse and fly around in a private jet. I'm not criticizing; I'm stating facts. You're young and hot and single and stupid rich. Why *wouldn't* you enjoy it? But you can't take a break from changing diapers and then go get arrested in Monaco for stealing a yacht—"

"That happened *once*, and I was sixteen."

I'd rather tease her about the *hot* that slipped out than defend my near criminal record, but that's not going to earn me any points in the *responsible adult* column.

I lean closer and continue, "I have a good job. My own place, and the *fact* that it's a penthouse just means it has plenty of space. I'm 'stupid rich,' as you put it. And I was raised by two amazing parents. Having a few wild years doesn't make you unqualified to have a kid."

"I didn't say it did. But do you know what babies are like? They're messy and loud and demanding. They're a permanent responsibility.

You can't possibly *want* that."

Wow. When Collins said she expected nothing from me, she truly meant *nothing*.

"Did I want to have kids? I don't know. Honestly, I'd never thought about it until Friday. But we're not talking about a hypothetical here. We're talking about *our* baby. I'm going to be a dad. That means I'm *going* to be a dad. And you should have fucking asked, Collins, before you assumed I wasn't."

"Well, silence and 'Fuck' didn't signify much enthusiasm about the prospect."

"What'd you do when you found out?" I ask.

There's a slight quirk to her lips. That tiny upturn fractures the tension a little bit. "I sat on my bathroom floor for two hours."

"I was shocked, Monty. Not bad shocked. Just … *shocked*. Telling me to sit was a solid call."

This time, she gifts me with a full smile. "I know."

"You told your family?" I ask tentatively.

She must have if she's made all these plans to move back to Connecticut.

"Yes."

"How much?"

"The PG version. Although the fact that we had sex was strongly implied."

I crack a smile. "Do they know I'm part of the we?"

"No. I just assured them it's not Isaac's."

Our waiter reappears to take our food orders. I haven't even glanced at the menu, but I've eaten here enough that I know exactly what I want.

Collins hasn't looked at the menu yet either, so she surprises me by saying she's ready to order.

I frown when she only requests a salad but say nothing until the waiter leaves. "That's all you want?"

"Yeah. Whoever named it 'morning' sickness was in serious denial. Or maybe just lucky. Mine's more of an all-day sickness."

My frown deepens. "Is that normal? Did you mention it to your doctor?"

"Yes, and yes. Supposedly, it'll get better once I'm through the first trimester. I'll just live on saltines until then."

I nod, making a mental note to request the break room be stocked with some of the crackers. "Do you *want* to move home, Collins?"

She plays with her napkin, avoiding my gaze. "I don't know. In some ways, it would be easier. In others, it would feel like backsliding. I'm going to be a … mom. It's time to grow up. Not to move home and rely on my parents. But the reality is, I don't know what the hell I'm doing. I barely know anyone in New York. And it's a lot more expensive to live here than—"

"You don't have to worry about money, Monty."

"*You* don't have to worry about money," she fires back.

"I'm not trying to sound like a rich asshole—"

"You mean your default setting?" There's no bite. She's teasing me.

I hide a smile. "But I have *a lot* of money. Money I inherited from my parents. Money that my kid will inherit. Since you and the kid are currently the same unit, *you* have a lot of money."

"That's twisted logic."

"Makes perfect sense to me."

"I appreciate you apologizing, Kit. And offering to be involved. But you have a clean out here. I'm prepared to do this myself. I'll sign whatever you want. I'll never ask you for money—or anything else. No one has to know you're the father. I'm *choosing* this. And you can *not* choose this."

I reach for my water, pretending to think about it. Part of me is pissed she thinks that's a decision I'd ever make. The rest of me is determined to do whatever it takes to convince her I want this.

"I'm in," I state.

Collins swallows. "You can't say that now and then back out later. I won't explain to my kid why his or her father is too busy to help with homework or show up at school plays or—"

"You think our kid will be an aspiring actor? You ran cross-country, and I played lacrosse, so I kinda figured we'd breed another athlete."

Collins tilts her head, a surprised look on her face. "How did you know I ran cross-country?"

"Even self-absorbed narcissists pay attention to other people *sometimes*, Monty."

She rolls her eyes, but some surprise lingers in her expression.

"You already run my calendar. Just block off the next eighteen years."

"*Kit.*"

"I don't want an out, okay? Not now. Not ever. My parents had help, but I wasn't raised by nannies. I know there's a lot more to parenting than writing checks. Kids are expensive, so I'm telling you that you don't need to stress about money. That doesn't mean I won't be there to watch Sesame break a leg as Hamlet. Although, hopefully, Dalton Academy will have moved on to a playwright other than Shakespeare by then."

She tilts her head. "Sesame?"

"You're about five weeks along, right? According to the Internet, that means our kid is about the size of a sesame seed."

Collins glances down suddenly.

I watch as she swipes a hand beneath her left eye, then sniffs once.

"Sorry. Hormones. I just … I kinda figured I'd be doing this myself. Please don't take that personally. I assumed *any* guy would run in the opposite direction."

"You don't have a lot of faith in men, huh?"

I say it teasingly, but her reply is serious.

"No, I don't."

There's weight—sadness—in those three words. About her ex? Or something else?

"Well, lucky for you, your taste has finally improved."

She snorts, then reaches for another piece of bread. "Yeah, lucky. We won the surprise pregnancy lottery. Woo-hoo."

"I'm not going anywhere, Monty," I state. "And I can't endorse my entire gender, but you *can* rely on me."

Collins chews, not appearing entirely convinced. I guess I should be grateful she's not shaking her head in disagreement. Baby steps.

"Okay," she finally says.

"Okay," I echo.

I suppose agreeing on something is a good start to co-parenting.

CHAPTER 22
Collins

"**Y**ou ready?"

I glance up at Margot. She's wearing a headband with bobbing pumpkins atop two antennas.

I smile at the sight, then ask, "Ready for what?"

Margot rolls her eyes. "Didn't you see the email? We're getting Halloween drinks. Let's go!"

I saw the email. But I wasn't planning on going because, one, I can't drink, and two, I'm worried about anyone at the office figuring out why.

Kit convinced me to remain as his assistant for the time being, saying it would raise fewer questions if I left after a few months than a few weeks. That the last thing I needed right now was the stress of switching jobs again. That I wasn't showing and there was no reason for anyone to suspect I was pregnant. That we could reassess after the holidays and decide what to do then.

So, I agreed to stay. Because he'd made valid points. And because … I like working for him. I like seeing him every day. I like hearing his deep voice in the background while I answer emails. I like that he brings me a sleeve of saltines every time he goes to the break room for a coffee refill.

"I have some work to finish up …"

Margot collapses on the side of my desk with an exasperated huff. "Collins! The mighty Mr. Kensington can wait until tomorrow. Everyone else is leaving on time tonight, so he can't expect you to stay late. And we haven't hung out in *forever*! Come on!"

She's being dramatic. We had lunch together two days ago. But I *could* use a fun night out. A brief distraction from reality. Lately, my life has followed a predictable pattern of work and home. Stress and sleepless nights. Naps and nausea.

"Okay," I agree. "Just give me a few minutes to finish things up."

Margot claps and straightens. "Meet us by the elevators."

I nod as I type. "Be right there."

From: ctate@kensingtonconsolidated.com
To: ckensington@kensingtonconsolidated.com
Subject: No subject
I'm heading out. See you tomorrow.
—C

I can hear Kit's voice. Know he's on a conference call from his calendar, so I'm not expecting my inbox to ping with an immediate reply.

> **From:** ckensington@kensingtonconsolidated.com
> **To:** ctate@kensingtonconsolidated.com
> Subject: Re: No subject
> Have a good night.
> —Mighty Mr. Kensington

I snort a laugh before I shut off my computer and gather up my stuff.

I scan the new notifications on my phone as I walk to the elevator. There's a photo from Jane—of her in a cute bunny costume posed with three other girls. I shoot her a *Happy Halloween!* text in response before moving on to the next message. My skin prickles unpleasantly as soon as I read it.

> **Sarah:** Hey, Collins. I hope you're doing okay. Wanted to let you know that Jeremy told me that Isaac is transferring to the firm's New York office. Just a heads-up.

I chew my bottom lip and slow my steps, rereading the message twice before I send a reply.

> **Collins:** Thanks for letting me know.

> **Collins:** Hope you're well too.

I blocked Isaac everywhere as soon as we broke up. I'm not sure he knows I moved to New York. If he does, he doesn't know where I work or where I live. I doubt Isaac would even try to contact me. *He* cheated on *me*, and he wasn't very careful about covering it up.

But still, the news is a damper on my cheerful mood.

My fresh start keeps getting staler.

I slip my phone into my bag before turning the corner to approach the elevator bank.

Margot cheers when she sees me. "You ready?"

"I'm ready!" I push my worries away like they're a physical layer I can shed, determined to be a non-pregnant, non-cheated-on woman for the night.

It takes us a half hour to travel to a bar in Greenwich Village. They're known for going over the top around holidays, Stella tells me, and the interior doesn't disappoint. Fake cobwebs cover the ceiling. Drinks are being served in miniature cauldrons. A smoke machine is set up in one corner, sending billows of gray mist into the air, and a spooky soundtrack pipes through invisible speakers.

We snag and settle at a large high-top table in one corner. The wooden surface is scarred from years of use, plus several sets of initials enclosed in hearts.

Everyone else reaches for a laminated menu, so I do the same. I pretend to scan it but mainly zone out, listening to the creepy soundtrack of creaks and groans.

"You okay?" Margot asks, bumping her shoulder against mine from her spot on the stool beside me.

"Yeah," I reply. "Just tired."

I yawn for emphasis, and it's not even fake. I almost fell asleep standing in the shower this morning.

"What's it like, working for Christopher Kensington?" Aimee's question burns with curiosity.

She's an attorney, part of Kensington Consolidated's legal department. I'd never met her before tonight, much less told her whose assistant I was. Which must mean people are gossiping about me.

Suddenly, I'm the center of attention, everyone abandoning their side conversations to hear my reply.

My fingers fiddle with the firm edge of the laminated menu. "It's fine. He's pretty easy to work for."

"Pretty easy on the eyes too," someone—Caroline, I think—comments with a laugh.

Fervent agreement echoes around the table.

I can't count the number of times I've gotten trapped in a conversation that included some mention of how gorgeous Kit is. The topic has come up at every event I've attended that he's also been at, including the party where he got me pregnant. He draws attention anywhere he goes.

But I *can* count the number of times there's been a hot twist in my chest that feels a lot like jealousy. A recent yet recurring occurrence that started when Sadie Carmichael showed up. The thought of Kit with other women bothers me, and that reality *really* bothers me.

"Is he dating anyone?" Stella wonders.

I shrug. "I don't know. We talk about spreadsheets and earning statements. Not his personal life."

Mostly true.

Ever since our dinner last month, my conversations with Kit have remained totally professional. Aside from Sunday mornings, when he texts me the size of our baby in food terms. I'm currently twelve weeks—a plum—almost through the first trimester.

"You manage his schedule and screen all of his calls," Aimee argues. "You must have some idea."

"Nope. Sorry. If he's seeing anyone, it's after hours and on his personal phone."

Everyone at the table appears disappointed by my lack of juicy gossip. God, if they only knew.

This is one of the few times I've been grateful for the frequent urge to pee. Hopefully, they'll have moved on to a different topic by the time I return to the table.

I lean closer to Margot. "I'm running to the restroom. Order me a ginger ale?"

"A ginger ale?" Stella's nose scrunches across the table. "What about the Halloween menu?" She waves it around like a sparkler. "At least get an apple cider spritz or something."

"Headache," I explain. "Alcohol will just make it worse."

"I think I have some painkillers in here ..." Margot reaches for her purse.

"I took one before we left the office," I lie. "But it hasn't kicked in yet, so I'm sticking to soda. I'll be right back."

The restroom line is long, at least ten other women waiting in front of me.

I lean against the wall, letting it support my weight, wishing I'd worn flats. The arches of my feet are aching even though I sat most of the day. I'm not sure if sore feet are a pregnancy symptom, but the changes to my body sure aren't making heels *more* comfortable.

Ahead of me, two girls are dressed as a campfire and s'mores. They're drafting a text to a guy one of them is meeting later, collapsing into tipsy giggles every fifteen seconds as their suggestions become increasingly bold.

I study them like a scientist observing a foreign species, realizing that'll never be me again. When I'm able to drink again, I'll have a newborn. Then that newborn will become a toddler, that toddler a teenager.

I'll always have a responsibility for someone else for the rest of my life.

Parenthood doesn't have an expiration date. It'll never only be me I have to worry about again.

It's a bizarre realization to have.

Almost as strange as the idea that I'll be buying a baby-sized costume a year from now.

By the time I return to the table, everyone's received their drinks.

I slide back onto my stool and take a long sip from the glass set at my spot. And then, as soon as the flavor hits, I cough, spraying liquid everywhere.

"Collins!" Aimee protests, sliding her sequined clutch farther from me.

"There's alcohol in this," I state.

Stella smiles as she tosses some napkins my way. "Only an ounce of vodka. The bartender didn't even charge for—"

Panic gathers in my chest, constricting my windpipe and making it hard to breathe. The smoky air feels suffocating all of a sudden.

I stand, grabbing my bag off the sticky floor. "I've, uh, I've gotta go."

Any replies get lost in the commotion of the bar as I spin and hurry for the exit.

I skirt around a plaid-wearing farmer and two cows before reaching the door and rushing up the steps to the street. Once I'm outside, I inhale a deep breath, the taboo taste of alcohol buzzing and bitter on my tongue.

"Collins!"

I glance over my shoulder, watching Margot dart up the stairs after me. She's not wearing a jacket, bare arms hugging her waist for warmth. I can see the raised bumps on her skin from here.

"Are you okay?" she asks, pausing a few feet away and scanning my face anxiously.

"I'm pregnant."

"Shit." Her face pales. "I had no idea they'd ordered a real drink for you. But I know they never would have if they'd known—"

"I know; I know. I'm just … I'm a little on edge tonight. This"—I point at my stomach—"has been a lot. And I found out earlier that my ex is moving here, and I …" I blow out a long breath. "Can we keep all this between us?"

"Of course," she assures me. "But if you ever need to talk or if you want to go out for a … ginger ale, I'm here. My sister had a baby last year, so I know a lot more about pregnancy than your average childless woman."

I muster a grateful smile. "Thank you."

"I'll tell the girls you got your period and needed to head out fast." Margot winks. "No one will suspect a thing."

"Thank you," I repeat. "And here, let me give you some money for—"

She shakes her head, shivering. "Don't worry about it. See you tomorrow."

"See you tomorrow," I echo as she hurries back inside.

I pull out my phone and order an Uber. The practical decision would be to walk to the subway from here, but my feet are going to protest each step. I can splurge on one ride.

When it shows the closest car as seven minutes away, I make another impulsive choice.

He answers on the second ring.

"Hello?"

Wherever Kit is, it's quiet. I was expecting raucous cheers, loud music, even a woman's voice—or several women's—in the background.

But all I hear is silence.

"Collins?"

"I accidentally drank vodka," I blurt. "It was only a sip, and I spit most of it out, but ..." *I'm freaking out about it.*

I don't say that last part aloud, but it's strongly implied in the panicked flurry of words.

"How do you accidentally drink vodka?"

Kit sounds amused, and the tight set of my shoulders relaxes.

"I went out for drinks with some of the other assistants. I asked them to order me a ginger ale before I went to the bathroom, and they got me a Moscow Mule instead."

"Ah."

Just a single syllable, but it drips with disapproval. Maybe even anger.

"They didn't mean anything by it," I rush to add. "I told them I wasn't drinking because I had a headache, and they didn't know I'm ..." I bite the inside of my cheek. "I told Margot the truth. I asked her not to tell anyone, and I don't think she will, but she knows."

"Is that why you're calling?" Kit sounds remarkably calm about the possibility of the entire office discovering his assistant is pregnant.

"Yes. I mean, no. I said I'd keep you updated, so ..."

"So, you thought you'd let me know about Plum's first taste of alcohol?"

I'm smiling.

I've *been* smiling, based on the soreness in my cheeks that I'm suddenly aware of. "That's this week?" I ask, like I didn't memorize Sunday's text as soon as I saw it.

"Uh-huh. Next week is a kiwi."

"Exciting."

"I hear the sarcasm, Monty, but I'm a visual learner. I can't picture our kid in centimeters or ounces or whatever you're supposed to measure babies in."

I laugh. "It's quiet. You're not going out for Halloween?"

"It's not even six. The good parties have barely started setting up."

"Oh. Right."

"But, no, I'm not going out tonight."

"Lose your cowboy costume?" I tease.

Senior year, I ran into Kit at an off-campus party. There was a Western theme.

"For the last time, I was Indiana Jones, not a cowboy."

"You had a lasso."

"It was supposed to be a whip. I would have put more effort in had I known you were going to memorize the entire outfit."

My cheeks burn as I clear my throat. "Well, I'll let you get back to

..."

"Wanna come over? I'm about to leave the office."

"That's …"

"A great idea? I know. I'll text you my address. See you soon."

He hangs up before I can respond.

CHAPTER 23
KIT

"Hey, Monty."

Collins glances up from her phone at the sound of my voice. She swallows twice before replying, "Hey."

She looks tired, leaning against the wall across from the elevator. And beautiful. So, so beautiful. Always, but especially waiting in my building's lobby. For a few seconds, I let myself fantasize, pretending this is a regular occurrence.

"You didn't have to wait down here." In addition to my address, I texted her the elevator code and where I keep a spare key.

"I didn't want to … invade your space."

"It's not an invasion if you're invited."

She bites on her bottom lip. "I'm not sure this is the best idea …"

So, *that's* why she's down here. Talking herself out of this.

"We said boundaries, Kit," she adds.

That was part of my pitch to convince her to stay in New York and at Kensington Consolidated. So far, it's been pretty successful. But …

"We also have a lot to talk about, right?"

All our last conversation established was that she was keeping the baby, remaining as my assistant—at least for the time being—and that I wasn't going to skip off into the sunset solo. We haven't discussed her moving. Her changing jobs. Telling my family. Not to mention what happens after the baby is born. Child support and custody arrangements and day care and holidays and birthdays and weekends.

It's one of the reasons I asked her to come here rather than offering to meet Collins at her apartment.

I want her to move in with me. Being in the same place will make co-parenting a lot easier. I have plenty of space. She'll save money on rent.

Practically, it makes sense. Realistically? I'm not anticipating an easy agreement.

Collins has focused on the paper bag I'm carrying.

"Hungry?" I ask, nudging the Up button on the elevator with my elbow. I'm not above luring her upstairs with the promise of food.

"Starving," she admits.

"Cocktail wasn't very filling?"

That comment earns me a dirty look. I don't miss the slight upward curve to her lips though, which tells me she found my question a *little* funny.

"No, it wasn't."

I chuckle as the doors slide open, stifling a sigh of relief when Collins follows me inside. The doors shut, and the elevator starts to ascend a second later.

I lift the bag I'm holding. "At least we have food if it breaks down."

She rolls her eyes. "Have you lived here long?"

"Since June," I reply.

Collins nods, sucking her bottom lip in between her teeth as she leans against the brass railing.

My money makes her uncomfortable, and it's one of many things that's always intrigued me about her. I'm accustomed to women treating time with me like literally winning the lottery—eagerly agreeing to luxurious vacations and ordering the most expensive wine on the menu and dropping hints about designer accessories they've always coveted.

So, it figures that the one woman I'm tied to for the rest of my life argues about me buying her dinner.

"There's a pool," I state. "And a full gym. Plus a twenty-four-hour doorman. My place has private rooftop access."

Collins's expression remains impassive as I list off the amenities. It sounds like I'm bragging, but this isn't me trying to impress her. I'm trying to highlight convenience more than anything. A safe, easy place to exercise. Someone to help with packages. The roof? Yeah, maybe that was plain old boasting. But she should see the nighttime view of Central Park. That's what sold *me* on this location.

The elevator stops a few floors shy of the top. The doors open to reveal Mrs. Van Lewan, dressed like a butterfly.

She waves when she sees me. "Hello there, Christopher!"

I smile back. "Edna! You look fabulous! Headed up?"

She preens in response to my compliment, then frowns and opens her purse. To search, I'm guessing, for the glasses perched on the top of her head. "You go ahead," she says, waving a wrinkled hand as she continues to rummage around. "Forgot my damn spectacles again and hit the wrong button. Aging is a clusterfuck."

Collins's eyes widen, and I swallow a chuckle.

Edna is a sweet old lady with a penchant for swearing like a sailor at the slightest inconvenience. Her family's wealth came from her grandfather's ship-building company, and we bonded over boats when she showed up at my door to welcome me to the building over the summer.

"Your glasses are on the top of your head," I inform her.

Edna's hand flies upward to pat her white curls, nearly losing one of her wings. She locates the glasses a few seconds later. "Thank you, darling. I'll just—" She smiles, catching sight of Collins. "And who's this?"

The doors start to close, so I stick a hand out to keep them open. "This is Collins. She's my *older* sister's friend."

Collins spares a tight-lipped look for me before aiming a polite smile at Edna. "Nice to meet you, ma'am."

"Ma'am? Psst. Call me Edna, dearest. It's *so* nice to finally meet a lady friend of Christopher's. The only person he brings around here is that handsome Flynn."

I beam at her.

"Really?" Collins sounds surprised.

I'm sure she pictured a rotating door of women coming in and out of my bedroom. But there are parts of my life I like to keep private, and where I live is one of them. If I'm hooking up with a woman—which hasn't happened in a while—I'll go to their place or a hotel.

Edna nods rapidly. "Oh, yes. I had half a mind to set him up with my granddaughter, but I thought he might be too spirited for her—" Edna's phone starts ringing, cutting her off. "Oh, dear. Where did I leave that blasted thing?" she wonders, patting the sides of her costume, which doesn't appear to have pockets.

Collins's smile is amused now, not just friendly. *Spirited?* she mouths at me.

Edna neglected to mention her granddaughter is in her mid-thirties.

"Happy Halloween, Edna," I say. "Have a good night."

"You too. You too," she mumbles, distracted by the hunt for her phone.

I drop my arm. The doors shut a second later, and we continue to rise.

"You're friends with your elderly neighbor?"

I glance over at Collins. "Yeah. Why?"

"Nothing."

"Oh, I get it." I grin. "You thought I was too self-absorbed to notice anyone else lived here."

"No. I *might* have assumed you only flirted with women under the age of forty."

"Fifty is my hard limit actually."

She huffs, shaking her head as the doors open again. This time, we're on the right floor.

"Home sweet home," I announce, striding down the hallway.

Collins trails behind.

I unlock the front door and push it open, gesturing for her to enter first.

She kicks her heels off as soon as she's inside, which makes me smile. I follow her as she pads deeper into the penthouse, flicking on lights as I go.

"Wow." Collins pauses when she reaches the edge of the living room.

The layout of the first floor is mostly open, mainly to maximize the aerial view of Central Park that she's currently admiring. The scenery was more impressive over the summer, when the leaves and grass were green, but it's still pretty spectacular.

"Not bad, huh?"

"Not bad," she agrees, continuing to look around. Her eyes land right where I expect them to. "Do you play?"

I study the Steinway in the corner. "Not really. I just like the way it looks."

Collins gravitates closer and closer to the instrument, an awed look on her face.

"Play it if you want," I offer. "It was tuned a few weeks ago. I'm going to go change. Want to borrow something to wear?"

She's still in her dress and blazer from work.

"Sure," she replies absently, lifting the fallboard that covers the keys and letting her fingers run over the ivory. Gliding across, not pressing down.

I continue into the kitchen, leaving the takeout on the center island, then down the hallway and into my bedroom. I change into sweatpants and a T-shirt, then grab a pair of joggers that have a drawstring and a college sweatshirt from my closet.

Halfway down the hallway, I hear the music start.

My steps slow as I absorb the sound.

Lili told me Collins was talented. But no one in my family is particularly musical, so that statement didn't tell me much. I've attended plenty of events where a professional was playing, but it never registered as anything more than pleasant background noise.

This is different. There's no crowd or commotion to distract me from the music. And it's *Collins* playing. I'd develop an interest in watching paint dry if that was an activity she was interested in.

I resume a normal pace, wanting a sight to accompany the sound.

I don't get much of a chance. Collins glances over her shoulder and pauses her playing when I enter the living room, pink flushing her cheeks as she quickly stands from the bench.

"You sound a little rusty," I comment.

She scowls. "I do not."

"Prove it."

Her laugh is wry. "I'm not falling for that trick again."

"Technically, *I* fell for it." I toss the clothes to her. "There's a guest room down the hall on the left, if you want to change in there."

Collins nods and starts that way. "Thanks."

I head into the kitchen as she disappears down the hallway, pulling two plates out of the cabinet and setting them on the counter. I grab the containers out of the takeout bag, fold it up, then walk down the hallway and tap on the closed door.

"Collins? Do you want—"

"One sec," she interrupts.

The door opens a second later, and it's a struggle not to react as I watch her tug the sweatshirt down and pull her hair free from the collar.

Meaning her hair is loose. The last time I saw her hair loose, it was spread wildly across white sheets.

And Collins Tate, standing in my home, wearing my clothes, *carrying my baby*? It ignites some primal, possessive urge I never knew existed.

I've felt jealous, seeing her with other guys, but I never had any real right to be. I still don't, I guess. Yet, for the rest of our lives, we'll share a kid. A bond that nothing—not time or distance or any other barrier—can break.

That's daunting. But it's also comforting. I *like* that we'll have that in common.

I'd step up and take responsibility in this situation with anyone. But it would be straightforward. More … clinical. It'd be easy to focus exclusively on the baby. With Collins, my brain gets too muddled with *her*.

I'm going to pitch her moving in as practical, but a large part of it is selfish. I want her here, with me, not across a bridge in Brooklyn. And full honesty? It's not entirely tied to the pregnancy. If this were happening with another woman, I'd offer to rent her an apartment near me, not suggest she move into my home.

"Kit?" Collins is staring at me, hesitation written all over her face.

Which is when I realize my reaction was freezing in place. Who knows how long I've been standing here, silent, just looking at her? So much for acting casual and making her feel comfortable.

"Right." I clear my throat. "I was checking to see if you wanted Parmesan on your pasta. Hard cheese is okay, right?"

"Uh, yeah. Parmesan is okay, and, yes, I'll have some."

"Great." I glance past her, at the bed. "Also … I'm thinking of this room for the nursery."

Collins spins to survey it. "This room? It's *huge*."

"This bedroom is smaller than the primary suite. And the rest of the guest rooms are upstairs. I should be close by, right?"

She gnaws on her bottom lip. "I guess you could add a crib in the corner?"

I laugh. "What? Monty, I'd get rid of all of this." I gesture toward the current furnishings. "My kid isn't sleeping in the corner. Plus, there needs to be room for toys and all the other baby shit. A guy I went to school with, Pierce, has a sister who paints. I was thinking of asking her to do a mural on that wall." I point toward the one the headboard is pushed up against.

"A mural. Wow."

"Is that a bad idea?" I wonder.

"No, I think that's a really nice idea. I just …" She glances around again, shaking her head. "This room is about the same size as my entire apartment."

I seize the perfect opening. "So, move in with me."

Her chin jerks in my direction. "*What?*"

Maybe I should have attempted a more gradual segue. Too late now.

"Move in with me," I repeat.

Collins is already shaking her head. "No, I—Kit, that's crazy!"

"What's crazy about it? I can't contribute much until you, you know, birth the kid, but I can do this much. And once Plum is born, we won't have to shuttle him or her between here and Brooklyn. You haven't even seen the upstairs. I've got plenty of space."

"We talked about boundaries, Kit. *Living together* is not boundaries."

I shrug a shoulder, attempting to act nonchalant. This is the exact response I expected. But I didn't realize how much I wanted her to say yes until she said no.

"It doesn't have to be a big deal, Collins. You moved in with Lili when you were eighteen, and she was a total stranger."

She clicks her tongue. "That was totally different, and you know it."

"It doesn't have to be. Pretend my apartment is a dorm and I'm your random roommate if it'll make you more comfortable. You need more space, and I have space. It's as simple as that."

"Plum is going to wake up screaming in the middle of the night, you know. Your neighbors will hate us."

"It's a penthouse. I don't have any neighbors. And I would hate missing the screaming."

Collins snorts. "Yeah, right."

She's *still* waiting for me to cut and run. It erases all my self-doubt that I'm bringing this up too soon. I'm limited with how much attention I can show her at work. Here? She's going to have a hard time missing my commitment, no matter how hard she tries to.

"Offer stands," I state. "Come on. Dinner's getting cold."

"You said pasta?" she asks, perking up as we enter the kitchen.

"Yeah," I reply. "Thought the carbs would help soak up the alcohol."

She sticks her tongue out as she opens the container, spooning spaghetti with meatballs onto one of the plates I set out. "Hilarious."

"Speaking of drinking, what do you want?" I fling open the fridge doors, doing a quick scan of the contents. "I've got—"

"I'm good with water."

"Sparkling or still?"

"Still's fine, thanks."

I nod and fill a glass. "Ice? Lemon wedge?"

Collins raises an eyebrow as she twirls some pasta. "Both, thanks. Was Edna wrong? Sounds like you do a lot of, uh, entertaining."

"Not here. Flynn has crashed a few times, and Bash squatted most of the summer, but I prefer my privacy. This is the first place that's all *mine*, not my parents'." I hesitate before adding, "I mean, I used money from my trust fund to buy it, so they contributed. I don't make enough to cover a place like this myself. Not *yet* at least. But I picked it out."

She nods, giving the kitchen a quick glance. "It's nice."

I snort. "Thanks, Monty."

I don't think many women would describe a sixty-five-million-dollar penthouse as *nice*, but it's more complimentary than I would have expected from Collins.

Ostentatious or *way too big* or *characterless* would also apply. I mostly use this gourmet kitchen for reheating. No bachelor needs seven bedrooms. And I hired an interior decorator who made this place look like the glossy pages of a design catalog. Pretty to look at, but not very welcoming.

I'm excited to set up the nursery. It'll be the first part of this place that will actually feel like a home.

"There's plain pasta too," I tell Collins as I set her water down beside her plate. "I wasn't sure if sauce would sound good."

"Thanks, Kit," she says sincerely.

"No problem." I fix my own food, then take the stool next to her at the counter.

Collins points her fork at the fridge. "What's the story there?"

I glance at the playing card taped to the stainless steel. "*That* is the playing card that Flynn snuck out of a casino in Vegas."

"Why?"

"I don't have an answer to that question."

She scoffs softly, then twirls some spaghetti. "How was Vegas?"

"Boring," I reply. "All the strip clubs were closed."

"I'm serious."

"So am I. I went to every single one, just to make sure."

She shakes her head, then takes a big bite of pasta.

"It was fine," I tell her. "I'd been before. My aunt and uncle actually got married in Vegas. The first time at least, and then they had a more traditional ceremony."

"*Oliver* got married in Vegas?"

I chuckle. "Surprising, right? And look at what a great CEO he's turned out to be. There's hope for me yet."

"I never said I thought you'd be a bad CEO."

"Plenty of other people have. And are hoping Bash will end up being the one who's next in line."

"I'm not."

I glance at her. "I'm sure he'd let you keep your job, Monty. Probably pay you more too."

Collins rolls her eyes. "That's not what I meant. Although this is probably a good time to tell you that I applied to a paralegal position yesterday."

I stiffen. "I thought we'd discussed—"

"We did discuss this. And we need to discuss it again. The clock's ticking. I have a better shot at getting hired before I start showing. I checked, and I'm not legally required to disclose a pregnancy to a potential employer."

"You're not legally required to leave either. We did nothing wrong. You can stay, and then I'll be there if—"

"I don't want to stay, Kit. Do I like working with—for—you? Yeah. Do I like that you're my boss? Not really. The … other stuff was questionable enough. But at least that happened before I started at the company. Before either of us even knew I'd be starting. Us working together during my entire pregnancy, with all the whispering? I mean, you should have heard what—" She abruptly stops talking.

I lift an eyebrow. "I should have heard …"

She stabs a meatball with her fork. "They were talking about you at drinks earlier. Asking me questions … and stuff."

"Questions about what?"

"It doesn't matter," she says, which only increases my curiosity. "The point is, people pay attention to you, and you *know* that they're going to talk about your unmarried assistant getting knocked up. I don't want to deal with that gossip, even if you're willing to."

Realistically, I know she's right. And the attention isn't something I necessarily *want* to deal with. But I've gotten used to having her as my assistant, to seeing her every day, and I'm panicked at the thought of losing that.

"Why are you applying to paralegal jobs? You should be looking for positions playing—"

Collins is already shaking her head. "I can't afford to focus on music. I was barely breaking even in Chicago, and my rent here is more. Not to mention the baby and all those expenses."

I rub the back of my neck, trying to temper my frustration. "How many times are you going to make me say this, Monty? I. Am. A. Billionaire. The fact that you're stressed about money is …" I search for a word that won't offend her. "You don't need to be stressed about money."

Collins exhales. "I know how much money you have, Kit. And I'll give a little on stuff for the baby, I promise. You can pay for an expensive day care and the fancy private school and designer whatever—anything that's truly important to you. But it's important to *me* that I be financially independent. That I be able to support myself. I need you to respect that."

I nod. "I will."

"Thank you. And for offering."

I nod again. "Pearson's the best law firm in the city. Nick Pearson is my godfather. I could give him a call. Mention you're looking and see if he knows of any openings."

And you'll have a job offer an hour later.

I don't say that last part—for obvious reasons. I admire Collins's determination, even if it exasperates me. But I need her to let me do *something*, to help her.

She takes a sip of water. "Maybe. Let me try myself first, before you start pulling strings."

I smile reluctantly. Busted.

While she's being amenable, I decide to push my luck. "And promise me you'll think about moving in. *Actually* consider it. Okay?"

She doesn't hesitate as long this time. "Okay."

CHAPTER 24
Collins

Perry: *Drinks on Friday?*

I stare at the message from Perry, then glance at the drooping leaves of the fern I brought in to decorate my desk. The tips of the leaves are curled and browning.

I've watered it once a week since I bought it. Is that too often? Too infrequent? I honestly have no clue. Just like I have no idea what to say to Perry. He's been politely persistent ever since I bailed on drinks, and

I'm not sure why I keep making excuses to avoid rescheduling.

Yeah, I'm pregnant, but I'm also *single*. My life isn't over. I can date and flirt and have fun. And I should do those things now—or at least soon, before my life's latest complication becomes obvious.

I sigh, stand, and stretch.

There's a big meeting happening with a bunch of important executives right now, so the hallway is quieter than usual as I head into the break room. Margot's rummaging in the fridge, her blonde hair braided back in a fancy twist that I'm instantly envious of. Lately, a smooth ponytail is the most elaborate style I can manage.

"Hey." Margot gives me a friendly smile when she spots me. "How are you?"

"Warm," I say with a laugh. My sweater sleeves are shoved up to my elbows, but I'm still stifling.

Margot nods vigorously. "Right? They're really cranking the heat. That, or we all turned into penguins over the summer." She glances around, then takes a tentative step closer. "And how are you *really*?"

"I'm better," I reply. "Thanks for asking."

All the women I went out for drinks with on Halloween came to my desk to check on me at different points the next day. Stella apologized profusely. Even Aimee stopped by, despite the fact we'd never spoken before that night. Cynically, I think her thoughtfulness might have had something to do with hoping to catch a glimpse of Kit, based on how many times she glanced at the door past my desk, but it was a nice gesture regardless.

I didn't tell any of them *why* I'd freaked out so much though. Margot is the only one who knows the truth, aside from Kit and my family.

"Good." Margot slips a folded piece of paper out of her pocket. "I was about to drop this off at your desk. My sister recommended this birthing class. And I assume you have a doctor already, but I put the number for her OB on there too, just in case."

"Thank you," I say, taking the slip from her. "I really appreciate it."

"How far along are you? If you—if you don't mind me asking."

I don't mind. It feels nice to have such a *normal* conversation about my pregnancy. The kind I might have if this had been planned.

"Thirteen weeks," I answer. "He—or she—is the size of a kiwi."

Margot smiles. "You think it's a boy?"

"Yeah. The"—I lower my voice to a whisper because saying this word feels weird at work—"sperm determines the gender, and I picture him with a son for some reason."

"You told your ex, then?" Margot asks sympathetically.

It takes me a few seconds to realize what she concluded. I completely forgot I'd mentioned Isaac to her during my Halloween freak-out. "Oh. My ex isn't the father."

When Margot's eyes light up with interest, I decide I might have taken this confiding thing a little too far. "What? You're seeing someone new?"

"Not exactly. It was a, uh, one-night stand."

"What?" Margot leans closer, her voice lowering conspiratorially. "Does the guy know?"

I nod. "He knows."

"Was he an ass about it?"

"No. He's been … he's been really amazing actually."

"You *like* him," Margot sings.

I shake my head rapidly. "No. No, I don't. It was just sex, and now we're co-parenting. Or we will be."

"Tell that to the dreamy look on your face."

I don't have a dreamy look on my face. I *can't* have a dreamy look on my face. Can't have feelings for Kit. And if I do have feelings for Kit, they're just pregnancy hormones. Another unfortunate side effect of incubating his offspring.

"I'm considering dating someone else."

Margot's eyebrows rise. "Really?"

"Yeah. I met him at a party over the summer, and he was really nice. We were supposed to get drinks a couple of months ago, but I canceled, and he's still asking to reschedule."

"A couple of months, and you canceled? Wow. He's super interested, then."

"Maybe." I worry my lower lip with my teeth. "I'm just not sure if I am."

"That's the point of dating, Collins. Get a drink with him and then decide if you're interested."

"I *can't* drink, Margot."

"Oh. Right. Suggest coffee, then? That's even more casual."

"Do I tell him *why* I can't drink?"

"Definitely not. I *would* tell baby daddy you're going out on a date with another guy though."

I shake my head and laugh. "Don't call him that."

"Fine. What's his name?"

On second thought … I dodge the question and ask, "Why would I tell him?"

"Because you can deny it all you want, but I think you like him. And men are simple creatures. If you want to know how he feels about you, let him know there's another guy in the picture. And, *bam*, you'll get your answer."

"You're ridiculous."

"I'm *right*. And if it doesn't work out with either guy"—she taps the piece of paper I'm holding—"I'm available to assist. Maureen loved me."

"Who's Maureen?"

"The birthing instructor."

"You took the class with your sister?"

"Uh-huh. Her boyfriend ran for the hills. Sounds like you picked a lot better." Margot glances past me and swears under her breath. "Crap. Meeting's done. I gotta go. Keep me posted!" She rushes into the hallway.

I fill a clean mug with cold water and head back toward my desk.

Kit's standing right outside his office, talking to his father.

My steps slow as I watch Crew clap a hand on his son's shoulder. Kit says something that makes Crew smile, and then they part ways. Kit heads into his office, and Crew turns in my direction.

Since I started working here, I've only attended one meeting where Kit's father and uncle were present. I'd met them both before, in more casual and chaotic circumstances, but that didn't make me feel any more comfortable. They're both intimidating. The entire Kensington family is intimidating, honestly. Kit's the most approachable one out of the untouchable group. Lili's warm, but only once you get to know her. And Kit's brother, Bash, is more serious and stoic than his siblings. At least he was two years ago, when I last saw him.

"Good afternoon," Crew greets as he passes me.

"Good afternoon," I echo, unable to tell if he recognizes me or is merely being polite.

Crew continues without another word, so I'm assuming the latter. Aside from our brief interactions at Lili's graduation party and his in-laws' patriotic bash two years ago, we haven't spoken since

Montgomery Hall. I'm unsurprised that he doesn't recognize me.

I take a seat at my desk, dump half the mug's contents on the fern, then decide to add the rest of the water. Unlock my phone and resume staring at Perry's most recent text.

I'm still studying the screen when Kit's door opens.

I glance toward the sound automatically, not expecting him to already be looking at me. When our eyes connect, there's a silly cartwheel in my chest.

Please don't let there be a dreamy look on my face, I pray.

"Hey," he says, approaching my desk.

I clear my throat, wishing I'd stopped by the restroom on my way back to my desk. My ponytail probably isn't that smooth still. "Hey. How'd the meeting go?"

Kit drums his fingers against the wood counter. "Good. Can you push the four p.m. call with Marshall to tomorrow?"

"Yeah, sure." I scribble down a reminder on a blank Post-it. "Any time preference?"

"No. Whenever I'm free is fine."

I nod. "Got it."

I'm expecting him to head back into his office, but Kit doesn't move. "You okay?"

I glance at my phone screen, then to the waterlogged fern. "I think my plant died."

"I'm sorry to hear that." Kit's lips twitch as he glances at the wet brown leaves.

"You should look more concerned," I inform him.

Another twitch. "Should I?"

"*Yes*. If I can't keep a fern alive, how am I supposed to take care of a … kiwi?"

"You can't compare ferns and kiwis. I'm not concerned."

I scan his smooth expression, finding no trace of falsehood. Laugh self-consciously. "You're a good liar."

"Or I've never lied to you." Kit holds my gaze for a few fraught seconds, then straightens and heads back into his office.

It would have been a lot faster for him to email me the meeting request.

I pick up my phone and finally text Perry back.

Collins: *What about coffee on Saturday?*

CHAPTER 25
Kit

Collins: The doctor's office just called. They want to do the ultrasound an hour earlier.

Kit: 9? That's fine.

Collins: You have a meeting at 9.

Kit: You're not the only one with access to my calendar and the ability to read, Monty. I know I have a meeting at 9.

Collins: You don't have to come.

Kit: What happened to no outs once I was in?

Collins: That kicks in after the baby is born.

Kit: It kicked in a long time ago. I will be there.

Kit: At 9.

Collins: Okay.

Standing outside an obstetrician's office solo is a unique experience. In the ten minutes I've been leaning against the brick exterior of Collins's doctor's office, I've received quite the array of looks. Some amused, others concerned. Five minutes ago, I pulled out my phone to answer emails as a temporary distraction.

"Sorry, sorry!"

I glance up to see Collins jogging toward me. She has a green scarf draped around her neck that's flying behind her like a kite. It's cold and gray and windy today.

"Train was late," she adds between rapid breaths, coming to a halt in front of me.

"Another reason you should have let me drive you," I tell her.

"Yeah, yeah," Collins grumbles. "Good morning to you too."

I smile, watching her glance at the building and then fiddle with the zipper of her jacket. "You ready?"

"Nope." She laughs, but it's thin. One for show, lacking any true substance. "Let's go."

"Okay." I slip my phone into my pocket and start toward the entrance. Only to get stopped by a quick tug on my sleeve.

Collins's eyes are wide and worried. "What if something's *wrong*, Kit? What if there's no heartbeat or it's an ectopic pregnancy or the baby has a disease that—"

"*Breathe*, Monty." I wrap her wayward scarf more securely around her neck, then use it to pull her a little closer. "Nothing's wrong."

"How do you know that? You *can't* know that! There could be something wrong, and I'm just trying to … prepare."

"You don't need to prepare for anything. On the *very* slim, *extremely* unlikely chance that there's anything out of the ordinary, we will handle it. And worrying won't help. Okay?"

Collins is gnawing on her bottom lip as she nods.

"Not good enough. Say it. *Everything is going to be fine.*"

"Okay, you're right—and enjoy hearing that because I might not ever have a reason to say it again."

I bite back a smile. "I know I am. So, say it. Tell me what I'm right about."

"Everything is going to be fine," she whispers.

"That's my girl." I kiss her forehead, then open the door and gesture for her to walk in. "Ladies first."

Her laugh is more solid this time. "Since when are you a gentleman?"

"I've always been a gentleman. Except"—I lower my voice and wink—"when you asked me not to be."

"A consequential request, it turned out." She gestures toward her midsection.

"I'm still glad you asked."

She tilts her head. "You are?"

"Yep." I nod toward the steps. "We're holding up traffic, Monty."

Collins glances over her shoulder at the woman waiting to enter the medical practice. "Oh. Sorry."

As she passes me, very quietly, I hear, "I'm glad you came."

And fuck if that isn't my second-favorite thing she's ever said to me. Right after, *"More."*

My knee won't stop bouncing.

Not only with nerves—although there are plenty of those. Despite what I assured Collins, there are a terrifying number of pregnancy complications according to the research I've done. And this pregnancy might have been unplanned at the start, but now it's very, very much planned.

Yesterday, when Andy Sanborn mentioned the trip to Italy he's planning next summer to celebrate his daughter's high school graduation, my first thought was, *I'll be a dad then.*

And the main reason my knee won't stop bouncing is the enormity of that.

Up until now, this pregnancy has felt manageable. It's often been overshadowed, honestly, by my dynamic with Collins. When I'm around her, I spend a lot more time memorizing her outfit or trying to make her smile than I do focusing on the fact that she's growing a kid that's half me.

In a sterile white exam room, that's all I can suddenly think about.

I'm about to *see* my kid. Hear its heartbeat.

"You're making me nervous," Collins states, glancing at my jumpy leg.

"Sorry," I say, focusing on forcing my knee to stay still.

"It's fine." She sighs. "I'd be nervous anyway."

"Wanna hold hands?" I suggest.

"Mine's all sweaty."

I grab it anyway, squeezing once. "I don't care."

The door opens, and the ultrasound tech returns. She's roughly my mom's age, I'd estimate, which is reassuring. It seems like she must have successfully done this many times before. Her attention is mostly on Collins, only sparing me a brief smile before she warns her about the cool gel.

Collins's fingers tighten around mine when it gets spread on her stomach, and I hide a wince.

She's strong. In every sense of the word.

I know she's worried because she told me, but she's calm and poised as she talks to the tech. Prioritizing the baby, like a mom.

The tech finishes setting everything up, then points to the screen and announces, "And … there it is. That's your baby."

"Holy shit," Collins whispers, and I couldn't have said it more succinctly myself.

It's surreal, staring at the shape on the screen. My eyes only leave it to check on Collins.

Silent tears are sliding down her cheeks. The tech notices, too, handing her a box of tissues.

"Sorry." Collins sniffles.

"Don't be," the tech replies. "It's a big moment. I've been doing this for thirty years, and I still get choked up sometimes. Here's the heartbeat."

A steady whooshing sound fills the room a second later.

Collins glances at me then, her eyes full of wonder. And she doesn't look away when she realizes I'm already staring at her.

"Wow," she says.

I'd agree, but my throat feels too thick to talk.

I thought I was prepared for this, that I was equipped for parenthood because I had good role models and can afford the best car seat and stroller and crib. But I suddenly feel totally inadequate. The anxiety I had about starting at Kensington Consolidated was nothing in comparison to the magnitude of *this* responsibility.

"You decided not to find out the sex, correct?" the tech asks.

Collins glances at me. "I said I wanted to wait and have it be a surprise. Is that okay with you?"

I wouldn't mind knowing. If nothing else, it'll make decorating the nursery much easier. But this is Collins's call. If she wants to wait, we'll wait.

"Good with me," I confirm, refocusing on the screen. Watching the blob shift feels like a rare event—a lightning strike or a meteor shower or a solar eclipse—that deserves to be fully appreciated for the limited time it lasts.

"Everything looks great, Collins. We'll print some photos for you and Dad"—the tech glances at me, and I startle at the unfamiliar title—"to take home. Dr. Bailey will review the images and give you a call later today or tomorrow."

"Why not now?" I ask.

"Kit," Collins chides softly.

"It's standard procedure, sir. If there was cause for concern, you'd be seeing a doctor now."

"Okay," I acquiesce. "Thank you," I add more politely.

"No problem." The tech wipes the gel off Collins's stomach, then leaves the room.

"Told you nothing would be wrong," I state.

She laughs. This time, the sound is suffused with relief.

"Yeah. Your knee didn't seem stressed *at all*."

Speaking of stress …

"You hungry?" I ask.

I was too anxious to eat this morning, and I'm guessing Collins felt similarly.

"Yeah, I am."

"Can I buy you breakfast?"

I hold my breath, waiting for her reply. Because she's been historically opposed to me spending any money on her and because this falls outside of co-parenting *and* work responsibilities.

She doesn't have to say yes.

She probably won't.

"Yes."

"What about whales?" I suggest.

"Whales?" Collins's nose crinkles.

"Yeah. Like an underwater theme. There could be fish and turtles too."

"I don't like the ocean."

"At all?" I ask, aghast.

Sailing's how I spent most of my summers growing up. I still go out every chance I get.

"I guess." She sips some water.

We finished our food over an hour ago, but we're still sitting in the back booth of the diner around the corner from her doctor's office.

I shake my head. "Why?"

"I …" She plays with the edge of one of the napkins on the table, curling the corner. "I almost drowned when I was nine. Jane and I swam out too far at Seabluff Beach, and there was a riptide, and … I haven't been in the ocean since. I'll swim in lakes and pools, but the sea? Pass."

"I'll pick a different nursery theme," I say hastily.

Collins smiles. "Thanks. I actually saw this cute mural online when I was looking at cribs." She pulls her phone out of her bag and thumbs at the screen. "What do you think?"

I take the phone and peer at the screen. "Mushrooms, Monty? You want to paint fungi on our kid's wall?"

"They're cute," she says defensively. "Look at the little spots."

"The *mold* spots, you mean?"

"They're not mold spots." She squints, considering. "Are they?"

"We're going to have to keep brainstorming," I say. "Maybe a forest or—"

A new message appears at the top of the screen.

Perry: I'll come to Brooklyn. Do you have a favorite spot?

It feels like a balloon just popped, all the excitement and anticipation and relief following the appointment evaporating into the grease-saturated air surrounding us. A bitter, unwelcome dose of reality.

"Or else what?" Collins prompts.

I pass her phone back. "You got a text."

Collins takes the phone, glances at the screen, then sighs. "I was going to tell you."

Her voice lacks any real conviction, and she twirls a piece of hair around her finger right afterward. Bullshit, she was going to tell me. Worst part, she didn't need to. It's not technically any of my damn business. Selfishly, I assumed—hoped—the fact that she hadn't mentioned Perry since their date meant it had gone poorly and she wasn't still seeing him.

"Tell me what?" I ask flatly.

"That I'm getting coffee with Perry this weekend."

Coffee is better than dinner. But way worse than nothing.

"You can't drink coffee," I point out.

Her lips flatten to a thin, irritated line. "I'll order decaf. Or a tea."

"Does Perry know *why* you can't drink coffee?"

"Of course not."

"Worried he won't be interested anymore?" I snark.

"And … we're done here." Collins stands, pulling her coat off the back of her chair and slipping it on. "Thanks for breakfast." She strides out the door without another word, the bell chiming cheerily in her wake.

Damn it.

I stand too. I grab my coat, toss some bills on the table, and hustle out of the diner.

Collins is halfway down the block already, meaning she's *really* pissed. When will I learn to keep my mouth shut? I knew, even as the words were coming out, that it was the wrong thing to say.

"Monty!" I call out, jogging after her. "Monty, wait!"

She doesn't stop. Not until I grab her elbow and spin her toward me. "I'm sorry," I state. "I shouldn't have said that. Perry's probably— Perry's probably prime stepfather material."

That last sentence burns like swallowing acid. The thought of another guy touching Collins makes me see red. But the idea of that guy also being around the perfect heartbeat I just heard? That's a direct stab to the heart.

Perry's a respectable lawyer. He's always polite to Flynn, despite Flynn mostly treating him like a fly that needs swatting away. I doubt he's ever been busted for underage drinking or talked his way out of a speeding ticket or had a misunderstanding with the Monaco police. He *is* prime stepfather material.

"It's *coffee*, Kit," Collins tells me. "I'm not marrying the guy."

She still sounds annoyed, but she's no longer actively glaring at me. More looking at me like I'm absurd. And overreacting.

It'd be different if I was free to pursue her myself. Her dating another guy would still suck, but at least I'd have a metaphorical hat in the ring. I'd have a *chance*.

That's all I've really wanted with Collins. A chance.

I stare at her, not really trusting myself to say anything.

"I'll see you at work," she states.

I don't think she means it as a reminder of our respective roles— that I'm her boss—but it serves as one anyway. We have to return to the office, and I'll have to pretend she's simply another employee. No special treatment.

We're not back at the office yet though.

"At least let me drive you," I plead.

Collins shakes her head. "I'll see you at work," she repeats more firmly, then walks away from me.

And it hurts a hell of a lot more than it has any of the other times.

CHAPTER 26

Collins

There's a convex curve to my stomach when I turn to the left. Barely a bump, but nearly noticeable. I'm sixteen weeks pregnant, and I'm starting to show.

I grab my phone and snap a photo, smiling as I zoom in on the small swell. My thumb hovers over the Text icon.

Is it weird to send Kit this?

Things have been off between us since the ultrasound. Stiff. Aside from his weekly fruit texts—we're up to an avocado—we haven't had a single conversation related to the baby. Or discussed anything non-

work-related.

And I miss it.

I miss … him.

My awkward coffee date with Perry wasn't worth this tension. I'm not even sure you could classify our brief meetup as a date. We mainly talked about our favorite spots in Chicago, reminiscing about living there. It lasted less than an hour, and he hugged me goodbye. The commute from Manhattan to Brooklyn and back likely took longer than he spent with me.

I drop my dress and toss my phone on the mattress with a huff, watching it bounce twice. Why did Kit have to be looking at my phone when Perry texted? Things went so well during the ultrasound, and then after …

I unzip my suitcase and rummage through its contents until I find the hardback I packed. Thankfully, the white envelope didn't slip out during the train ride. It's perfectly preserved on the title page without a single crease.

My mom is standing in the kitchen, chopping celery for the stuffing and listening to NPR. Jane is sprawled on the living room rug, painting her nails and watching the parade. And my dad … no sign of him.

"Where's Dad?" I ask, heading into the kitchen and propping a hip against the butcher-block counter.

My mom glances up from the cutting board. "He's walking Newton."

"Oh."

I scan her serene expression as she continues chopping.

I can't tell if she knows. I've never been able to tell if she knows.

Having been cheated on myself, I can confirm that the *women's intuition* thing doesn't exist. Or if it does, I didn't have it. I wish someone had told me about Isaac's philandering so I didn't have to see it for myself. But this is different. This isn't a friend; it's my mom. If she doesn't know, I don't want to be the one who tells her.

I fiddle with the stiff edge of the envelope for a few seconds, watching her prep for dinner, then hold it out. "Well, this is for you guys."

One of her eyebrows lifts as my mom dries her hands on the brown gingham towel on the counter. She lifts the flap and inspects the contents.

At first, her expression doesn't change. It shifts, bit by bit, as she pulls the sonogram out. Her lips part, and her eyes mist. "Oh my," she says softly, raising a hand to cover her mouth. "Oh my," she repeats, swiping a finger beneath her left eye.

It's the first time I've seen my mom cry since we had to put down Newton's predecessor, Einstein, when I was a junior in high school.

I clear my throat to get rid of the lump, recalling the same surreal moment of seeing my child for the first time. "He—or she—isn't very big. But you can sort of see its face, I think, right *there?*" I point to the spot the tech indicated during the ultrasound, which looks like a gray blob to me.

My mom sniffles, reaching for the dish towel and dabbing at her nose.

"I cried too," I admit. "At the ultrasound. We heard the heartbeat, and …" I swallow hard when my mom's attention jumps from the photo to me.

"We?"

I haven't made a paternity announcement to my parents yet. I've been putting it off, honestly, hoping our relationship would magically become easier to explain before the conversation needed to take place.

"Yeah. We. The father is involved."

"How involved?"

For some reason, the mural Kit is determined to paint in his professionally decorated guest room is what pops into my head first. No matter how hard I try, it doesn't fit with the immature playboy puzzle. I thought Kit's involvement was too much to expect. It never occurred to me he'd be *excited* about the prospect of parenthood.

I feel guilty for misjudging him, and it comes through in my confident, "Very."

"Mom, is there more of that cheese you got at—what's that?" Jane enters the kitchen, carrying a cloud of chemicals with her.

I cough and walk over to the sink to crack the window above it. Then start breathing through my nose, same as I have to do on the subway. Pretty sure I could out-sniff a bloodhound. At least, that's how it feels.

A gust of clean, cold air blows through the opening, and I inhale deeply.

"It's your sister's sonogram," Mom answers.

"Ooh, let me see!" Jane reaches for it eagerly.

"Not with wet nails, Jane!"

"They're basically dry," my sister retorts.

"They don't smell like they're almost dry," I mutter.

"It's cute," my sister states, peering over Mom's shoulder as she frantically wiggles her fingers. "I think. Kinda hard to tell yet. But with *that* gene pool ..." She sighs dreamily.

I shoot her a *shut up* look that my mom catches.

"What gene pool? Jane knows the father? Is he a student at Yale?"

Sorry, Jane mouths.

I swore her to secrecy during my last trip home, but I knew that couldn't last forever. My mom was about to ask the question anyway, as soon as I let that *we* slip.

"No," I answer. "Well, not anymore. It's, uh, Kit Kensington?" That last sentence comes out like a question, even though it's not really one. I ordered a paternity test so I was prepared for the Kensingtons' lawyers with proof that I wasn't a gold digger, not because I had any doubts.

Jane flashes me an encouraging thumbs-up.

My mom blinks rapidly.

"Kit Kensington," I prompt when she says nothing. "You met him my freshman year, during move-in. He's Lili's brother."

"Smells good in here, Mandy."

I glance at the doorway. My dad's returned, bent over, unclipping Newton's leash from his collar.

"Did you know?" Mom asks Dad.

"Know what?" he replies, hanging the leash up on a hook.

"That Collins is having a child with her *boss*?"

I swallow hard. I guess she knows *exactly* who Kit Kensington is. Knows my direct superior, not just the company I work at. I was hoping to ease into that part a little more. Emphasize the *I'm friends with his sister* part before revealing the whole *I work for him* bit.

Embarrassment prickles in my chest. "He wasn't my boss when we—" I clear my throat, losing some steam when I realize I'm treading dangerously close to revealing details about my sex life to my parents. "It sounds bad, but nothing unprofessional took place. It was unfortunate timing, is all. I'm looking for a new job. He won't be my boss for much longer."

I hope, I add silently. I didn't get the paralegal position I'd applied to last month. Or any other jobs I've pursued. But mentioning that now isn't going to reassure anyone.

"Oh, Collins. You're changing jobs *again*?"

The way my mom says *again*, you'd think I was swapping out careers on a weekly basis. My parents were so relieved when I told them I was double majoring in college, happy I'd have a fallback career if—when—music wasn't paying the bills. I prided myself on not worrying them, and now it feels like it's all I'm doing.

"Lots of people change jobs in their twenties, Mom," Jane says. "It's like dating, but for a career. How many people marry the first person they go out with?"

My parents exchange a look.

They did, which I used to think was sweet. Now that I'm older and far more jaded and aware of mistakes my father has made, I don't.

"Also, Kit's a *billionaire*," Jane continues. "Linny won't have to worry about money. She could play piano again."

I suck in another deep breath of fall air. All the heat in the kitchen is getting sucked out the open window, which would ordinarily make my frugal father fret. But I'm the only one who seems to notice the dropping temperature in the room.

Jane is trying to help. She's trying to spin this into a fairy tale. But I know, even before I see my mom's pursed lips and my dad's furrowed forehead, that was the wrong argument. Our parents raised us to be independent and proud, not reliant. To work for what we received. The net worth of my baby daddy isn't an important factor in their minds.

Mom focuses on me. "If you're leaving your job, you should reconsider moving home."

"I'm not moving home," I state. "I like living in New York. And it's where Kit lives. He chose to be involved, and I'm not going to make that harder than it needs to be."

"Have you discussed custody?" my dad asks somberly.

"Not … specifics," I admit.

Another loaded look is exchanged between my parents.

I glance at the sonogram my mom is still holding.

I know they have my best interests at heart. That their doubts are rooted in a place of love and concern. But their lack of confidence—in my ability to manage this situation and in my relationship with Kit—stings.

"Do you need help with the food, Mom?" Jane asks, glancing at the clock on the wall. "I'm starving."

"Right. The cheese." Mom walks over to the fridge, grabbing an unused magnet off the steel surface and using it to affix the sonogram. She opens the door next, removing a plastic package and passing it to Jane. "Don't ruin your appetite. I just have to finish the stuffing. Everything will be ready in another hour."

Jane shoots me a half-apologetic, half-encouraging look, then scurries out of the kitchen with her snack.

My mom heads back to her cutting board. Dad's still standing in the doorway, uncertain.

"I'd like to meet him, Collins," Mom tells me as she resumes chopping. "*Re*meet him, rather."

"Okay," I say.

My father moves then, heading over to the pile of papers stacked at the far end of the kitchen table. He hunts through the stack, ripping the bottom off a bill and then writing something on it. He folds it in half, walks over to the sink, and hands it to me.

"John Williams is a good friend. He's the dean of the law school. If you need an attorney, you call him. Number should be on the school website."

"Thanks, Dad."

Absurdly, I feel the hot prick of tears start to form. He's not telling me to call. Not chastising my choices. Not checking out either. It's been a long time since I felt like I had that sort of support. It's been a long time since I confided in my parents too. Since I let them see the struggle instead of showing off the solution.

He nods. "Anything else your mother or I can do, you let us know."

"I will."

"And close that window, or the next propane bill will be astronomical."

He heads toward the living room, and I smile.

CHAPTER 27

Kit

"We're going to be late!" Bash bellows.

I ignore my brother and continue staring at my phone. Keep hoping the perfect text will magically appear on the screen.

I'm losing confidence in that by the second.

"Did you hear me—the fuck?" My brother skids to a stop, tie undone and hair mussed, in the doorway. "You're not even dressed yet? You know Mom will notice we're late even though she invited a hundred other people, right?"

"I'm busy."

"Doing *what*? Posing for a portrait?" He guffaws.

I glare, not appreciating the interrogation. "You want to be on time for dinner? Stay at Mom and Dad's instead of crashing here."

Bash flashes a carefree grin. "No, thanks. You're my favorite brother."

Conveniently, I'm also his *only* brother. Not much of an endorsement.

I sigh and stand. He's right about Mom noticing our absences. This is the first Thanksgiving Lili is missing, so us being there is extra important to her.

"Give me ten minutes."

It'll probably only take me five to change, but Bash can learn some patience.

My brother sighs. "I'm not taking the blame for being late if Mom asks."

"While I'm getting ready, why don't you pack your shit?" I retort.

He holds both hands up hastily. "Hey, hey, I was kidding. See you in ten. Take fifteen if you need to."

It feels like a long, long time ago that I was that excited about living someplace with no parental or collegiate supervision.

As soon as Bash is gone, I rake my hands through my hair. I can't come up with a single meaningful or memorable thing to say, and I'm out of time. With a frustrated groan, I send the unoriginal message I've spent the past twenty minutes staring at.

Kit: Happy Thanksgiving! You feeling okay?

Collins is in Connecticut with her family. I'm in New York with mine. This time next year, we'll have a kid.

Do we split up holidays?

Do we spend them together?

We still haven't discussed custody or childcare or had any of those important conversations about our shared future for the next eighteen years. And May isn't getting any farther away, only closer.

I watch the screen, but no reply comes through.

She's probably busy with her family. I've only met Collins's mom and sister once, when Lili moved into the dorms freshman year. Her dad I know as a stoic professor, who I'm unsure ever made the connection my sister roomed with his daughter. When I asked him to say hello to Collins for me at graduation, he hardly reacted, and the ceremony was too chaotic for me to explain why.

I head into the closet and change into a navy suit on autopilot.

I moved the sonogram from my bedside table and into my sock drawer before Bash arrived yesterday. The pregnancy books are hidden under the bed since no one in my family knows about the baby. My parents would probably provide notice before showing up, but my siblings both have keys and probably *wouldn't*.

As far as I know, Collins is still intent on changing jobs. Telling my family I knocked up my former assistant sounds slightly better than my current one. And so will having answers to all the open questions about what us co-parenting will look like when I share the big news.

I pull the photo of my baby out of the drawer and stare until it blurs.

I wish there were a way to go back to the morning I received it. To ignore Perry's message when it popped up on her phone.

That argument isn't the only reason things are strained between us right now. Everything felt more real after the ultrasound. At least for me. I'm not the one having to deal with nausea and heartburn, so it's probably felt pretty real to Collins for a while.

I've been trying to give her space, to respect her boundaries and follow her lead. But we're overdue for a big conversation, and the perfect text was supposed to set the tone for it.

There's still no reply from Collins when I slip my phone into a pocket, along with my wallet, and walk down the hallway. Not entirely unexpected. Even if she has seen it, it's not like I sent anything that required an immediate response. But the lack of one still chafes.

Bash is waiting by the door, tossing a glass paperweight the interior decorator placed on the entryway table between his hands.

I grab my keys out of the matching bowl and head out the door without saying a word.

"Everything okay?" Bash casts me a worried look as we wait for the elevator to arrive.

"Fine," I answer.

He appears unconvinced. "You're acting weird."

"No, I'm not."

"Yeah, you are. Is it work? Bosses being dicks or something?" He chuckles at his own joke.

My bosses are Dad and Uncle Oliver, technically.

I don't crack a smile as I shove my hands into my pockets, leaning back against the wall. "Or something."

Bash is right; I'm acting off. I'm accustomed to having control in certain circumstances. This situation is the first time I've felt so limited. What if Collins is reconsidering moving back to Connecticut right now, and that's why she's not replying? Her living in Brooklyn feels close by comparison.

The elevator stops a few seconds later. Not in the lobby, unfortunately.

Sadie smiles wide as she steps inside. She's dressed up, same as we are, her hair in a fancy twist and a full face of makeup enhancing her pretty features. "Hey, Kit," she greets cheerfully.

I manage a friendly smile in response. "Hi." I nod toward Bash, who's attempting to look cool and uninterested. "This is my brother, Bash. Bash, this is Sadie."

She giggles, glancing between us. "I would have guessed you two were related. Nice to meet you, Bash."

He grins. "You too, Sadie."

She refocuses on me. "How are you, Kit? How are … *things*?"

Bash glances between us, brows raised, no longer faking nonchalance.

"They're, uh …" My mind goes straight to the unanswered text. "They're still complicated."

Sadie makes a sympathetic face. "Sorry to hear that. Edna said she saw you with a 'special lady friend' on Halloween, so I figured that meant things were going well."

"Not exactly." I avoid looking at Bash, who's sure to have more questions about this conversation.

"Sorry to hear that," Sadie says, and then, thankfully, she moves on to a different topic. "Where are you guys headed?"

"Thanksgiving dinner with our folks," Bash answers. "How about you?"

"Same. Well, I'm meeting some friends for drinks first, then having dinner with my parents."

The elevator doors open again, this time at the lobby.

"Happy Thanksgiving!" Sadie exclaims, exiting first.

I follow, avoiding Bash's curious gaze.

I'm not used to my parents' new place yet. They still own the penthouse that was our East Coast home base, growing up, but their main residence now is a six-story townhouse in Greenwich Village.

My mom claimed she wanted to experience a new neighborhood. My dad said it would be a shorter commute to the office. But I have a sneaking suspicion the real selling points were the walled gardens and terrace past the private patio. And I'm pretty sure they prioritized the easy outdoor access for Ben and Jerry, not themselves.

I'm used to people mentioning my parents to me in reverent, awed tones. Amid the privileged and the powerful, my parents are at the top of the pyramid. Everyone knows the names Crew and Scarlett Kensington. And I find the fascination amusing, mostly. So separate from the present, loving parents I know.

"So, you're *not* dating someone?" Bash wonders as we walk up the front steps to the double doors.

He spent the entire drive here badgering me about Collins. Or rather, about my "special lady friend" who he doesn't know is Collins.

"Nope," I state, stabbing the doorbell before glancing at a tight-lipped Camden.

My driver hasn't said a single word since wishing me and Bash a happy Thanksgiving when he picked us up outside my building. It's why he and his family were invited to Thanksgiving at my parents'. In the world of money, loyalty is priceless.

"Surprise!" The left side of the door flies open, revealing Lili.

Bash and I exchange a confused look before she flings her arms around him.

"Mom said you couldn't make it," he says, the statement muffled against her hair.

My sister releases Bash and reaches for me next. "I decided to hop on a flight at the last minute. I leave tomorrow. The jet lag will be hell, but I'll survive."

"Is Charlie with you?" I ask.

Lili shakes her head. "He couldn't get away from classes this week. They don't celebrate in the UK, you know."

"I know," I state dryly, heading inside.

Bash wasn't exaggerating about the number of people here. I lose track of my siblings as I hand my coat off to one of the staff and continue into the living room.

My parents have invited other families to join ours in the past, but the crowd has never been this big. This place has a better layout for entertaining than their old one. I recognize all the surrounding faces, but don't see any sign of my uncle and his family. Then recall Dad mentioned they were traveling to California to spend the holiday with Aunt Hannah's family.

I get pulled into three separate conversations with friends of my parents on my way over to the bar set up by the arched bookcases in the living room.

With a glass of my favorite scotch in hand, I gravitate toward the piano. Classical music is piping through the speakers, but it's hard to hear over the murmur of dozens of voices. So are the random notes I pluck.

A few minutes later, I slip my phone out of my pocket and check the screen. I have new messages, but none of them are from her.

Another hearty swig of scotch washes down my disappointment.

"I didn't know you played piano." Fran appears, resting her elbows on the edge of the upright.

"I don't," I state flatly, reaching for my drink again.

She tilts her head. "Happy Thanksgiving to you too."

I sigh and set the glass down. "Sorry. If you're looking for cheerful company, keep looking. Lili's pretty chipper."

Fran laughs. "Lili's bloodstream is half caffeine and half alcohol right now. No one's as chipper as she is."

"Did you know she was coming home?"

"Nope. We brunched earlier, caught up. She said you're doing really well at the company."

"After how many mimosas?"

Fran smiles. "She was sober. *And* she showed me the photos of you in your office."

I groan. "Are my eyes closed in every single one, or was Bash exaggerating?"

"Don't worry; you looked hot. Then again, you always do." She winks, drawing a startled laugh out of me.

Fran—and several of Lili's other friends—have flirted with me before.

But the only one I've hooked up with is Collins, which also happens to be the last time I had sex. The longest drought since I *started* having sex. I should be dying to get laid. But just like at Proof with the gin-and-tonic girl or around Sadie, my dick doesn't react.

Collins might not want me, but I don't want anyone else.

"Thanks," I say.

"*Thanks?*" Fran repeats incredulously. "You're not going to compliment me back? Or invite me upstairs?"

"I can't," I say, which sounds marginally better than *I don't want to.*

"Oh. My. God. You're dating someone?" Fran's voice is low. Shocked but low.

Still, I glance around to make sure no one else is in hearing distance before saying, "No, we're not dating. But I am interested in someone, so …"

Fran shocks the shit out of me by asking, "Is it Collins Tate?"

I blink rapidly, convinced I somehow misheard her. "What?"

She rolls her eyes. "I was totally interested in hooking up with you at that party in the Hamptons. You were too busy sneaking looks at her to notice. And *I* noticed you left right after she did. Lili said she's your assistant now?"

I sigh.

I'm starting to really hate that word. Assistant. I don't want Collins to assist me with anything. I want to be the one who helps *her*. Who *she* relies on.

Fran's waiting for an answer, so I acknowledge, "Yeah, she is."

"Why would you hire someone you have feelings for?"

I revert to my default, "It's complicated," then add, "And it doesn't really matter. She's not interested."

I flipped out about Perry because I was jealous. There's no way Collins didn't realize that, and her response has been to act as professional as possible ever since. So, I need to get over my silly crush on her before it permanently affects our co-parenting relationship. If it hasn't already.

Fran scoffs. "Yeah, she is."

I raise my eyebrows. "You've met her, what, twice?"

"And I saw her face when I came over and started talking to you."

"That was probably disgust," I say. "She thinks I'm a player."

"*Should* she think that?"

"No."

"Does she know she shouldn't think that?"

I stare at the smooth ivory keys, considering. I've flirted with Collins at every opportunity since we first met. I've made it clear—at least, I hope I've made it clear—that I'm in this kid thing for the long haul. That she can trust and rely on me. But have I told her I have trouble focusing on anything and anyone else when she's around? That I've become abstinent at age twenty-three because touching a woman who isn't her feels wrong? That I've memorized every single outfit she's worn since she started working for me because I stare at her so often? That the photo on my desk is of me, my siblings, my best friend, and … her?

No, I haven't shared all—any—of those details. Partly because I'm embarrassed. Mostly because I'm worried I'll freak her out, affecting our professional *and* parenting relationships. I can handle Collins avoiding me at work. But I don't want to put her in that position. And I *can't* handle missing moments like the ultrasound or discussing the nursery decorations.

"I'm going to take that *very long* pause as a no," Fran says. "So, I'd start there."

"We work together, Fran."

"So? Wouldn't be the first time it happened. Bridget's ex got all chummy with a waitress he worked with."

I lift an eyebrow, and she laughs.

"Okay, yeah, that was a bad example. But my point is, it's natural—common even—to develop feelings for someone you spend a lot of time around." Fran straightens, leaning her hip against the side of the piano instead of resting her elbows on it. "Plus, you've never struck me as someone worried about breaking a few rules."

I muster a smile.

"I've been looking everywhere for you!" Lili appears, one hand holding a cherry-red cocktail and the other stuck in her hair. "One pin was stabbing my skull, so I pulled it out, and the whole braid's falling apart now."

"What an emergency," I drawl.

Lili glances down at me, eyes narrowing. "You can't play piano."

"I'm not playing; I'm sitting."

"I think I have a mini hair spray in my bag," Fran says. "I'll go grab it."

She disappears through the doorway, and Lili focuses on me.

"You look tired."

"So do you."

My sister scowls. "I'm running on four hours of sleep. What's your excuse?"

"Late night at Proof."

I don't want Lili wondering or worrying about me. Staying out all hours partying isn't behavior she'll blink twice at. The truth—that I read about Braxton-Hicks contractions and congenital disorders, then stared at the ceiling for a few hours, brainstorming what to send Collins today (whole lot of good that did me)—would elicit a very different reaction.

Sure enough, my sister shakes her head and spins to follow Fran. "Mom's looking for you," she calls over one shoulder.

I sigh, stand, and head deeper into the house.

Bash wanders into the living room while I'm staring into the fire. He's changed into sweatpants and a green hoodie. I'm still wearing my suit even though we got back from Mom and Dad's over an hour ago.

My brother surveys me for a few seconds. He scratches his jaw, then flops down in the armchair opposite mine, resting his socked feet on the coffee table. "Dude, I'm stuffed."

I nod in agreement. "Yeah, me too."

"You going out tonight?"

"Nah."

"Lili asked if I was at Proof with you last night. Unless you snuck out after telling me you were going to bed at eleven …"

I say nothing.

"I covered for you. Said you went with Flynn."

I nod. "Thanks."

"So, you ready to tell me what the hell is going on with you?"

I lean forward, resting my elbows on my knees. Deliberating. If I'm going to tell someone, my brother is my best option. He's not my boss, like Dad. He's not connected to Collins, like Lili. He won't get emotional, like Mom.

"I got a girl pregnant."

It's a sick relief to finally say the truth aloud, like pressing on a bruise. A painful release.

Bash laughs once, settling deeper into the chair. "Ha. Good one. Okay, I'm invested. What's *really* going on?"

"I'm fucking serious, Bash. That *is* what's going on."

The broad smile slides right off my little brother's face.

Wordlessly, he stands and strides over to the bar cart in the corner. He fills a crystal tumbler with my favorite single-malt scotch—almost to the brim—then returns to his seat and downs a healthy amount.

"Don't overreact," I warn.

He makes an incredulous sound in the back of his throat between sips. "She's keeping it?"

I nod. "She's due May 18."

"May 18." Bash whistles, long and low. "Holy fuck. Who knows?"

"She told her family. You're the first person I've told."

He downs more scotch, inhaling it like oxygen.

Unease swims through my bloodstream. If *Bash* is reacting like this …

"Mom and Dad are gonna freak out," he tells me. "You're twenty-three."

I shrug. "So? Mom was twenty-five when she had Lili. What difference does two years make?"

"Mom and Dad were also married."

"A piece of paper doesn't make you a better parent," I snap.

Bash sets down his drink and holds up his hands. "Whoa, whoa. I'm just saying, that's what other people are going to say."

"Well, don't."

He crosses his ankles, studying me speculatively. "Is it the blonde from the elevator earlier? Was 'special lady friend' some kind of weird code between you guys?"

"No, it's not Sadie."

Silence.

"C'mon, Kit. You're really gonna make me ask who?"

I tug at my tie, loosening it a little, then state, "It's Collins Tate."

"*Collins Tate*, Collins Tate?"

I cock an eyebrow. "You know more than one person named Collins Tate?"

"No. But I'm hoping *you* do or else you're telling me the girl you knocked up is your *assistant*."

I slouch in my seat, tilt my head back, and blow out a long breath. "It happened *before* she was my assistant."

Bash barks out a stunned laugh. "And then you *hired* her? What the fuck, Kit?"

"I didn't know she was pregnant."

"You knew you'd screwed her."

"I know." I drag a palm down my face. "It was a bad judgment call. But it was only one night. We weren't in a relationship or anything. If she was willing to work with me, I knew I could be professional."

"Professional," Bash echoes, dubious. "You're full of more bullshit than scotch right now. You know that, right?"

I reach for my empty glass, stand, and head toward the bar cart to even out the balance.

"What's the plan, Kit?" Bash calls after me.

I'm silent, watching the liquor splash in the glass.

"I don't know," I admit. "She tried to quit, to leave New York, and I asked her not to."

"Why not? Wouldn't that be for the best?"

I spin back around. "No, it wouldn't be 'for the best.' She's *pregnant*, Bash. When she's not pregnant, there's going to be a baby. *My* kid. I'm not going to write a check and help her pack. I'm not going to miss everything. I want to be there when he or she is born. When it talks. When it takes its first steps ..." My voice trails off.

I've been too preoccupied with current crises to truly think about what life past approximately May 18 will look like. Joking about our kid acting or playing sports felt abstract when Collins and I had dinner. But all those milestones will actually take place.

"So, you're going to share custody?"

My grip tightens on the tumbler as I walk back to the armchair. "I guess," I mutter, sinking back down.

But I don't *know*. And I doubt Collins is going to want to be separated from our newborn often or for long. If she's still living in Brooklyn, where does that leave me? Camping out on her floor to help with whatever I can? I will, but it doesn't feel like a sustainable solution. It'll be years until our kid is old enough to understand parents sometimes live in different places.

"Did you ask for a paternity test?" Bash asks.

I swirl the contents of my glass, avoiding answering.

This is another reason I've told no one. Because in my world, that's one of the first questions—if not *the* first question—that gets asked. Any kid I have stands to inherit a lot of money, and a lot of people know that fact.

"Kit." My name is weighed down with the heaviness of disappointment as Bash correctly reads my silence.

My little brother sounds *exactly* like my dad when he disciplines me.

"Bash." I match his tone.

"You have to get a paternity test. You'd be crazy not to."

"I don't *have* to do anything."

"I'm not saying she would … you know, lie, on purpose … but she might not be sure and scared to tell you. It's a messy situation. You're her boss too. Finding out for sure is—"

"I'm not asking her for a paternity test," I state.

Bash sighs. "You barely know her. She lived with Lili for a couple of semesters *years* ago and now—"

"I *do* know her," I insist. "And she wouldn't lie to me. Not about this."

"What if it were me? What if I told you I'd knocked up a girl?"

"I'd …" I exhale, opting for honesty. "I don't know what the fuck I'd say now that I'm on this side of it."

"And before? The first thing you would've said was to get a paternity test."

He's not wrong, and I hate that he's right. But it doesn't shake my resolve.

"It's *mine*, Bash. I'm sure."

"Well ..." He drains the rest of his drink. "We both know I'm not the one you're going to have to convince."

I hate that he's right about that too.

Bash chuckles. "Thanks, by the way."

"For what?" I question, confused.

My brother grins. "Are you kidding? This is the best gift you ever could have given me. A lifetime *get out of jail free* card."

I scowl. "You're a dick."

"We both know where I learned it from."

I roll my eyes, then focus on the flickering flames. A log crackles and pops, creating a cozy ambiance. The alcohol is making me feel warm and sleepy, and so is the relief of having finally told someone the truth.

"You got a photo?" Bash asks suddenly.

I glance at him. "Huh?"

"Of the baby. Have they given you a picture of it yet?"

I stare at my brother for a few seconds, then clear my throat. "Uh, yeah. They gave us a sonogram after the first ultrasound."

Bash waits expectantly.

"You want to see it?"

"Might be your kid, but it's *my* niece or nephew."

I clear my throat again and stand. "One sec."

The sonogram is tucked in the same spot I left it. It only takes me a few minutes to grab it and return to the living room.

Bash hasn't moved.

I hand him the sonogram, then continue toward my seat.

"Wow, I can see the resemblance," he jokes, squinting at the blob.

I flip him off, then reach for my phone when I feel it buzz. Stiffen when I read the name on the screen and hastily unlock it.

Collins: Happy Thanksgiving!

Below it, she's sent a photo of her stomach. In profile, so the subtle bulge of her midsection is more obvious.

Collins: Too much turkey.

I grin.

"Oh, I get it now," Bash says.

I glance at him. "Get what?"

"You *like* her. That's why you're so defensive."

"I'm not defensive. And of course I like her. We work together, and she's the mother of my child."

"Nope." Bash shakes his head. "It's more than that."

"Whatever. I'm going to change. Leave that"—I point at the sonogram—"in the kitchen when you're finished looking at it. Been meaning to put it up on the fridge."

Bash salutes me. "Will do. And congrats, by the way, on the whole baby thing."

"Thanks," I reply, then head down the hall.

CHAPTER 28

Collins

I reread my letter of resignation yet again, a surprising amount of sadness and dread warring with relief.

When I received an offer from Bradford, Nash, & Monroe LLP yesterday, I *was* relieved. Grateful. Everything felt a little lighter.

But now, faced with the prospect of telling Kit, I'm mostly apprehensive.

I already attempted to quit once. He knows I've been actively looking for other jobs. This position doesn't start until early January, so I'm not leaving him in a lurch. I'm giving him a full month to find a

replacement, not just the traditional two weeks.

Kit and I don't have a standard boss-employee relationship, however.

Which means I have no idea how he's going to react. I also don't know if he's aware Bradford is the firm Perry works at. Or if I should disclose that, considering the subject of our last argument. Or if I should tell him Perry and I are friends, nothing more.

Ever since the ultrasound, I've inserted an extra layer of space between us. I know Kit thinks it's because of how he reacted to Perry's message. But I basically used that as an excuse. I was a lot more freaked out by what'd happened earlier in the day.

When I had decided to keep this baby, I had been prepared to do it alone. Even after Kit committed, I was prepared to do it alone. But I'm not sure I would have walked into Dr. Bailey's office without his reassurances.

And *that* scared me a lot more than single parenthood.

I wanted him there for *me*, not as the baby's father. And if there's a more potentially catastrophic choice I can make after the series of events that landed me as Kit's pregnant assistant, it's falling in love with the man.

Not because he's my soon-to-be former boss. Or Lili's brother. Because he's the *father of my child*, and that's not the guy you can casually date without consequences.

"You almost ready?" Margot asks, popping over the ledge of my desk.

I startle, nearly upending my water bottle with my elbow. "Margot! You scared the shit out of me."

"Sorry." She giggles. "I'm trying to be stealthy."

We're throwing a surprise engagement party for Aimee tonight.

Her boyfriend proposed when they were visiting her family for Thanksgiving.

"So?" Margot prompts. "Are you ready to go?"

I glance at the clock—5:02. Stop deliberating and hit Print on the letter. "Yeah, almost. Five minutes." I stand. "I just have to give something to Kit."

"Okay. Hurry, yeah?" Margot rushes down the hallway.

I head for the copy room. It's empty and noticeably warmer than the already-toasty office. The massive machine is churning out documents at a rapid pace.

I tap the screen, sighing when I see two-hundred-plus-page contracts are in the queue ahead of my job.

"Hey."

I glance over my shoulder at Stella.

"Hey," I reply, trying to ignore the quickening pace of my heart.

I'm not doing anything wrong, but I feel jumpy. Guilty. I'm closer with Margot, mainly because of what I confided in her, but I consider Stella a friend too.

She glances at the growing stack of paper. "Sorry. I didn't think anyone else would be trying to print this late in the day."

"Don't worry about it," I say, then glance at the clock. The five minutes I promised Margot have already passed.

Stella catches me and smiles wryly. "Margot stopped by your desk too?"

I smile back. "Sure did."

"Do you *ever* leave by five?" Stella's teasing, but there's also curiosity in her tone.

I keep my expression neutral as I shrug a shoulder. Kit tends to work later than any other executive on this floor. I'm usually the last assistant to leave. Stella isn't the first person to comment on it.

The printer pauses for a few seconds.

Stella strides toward it, glancing over the documents. "That should be all of mine," she tells me. "If anything else comes out, just drop it at my desk?"

I manage a nod, trying not to look *too* relieved. "Will do."

"See you in the lobby," Stella tells me, then walks out.

The printer whirs to life again, spitting out my single sheet of paper. I grab the warm letter from the tray and hurry back to my desk, scanning the lines of text one final time. I slip an envelope out of my bag and knock on Kit's door. Might as well give this to him now too. Stop avoiding and lay everything out on the table.

"Come in," Kit's voice calls a second later.

My fingers fumble with the handle as I open it and step inside his office.

"Hey." He glances up, giving me his full attention as I close the door.

I swallow nervously. "Hey."

Kit leans back in his chair, holding eye contact. "What's up?" he asks cautiously.

The last time I entered his office without a professional reason was with my first letter of resignation. The time before that, a pregnancy announcement. So, I understand his apprehension.

"I have a couple of things to give you," I state. Fake a cough to clear my throat. "They're, uh, non-work-related."

He straightens in his chair, focus sharpening as he nods once.

"Is now an, uh, okay time?" I question.

"Of course. Take a seat."

I do, fighting a strong burst of déjà vu as I pass him the envelope with the paternity test results first. Dr. Bailey's office did the test when I was eight weeks. I've had the results for more than two months, waiting for Kit to bring it up. He still hasn't.

Kit takes the envelope, a crease appearing on his forehead as he studies the outside. "This is addressed to you. And"—he flips it over—"it's unopened."

"We need to have a custody conversation soon," I start.

"What does this"—he holds up the envelope—"have to do with custody?"

"It's a paternity test."

The explanation doesn't clear the confusion. Kit's frown deepens instead. "What?"

"It's a paternity test," I repeat. "For your lawyers or whoever needs to see it."

He tosses the envelope on his desk with a low scoff. "I didn't ask you to do a test, Collins."

"I know you didn't. But I'm sure you wanted to. We've never been in a relationship. We *weren't* in a relationship when … it happened. I'm sure you've wondered if—"

"I haven't," Kit states flatly.

"Okay." I swallow hard, completely thrown by his reaction. And increasingly concerned about how the letter is going to land next. I thought handing him the test results was going to be the easy part. That he'd nod, thank me for taking care of this, and tuck the envelope in a folder for safekeeping. "Well, even so, this way, there's no doubt about—"

He interrupts, "I didn't *ask* you to do this, Collins! And I'm pretty sure collecting my DNA without permission is a federal crime."

I blanch. Swabbing one of his coffee cups while he was in a

meeting seemed simple and harmless, not criminal. Something I thought Kit would laugh or joke about.

"You're *mad* that I—"

"You're damn right I'm mad." He roughly runs a hand through his hair. "What the hell happened to making decisions together?"

"This—I—this had nothing to do with the baby. It was about—"

Again, he interrupts, "Nothing to do with the baby? It has *everything* to do with the baby. Because I trust you, but you don't trust me."

Now, *I'm* mad. "Because I gave you *proof* you can trust me? That I told you the truth? That means I don't trust you? That doesn't make any sense, Kit!"

He shakes his head. "You didn't take this test for me. It's insurance—for *you*. If anyone asks the question, you wanted to have the evidence handy. And the only reason you'd need evidence was if you didn't trust me to protect you."

"That's not ..." I chew the inside of my cheek until I taste copper. "I can't believe you're *upset* about this. I thought you'd ask me to take one, but you never did, so I figured I'd just ... handle it."

"If I'd wanted a paternity test, I *would* have asked you for one. So, are you sure you didn't do this to reassure yourself?"

My spine snaps straight. "How long have you been waiting to ask me that?"

I've been waiting for him to ask me that.

I never expected Kit not to question me about paternity. A leading *you're sure ...* when I said it was his. Or a question at a doctor's appointment, clarifying the conception date.

We hadn't seen each other for two years before that night. He knew I'd recently gotten out of a relationship with someone else. And he's rich, with obvious assets to protect.

Not asking is careless, and Kit is smart.

"How long? Since you handed me this." He nudges the offending envelope with the tip of a pen.

"If I needed *reassurance*, I would have opened the results before I gave them to you."

I stand, still clutching my letter of resignation. I'll have to give this to him tomorrow. I don't have the time or the energy to handle another argument right now. Everyone else must be down in the lobby already, and tonight's supposed to be a celebration.

"And *you're* the billionaire who's slept with half the women in this city and every sorority girl at Yale. For all I know, this has happened to you before. Stop acting like I'm being unreasonable. This situation is complicated, and I'm trying to make it a little more straightforward. Don't pretend you don't know how the world—*your* world—works. A paternity test is the first thing your family's team of lawyers is going to ask for, and that's not *my* fault."

I stride out of his office as fast as I can without jogging, blinking away the tears before they have a chance to fall.

CHAPTER 29
Kit

At eight fifteen, she finally shows up.

I don't move from my current spot, watching her say something to the cab driver before closing the door and turning this way. She sees me two steps later, lips pressing tight together as she continues toward the stairs I'm sitting on.

"Those are filthy," she states when she reaches me. "You'll ruin your suit."

Still, I don't move.

Collins heaves out a sigh before she climbs and sits next to me,

setting her bag between her feet. As per usual, it's stuffed full. "How long have you been here?"

"A while."

"I had an engagement party to go to after work."

"Whose party?"

"Aimee." Collins shifts, tightening the strip of wool holding her coat together. "She's part of the legal department. She has quite the crush on you actually. She'd probably leave her fiancé if you asked."

I say nothing.

I've had two and a half hours to decide what to tell her, but I'm still struggling for the right words.

I exhale, resting my elbows on my knees. "I hate fighting with you, Collins. I've always liked arguing with you, but fighting? For real? I hate it."

"I do too." She bites her bottom lip. "I'm sorry about the paternity test. I really—it never occurred to me that you'd be *upset* about it."

"I know." I reach for her hand, lacing our chilly fingers together. I think it's above freezing out, but not by much.

Collins releases a surprised breath at the contact, but doesn't pull away, which I take as an encouraging sign.

"I *chased* you because I wanted to be around you, Collins, not because it was a game. You are the one person I've ever met who doesn't *want* anything from me. Who doesn't expect me to be … Kit Kensington. My friends want me to party with them, and my family wants me to grow the hell up. Strangers think they know me because we were at the same club once. This baby is the first thing in my life that's been … a fresh start—almost. Pomegranate doesn't know how much money I have or that I was *almost* arrested in Monaco once."

She smiles reluctantly.

"I got used to the baby being separate from the rest of my life. From it being in this special, protected bubble. You said you got the test because you know how my world works. And you were right; a paternity test is probably going to come up at some point. But I didn't *want* it to. It caught me off guard—that things weren't staying separate anymore. I was mad you'd felt like you needed to get one, not mad at *you*. I'm sorry I overreacted."

"Why-why didn't you ask me for one?" she asks tentatively. "Were you worried about … offending me? Because I want us to be honest—"

I shake my head. "You want honest? I didn't ask you for a test because, if you were pregnant, I wanted it to be mine. No one gets handed a present they really fucking want and asks for a gift receipt, Monty."

She glances down at our joined hands, hiding her expression from me. I wait, holding my breath, terrified the next words out of her mouth are going to include *boundaries* or *line*.

Instead, she tells the ground, "I'm not dating Perry."

A spark of hope flares to life in my chest. "You're not?"

"I'm not. Because I don't *want* to date him … not because I'm going to be working at the same law firm he does, starting in January." Collins reaches into her bag with her free hand and extracts a folded sheet that she smooths and sets on my lap. "One of the paralegals in Perry's department is leaving at the beginning of next year. He recommended me for the position. They offered it to me yesterday."

I stare at her creased resignation letter.

"I can print a clean copy," Collins adds hurriedly. "I was going to give it to you at the office earlier. When things … derailed, I decided to wait until tomorrow."

"Congratulations," I say.

Her forehead furrows. "Really? That's it?"

"I told you, I'm sick of fighting. As long as this is what you want, I'll support it."

She exhales in obvious relief, and I hate the sound of it. Hate that she was so worried about telling me.

"Thanks," Collins whispers.

"Anything for my favorite baby mama."

She laughs, then winces. "Sorry I, uh, brought that up."

"It was a fair shot. I was acting like an ass."

I glance at her.

"Oh, sorry, were you waiting for me to disagree?"

I laugh.

I like Collins Tate. I like her *a lot*. I might even love her.

"For the record, you're also my *only* baby mama. I've always been … careful."

Collins hesitates before saying, "We were careful too."

"Three times increases the odds."

Once again, she pauses before speaking. "So, you don't usually …"

I wait, but she doesn't finish. Just blushes.

We haven't discussed *that* night in any detail since it happened. Her fishing for information, paired with the revelations she's not dating Perry and will no longer be working at Kensington Consolidated in a month, has me in an excellent mood all of a sudden.

"That wasn't a normal night for me, Collins," I state.

Something I would have said sooner had she stuck around the next morning.

She's avoiding my gaze, but I don't think she's uncomfortable. The corners of her lips are curved up, and she's still flushed. I think she's flustered.

Maybe Fran and Sadie were right, and I should spell the whole truth out.

"I hope you're ready for January," I tell her.

She glances at me in response to the rapid subject change. "Uh, yeah. I should be. The responsibilities they went over during the interview sounded pretty similar to what I was doing at—"

"I'm not talking about your new job," I clarify. "I'm talking about how, starting in January, you *won't* be working for me."

Her head tilts. "What does that mean?"

"You know that's the only reason I haven't *chased* you since August, right?"

Shock spreads across her face, like ink spilling in water. Then gets hastily wiped away.

Collins's fingers fidget, like she's contemplating pulling her hand away. "I'm not sure that's a good idea," she says softly.

"Why?" I challenge, undeterred.

She opens her mouth. Closes it. Opens it again. "It would complicate co-parenting if we were … involved."

I nod in agreement. "That must be why couples never have kids together. Can you imagine? The hassle of *not* having two houses and a custody agreement and separate finances—"

"It would complicate *our* co-parenting. There was nothing to separate. We were never a couple to begin with, Kit."

"That was your choice. Not mine. You knew I was interested."

She scoffs. "So *interested* that I never heard from you after that night? It took me walking into your office as your *assistant* for us to have a post-sex conversation."

I exhale. "I know. And I'd change that if I could—and not just because you're pregnant. I'd flirted with you for years, and you shot me down every time, except once. I figured you wanted a one-night stand, and waking up alone pretty much confirmed that. Monday, I started at Kensington Consolidated, work got crazy, and then the next thing I knew, you were accepting the job. I never *lost interest*, and there's no chance I wouldn't have begged for another night the next time I saw you if it were under different circumstances."

A reluctant smile plays across Collins's lips. "Begged, huh? I would pay to see that."

"For you? I'd do it for free."

"For sex, you mean."

"Do I want to have sex with you again? Fuck yes. But I'm talking about a relationship, Monty. Exclusive, monogamous, committed. The real deal."

"Have you ever been in a relationship?"

She already knows the answer, and I'm sure it's contributing to her uncertainty. "No. If I had been in a relationship, I wouldn't have been free to flirt with you."

Collins rolls her eyes. "You're ridiculous."

"I'm also completely serious. If I'd met a woman I wanted more than you, I'd have dated her. Never happened."

"You're serious," she realizes, almost to herself.

"I'm serious," I confirm.

"Can I think—I just need to think." She squeezes my palm. "Not because I don't—I'm just a little overwhelmed."

"You can think about it as much as you want," I reassure her. "But fair warning: I'm taking you out on a date the first weekend you don't work for me. We never properly celebrated the pregnancy, and we're going to. After that, you can decide if you want this to go anywhere."

"Like a trial run?"

"Sure," I agree. "If a trial run ruins you for all other runs."

She laughs. "Okay."

"Okay," I echo.

I've said everything I needed to. I should stand. Leave. Let her head inside and get warm. But despite the fact that my butt went numb a couple of hours ago and my stomach's rumbling, I'm hesitant to leave.

"I was thinking …" Collins starts.

"Yeah?" I prompt.

She glances at the ground, then meets my waiting gaze. "I was thinking that since I won't be working for you, starting next year, it might be a good time to give the *living together* thing a try. That way, if it doesn't go well, we'll have time to figure something else out before the baby arrives."

I blink at her.

Collins misreads my stunned silence. "If you've changed your mind, that's totally fi—"

"I haven't changed my mind," I tell her hastily. "In fact, when your landlord came home an hour ago, I pretended I was interested in living here. He said he had thirty applicants for a unit that changed tenants a couple of weeks ago. Doesn't sound like you'd have any trouble breaking your lease."

And if you do, I'll take care of it.

She shakes her head in exasperation, but she's smiling. "Okay. I'll talk to him. One other thing …" She bites her bottom lip. "My, uh, parents want to meet you. *Remeet* you, I mean. It's not urgent; I've just been meaning to mention it."

"What about next weekend? Does that work?"

She blinks rapidly, clearly taken aback. "Uh, it should. I'll check with them, but it should."

I nod, squeeze her hand one final time, and stand. "Great. Set it up."

CHAPTER 30
Collins

My heart trips in my chest when he steps out of the driver's seat.

A ridiculous reaction, which is how I wound up needing to use an elastic hair tie to close my jeans this morning.

If I'd never started working for him—if I hadn't wound up pregnant—I probably would have convinced myself that night in the Hamptons was simple lust. But Kit has depth. He's just selective about when he shows it. Or maybe I never looked hard enough. Maybe I subconsciously knew, if I did, I'd wind up in love with him.

Falling is an accurate verb. It's a loss of control. Walking into water, deeper than your feet can touch.

"Hey, Monty," Kit greets casually.

My, "Hey," comes out breathless, and it has nothing to do with the flights of stairs I just hustled down.

Ever since our conversation on the steps behind me, I can't be around him—can't even think about him—without my body reacting. It's like he lit the end of a fuse. A very *long* fuse that's going to take three more weeks to burn.

Even more frustrating, Kit appears unaffected. All week at work, he acted completely normal, like our conversation never happened.

Which might have factored into my decision to wear a V-neck shirt today that shows off the fact that my boobs are twice their former size.

"Ready for our road trip?" he asks, flashing that billion-dollar smile my way.

"I don't think a two-hour drive really constitutes a road trip," I say dryly, setting my suitcase on the curb.

Kit frowns, glancing between the luggage and my building. "Does your building have an elevator?"

"Yes," I lie, reaching for a strand that's come loose from my bun.

He lifts a knowing eyebrow, and my hand immediately falls to my side. My cheeks warm as I recall the last time he called me out on doing the same thing.

I sigh. "No, it doesn't. My bag isn't that heavy, and cardio is good for you."

"Let me help sometimes, Collins. It's good for my fragile male ego."

At that, I scoff. "A hurricane couldn't wreck your self-confidence, Kensington."

He tilts his head. "Thank you?"

I smile. "I'll use the elevator at your place, okay?"

Not like I'll have a choice since his unit is the penthouse.

"Does that mean you talked to your landlord?"

"Yes," I say as I climb in the front seat, pulling my hands out of my pockets and holding them in front of the vents.

This is a different car from the one Kit drove me home in before. Just as sleek and luxurious, but a little roomier. I don't know enough about automobiles to recognize the logo on the steering wheel, but my guess is, it's European and expensive.

"And?" Kit settles in his seat, clicking his seat belt into place.

"He's already found a new tenant."

Which is ideal because it means I won't be penalized for breaking my lease. But also nerve-racking because I no longer have an alternate living option. Moving in with Kit is happening.

"I have to be out by January 4," I add.

I start my new job on January 3, so it's going to be a hectic start to the year. At least there's not much to move. I haven't had the energy to decorate my apartment, and I only bothered bringing the bare necessities from Chicago to begin with.

"Did he give you any problems with the lease?"

"No."

Kit nods. "Good." He shifts the gear into drive, then adds, "You look nice."

I'm completely caught off guard by the compliment. I haven't even taken my parka off yet. "Thanks. So do you."

It's the first time I've seen him out of a suit since Halloween. And while he wears them exceptionally well, I prefer this sweater-wearing, stubbled version. He seems more mortal. Touchable.

"You're making me blush, Monty," he teases.

I shake my head, dropping my warmed hands into my lap. "Did you see that James Dennis emailed this morning about changing—"

"What happened to nothing professional on the weekends?" Kit interrupts.

"It's time sensitive."

"Forget about it, Collins. It can wait until Monday."

"Fine." I fiddle with my zipper, staring out the windshield as he navigates through my neighborhood.

"You nervous?"

"A little," I admit. "I know you've met them before, but this is different."

I've only spoken to my mom once since Thanksgiving—to run this visit by her. I haven't talked to my dad at all. And Jane has been quieter than usual, busy with finals. She has one tonight. She's going to try to stop by our parents' after, but she won't be there for dinner.

"It's gonna go great." Kit's voice is pure confidence, and I relax into it, like slipping into a warm bath.

"Have you thought about when you're going to tell your family?" I ask.

"I was thinking after the holidays. Lili will be back home ... unless you wanted to tell her?"

I shake my head as I slip off my coat. I'll say this for his fancy car: the heat works really well in it. "She's your sister. You should tell her."

I don't think Lili's absence is the only reason Kit's waiting. Telling his father, who's technically his boss, that his *former* assistant is pregnant sounds slightly better than announcing he knocked up his *current* one.

"Bash knows. I told him when he was home for Thanksgiving."

"How did he react?" I can't tell based on Kit's cavalier tone.

"He's stoked."

"*Really?*"

The few times I've been around Bash, he's acted polite and reserved. I can't picture him and *stoked* in the same room together.

"Really." He glances at me and grins. "He thinks it'll mean a *get out of jail free* card on any future indiscretions."

"Like a *sorry I crashed the Benz, but remember Kit knocked up his assistant* kind of thing?"

Kit chuckles. "Yeah, exactly. I don't know what he's worried about though. Bash has always been an angel compared to me."

I smile. "Does that mean you're a devil?"

"Baby, I'll be whatever you want me to be," he drawls.

A full acrobatic routine is taking place in my chest right now. I clear my throat in an attempt to regain some composure. "Calling me *baby* isn't very professional."

He glances at my chest before refocusing on the road ahead. "Neither's that top."

It's raining when we reach New Haven. The town looks dreary and gray and damp. Same with the street I grew up on, the branches of the few trees that line it bare and brown.

"It's that one." I point. "With the yellow door."

Kit nods, then pulls into the correct driveway.

I stare at the split-level, trying to view it from a stranger's perspective.

I've never been to Kit's parents' home, only their summer place. The house I grew up in could comfortably fit in the foyer of that mansion.

And I'm suddenly very aware of the fact that we always interact in *his* world. I've attended events Lili invited me to, hosted at their family's homes. The party in the Hamptons I was so uncomfortable at was typical for him. Despite his confession in the elevator, Kit always appears completely at ease in the skyscraper that houses Kensington Consolidated's corporate headquarters. We went to his favorite restaurant. Met at his penthouse. The closest we've come to my world, until now, was sitting on my apartment steps.

We're different. And that's not a bad thing, but it's *noticeable*. Especially right now.

"Still sure you don't want a hotel room?" I check.

Two bedrooms don't allow for a lot of guest space. And since my parents know we're not a couple, sharing a bed seems strange.

I offered to take the couch, and Kit said, "Absolutely not," in a tone that brooked no argument. He also turned down sleeping elsewhere.

He just laughs now, climbing out of the car and stretching. His sweater rides up a few inches, flashing a strip of firm muscle, and I quickly open my door to counteract the immediate heat flash with some December air.

It's for the best that I'm unable to drink. I need full control of my faculties. All the pregnancy books I've read mentioned an increased sex drive being common in the second trimester.

I thought they were exaggerating.

They weren't.

"You're here!" My mom is rushing down the front walk, her cheeks rosy from the cold.

I smile as I step out of the car, pulling my hood up and over my hair. "Hi, Mom," I greet, giving her a hug.

"How are you feeling?" she asks as soon as we separate.

"Good. No more nausea."

"That's great." She smiles, then glances at Kit, who's appeared on my left.

He holds out a hand. "It's very nice to see you again, Professor Tate. Thank you for inviting me."

"Amanda. Please, call me Amanda." My mom glances at me quickly before shaking Kit's hand. I don't think the color in her cheeks is entirely from the cold anymore.

"Hello, Kit." My dad's appeared, umbrella in hand, holding a palm out to him.

I watch them shake hands, chewing the inside of my cheek anxiously. My relationship with my dad might be messy right now, but he's still my dad. I want him to like Kit.

"Good to see you, Professor Tate," Kit greets politely.

My dad harrumphs in response. If I didn't know their personalities, I'd think my parents had designated *good cop* and *bad cop* roles before we arrived.

He glances at me next. "Hello, Collins."

"Hi, Dad," I reply.

Kit looks over, a small furrow forming between his eyes as my cool tone registers.

"Let's head inside before we're all soaked," Mom says, filling the lingering pause.

"Go ahead," Kit tells me. "I'll grab the stuff from the car."

I open my mouth to argue, then remember what he said earlier. I close my mouth and nod.

Kit smiles, like he knows what I was thinking.

I follow Mom up the brick path. My dad lingers by the car with Kit. From the strain of their conversation I catch before exiting earshot, it sounds like my dad is asking Kit a question about the vehicle. What question that might be I have no clue. My dad has driven the same station wagon since he was in grad school.

My parents' house might be small and shabby, but it's cozy. Stepping inside is an immediate relief, warm, dry air chasing away the chilly dampness outside.

"I see what Jane was going on about," my mom says as she hangs her coat up in the closet. "He's very attractive."

I groan. "*Mom*."

"What? I don't want an ugly grandchild."

I'm torn between amusement and horror. There's some happiness too. This is the first time anyone, except for Jane or Kit, has acted *excited* about the baby. The repressed laughter in my mom's voice as she teases me is as comforting as the hiss of the ancient radiators working overtime.

"That's—he's my boss," I remind her. I told my mom about the new job I'd accepted when we discussed this visit, so at least my parents know that's a temporary statement. "Don't talk about how hot he is."

"You're having a child with the man, Collins. Clearly, you noticed."

I grimace. "Something smells good."

My mom laughs, but she lets me change the subject. "I went a little overboard on food. I wasn't sure what would sound good to you—*oh*."

Impulsively, I pull my mom into another hug.

She's silent for a few seconds, petting my hair the same way she did when I was younger. "Everything okay, honey?"

"Yeah." I pull back and sniffle. "I'm hormonal. And it's nice to be home."

Mom smiles. "It's nice to have you home. You seemed happy in Chicago, but I have to admit, I'm really glad you ended up in New

York."

"I am too," I say truthfully.

And honestly? I'm not sure I *was* happy in Chicago. I was content, until things imploded because I didn't know it could be this much better.

"… has a 4.0-liter twin-turbo V8 engine with …"

I tune in and then tune right back out of my dad and Kit's car conversation as they enter the house, dripping rainwater all over the mat.

My mom and I hastily move to the side as they pull off their coats and set down the luggage. I catch Kit call my dad Gerald and still with surprise. A glance at the clock above the mantel confirms we haven't even been here ten minutes. My dad's had teaching assistants last an entire semester who were never on a first-name basis with him.

I catch a quick smile when Kit spots the doorway that leads into the kitchen, where eighteen years of heights are marked. Five months ago, I would have laughed at the idea of Kit Kensington defacing his penthouse—which undoubtedly cost tens of millions of dollars—with permanent marker. Now, I can picture him suggesting it.

Kit reaches into one of the bags he brought, retrieving two bottles of wine. One is wrapped, which he hands to my mom. "This is for you, Amanda."

"Oh, thank you so much," my mom says, taking it and beaming.

She tends to buy whatever wine is on sale, but my mom studies the ornate label like she's a sommelier.

"It's my mom's favorite, and she tends to have pretty good taste in that kind of thing," Kit tells her, then holds the other bottle out to me.

I raise an eyebrow.

He winks. "It's nonalcoholic, Monty."

As I take the bottle, I can't believe there was a time when I thought Kit wasn't capable of thoughtfulness. "Thanks," I whisper.

"Monty?" my mom repeats. "What does that mean?"

This is one of the rare occasions I've seen Kit look embarrassed. He's rubbing the back of his neck, which he only does when he's uncertain.

I guess I've memorized some of his tells too.

"Kit calls me Monty because …" My voice trails because I don't actually know *why* he gave me a nickname, just what it's short for.

"Because we met at Montgomery Hall," he finishes.

"That's sweet." My mom smiles, glancing between us, and I'm quite certain she's getting the wrong idea.

Or is it the right idea? I'm retraining my brain when it comes to Kit, ever since our conversation last week.

I'm so used to him calling me Monty that I never searched for a deeper meaning. Never wondered why he gave me a nickname at all. But now? It's like it's hitting me for the first time that the moniker is a reference to our first meeting. And that *is* sweet. Romantic even.

My mom pours the wine Kit brought, and we sit down for dinner. She made lasagna—another one of my favorites—and I demolish two servings. My body is trying to make up for the last three months of crackers because, lately, my appetite has returned with a vengeance.

The evening isn't awkward, the way I was worried about. Kit's charming. I guess I thought that might change because we're in my world. But he fills every pause with questions, appearing entirely absorbed as my mom talks about the courses she's teaching this semester. He and my dad discuss the book Kit brought him—a new release by a scientist my father admires. A thoughtful gift I wouldn't have known to get him.

When Jane arrives during dessert, Kit answers all her eager queries about his "rich and fabulous family"—Jane's words, not mine—with patience and humor.

Even Newton is enamored by him, lying on the hardwood right next to Kit's chair, even after all the food has been cleared.

"He's *way* better trained than my parents' dogs," Kit comments at one point, glancing down at the fluffy pile on the floor. "They're a couple of hellions. I took them out for a bathroom break once, and they dug up half of my grandfather's yard."

He glances at me, flashing my favorite boyish grin, and I decide maybe falling isn't so scary after all.

I wake up in the middle of the night to pee, which has become a regular occurrence that research has told me will only become more frequent. Right as I'm slipping back under the sheets, hoping I'll fall back asleep quickly, there's a strange sensation in my stomach. A gentle nudge, barely more than a flutter.

I instantly stiffen, pressing a palm against my small bump.

Holy shit.

Before I can second-guess it, I slide out of my bed and tiptoe down the hallway. My dad always leaves the kitchen light on overnight, so there's enough illumination to avoid bumping into any furniture.

Kit's fast asleep on his back, one arm tucked behind his head and both feet hanging off the end of the couch.

I tap one of his ankles. "Kit."

His head turns, but his eyes don't open.

I tap him again, a little harder. "*Kit.*"

A groan this time. Then he squints. "Collins? What—" He's suddenly upright at a speed that startles me into stumbling a step back.

"Fuck, is something wrong—"

"Nothing's wrong," I say hurriedly. "Nothing's wrong. I just … the baby's kicking. I thought you might want to feel."

Kit swipes a hand through his hair. "Thank God. You scared the shit out—the baby's kicking?" The rest of what I said finally sinks in.

It takes me a second to respond because the fact that he's shirtless just registered with *me*. And my memory of our night together didn't really do his abs justice.

I manage a weak, "Yeah," as I take a seat on the couch. He sinks down beside me. Old cushions sag beneath us. "It feels weird. *Good weird*," I hasten to clarify when he frowns. "Kind of like bubbles are floating around in there."

I pull my T-shirt up, knotting it under my boobs.

Kit stares at my stomach. I ended up sending him a photo on Thanksgiving, but he hasn't seen my bump in person since the first ultrasound. And there wasn't much to see then. Now, there's a noticeable bulge.

"Wow," he whispers, pressing his palm flat against it.

I suppress a shiver that has nothing to do with how low my dad turns the heat at night. And suddenly, there's another flutter, like the baby is reacting to his touch too.

"Did you feel that?" I ask softly.

Twin lines of concentration appear as he shifts his palm a little to the left. He's staring at my stomach. *Staring*, not just looking, like it happens to be the Eighth Wonder of the World.

My thighs clench tight, my hormones mistaking the sweet moment for something sensual.

"No," he finally replies. "I don't feel anything."

"It must be too early," I say. "The kicks will get stronger as the baby gets bigger."

His thumb moves in a tiny circle. "Hey, Orange. It's your daddy. Kick harder next time. It's probably pretty boring in there, but things will get more interesting soon."

I have to blink rapidly a few times. I also clear my throat, dislodging the lump that formed there. Seeing Kit *excited* about this pregnancy has my whole heart expanding, making my chest feel too small to contain the spreading sensation.

"It might also be too early for them to hear," I say softly.

"Yeah, I know it can vary a little. But our kid is probably pretty advanced." Kit shoots me a grin that requires me to clench my thighs again.

"You … know? Like, you bought a baby book?"

"No. I bought baby *books*."

All I can think to say is, "Oh."

I'm surprised, and I shouldn't be. Kit's been nothing but committed. I thought his involvement was too much to expect, let alone the mural, or the coming to doctor's appointments, or the meeting my parents, or all the ways he's continued to show up.

My life isn't the only one that was completely upended. His was too. And I'm worried, at some point, this excitement will spoil. Become resentment instead.

"Exceeding your low expectations is entertaining, Monty. But you'll save yourself some surprise if you stop expecting the worst from me."

The words are light. Drawled with an edge of amusement.

But I can feel the tension humming in his body. Can sense the edge behind the flippancy. And wonder how many times I missed it before, when I wasn't paying this close of attention.

"I *do* have expectations of you, Kit. High ones even. And you're still exceeding them. Still surprising me, which isn't always a bad thing. It means a lot that you bought books."

I swallow hard, glancing down at my stomach. His hand is still resting there. He's touched me a lot more intimately, but this feels even more vulnerable than sex.

"Sorry I woke you up for no reason," I add.

"You can wake me up for any reason anytime you want."

I'm not sure if I'm projecting the innuendo in his voice or if it's really there, but I flush regardless.

"Kit?"

"Yeah?" He's looking at his hand on my stomach, not at me, which makes this a little easier to say.

"I want to date you."

He glances up so fast that I swear I hear a crack. A stray section of hair flops onto his forehead. "What?"

"You heard me."

"Yeah, I did. But I could be dreaming." He leans closer, the blue of his eyes all I can see. One ocean I'd happily get lost in. "So, *say it again,* Monty."

I comb the wayward section back. "I want to date you, Christopher Kensington."

"All it took was me taking off my shirt, huh?" He smirks. "I caught you looking."

"I'm hormonal."

"You mean, you're using our unborn child as an excuse for your horniness?"

I scoff at that framing, but I'm smiling. I'm *usually* smiling around Kit. Sometimes, I have to remind myself to stop. "Fine. It's not *just* pregnancy hormones. That's how I wound up pregnant, remember?"

"Yeah, I sure do." This time, the innuendo is absolutely there.

The heat in his gaze is burning through all the oxygen in this room. No matter how fast I breathe, my lungs can't seem to pull enough air in.

"It's not January yet," I murmur.

But I'm already compiling excuses in my head. I handed in my resignation. We've worked together for months, successfully, after having sex. And we're not at work. We're a state away, and it's the weekend.

I can feel the tension radiating off his body, but Kit doesn't move. He's waiting. Letting me be the one to make the decision.

I'm home, in the house I grew up in, and Kit is still the place I'm drawn to. He's become my safe harbor.

I lift my feet off the floor and slide them under me, then shift my knees so they're on either side of his hips. When mine lower, a startled gasp leaves my mouth.

"*Please* tell me your parents are deep sleepers," Kit says somberly.

I grin as I grind against his erection. "Not exactly. My dad leaves the kitchen light on because he sometimes wants water in the middle of the night. And my mom has been known to get up and read sometimes."

He groans, low and tortured, as I lean forward. My bump presses against the ridges of his bunched abs.

"Don't worry," I whisper, tilting my head so I can trace the taut line of his jaw with my tongue. "He's a scientist. He knows you can't knock me up twice."

"You're going to fucking kill me," Kit mutters. "Or *get* me killed."

And then his hand is in my hair, tugging my mouth down until it's covered by his.

With one kiss, Kit seizes control. His tongue coaxes my lips apart, invading my mouth with purpose and skill. His hands angle my head to the precise position he wants.

One second, he's stroking my tongue. The next, he's pulling my lower lip between his teeth and biting gently. My overstimulated body can barely keep up, most of my brain busy processing that this is really happening.

It feels right, letting him lead. Kit said I didn't trust him during our latest fight, but he was wrong. I hope he knows how wrong he was, that my pliancy in his arms is making it obvious. It's never been like this with anyone else. This blissful and consuming and safe.

Kit's seen me cry and yell and panic. I've seen him stressed and embarrassed and uncertain.

And there's something so reassuring about knowing someone has witnessed moments you wish they hadn't and is acting like you're more essential than oxygen anyway. There's a beautiful comfort in experiencing an easy moment with the same person who stayed during a hard one.

My knees spread wider, my pelvis connecting more solidly with his. I'm so *sensitive*; it doesn't matter that his cock is under layers of fabric. This is the most action I've gotten in months, and my body is primed and desperate for any form of relief.

His hands slide up my rib cage, cupping my boobs, which are *also* extremely sensitive. I arch into his touch, moaning as his thumbs rub the aching points of my nipples.

"Don't make me gag you," Kit says in a tone that I think is meant to discourage me from making noise but really has the opposite effect.

"You're not into exhibitionism?" I tease.

Of the two of us, I never would have guessed Kit would be the more reserved one.

He shifts so his mouth is right by my ear. "Not in my future in-laws' house."

My breath catches, and we're so close that there's no chance Kit didn't hear it.

"Did I freak you out?" he asks.

"I'm not sure," I say honestly. I'm not exactly thinking straight right now.

"I can work with that."

His hand slips into the front of my pajama pants. I'm wearing boring cotton panties instead of anything sexy, but I don't even care about my lack of lingerie. I just need him to touch me lower. *Now.*

My eyes close when he hits the perfect spot, the satisfaction immediate but the desperation even wilder.

"You're so fucking beautiful," he murmurs, circling his thumb.

I could cry; I'm so close to coming. My legs start to shake, the pressure building to an explosion that ripples through my body in ruthless, devastating, satisfying waves.

I drop my face against Kit's shoulder, muffling my moans against his warm skin.

Even once the tremors stop, I don't move. Why would I?

When I lift my head to look at Kit, he's smiling softly at me. I rest a palm on his chest, appreciating the steady thud of his heartbeat before sliding lower down his abdomen.

Kit grabs my wrist before I can reach my destination. "Not tonight."

"But you didn't …"

His smile's a little pained now. "Well aware. But if you touch my cock, I'm going to end up fucking you, and that's going to ruin the wonderful impression I made with your parents because I remember how loud you are."

"I'm not loud," I say defensively.

"With me, you are," he replies smugly.

I'm too tired to argue and not entirely convinced he's wrong, so I lie down on the couch. "I'm too sleepy to walk back to bed."

"Want me to carry you?"

My eyes are closed, but I hear the smile in Kit's voice.

This couch is too small for him. It's *way* too small for both of us. But neither of us mentions that.

I yawn. "In a little bit."

"Okay."

Right before I fall asleep, a random thought occurs to me.

I would have picked Kit to be the father of my kid. On purpose.

CHAPTER 31

Kit

A sparrow lands on the bird feeder attached to the window above the kitchen sink, pecks at the seed once, then startles away. Next, the bird lands on the browning grass, coated with frost and sparkling in the sunshine.

"Coffee?"

I glance over my shoulder at Professor Tate. Gerald—I guess I should get used to calling him that.

"Coffee sounds great," I say. "Thanks."

Gerald nods, hitting a button on the coffee maker. He pulls two

mugs out of a cabinet, setting them on the counter. "Sleep okay?" he checks.

"Great," I lie.

I dozed on and off until around seven, when the sun started streaming through the living room windows. I carried Collins to her bed but quickly gave up on falling back asleep myself. There's a crick in my neck that's going to make driving home later hurt like hell, and my balls ache in a way that make me wonder if I'll ever be able to give Gerald more grandkids, but I wouldn't change a thing about last night despite the discomfort.

The coffee maker starts gurgling, the heavenly scent of a fresh brew filling the kitchen.

"Chilly morning," Gerald comments, glancing past me at the yard.

"Looks that way," I agree.

"Girls complain I keep the heat too low this time of year."

I'm not sure if he's looking for an agreement or not, so I just say, "I run warm."

He chuckles, then hands me a steaming mug.

"Thanks," I reply, hiding the wince when I lift my arm to take it. My shoulder's tweaked from the cramped sleeping position too.

"You didn't wind up doing much with that chemistry degree."

"Uh …" I swallow some hot coffee, scalding my tongue in the process, buying myself some time to reply.

Again, it wasn't really a question. Or a condemnation. Simply a statement. There's no obvious indication of how I'm supposed to answer.

I don't think Collins's dad *dislikes* me. I caught him smiling a few times last night. And I had done well in his classes, wanting to prove to myself I was capable of succeeding at something I wasn't set to inherit, so he has no reason to think I'm a slacker. But I knocked up his daughter. There's no way I'm one of his favorite people.

I like how he's broaching the topic though. Giving me an opportunity to talk rather than making assumptions.

"A chemistry degree didn't fit in with the rest of the plan," I finally say.

I knew before I started college—before I started high school—that I'd wind up working at Kensington Consolidated, not in a lab.

Gerald nods. "Does my daughter fit in your plan, Christopher?"

I'd know the seriousness of his question from his tone alone, not just his use of my full first name.

I hold his gaze as I answer, "She *is* the plan, sir."

"Good morning!"

Amanda bustles into the kitchen, grabbing an apron off a hook by the fridge and breaking the heavy moment. I didn't notice last night, but a copy of the sonogram is displayed next to the college calendar. The sight makes me smile.

"What can I get you for breakfast, Kit?" she adds.

Before I can reply, Gerald asks, "You like eggs?"

I nod, and Collins's dad squeezes my shoulder. I hide another grimace.

Something that looks similar to approval glimmers in Gerald's eyes as he heads toward the stove. "I'm making eggs, Mandy."

Rather than drive straight home after dropping Collins off at her apartment, I head to my mom's office. It's a Sunday, but I'm not surprised to see her car parked in the garage.

When I walk into the headquarters of rouge—my mom's fashion label—she's standing in the middle of a tornado.

I lean a shoulder against the doorway, watching as she directs fabric samples one way and a rack of jackets in the opposite direction.

Growing up, I witnessed my mom work a lot more than my dad. Bash, Lili, and I all went to school in New York, spending more than half of the year here, and Dad was often called back to the West Coast for work. Since both rouge and her magazine, *Haute*, were New York–based, I saw more of Mom's work up close.

A lot of my friends resented their parents' busy schedules. Hated how they were rarely around or hardly involved.

I love my parents. But I also respect them. I saw how hard they worked to juggle being present and being successful.

A balancing act I'm going to have to figure out for myself soon. The hours I'm currently logging at the office are going to be difficult to sustain come May.

My mom spots me a second later and smiles, holding up one finger and mouthing, *One sec.*

I nod an acknowledgment, surveying the mess of swatches and drawings and measurement tapes strewn across the long table.

"Hey, Kit. Need anything?"

I glance at the woman who's appeared beside me. "Hey … Josie."

She smiles when I get her name right. My mom has four assistants, so I had a twenty-five percent chance of guessing correctly.

"I'm good, thanks," I add. "Just stopped by to say hi to my mom."

"That's so sweet," Josie gushes.

I nod in agreement. "I'm a sweet guy. Sometimes."

Josie's smile expands. I straighten, subtly adding some distance between us.

My mom's voice interrupts, "Hey, honey. How are you?"

"Great." I hold up the bag from the bakery in Stamford, where

Collins and I stopped to have lunch. "Just stopped by to bring you this."

"Really?" My mom lifts one eyebrow. "What a lovely surprise."

I grin. "That's me."

Mom glances at her assistant. "Josie, did the art department review the new sketches yet?"

"I'm headed there now to check," Josie says quickly, then takes off like a shot.

"You've been busy lately," Mom comments as she heads for her office.

I trail after her, glancing over the framed sketches decorating the walls.

"Just trying to set a good example for this family of underachievers," I state, dropping the bag I brought next to a vase of peonies. I sink on the couch, covering a yawn with my left hand. I might have to take a nap when I get home.

Mom laughs. "Please make sure you're balancing work with some hobbies. And that is *not* an endorsement of you partying at Proof every night."

"But that's my *only* hobby."

She sighs. "Kit."

I smile. "Relax, Mom. I've been to Proof *once* since September. You definitely don't need to worry I'm partying too much. I've been reading, uh, nonfiction. And trying some redecorating at the penthouse. The designer's style felt a little … austere. Also, I'm teaching myself piano."

"Wow," she states. "You really have been busy."

"Sure have," I say cheerfully, glad she isn't asking for details about what nonfiction I'm reading or what redecorating I'm doing. "And since you're the one at work on a Sunday, seems like you're the one who needs to pick up some new hobbies."

Mom gives me her trademark exasperated look, but the corners of her mouth are curved up as she reaches into the mini fridge and pulls out a sparkling water. She holds a second one my way, and I shake my head.

"I had a call with Charlie's sister, Blythe, this morning," my mom tells me. "She's interested in fashion and in possibly doing an internship here next summer. It was easiest to do the call here, and once I was here …" She shrugs, then sips some water. "I'm headed home soon."

"Lili set that up?" I surmise.

Mom smiles and nods. "It's sweet. I could tell Blythe really looks up to her. And speaking of Lili, she and Charlie are planning to spend a couple of weeks in New York next month. Charlie has a winter break from school, and Lili's project is wrapping up this week."

"Sounds good," I say, shoving the niggling nerves away. Once Lili's home, I'll need to share the news with my family.

"What's this?" Mom takes a seat next to me on the couch, reaches for the bag, and opens it.

"From a bakery I went to earlier."

She pulls the chocolate sea salt cupcake out, then glances at the logo stamped on the paper bag. "In Stamford?"

"Felt like a drive. Getting out of the city."

"Hmm." She takes a bite. "It's delicious. Do you know when you're headed to Aspen? Before the thirty-first?"

"I, uh … I was thinking I'd hang out at the Hamptons house instead this year. Is that cool?"

"The Hamptons house? This time of year?"

"It'll be a bigger crowd this year. And most everyone lives in New

York. The Hamptons are a lot closer than flying everyone to Colorado."

She takes another bite of the cupcake, considering. "I'll check with your father. Assuming he's fine with it, so am I."

"Great. Thanks." My knee bounces once. "I have a favor to ask."

"Another one?" Mom teases, holding up the half-eaten cupcake. "This is tasting like a bribe."

"It wasn't a bribe. Just a reminder I'm your favorite child. I don't see Bash or Lili stopping by with baked goods."

She smiles and reaches for her water. "Parents don't have favorite children, honey. You'll find that out one day, maybe."

I stiffen.

My mom doesn't notice, busy taking a sip.

One day. Maybe. I'll find that out on or around May 18.

And I want to tell my mom all of a sudden.

When I was eating dinner with Collins's family last night, I kept thinking how odd it was that those near strangers all know I'll become a dad in May, but the people who raised me don't.

I've never hidden anything this huge from them. This secret isn't swiping my dad's most expensive scotch or sneaking into a club on a school night. It's big, and it's important, and it'll affect my life—and theirs—forever.

But I can't say anything now. Not like this. I should tell my parents together, and it'll feel a lot less like I'm sharing the news with the COO of Kensington Consolidated if my father finds out when Collins is no longer my assistant.

"What's the favor?" my mom asks, and I refocus.

"Right." I clear my throat. "I'm trying to find a dress."

"A *dress?*"

"Yeah. I kinda drew what it looked like." I shift so I can pull a piece of paper out of my pocket and hand it to her.

It takes a few seconds for my mom to react. She still looks dumbfounded as she takes the sheet.

"It was gray," I add. "A bluish gray. The color was called pewter."

"Pretty," my mom murmurs, staring at the rough sketch. She glances up at me. "What is—"

"It's a Christmas gift," I state.

Both eyebrows rise. "For a woman?"

"No, for Ben and Jerry. I thought the silver would complement their coats."

She huffs. "Kit."

"I'll tell you the whole story soon. But for now, can you just find the dress? Please."

Mom nods, her brisk, businesslike mode appearing. "I'll have the details for you by tomorrow."

"I knew you were the right fashion designer for the job," I tease, then stand and stretch. Driving for two hours didn't do wonders for my sore muscles. "Thanks, Mom."

"Of course." She tilts her head, studying me with a speculative expression. "I'm proud of you, Kit. We both are. I know your dad has noticed how hard you've been working."

I smile back, but it takes some effort. "Thank you."

I don't think my parents will be proud of the secret I'm keeping from them.

CHAPTER 32
Collins

"I'm here to see Christopher Kensington."

I glance up from the papers I'm organizing, straight into a steely-blue gaze. I've never met Arthur Kensington before, but I recognize him instantly. His eyes are a cooler version of Kit's.

His grandfather wasn't on the approved list Kit gave me on my first day of work. There's no visitor badge clipped to the lapel of his tailored suit. But I doubt that's because Arthur wasn't offered one. He's Arthur Kensington. He doesn't need one.

"I'll check if he's available," I state, sneaking a quick look at Kit's calendar as I reach for my phone. According to it, he's free right now. No meeting with his grandfather was scheduled.

Arthur appears mildly entertained by my response, but doesn't comment as I dial Kit's direct line. He glances around the immediate vicinity instead. The two women walking down the hallway, staring this way, quickly avert their gaze and speed up their steps.

Kit answers on the third ring. "Kensington."

"Hi. I—your grandfather is here. Should I, uh—are you available?"

"My *grandfather* is here?" There's a stunted, stunned cadence to the question that tells me this wasn't a visit he simply forgot to add to his calendar. Or have *me* add to his calendar.

"Yes," I confirm.

Kit clears his throat. "I'll be right out."

"Okay." I hang up, meeting Arthur's hawkish gaze, which has refocused on me. "He's free."

"I would hope so since he answered his telephone." Arthur glances at the files I was paging through. "How long have you been working for my grandson, Miss …"

"It's Collins. I mean, my last name is Tate. My first name is, uh, Collins. You can call me Collins." Frantically, I count backward in my head, trying to come up with an answer to his question. "Almost four months?"

"Are you asking or telling?"

I swallow. "Telling. Four months."

"Grandpa."

Arthur and I both glance to the left, where Kit has appeared in the doorway of his office. He tucks his hands into the pockets of his slacks, studying his grandfather.

"It was nice to meet you, Collins," Arthur states, then continues toward Kit. "Do you always greet visitors *outside* your office, Christopher? It's rather over-accommodating."

"You're the only one I over-accommodate, Grandpa," Kit replies. "Most visitors have to wait until I've played a few rounds of solitaire for an unscheduled meeting."

"I've heard reports that you're more focused on your responsibilities than playing games."

Kit raises one eyebrow, surprise—and some pride—flashing across his face. "Is that why you're here? To see if your spies reported accurately?"

"You suggested I stop by," Arthur states. "So, here I am."

Kit hooks a thumb over his shoulder. "Dad's old office."

"I remember."

"Want to see what I've done with the place?"

In response, Arthur enters the office. Kit follows his grandfather inside and shuts the door.

He wasn't exaggerating about his grandfather's demeanor. But Arthur stopping by doesn't seem meaning*less*.

I stand, grab my empty mug off the desk, and head toward the break room for a fresh cup of tea. While I'm waiting for more water to boil, I walk over to the windows that line the exterior wall. Like the ones in Kit's office, they offer an impressive view of the skyline.

It's snowing, fluffy flakes drifting down from the sky. There isn't any accumulation on the street, but up here, it feels like standing in a snow globe. I watch the flakes fall, wondering how Kit's conversation with his grandfather is going.

Maybe he'll tell me later.

Probably not.

Ever since our trip to New Haven, things between me and Kit have reverted to professional. As soon as the sun rose and we were back in the city, my fears reset. I remembered that I have to work with Kit every day, focusing on spreadsheets and calendars and important deals worth tens of millions of dollars. I remembered that the small bump I'm sporting is going to become a living, breathing human being that's relying on me to not mess up.

I want Kit to be this kid's dad. I'm *grateful* he's this kid's dad.

I'm scared I'll do something to ruin my relationship with him, and it'll affect our child in some negative way. And I'm scared I'll do something to ruin my relationship with him, and it will ruin *me*.

It was so easy to *leap* that night at my parents'. To admit I wanted him. To show I wanted him. To forget all the complications and pretend it was that night in the Hamptons again. To be selfish and to take exactly what I wanted.

I don't regret it. And I meant what I told Kit—I *want* to date him.

But it's not that simple. I wish it were.

The electric kettle shuts off. I fix myself a fresh cup of chamomile and return to my spot by the windows. Stare outside, savoring the peaceful scene for a few more seconds before I go back to staring at a screen.

"Stella said Arthur Kensington is here?" Margot appears next to me, peering out at the snow. "Wow. It's really coming down."

"Yeah, it is," I agree. "And, yeah, he is. He's in Kit's office right now."

"He *is*? I thought Stella was hallucinating."

"He is," I confirm.

"Well, that's interesting. Sanborn said he hasn't been here in years. Decades. Do you know what he's doing here?"

"No clue," I reply, stirring my spoon in my tea.

Margot glances at my abdomen. "You're showing a little."

I make a face. "I know."

Friday is my final day, and I couldn't be cutting it much closer. Sucking my stomach in isn't really cutting it anymore. Chunky sweaters are the main reason everyone isn't suspecting what Margot knows.

"If you hadn't told me, I wouldn't have … it's not *very* noticeable."

I laugh. "Convincing. Thanks."

"Seriously, how are you feeling?"

I glance over my shoulder, making sure we're still alone. "Better. Physically at least. No more nausea and vomiting. But emotionally? Each week, I'm getting closer to the whole *having a baby* part, and that's … terrifying."

"How's baby daddy dealing?"

"He's great. He's …" I exhale. "It seems like nothing fazes him, and that's reassuring. It also makes me feel a little crazy sometimes. Like, why am I panicking about every little thing and he's just … steady? Also, I kissed him." I take a hasty sip of my tea, wincing when my tongue registers how hot it is.

"That's norm—wait, what? You kissed him?"

I nod. "Last weekend. He came home with me to meet my parents, and we made out on the couch while they were sleeping."

"Sounds like high school."

I laugh. "Yeah, it was, kinda."

Kit makes me feel younger. Maybe it's because he's younger than me. Maybe it's his playful personality. I feel more like myself when I'm around him and act nothing like my normal behavior. I've never even kissed a guy in front of my parents before, and Kit's refusal was the only reason we didn't have sex in their living room.

"Was it good?"

"Yeah. It was … special. But then I woke up the next morning, and it felt hazy. Like this really good dream had ended. And I don't know how to get back there and stop overthinking everything."

"Kiss him again," Margot suggests.

I laugh. "That's your advice?"

"It sounds like you're putting up extra caution tape because he's the father of your kid. But that doesn't mean you can't have some fun, Collins. Are you seeing him around the holidays?"

"New Year's Eve, I think."

Yesterday, I fielded several phone calls from an event planner named Lucy, who is organizing a New Year's Eve party that Kit is throwing. He made it clear that I was invited and also mentioned Lili wouldn't be back from London yet, as if anticipating me using that excuse. Technically, I'll no longer be a Kensington Consolidated employee by then.

"That's perfect!" Margot exclaims. "Kiss him at midnight. Why don't we get drinks—I mean, ginger ale for you—next week and make a plan?"

I exhale, chewing on my lower lip. Aside from human resources, Kit is the only one who knows this is my last week at the company. I haven't told Margot or anyone else I've gotten to know here because I've been debating how much to say. Especially to Margot, who knows about the pregnancy.

"I, uh … I need to tell you something."

Margot raises an eyebrow. "Okay …"

"I'm changing jobs. I accepted a paralegal position at a law firm. Friday is my last day, and I start at the firm right after New Year's."

She blinks rapidly. "You're leaving Kensington Consolidated? Why?"

I shrug a shoulder. "I preferred that work. The only reason I started here was because I couldn't find a paralegal job in September. With everything …" I gesture toward my abdomen. "It just makes more sense for me right now. But I'll still be in the city. We can still be friends? Meet at sample sales after work? Elastic waistbands aren't going to cut it for much longer. I'm going to need to shop for actual maternity clothes soon."

"*Of course* we'll still be friends, Collins." Margot pouts. "But I'm going to miss having you just down the hall."

"I'll miss it too," I admit.

Leaving Kensington Consolidated is the right decision. For me and for Kit. He's worked incredibly hard the past few months for everyone to take him seriously. To admire him for more than his last name. Whatever way I can shield him from the scandal of an unplanned pregnancy, I will.

But I'll also miss working here. My desk and its brown fern. The glass offices that don't appear as intimidating anymore. Margot and Stella and Aimee and all the other colleagues who I've gotten to know since reluctantly starting here in September.

Margot tilts her head. "Does Kit know?"

"He knows."

"How did he take it?"

She *knows*, I realize. Maybe she's wondered all along. Maybe my sudden departure, right as I start showing, has confirmed a hunch. But I'm suddenly positive Margot is aware Kit's more than simply my boss.

"Uh, fine," I respond carefully.

Margot nods. "Be careful, Collins." She glances at the snow.

"People aren't talking about Arthur because they're excited to see him. They're talking because they're afraid of him. People with that much money and power … they live in a different world."

I keep a smile fixed on my face, attempting to ignore the ominous echo in her words. "I'm always careful."

"… *you didn't trust me to protect you.*"

Kit's angry words from our paternity-test argument echo in my head. At the time, it didn't occur to me to ask what he'd need to protect me *from*.

Kit fit in my world seamlessly. I don't think the same can be said about me in his. Starting Saturday, I might no longer be Kit's subordinate in the office, but I still will be when it comes to everything else. Money, influence, resources.

"Text me about getting together, okay?" Margot says. "Or if you need to talk."

I set my mug down on the window ledge and give her a quick hug. "Thank you," I whisper.

"I'll miss you," she whispers back.

I smile sadly over her shoulder, at the snow.

CHAPTER 33

Kit

Kit: New Year's Eve party is in the Hamptons this year.

Flynn: What?

Flynn: I thought we were going to Aspen for New Year's. Like we do EVERY year.

Kit: Not this year.

Flynn: It's gonna be cold in the Hamptons.

Kit: And Aspen's a sauna?

Flynn: I can't snowboard or hot tub in the Hamptons.

Kit: You can go to my party.

"This party is awesome!" Flynn shouts, adjusting the golden top hat he's wearing.

Flynn has rapidly rallied from his disappointment over this year's change in venue. Everyone else seems to be having fun too. The music is blaring, the alcohol is flowing, and countless balloons filled with gold glitter decorate the living room of my parents' Hamptons house. Hundreds of people pack the space. Some friends, some former classmates, some total strangers.

No sign of the reason I moved my annual party two thousand miles.

I wanted to spend New Year's Eve with Collins. And I didn't think she'd be willing to travel all the way to Colorado. She's been in New Haven for the past week, spending Christmas with her family. It's possible she decided to stay in Connecticut longer. Or simply decided not to come tonight.

I check my phone for the tenth time in as many minutes.

We haven't texted since I sent her *Mango* on Sunday.

I thought Collins leaving Kensington Consolidated was going to bring us closer together. Remove a boundary. Instead, it feels like we've drifted further apart. Like there's a new vagueness to our interactions now that we're no longer required to spend forty-plus hours a week in the same space. She's supposed to move into my penthouse in a matter of days, and we've only discussed the most basic of details about becoming roommates. Even during the anatomy scan last week, she felt distant. She didn't lean on me the way she did during the first ultrasound.

I should have felt relieved she was more confident. Instead, I was disappointed.

"Here. You look like you could use this." Flynn shoves a shot my way, and I don't even check what type of liquor it is before sucking it down.

Vodka, it turns out.

"You having trouble deciding?" Flynn shouts, gesturing toward the crowd of scantily dressed women dancing in my living room. "Because that's my dilemma right now. They're all so hot."

"Too many hot women," a female voice says dryly. "What a *complicated* life you lead, Parks."

Flynn rolls his eyes as he grabs another shot. "I hope you invited your *fun* cousin too, Kit."

I elbow him in the ribs before hugging Rory. I'm surprised she came with Wren, but I don't mention that in front of Flynn. I'm too distracted by Collins's absence to play referee.

"How were the Bahamas?" I ask, remembering she just got back from a trip there with college friends.

"Amazing," Rory gushes. "I missed the sun. And it was really nice to get away and take a break from studying."

To my left, Flynn snorts.

I elbow him again before asking, "You hear anything yet?"

"Not yet," she says, managing a nervous smile. "They start sending decisions at the beginning of January, so …"

"You'll get in," I tell her, and that's not even me being reassuring.

Rory's brilliant. And for as long as I can remember, she's been intent on becoming an attorney. She would try to talk Lili, Bash, Wren, and me into playing courtroom when we were younger. I was usually the accused. Lili was always the arresting officer.

"Thanks, Kit."

"Harvard will be lucky to have you," I add.

"You applied to Harvard Law?" Flynn interrupts rudely.

"I'm *going* to Harvard Law," Rory replies with the trademark Kensington confidence.

There's no sign of Flynn's normal nonchalance as he responds, "I'll see you in Boston, then."

I lift an eyebrow, but keep my mouth shut and stay out of it.

Last I knew, Flynn only applied to gain access to his trust fund. He's never mentioned actually *wanting* to go to law school, and I was pretty sure he was working up to tell his dad to fuck off and stop pulling strings.

"Where's Wren?" I question, cutting through the tension in the air.

"Yeah. Where is Wren?" Flynn mutters.

Rory scowls at him before focusing on me. "I don't know."

I frown, not expecting that answer. I've never heard Rory say *I don't know.* "What do you mean?"

"I mean, I don't know where Wren is." Rory enunciates each word, then reaches past me to grab a flute of champagne off a tray being circulated by one of the servers. "She disappeared as soon as we arrived."

I survey her calm expression. "Shouldn't we be … concerned about that?"

Rory sips her champagne. "You haven't noticed Wren is rarely around whenever we're in the Hamptons?"

"Uh … not really." Now that she's bringing it up, I guess I don't remember Wren being around much last summer. I think she also got grounded for sneaking out a couple of times. "Does that mean you *do* know where she is?"

Rory sighs. "She's probably at the marina."

The marina?

"It's December. The marina closed *months* ago." I point out the obvious.

"Uh-huh," Rory agrees. "I'm gonna go grab some food. I'll see you later, Kit." Pointedly, she ignores Flynn as she brushes by him and heads toward the buffet set up across the room.

"Why didn't you tell me Rory was applying to Harvard Law?" he asks as soon as she's out of earshot.

"Why would I?" I reply absently, busy typing out a text to Wren.

> **Kit:** Hey, everything okay? I just saw Rory, and she said she wasn't sure where you had gone.

Wren replies instantly.

> **Wren:** All good.

> **Wren:** I'll be home by curfew, DAD.

I roll my eyes and slip my phone back into my pocket. Out of the five of us, Wren and I were always the main troublemakers. Least likely to play the part of responsible adult. I'm not a teenager anymore though. Wren is.

"Everything good?" Flynn asks.

"Yeah. Fine."

"Something else bugging you? You still weirded out about your grandfather's visit?"

I reach for another shot. "A little."

Flynn's the only one I've told about Arthur's unexpected appearance at the office. When I suggested he stop by the office back in September, it never occurred to me that he *would*. And it was awkward, and he made some of his usual judgmental comments, but he'd shown up. He had come all the way to the office just to see me. And it was nice, showing him around my office.

Flynn claps me on the back. "Don't overthink it. He'll reset to his usual grumpiness pretty soon. Every now and then, my dad decides to act like a dad, but it passes fast."

I muster a smile. "I'm going to do the rounds."

"Have fun."

After a trip around the first floor reveals no sign of Collins, I decide to head outside for some fresh air. It's cold and salty, each inhale burning my lungs. The pool is covered, and the patio furniture is stored for the winter. My steps echo on the pavers, the only other sound the distant roar of the ocean.

I take a seat on the stone wall, wishing I'd thought to bring a drink or a jacket out here.

Rhythmic clacking announces someone else's arrival. Hope balloons in my chest, even though I know it's probably pointless.

Sure enough, it's not Collins's voice that asks, "Got a light?"

Hope deflates as I glance over my shoulder at the woman approaching. It takes me a minute to place her. "Camila, right?"

"Cammie," she corrects, taking a seat on the wall next to me. "Good memory."

"Flynn's inside."

Cammie lets out a husky laugh. "Oh, I didn't come for Flynn." She glances at the house. "Always wanted to see the inside of one of these places."

"You're a local, right?"

That's basically all I know about Flynn's summer fling, aside from where she worked. Or works—I don't know if she's at the hotel year-round. She looks younger, so she might be in college.

"Born and raised," Cammie confirms, then holds up an unlit cigarette. "Lighter?"

"Don't have one."

She sighs, then tucks the cigarette away.

We sit on the stone wall in silence, which is nice. And strange. Cammie has a down jacket on, but it's been patched in several places. I'm not sure how warm it is.

She pulls her phone out of her pocket, glances at the screen, and mutters something under her breath that gets lost in a gust of bone-chilling wind. "I've gotta go," she states.

"Yeah, I should head in before hypothermia hits." I glance at the house.

Glass sliders separate the kitchen from the patio. At night, the lights inside make them look like a massive picture frame. I survey the party, doing a double take when I glimpse a shade of distinctive hair through the glass.

I stand, in an immediate rush.

I have to force myself to focus on Cammie for a minute. "Do you need me to call you a ride or anything?"

"Nah, I'm good. I drove, and the marina's not far. Thanks."

I frown. What the hell is happening at the marina?

If Collins wasn't here, I'd ask. But I'm too impatient to get inside. So, I just nod and beeline for the closest door after saying goodbye to Cammie.

The heat and commotion inside the house are a shocking contrast to the freezing quiet outside. I push through the crowd, scanning the room as quickly as possible, finally spotting Collins standing under the dining room chandelier, talking to Indy and her fiancé, Tony.

Collins looks stunning. Her auburn hair is curled, falling in loose waves over her shoulders. She's wearing a short, sparkly dress with a flared fit that conceals her baby bump.

I stall in place for a few seconds, watching them converse,

wondering if I imagined Collins by the doors.

Someone jostles into me from behind. "Sorry, man!"

I wave a hand in acknowledgment, then continue walking, passing through the living room and into the dining room. The party planner, Lucy, had most of the furniture cleared from the first floor, including the massive table that's usually centered in here. A champagne tower has taken its place tonight.

Indy spots me first, waving as I approach. "Kit! Hey! Awesome party!"

"Thanks, Indy," I reply, holding a hand out to greet Tony once I'm close enough. "Nice to finally meet you, man."

"Likewise," he responds, grinning. "Thanks for inviting us."

"No problem." I glance at Collins, who's sipping what looks like sparkling water from a flute.

It feels like déjà vu. Like the last time we were in the Hamptons together.

"Collins was just telling us about her new job," Indy informs me, then glances at Collins. "I was bummed to hear you were leaving, but it sounds like a great opportunity." Her attention returns to me. "Have you lined up a replacement, Kit?"

"Not yet," I mutter, the feeling of déjà vu increasing when Collins swallows and still doesn't meet my gaze.

She's talking to one of the waiters now, asking him about the appetizers on his tray.

Indy glances between me and Collins, a knowing look flashing across her face before she looks at her fiancé. "We haven't made it to the buffet yet, and I should probably have more than champagne for dinner if I'm going to make it to midnight. Nice talking to you, Collins. See you later, Kit."

Tony echoes Indy's goodbyes before they move into the living room.

Collins is staring at the champagne tower.

She saw me outside.

I clear my throat. "Hey."

I can hardly hear her answering, "Hey," over the loud music.

"Wasn't sure you were going to make it."

"Traffic was bad. Don't let me keep you from outside."

I sigh. "Collins …"

"Don't worry about it, Kit." She glances around the dining room. "I forgot how huge this place is. Lucy did a great job decorating."

I take a step closer, erasing the polite distance between us. "I *am* fucking worried about it. I don't want you to think—I just went outside for some fresh air. She—I barely know her. I *don't* know her. She dated Flynn. Well, not really dated."

"People are staring."

I don't move. Or look around to confirm. "So?"

"Is Indy the only other person you invited from the company?"

"No," I admit. Levi and a few other guys I've been on teams with are around here somewhere. "You don't work for me anymore, Collins."

"I know," she says, glancing around like she's cataloging everyone who's seeing us together.

My irritation grows. "Did you mean it? What you said in New Haven?"

Right now, it feels like she doesn't want to be seen in the same room as me, let alone date me.

"You want to have this conversation in the middle of your party?" she asks incredulously, which isn't the *yes* I was hoping for.

"You've been avoiding me, so I'm not sure where else to have it."

Collins bites her bottom lip. "I've just been—"

"Hey! Here you are." Flynn picks the worst possible moment to appear, slinging one arm around my neck and straightening his ridiculous hat with the other. He squints at Collins. "Hey, Collins."

"Hi, Flynn," she replies, a smile fracturing her serious expression. "Nice to see you. And if you'll excuse me, I need to find the bathroom."

Flynn glances at me as soon as Collins is out of earshot. "You invited your assistant?"

My jaw works. "She's not my assistant anymore."

"What? Why not? Since when?"

I pretend not to hear his questions as I watch Collins weave through the crowd. "You were looking for me?"

"Oh, yeah. Head caterer needs to talk to you."

I nod, then head toward the kitchen.

CHAPTER 34
Collins

A sudden thud, followed by, "The fuck?" has me sitting straight up in bed.

I'm paranoid and pregnant and alone in a mansion that belongs to strangers—okay, *technically*, that belongs to my baby's grandparents—but is, or was, full of strangers.

So, when I discovered my bedroom door didn't lock, I did what any reasonably cautious woman would do—I pushed the armchair in the corner in front of the door so I'd hear if it opened.

And the only reason I'm not screaming right now is I recognized

that muttered swear.

"What are you doing, Kit?" I ask wearily, lying back down in bed. Maybe if I pretend he woke me up, he'll feel bad and leave faster.

"Navigating an obstacle course, apparently."

His voice is louder now. He's moving closer, not farther away.

"I was worried about someone breaking into my room. Clearly, that fear was warranted."

The sound of rustling fabric has my heart rate skyrocketing. I can't see much because Kit closed the door behind him. A sign he's not departing imminently, I belatedly realize.

I sit up in bed again, this time clicking on the lamp sitting next to the bed.

"What are you …"

My voice trails as I realize exactly what Kit is doing.

He's getting undressed. He *is* undressed actually, aside from a pair of black boxer briefs that cling like they're getting paid to show off how generously endowed he is. He looks like a goddamn underwear ad, and what is that blatant attractiveness doing in *here*?

Before I can voice that question aloud—in less complimentary phrasing—he's lifting the covers and climbing in bed beside me.

"Did you have fun at the party?"

"It was nice," I say stiffly.

My voice might be tense, but the rest of me isn't. His body heat is bleeding over to my side of the bed, an immediate gust of comfort. Like I've been bundled by a cozy blanket or stepped under the warm spray of a shower.

"*Nice*," Kit muses. "What was lackluster? The fireworks? The champagne tower? The—"

"Did you forget where your room was?"

Or that we fought earlier? I add silently.

He should be mad at me. *I'm* mad at me. Yet he's acting … normal.

"My room's occupied."

"By …"

"By people not sleeping."

"Doesn't this place have, like, twenty bedrooms?"

"Twenty-four, yeah. I wanted to check on you."

"Well, you didn't have to climb into bed with me to do it."

I hear the rustle as his head turns on the pillow. Feel the weight of his eyes tracing my profile as I stare at the ceiling.

"Do you want me to go?"

"Do you snore?"

"You tell me. You're the only person I've slept with before."

I blink rapidly at the ceiling, trying to clear the tears before he notices. "I'm sorry about earlier."

Kit lets out a long exhale, tucking an arm behind his head. "I don't want you to be sorry."

"I'm pregnant."

"Still?"

That coaxes a small smile out of me. "I'm pregnant, Kit. I'm hormonal, and I'm tired, and I'm stressed, and I'm getting fat, and I really did not need to see you out on the patio with another woman. It's not that I don't trust you. I don't trust me. I'm waiting for you to realize I trapped you with this kid, and I … I … I *do* want to date you. I'm just not sure why *you* want to date *me*. You could have anyone."

I wasn't enough for Isaac, and he was inferior to Kit in every way.

I can't hold the tears back anymore. The salty water slips down my face silently, dampening the pillow and dripping into my ears.

"*Collins*." His tone is tender. "C'mere." Kit untucks his arm, holding it out to me.

I roll so my face is resting on his chest. His arm curls around my waist, tucking me securely against his body. His other hand swipes across my cheeks, clearing the wet tracks.

"I trust you," I tell him.

"You should. I'm not your ex."

I blow out a long breath. "Isaac isn't the only reason I have trust issues."

Kit's silent, waiting for me to continue.

"The spring of my senior year of college, I was headed to the library to study one weekend. I decided to stop by my dad's office to say hi. He wasn't there, but he was in one of the labs across the hallway. Kissing some woman who was *not* my mother."

Kit's chest lifts with a sudden inhale, but he says nothing.

"I don't know who she was. I'd never seen her before, and I haven't seen her since."

"What did you do?"

"Nothing. I just … left."

That haunts almost as much as the moment itself.

"Did you tell anyone?"

"Not until now. It's this awful secret I'm *stuck* with. I don't want to be the one to tell my mom … if she doesn't know. Same with Jane. And my dad?" I rest a palm on Kit's chest, right above his heart. The steady beat is reassuring. "I … I want to pretend it never happened. That I never saw anything. But it's been almost three years, and I haven't been able to forget." I sigh. "I wasn't totally honest when you asked me about moving to Chicago. I did want to live somewhere different after staying in Connecticut for college. But it was also a way to distance myself from my dad. I needed space."

"I figured something had happened," Kit says, playing with a strand of my hair. "The way you acted around him when we visited … I remembered you guys being closer than that."

He's referring to the day I moved into Montgomery Hall. My dad was so proud. Both of my parents were.

"We were closer," I say. "And I wish we still were, especially now, with the baby coming. But I … it's a new chapter in some ways, but I don't know how to just get over that part of the past."

"I'm sorry about your dad, baby."

I sniffle. "Stop being so understanding. You're supposed to be mad at me."

"I am?"

"Yes."

"You *want* me to be unreasonable and angry?" I can hear the smile in the question.

"I guess."

"Okay, I'll work on it." The hand on my hip moves, splaying across my stomach. "You're not fat, Monty."

"I'm *going* to be."

"Well, I hope so. I don't want an abnormally small kid."

"You're six-two, so statistically speaking, I'm going to get a lot bigger."

"Six-three."

"Huh?"

"You said I'm six-two. I'm six-*three*."

I laugh, but he doesn't.

"Did you feel that?" he asks suddenly. Excitedly.

"Feel what—oh. Yeah. You can feel it too?"

"Yeah." He nods, glancing down at my stomach as there's another soft tap. "Yeah," he repeats more quietly. "Holy crap."

"He—or she—seems to like kicking at night," I say. "Or … when you're here."

The look on Kit's face makes it hard to breathe. It feels like my heart is expanding, crushing my lungs. His expression is overflowing with tenderness. A focus that's bright but also inviting, like a sunbeam.

"Wow," he whispers when there's another kick against his palm. "Mango is really strong."

I giggle, melting at the wonder and admiration in his tone. "You know we're going to have to call the baby something other than fruit at some point, right?"

"It'd be easier to pick a name if we knew what we were having …"

"I want it to be a surprise," I say.

"Okay." He capitulates, same as he did at Dr. Bailey's office.

They could have told us the gender at the twenty-week scan, but I didn't want to know. I still don't. I probably should, considering this pregnancy was surprise enough. But something feels special about finding out at the same time we get to meet him or her.

We lie like that, Kit flat on his back and me using him like a pillow. My bump cradled between us, Kit's hand partially covering it.

He shifts so he can turn off the lamp. "Okay, *fine*. I'll stay since you begged."

"That was *not* me begging."

"Oh, I know. I remember what you begging sounds like."

His lips brush my hair. I relax against him, more tension seeping out of me. He's warm and solid and steady and … hard.

A flash of heat suffuses my system.

"Ignore it," he tells me. "It's just … been a while."

"A while? Like, a whole week?" I tease. My voice is light, but my heart is heavy.

I believe him—that nothing happened with the woman outside. I'd even guess he hasn't been with anyone since we talked on my steps, which was a lot longer than a week ago. But even hearing it's been a couple of months would bother me. I don't want to think about him with anyone else—ever.

"Sure," Kit agrees easily. "A whole week, plus the twenty-four you've been knocked up."

I'm … stunned by the revelation. *He's been celibate since we hooked up?* Forget our talk on the stairs. That means he hasn't been with anyone else since August, weeks before he even knew I was pregnant.

"Really?"

"I don't want *anyone*. I want *you*. If you think that's new or temporary, it's not." He shifts under the sheets, his sincerity settling over me like another blanket. "Happy New Year, Collins."

"Happy New Year, Kit," I whisper.

CHAPTER 35
Kit

Kit: Cantaloupe.

Kit: How big is a cantaloupe? I've only seen it cut up.

Collins: Big enough that none of my clothes fit.

"**T**here was a package delivered for you earlier, Mr. Kensington," the doorman tells me as I enter the lobby of my building. "It was oversize, so I had it moved to your hallway."

"Thanks, Samuel," I say, continuing into the elevator. As it rises, I text Bash.

Kit: You ready?

It's Sunday, but I had to go into the office to prep for my trip to Phoenix tomorrow. I have a meeting with several board members of a newspaper we're in negotiations with. Eight hours of travel for an hour-long meeting. I should be excited about the opportunity, but I'm kind of dreading the trip.

No immediate response comes through from Bash.

I sigh. He's home on winter break, crashing with me again, and annoyed I told him he needs to move out by tomorrow. Not only is Collins moving into my place in a few days, but Bash is currently sleeping in the room that's going to be the nursery. If he continues pouting during dinner, Dad's going to get suspicious.

The doors open on my floor. I glance up from my phone, startled by the sight of my dad standing in the hallway.

"Hey. What are you doing here?" I ask. "I thought Bash and I were meeting you at the restaurant."

"I was running early," my dad clips. "Thought I'd pick you boys up instead."

I frown, confused by his curt tone. He was the one who planned this guys' night, and now he's acting like—

"Care to explain this?" My dad steps to his left, revealing the package Samuel must have been referring to.

It *is* oversize. I can see why they didn't store it behind the desk downstairs. And the crib printed on the side of the box is a dead giveaway about its contents.

I swallow hard. Fuck. Fuck. *Fuck.* "Any chance you can pretend you never saw that?"

"What is a *crib* doing in your hallway, Christopher?" he thunders.

Guess not.

I drag my thumb along the bottom of my mouth, searching for the right words. I've had months to figure out how to break this news to my dad, and I still haven't come up with the right way to. "This wasn't how I wanted you to find out," I finally state.

"Find out *what*? Is your housekeeper expecting? Did they deliver to the wrong address? Please, tell me this is not what it looks—"

"She's due in May," I state. "And I wanted to tell you and Mom sooner—I *planned* to tell you sooner—but I needed time to wrap my head around it first."

Total silence follows that admission. It expands, filling the hallway with its suffocating weight.

I try again, aiming for a little levity. "So, uh, congrats. You'll be a grandfather soon."

More silence.

My dad's expression might as well be carved from marble.

Maybe I should have held off on dropping the G-word.

Uneasily, I realize this is probably what Collins was looking at when she told me the news. I've never seen my father freeze before. He's always competent. Always prepared. Always expecting the unexpected.

I scramble for something—*anything*—reassuring to say. "I was going to tell you and Mom later this week. Once Lili was home."

Still, he says nothing. I might as well be conversing with a statue.

My front door opens.

"Kit? What's—Dad?" Bash glances back and forth between me and our father, his phone in one hand. I didn't even realize mine had been buzzing in my pocket. "Weren't we meeting you at the restaurant?"

"Uh …" I rub at the back of my neck.

Dad unfreezes to point at the crib leaning against the wall. "Your brother was just explaining *this*."

Bash follows his finger. "*Oh*. Right."

Dad reads his lack of reaction correctly. "You *knew* about this, Sebastian?"

Bash grimaces, glancing at me, then back at Dad. "Well, uh, sort of. I mean, Kit mentioned it at Thanksgiving, so I've known about it for a little—"

"Thanksgiving? You've known your brother was expecting a baby for *six weeks*?"

"Wasn't my news to share, Dad. Kit and Collins are the ones who … yeah. I'm gonna go … anywhere else."

Bash spots the same switch on my dad's face I do when he mentions Collins's name. And comes to the right conclusion—I hadn't gotten around to the whole *who's having my kid* part of the story yet.

The front door closes a second later, emphasizing the total silence that follows the soft *click*.

At first, I think I'm in for another round of silent treatment.

When my dad speaks, his voice is dangerously low and even. A tone I haven't heard since the whole Monaco police incident Collins loves to rib me about. "Collins? Collins *Tate*?"

I exhale. "Yes."

He laughs. It's incredulous, not amused. "You knocked up your *assistant*, Christopher? An employee at the company?"

"She wasn't my assistant at the time." I doubt my dad's bothered to do the math back from May yet. "And she's not my assistant anymore."

They're both weak arguments, but technically true. It could be worse.

Dad frowns. "Not your assistant anymore? What do you mean?"

"Her last day was the week before Christmas. She's working at a law firm now."

Rather than appear relieved, my dad looks even angrier. "You *fired* her?"

I scowl, pissed off by the assumption. "What? No. Of course not. She wanted to leave. Changing jobs was her decision."

"This is unbelievable. A lawsuit waiting to happen. You understand that, right? I can only assume that's why you hid—"

"I didn't hide anything," I retort. "I've just been waiting for the right ... time to tell you."

"You mean, you were waiting until she no longer worked for you." My dad shakes his head. "That's not a magical solution. How could you have been so ..." My dad tilts his head back, staring at the ceiling.

"I get you're upset, Dad. But a lawsuit isn't something you need to be concerned about. Collins wouldn't—"

"You don't know what she would or wouldn't do. You're not married to this woman, Christopher. You've known her for a few months! We're not just talking about your trust fund, although your personal finances are a concern. You've opened the *entire* company to a massive liability. I thought you'd outgrown being this careless and irresponsible and—"

"She. Wouldn't. Do. That." I emphasize each word my father doesn't seem to be hearing.

He pulls his phone out of his pocket. "I need to let Oliver and the legal department know about the situation immediately. After she signs an NDA, then we can deal with—"

"She's not signing a damn thing, Dad. You want to know why I didn't tell you sooner? *This.* We're not talking about a business transaction here. We're talking about the mother of my child."

"If you hadn't hired her at Kensington Consolidated, I'd agree this was your decision, albeit an ill-advised one. But your naivete is not going to be what topples a company worth billions, employing thousands, that's been in our family for generations. And your recent choices have me second-guessing if you should be a part of that company at all."

He strides past me, toward the elevator.

"*Dad,*" I snap.

"What?" He turns, focused on his phone. Probably emailing his legal team.

"Aren't you forgetting something?"

He glances up. "Forgetting what?"

"We can cancel dinner. But I thought somewhere between lecturing me and legal documents, it might occur to you to say *congratulations.*"

My dad shakes his head. "Don't try to turn this around on me, Christopher. You are the one who lied for months. If I hadn't seen that"—he points toward the crib—"I'd still be in the dark. Keeping a secret like that? That's not the son I raised."

I stare, stunned and pissed, as my dad disappears into the elevator.

When I carry the crib into my penthouse, Bash is leaning against the entryway wall.

He raises an eyebrow. "Dinner's off?"

I huff a laugh, yanking harshly at my tie. "Yeah."

"Dad took it well."

I snort.

"He'll get over it, Kit."

I lean the crib against the wall. "We'll see."

"Can I be there when you tell Lili?"

"After your super unhelpful contribution earlier? I'm going to tackle it solo, thanks."

"Dad was going to find out it was her, Kit."

I sigh. "I know."

"Want help with that?" He nods toward the crib.

"Maybe later," I respond.

With the mood I'm currently in, I'm more likely to break the bars than assemble it correctly.

Bash nods and pushes away from the wall. "I'll order us some pizzas."

CHAPTER 36

Collins

"And here is your office!"

For the second time in less than six months, I'm starting a new job. This time, I'm a lot less nervous and a lot more pregnant.

"I wasn't expecting to have my own office," I say, glancing around it.

It's small and windowless, and it smells strongly of Lysol, but it's an entirely enclosed space that belongs exclusively to me. I could decorate with more than an ill-fated fern if I wanted.

"You lucked out," Marcie, another paralegal and my tour guide for the morning, tells me. "Most paralegals start in cubicles. But since Derek had an office and you're his replacement, it was the easiest swap. Your phone and computer should already be set up. If you have any issues, there are instructions in there." She points to the packet that I received during orientation this morning. "Or you can call IT. Their number should be preprogrammed in your phone."

"Great. Thank you."

"My extension is 2504 if you have any questions." Marcie smiles. "Welcome to Bradford, Nash, & Monroe."

I smile back. "Thanks."

I settle at my desk, log in to my computer, set up my voicemail, then start reviewing documents for the first case I was assigned. I'm sixty pages into a deposition when a knock pulls my attention away from the screen.

"Knock, knock," he narrates, making me smile.

"Am I supposed to say, *Who's there?*"

"Don't worry about it." Perry shoves his hands into his pockets. "I don't know any good jokes."

My smile grows. "Hey, Perry."

"Hey." He glances around my office, tapping a sheaf of papers against his thigh. "They gave you your own office. Nice."

"Isn't it? I've never had my own office before."

"Me neither," he says sheepishly.

"Really?"

"I'm a first-year associate, Collins, not a name partner. Not all of us start out owning the place, like Kensington."

I stiffen when he mentions Kit, and Perry notices.

"Sorry. I didn't mean to … it's just—he and Flynn are best friends.

I grew up an only kid. Always wanted a brother. And the closest thing I have, he wants nothing to do with me. So, I'm a *little* bitter about the guy who Flynn does want to be around. Nothing personal about Kit."

"I'm sorry, Perry."

He nods in acknowledgment. "Ignore my pity party. I just wanted to check in. Say hi. Finding everything okay?"

Macie reappears before I can reply. She pauses, blushing when she spots Perry. "Hi, Perry."

"Morning, Macie," he replies, giving her a shy smile that suggests her interest is reciprocated.

They stare at each other for a few more seconds, before Macie remembers me.

"Uh, Collins, there's someone here to see you."

"To see *me*?" I clarify, confused.

Outside of my family, the only people who know where I work are Kit, who's currently in Phoenix for a meeting, and Margot, who I texted with this morning and made no mention of stopping by my new office.

"Yes. It's Crew Kensington."

Apprehension unspools in my chest. "*Oh.*"

Perry's studying me, his forehead furrowed. "What is—"

"He's being rather insistent," Macie continues. "Should I show him—"

"Uh, no. I'll go." I stand, smoothing the wrinkles in my pencil skirt with both hands. It's held together by safety pins, and I'm wearing my boxiest black sweater with it.

I let my new supervisor know about the pregnancy shortly after accepting the position here, wanting to be as up front as possible. The firm offers eighteen weeks of paid parental leave for all employees, including supportive staff in non-attorney positions. I don't have to hide my pregnancy anymore, but I'm not ready to announce it yet either.

Not until Kit's family knows at least. And they *don't* know, right? That can't be why Crew is here.

Macie has disappeared, but Perry walks with me toward the lobby.

"My cubicle's at the other end of the floor," he states. "I promise I'm not stalking you."

"I believe you," I assure him, smiling. Then add, "Macie's really nice."

Perry clears his throat. "Yes, she is. She showed me around my first day too."

"Do you want me to find out if she's single?"

The tips of Perry's ears turn pink. "Oh. I, uh … we work together, so … that's a bad idea."

"It's not *always* a bad idea. Sometimes, it works out. Sometimes, it's … really nice, spending so much time with the person you love every day."

"You're in love, huh? Guess that means I should officially retire my crush."

I glance at him, startled. Both by his joking—at least, I hope he's joking—and by the realization that four-letter word slipped out.

Perry smiles. "I'm kidding, Collins. Was I interested? Yes. But I realized friendship was all you were interested in pretty fast. I'm happy you're happy."

"Thanks, Perry," I say sincerely.

We've reached the lobby. Talking to Perry was a welcome distraction, but my apprehension returns in full force now.

There are several clients seated, plus a few suits who look like they're here for job interviews, but Crew Kensington isn't hard to spot amid the crowd.

Everyone in the waiting area is staring at him.

He strides in this direction as soon as he spots me, hand outstretched. "Ms. Tate."

"Mr. Kensington."

I'm proud my voice doesn't waver and betray my nerves. Crew doesn't look angry, but he doesn't appear friendly either. He glances at Perry, expression neutral.

Perry straightens his tie before sticking out a hand. "Perry Parks. Pleasure to meet you, Mr. Kensington."

"Parks." Crew tilts his head, studying Perry. "Are you related to Flynn?"

I think I'm the only one who catches Perry's subtle wince before he answers, "Yes. He's my cousin, sir."

"I see. Small island." Crew smiles, but it doesn't reach his eyes.

Just like Kit when he's being polite. Their eye color matches too.

Perry isn't oblivious to social cues, but I sort of wish he were.

"I'll see you later, Collins," he says, giving Crew a respectful nod before continuing in the opposite direction.

Once Perry is gone, Kit's father focuses on me. "Do you have a minute?"

It's phrased as a question, but not really a request.

"Of course," I reply. "We can talk in my office."

Crew nods, following me as I spin and retrace my steps. The walk feels a lot longer with Crew than it did with Perry, like the distance doubled in the past few minutes.

"I was surprised to hear you'd left the company," he states.

Is *that* why he's here? I have no idea how Crew would have found out I'd left. He's too high up at Kensington Consolidated to be bothered by or informed of changes in assistant positions. It's *whose* assistant I was, I guess.

I clear my throat. "I was a paralegal before I started at Kensington Consolidated. Just … returning to my roots."

"I see."

Finally, we reach my office. I'm sure Crew's office is as large and luxurious as Kit's, but he doesn't comment on the small size or plainness of mine.

Kit would have made a joke. Asked if I accidentally brought him to a closet or something.

"Can I get you anything to drink?" I ask.

"I'm all set, thank you." Crew takes a seat in the wooden chair opposite my desk, resting his elbows on the arms and steepling his fingers under his chin.

I sink down in my swivel chair, faking a cough to fill the oppressive silence.

"I'm aware this isn't the first time we're meeting. I'm sorry we never had a conversation while you were at the company."

"That's all right, Mr. Kensington."

For the first time, he smiles. Crinkles appear in the corners of his eyes, like it's a common occurrence. "Please, call me Crew. It's been, what, a few years?"

I nod. "A couple. It would have been the Fourth of July. Lili invited me to the Red, White, and Blue party her grandparents hosted the summer we graduated."

Crew nods too. "Right, of course."

I doubt he really recalls me from the hundreds of people who attended that party, but I appreciate him pretending I was memorable.

"Do you and Lili talk often?"

"I …" I'm becoming more confused about the nature of this visit by the second, but can't come up with any polite way to ask why Crew is here. "We try to."

He nods. "Lili's always spoken very highly of you. And everyone who interacted with you at the company spoke very highly of you as well. I've heard nothing except impressed accounts of your work as Kit's assistant."

"I—that's nice to hear. Thank you."

Crew opens his briefcase, slipping a manila envelope out and setting it on my desk.

I stare at it.

He stares at it.

Finally, I ask, "What's that?"

Crew sighs. "I had a plan coming here, Collins. Is it all right if I call you that?"

I clear my throat. "Of course. Yes."

"Last night, I found out you're expecting a child with my son."

I suck in a startled breath. "Oh."

"I was planning to come here, ask you to sign an NDA, and say it was an oversight that should have been part of your exit process. Tell you to advise a lawyer before signing, if you wanted."

I think of the slip of paper my dad handed me. I never called. Never felt like I needed to. Should I have?

Crew exhales. "It's been a long time since there were any big surprises in my life, Collins. I grew up knowing where I'd go to school. Where I'd work. Who I'd marry even. Finding out I'm going to be a *grandfather* in a few months? That was a shock."

"Multiply it by ten, and you'll have a clue how I felt when I found out."

He smiles again, then sobers. "I'm sure. How-how are you feeling?"

"I'm good. I feel good." I hesitate. "I don't know how much he told you, but Kit's been … he's been amazing. He's held my hand at every appointment. I'm not sure I even would have made it to the first ultrasound if he hadn't been there. Every time I freak out, he talks me down. He bought pregnancy books. As in multiple. He looks up the size of the baby every week and texts me it in terms of fruit. He completely charmed my family. He's having this *massive* mural painted in the nursery, and I'm …" I let my voice trail, embarrassed. "Sorry, he probably told you all of that already."

"No." Crew drops his hands from his chin to his lap. "No, he didn't tell me all of that. *Any* of that. I reacted … badly to the news. And I regret that."

"Oh."

That explains why Kit said nothing to me about his dad knowing. And my heart constricts painfully in my chest as I worry how that conversation going badly affected him.

Kit is close with his dad. He admires him. Respects him. Their relationship is much closer than my current one with my father. Yet the first thing my dad asked was if I was okay. Based on the contrite look on Crew's face, that wasn't the first question he asked Kit.

And Kit didn't tell me.

He knows about my dad's infidelity. About Isaac cheating. About … everything. But he didn't tell me this. Because he didn't want to worry me? Because he didn't want me to know?

"You don't have to sign this, Collins," Crew says quietly, nodding toward the folder. "I'm here on business because you worked at my family's company while also having a personal relationship with my son. I don't need details. I don't *want* details, frankly. But I have a responsibility to …"

His voice trails as I flip open the folder. I scan the page, confirming the document's contents, then scribble my signature and the date at the bottom. "There you go." I push it toward him. "And whatever you said to Kit? You'd better fix it."

I'm certain Crew isn't accustomed to taking orders.

But he nods. "I will."

Kit calls while I'm walking down the steps into the subway. "I just landed," he tells me. "And fuck did I forget how cold it was in New York. Phoenix felt like an oven. We should go somewhere warm soon, where you can wear nothing except a bikini all day. How was your first day?" He finally takes a breath.

"It was good," I reply. "I have my own office."

"Yeah? Does that mean you need a new fern?"

"A fake one maybe. My office has walls, but no windows. I don't know much about plants, clearly, but I do know they need light."

His chuckle warms me more than the scarf wrapped three times around my neck to combat the January chill. "You could put up some photos of plants. Or paintings. Or a mural."

"Another mural, huh?"

"Why not?"

I tap my card against the terminal and push through the turnstile. "Why didn't you tell me about your dad?"

"My dad?" Kit repeats.

"Yeah. He came to see me at work, and—"

"He came to see you at work?"

"This morning. And I wish you'd told me he knew. You don't have to tell me what happened—he said it went … badly—but you *can* tell me if you want to talk about it."

No response.

"Kit?"

Still nothing.

I pull my phone away from my ear and realize the call disconnected. I try to call him back, but it doesn't ring once.

No service.

Kit

"You sure you're all right, Mr. Kensington?"

My fingers, already curled into a fist, clench even tighter. "I'm fine, Camden, thanks. This won't take long, and then we're headed to Brooklyn."

"All right, sir."

I climb out of the car and stride toward my parents' townhouse. I didn't button up my coat, but I'm oblivious to the harsh wind as it cuts through my suit. I'm too angry to feel cold. Walking too fast to see my breath hover in the freezing air.

I do feel my phone buzzing in my pocket, but I ignore that too. Collins has been trying to call me back ever since we got disconnected, but I need to deal with this first. And we'll be able to talk in person soon. I'll be picking her and the last of her belongings up at her apartment shortly. I was planning to head straight to Brooklyn from the airport, but I need to speak to my dad first.

I rap on the front door twice, jaw ticcing as I stare at the glossy black paint.

A few seconds later, Charlie opens it.

I stare at Lili's boyfriend, surprise temporarily dulling my anger. "Hey."

"We flew in this morning," he explains. "Lili wanted it to be a surprise."

"Oh. Nice. I mean, nice to see you."

"Likewise," Charlie replies, smiling. "Lili and your mom left to do some shopping about"—he checks his watch—"four hours ago. I thought you were them."

I nod. "Is my dad home?"

"Yeah. He's in his office, I think. He said he had a couple of work things to catch up on."

Probably a custody agreement he had his lawyer draft.

"Thanks," I reply, already headed for the stairs.

The higher I climb, the hotter my temper flares. I've never been so furious with my father. The constant comparisons to him get tedious, but I've always found a measure of pride in them too. Not now. Not about this.

The door to his office is shut, but I barge in without knocking.

My dad's seated at his desk, scanning some papers. He glances up, saying my name with obvious surprise as he checks the clock above the fireplace mantel. "You weren't supposed to land for another hour."

"Sorry to disappoint," I say snidely. "Were you trying to sneak in something else behind my back before I got back to town?"

He sighs. "Kit …"

"Her new job, Dad? You show up at her new job, on her first day? What the fuck were you thinking?"

"I was trying to grasp a better understanding of the situation. This is a time sensitive—"

"It hasn't even been twenty-four hours since you found out! And I've been in another state for half of them! You had no fucking right to—"

"I had *a responsibility* to. You're not CEO, Christopher. Decisions concerning the company are not for you to make alone."

"*You're* not CEO, Dad. You never have been, and unlike me, you never will be."

It's a cheap shot, delivered way below the belt.

I don't know all the details of what happened to cause Dad to leave Kensington Consolidated in the first place, but I've pieced together enough to know it was related to the CEO position and conflict with Grandpa and Oliver. Enough to know it's a sore spot.

Dad rubs his chin before telling me, "I talked to Oliver this morning. He agreed with me speaking with Collins directly was a necessary step—"

"Speaking with her? You *ambushed* her!"

"Is that how she described it?"

I say nothing.

"I was very impressed with how she conducted herself."

A brief flicker of pride breaks through my anger, but not enough to douse it.

"She also signed an NDA."

"Of course." I scoff, shaking my head. "Of course you didn't go over there for a social call. It was to make sure she keeps her mouth shut."

"I'm just trying to protect—"

"This family and this company. Yeah, I heard you loud and clear last night. I'm trying to protect *mine*, Dad. *My* family. Do you have any idea how hard I've worked to show Collins she can trust me? That she can rely on me? I hadn't even had a chance to tell her you knew about the baby, and you show up at her new job? You know that whole firm is probably speculating about why you were there, and that is the last thing she needs right now."

"That wasn't my intention. I'm trying to catch up, Kit. You've known about this for months, and I—"

He pauses when I toss the envelope on his desk. "Those are the paternity test results," I state. "I'm assuming that was next on your to-do list, after the NDA, right?"

"It's sealed." He holds the envelope up, as if I'm unaware of that fact.

"Because I didn't need to look at the results. I know what it says. And if there's anything else you need to absolve the company of any liability, ask *me*. Don't show up at Collins's work again." I spin on my heel and stalk out of the room.

"Christopher."

I continue walking.

"Christopher!" Heavy footfalls pound the hallway as he follows me.

"Is this what you would have done if you'd found out Levi Jenkins had gotten his assistant pregnant?" I call over my shoulder.

"Levi doesn't have an assistant."

"That's not the point!"

"That's *exactly* the point. You have an assistant already because you're a goddamn Kensington. Start acting like it."

"You wanted me to be responsible? This is me taking responsibility, Dad." I walk faster, hell-bent on getting out of this house now that I've said what I came here to.

"We're not finished discussing this."

"Well, I'm done. We could have talked last night, but you had to go off and consult your legal team, remember?"

"What if you'd been wrong, Kit? What if she was trying to take advantage of you? I'm on your side here, son."

I turn to face him. "No, you're not. If you had been, you would have trusted me when I told you I trusted her. Do you know how many women have made it clear they only see my last name when they look at me? Collins sees *me*. Do you know what she did right after she found out she was pregnant? She made this plan to move back to New Haven and work at Yale and have her mom watch the baby. She didn't expect *anything* from me. Not a single cent. When I told you not to be concerned about the company, I fucking meant it. And you should have believed me, not printed an NDA."

I resume walking toward the stairs.

"Can you just stop for a second—"

"No, Dad, I can't. I need to go check on Collins. Find out how much damage you did."

"We had a nice conversation, Kit."

I pause again at the top of the steps, hand on the railing. "A *nice conversation*? During which you asked her to sign an NDA? Did you ask about a paternity test too?"

"No, I—"

"Did Grandpa ask Mom to sign an NDA, Dad? Did she take a paternity test when she got pregnant with Lili?"

Dad's expression darkens. "You are *way* out of line, Christopher."

"I'm not the only one. I used to think you were nothing like Grandpa. People always compare me to you, but I've never heard anyone compare you to him. But I changed my mind when my child became a fucking *liability* to you."

"*Christopher,*" he calls again, but I don't pause this time.

I continue pounding down the curved stairs, not even stopping when I have a clear shot of the entryway.

The three shocked people standing in the entryway, specifically.

Well, my mom and Lili look shocked. Charlie looks serious. And uncomfortable.

Welcome to the shit show, Duke.

I shake my head and continue down the rest of the steps.

Mom recovers the ability to speak first. "Kit, what on earth—"

I reach the entryway and blow out a long breath. "I'm really sorry you found out this way, Mom." I glance at Lili, who appears comically stunned. "You too, Lili. But I can't discuss this anymore right now." I continue toward the door.

"Kit!" Mom's voice is louder now, the surprise in it starting to fracture. "I'd like an explanation of what—"

I twist the handle. "Ask Dad."

Mom glances at him. Dad's reached the bottom of the stairs too.

"Crew, what's—"

"Not now, Scarlett," is the last thing I hear before stepping outside.

The front door opens again a few seconds later.

"*Stop,* Christopher." There's an undertone of steel in my dad's voice that's startling enough that I stall on the sidewalk.

I can see Camden peering through the windshield, no doubt wondering why my dad is literally chasing me out of the house.

"You're upset with me," he continues. "I get that. But I'm your father. Would you let your child storm out of the house?"

"You mean, my *liability?*"

Dad exhales. "I'm sorry, Christopher. I. Am. Sorry. Sorry for how I reacted. Sorry for some of the things I said. I always judged my father for treating me and Oliver a certain way when it came to the company. And I was so certain, so arrogant, that it would be different for you and me. Your mother didn't sign an NDA. But our prenup had too many confidentiality clauses to count, even though she never worked at Kensington Consolidated. And if she'd gotten pregnant with Lili before we got married, I'm sure a paternity test would have come up. Your grandfather hired a private investigator to follow her around, and I was furious. I felt so betrayed that he'd inserted himself into our relationship."

I lift an eyebrow, and he nods.

"I know. I see it. I reacted like *my* father would have, and I always swore to myself I'd be a different kind of parent than he was. I *do* wish that you'd taken more responsibility, handled things a little bit differently, *told me sooner*, but I understand it was a complicated situation. And it didn't occur to me … you care about her. There's more than just trust there."

"I'm in love with her," I state.

Dad glances at the ground, then back up to me. "You're going to find this out for yourself—soon—but there's no guide to being a parent. It's half instinct, half trial and error. I thought you needed my help. I was trying to protect *you*, Kit, not just this family or the company. I went about it the wrong way. Please apologize to Collins for me. And I'd like to say it directly to her, when you're ready for that conversation to take place. And get to know her better. I'm sure your mother will feel the same way."

I nod stiffly, still on edge from our fight.

I've always looked up to my dad. From my vantage point, he appeared pretty damn close to perfect. Infallible. For the first time, it feels like we're standing on the same plane. I'm realizing no one is incapable of making mistakes.

Dad lifts his left arm. "Come here."

I hesitate for a second, but I step forward, allowing him to clap my back a couple of times.

"Congratulations, son," he says thickly.

I clear my throat to dislodge the lump stuck there. My, "Thanks," still comes out husky.

Then I step back and head for the waiting car.

CHAPTER 38

Collins

There's a fashionably dressed, fast-asleep woman slumped next to the front door of Kit's penthouse when I arrive home after work. Next to the door of *our* penthouse, I guess, since we officially moved the last of my stuff over here last night. The stack of my belongings takes up approximately one-tenth of the space in the guest room that's going to become the nursery. I donated or left all my furniture since Kit's place is fully furnished. The biggest item I brought was my keyboard.

I crouch down on the carpet next to Lili, resting a hand on the rug

so I don't accidentally topple over. "Hey."

Lili groans, blinks, then rolls her head this way. Her eyes flutter open a few seconds later. "Hi." She yawns, raising a hand to cover her mouth. "Welcome home."

"You too. You didn't tell me you were coming back."

"Well, you didn't tell me you were having a baby with my brother, so I think we're even."

I exhale. "Right."

Lili opens her Birkin and pulls out a bottle. "I brought sparkling cider to celebrate."

I smile.

"Although I might need to drink something stronger if we're going to delve into certain details. All I know is what I overheard of my dad's screaming match with Kit."

I frown. "Kit and your dad were *screaming* at each other?"

Kit told me he went over to his parents' to talk to his dad. And that he told his mom about the baby. And Lili since she was there. There was no mention of any yelling in his recap.

"Yeah. But don't worry. Mom and I peeped on them hugging it out on the sidewalk after. They both have quick rebound rates. Although …" Lili tilts her head. "I'd never seen Kit that mad—*really* mad— before. So, that was interesting."

I bite my bottom lip hard. "Do your parents hate me?"

"*Hate* you? Why?"

"I mean, are they mad about the pregnancy?"

Lili doesn't reply right away, which rachets up my anxiety. "Are they mad Kit didn't tell them sooner? Most definitely. Charlie and I didn't get much sleep—and not for any fun reasons. We're staying in the room next to Dad's office, and he and Mom had a long, *loud* conversation after Kit left last night. But mad about the pregnancy? No. Dad hauled the rocking chair that was in our nurseries down from storage this morning. Pretty sure he's planning to bring it over here. Mom went into work at seven a.m. so she could sketch clothes for a possible children's line. They're excited. Probably still processing—I know I am—but excited."

I release a relieved sigh. "Okay. Good."

"How did your folks take it?"

"Uh … concerned at first. I'd just started working at Kensington Consolidated, so—"

"You'd *just* started working at Kensington Consolidated?"

I chew on the inside of my cheek. "Yes."

"Okay, now I get why Mom and Dad were freaking out so much. You're *pregnant*, pregnant."

I take a seat next to Lili, back against the wall, and unbelt the wrap coat that's one of the few items of clothing that still fits me. "Twenty-two weeks."

"Wow." She's staring at my bloated stomach.

The structured blazer I'm wearing disguises the curve a little bit, but the way I'm sitting makes my bump more noticeable. No clothes from my wardrobe, no matter how big or boxy, are going to cover it soon.

"Can I …" Her hand hovers hesitantly, which is rare for Lili. A reassuring reminder that this is as new for her as it is for me.

"Yeah. Of course. Here." I open my blazer and unbutton the bottom few buttons of the blouse I'm wearing under it. "You might feel a kick. Eggplant tends to be more active at night."

"Eggplant?" she questions.

"Yeah. We decided to keep the gender a surprise, so we refer to the baby in food terms. Last week, it was a cantaloupe."

Gently, Lili places her palm against my bump. "Wow," she whispers again, rubbing her hand in a small circle.

"Right?" I whisper back. "It's pretty cool. Crazy and scary sometimes, but also cool."

Lili withdraws her hand, and I tug my shirt back down.

"So, how'd you and Kit wind up …"

I glance at the penthouse door. "The hard liquor's inside."

Lili laughs, then sighs. "I'm too exhausted to move right now. Jet lag isn't always a choice. Just tell me."

"*You're* tired? I'm the one with an eggplant in my uterus."

"Yeah, and how'd it get there?" She lifts an eyebrow.

"Tequila."

"You were drunk?"

I chew on the inside of my cheek. Lili and I have shared stories about guys before, but this is different. This is her brother.

"Drunk? No. Tipsy? Yes."

"You'd been tipsy around Kit before, and I didn't wind up an aunt."

I smile, then shrug a shoulder. "I'd just moved to a new city. Everything with Isaac was still fresh. I know you're supposed to blame the cheater, not question what's wrong with you, but I hadn't felt *wanted* in a while. We were at the same party at the end of the summer. It just … happened. I only expected it to be one night, and it was. Then I wound up as his assistant."

"In my defense, you'd always ignored Kit. I had no idea you'd—"

"I know you didn't. And I probably should have turned the job down after what happened, but I'm glad that I didn't. I found out I was pregnant a couple of weeks later. Anyway, you know the rest."

"Actually, I don't. You're *living* here?" She waves a hand toward the wall we're leaning against. "And is that a convenience thing, or are you together?"

"My old apartment was in Brooklyn. It made sense for me to move closer."

"So, you guys aren't together?"

I fiddle with a button. "I'm not sure what we are. I don't want him to feel trapped. I know he chose to be involved, but he didn't choose this pregnancy. And I don't want him to think he has to commit to me to prove he's ready for this responsibility or to be a good father. Or to confuse lust with other feelings because we're going through this experience together."

Rather than look sympathetic, Lili laughs. "Are you serious?"

"*Yes*," I reply, a little affronted by her amusement. That was all honest.

"Kit has had 'other feelings' for you since he was sixteen, Collins. It doesn't have anything to do with you being pregnant." She crosses her ankles. "Okay, I went to Kit's office at lunchtime. He was in a meeting, so I talked his new assistant into letting me into his office. I was going to nap on the couch but decided to relax in his chair instead. You should have seen the look on Kit's face when he walked in and saw me sitting there." She giggles. "Anyway, you never looked at the photo he keeps on his desk next to his computer?"

I shake my head. "No. I would just stack papers on his desk. I never went behind it."

"Well, that makes me feel better because it crossed my mind that maybe you guys used to do *stuff* in his chair, back when you worked there, after I already sat down in it."

I make a face. "Lili."

"That wasn't my point. The point is, it's from my graduation party. Me and him and Bash and Flynn." She unlocks her phone and hands it to me. "And you."

I stare at the screen. I have a vague recollection of taking pictures at Lili's graduation party—there was a professional photographer in attendance—but I never saw any of the shots.

"Kit has this on his desk?"

Lili nods. "It was there the first time I visited him. Before you started working for him."

Before he knew I was pregnant, she means.

"You know, Kit called me twice as much freshman year as he did the rest of college, and it wasn't because he missed me more at first. The only time he voluntarily helped me move was when I was leaving Montgomery Hall. The only Red, White, and Blue party he didn't immediately disappear from was the year you came. Kit's blunt, Collins, and you know that. He's always acted differently around you, but I don't think I realized how serious he was about you until last night. Dad's his hero, and Charlie said he'd been yelling for a while before Mom and I got home. That should tell you everything you need to know." She yawns. "Okay. I've gotta go before I fall asleep again."

I start to stand as Lili does.

"Careful," she says, steadying me before reaching down for the cider. She hands the bottle to me with a broad smile. "Congratulations."

I smile. "Thanks."

We hug, and it feels different from all the times before. When I was randomly assigned to room with Lili Kensington, I wasn't sure we'd wind up as friends. I never could have predicted we'd end up *here*. Family.

"I'll see you next weekend," she says as she releases me.

"Next weekend?" I question. "What's next weekend?"

"Dinner at my parents'. They wanted to have you and Kit over *this* weekend, but he was very insistent you guys had plans that couldn't be changed?" Lili arches an eyebrow.

For a moment, my mind is blank. And then I realize … this is the first weekend I don't work for him.

"Oh. Right. Yeah, we're, uh, busy."

I think I'm blushing, which Lili confirms when she smirks.

"You're good for him, Collins. And I think he's good for you." She pats my belly. "I can't wait to get back to London. There's this store on Bond Street with the cutest baby clothes, and I've been *dying* to shop there."

I watch Lili bustle down the hallway, whistling merrily as she steps into the elevator. She waves, then yawns before the doors close.

Stepping into the penthouse is strange. I've never been here alone before.

Kit texted me earlier, letting me know he got pulled into a project at work and wouldn't be home until late. I was disappointed earlier. But now it's nice, having some time alone to think about what Lili said.

I think part of me has been using this pregnancy as an excuse. Allowing it to tether me to Kit without having to fully commit. Using reasoning like he should be near the baby to justify my sleeping in the same bed or agreeing to move in with him.

But the baby isn't here yet. He or she won't be here for months. I keep choosing to be around Kit because *I* want to be around him.

And Kit deserves to know that.

Excitement wars with nerves as I head into the bedroom. I undress and toss my clothes into the hamper, then head into the bathroom.

The shower connected to the primary suite might be my favorite part of Kit's penthouse, second only to the piano. It's huge and decadent, approximately the same size as my entire former bathroom. I stand under the steaming spray, letting the water pound my scalp and shoulders, wondering what I should say when Kit gets home.

I'm used to him being the instigator.

He's hit on me dozens of times. Surely, I can initiate things *once*?

I suds my hair, watching the white lather slide down the drain.

It's just Kit. A thought that used to provide reassurance and incite easy dismissal weighs a lot more than it used to. It sounds important—*he's* important.

And I'm scared.

But it's not fair to expect him to keep being the one who puts himself out there first. If I were him, I would have given up on me a long time ago.

Time to show him that wasn't a mistake.

CHAPTER 39

Kit

"**A**nything good?" I ask the fridge door.

It shuts a few seconds later, revealing Collins. "Hey. You're here."

"I live here, remember?" I tease her as I tug at my tie so I can undo the top button. "We wrapped up earlier than expected."

I reach past her to reopen the fridge, pulling a bottle of water out. There's a plate covered with foil sitting on the shelf.

"I made dinner," Collins says almost shyly. "Those are leftovers if you haven't eaten."

I did eat at the office because I'm not used to having food waiting for me, but if she cooked for me, I'll eat every bite.

"I didn't know you cooked."

"Try it before you say that," Collins cautions.

I smile, watching her play with the sash holding her robe together.

The robe is short, stopping just above her knee. If she's wearing anything under it, it's not very long. And I'm having a hard time focusing on anything else.

"Are you naked under that?" I ask, twisting the cap off the water bottle.

"Yes."

I cough, caught mid-sip, then guzzle some more water to clear my throat. I said it as a joke. I wasn't expecting her to answer, let alone in the affirmative.

We stare at each other.

Collins hasn't initiated anything sexual since that night on her parents' couch. But her gaze drops, very deliberately, and sudden hope flares in my chest.

"Do I have something on my dick?" I ask innocently.

"I can't tell with your pants on."

I smirk, abandoning my water bottle on the counter and closing the few feet of distance between us.

Her head tilts back to hold eye contact, lips parting to release the sexiest little whimper when my growing erection presses against her stomach.

She's naked under this, I think.

She's naked.

She's naked.

"Should I take them off, then?" I ask.

"Yes, please," she whispers.

I raise a hand, rubbing my thumb along the line of her jaw. Her head tilts back even farther, auburn strands brushing against my wrist. The reddish tint to her hair is barely noticeable, unless you're looking closely.

I'm looking closely.

"So polite," I muse. "Remember when you used to argue with every single word I said?"

My thigh presses between hers, and her breathing quickens. She reaches for my tie, loosening it enough to tug it over my head before working her way down the buttons of my shirt.

I grunt when her hands find my bare stomach, fingers lingering in the ridges of my abs.

"It's so unfair that you look like *this*," she bemoans. "So unfair."

I grin. "*And* you've stopped shredding my ego for sport? Excellent."

"*Why* are your pants still on?"

"Uh, because I wasn't planning on fucking you in our kitchen?"

That appears to be her plan though.

Collins rises up on her tiptoes, looping her arms behind my neck and colliding our mouths together impatiently. I groan into her mouth, and she tugs on my bottom lip with her teeth.

I can barely think straight.

I've spent the past five months fucking my hand to memories of fucking this girl. Six years before that, fantasizing about fucking her. There are too many places I want to touch her. Too many ways I want to tease her. And all I can focus on is the blinding need blazing through my body in response to the green light she's giving me.

She gasps for air when my lips leave hers, my tongue swiping a wet path down the side of her neck. Her hands grab my biceps for balance when my hands sneak under her flimsy robe, cupping her ass and tilting her pelvis so it connects more solidly with mine.

"I, uh, I'm more pregnant."

I have no clue what that means. "Are you actually worried I'm going to knock you up again? I don't think that's physically possible, but it sure won't be for lack of trying."

Collins rolls her eyes. "I mean … my body's different. I don't look like you're … used to. Like I did last time."

Realization hits.

"You're gorgeous, Collins. Always have been. Always will be. I'd think that even if your body wasn't changing because you're giving me the best gift anyone could give me."

She scans my expression, testing my sincerity.

I meant every damn word, which seems to register. I didn't know it was possible to crave someone this much. I want her just as much as I always have. Maybe even more. There's something primal about the knowledge that her body looks different because she's carrying our baby.

"Promise me this won't mess anything up," she whispers. "That whatever happens between us won't affect the baby."

"I promise."

"And if you change your mind or want to be with someone else, you'll tell me."

I snort. "Not gonna happen."

"Promise anyway."

"I promise, Monty."

She exhales unsteadily, then unzips my pants and reaches into my boxers to tug my erection free. I grind my molars as her thumb circles the leaky red tip. If I'd had *any* idea this might happen, I'd have woken up early enough to take care of business in the shower this morning. There's a legitimate concern I might come the second I'm inside of her after months of abstinence.

Collins smiles, seeming to sense the power she has over me. And then she's pulling at the tie of her robe. The front falls open, still covering her breasts, but not much else. She slips it off her shoulders, letting the fabric puddle at her feet.

I'm used to seeing her in bulky sweaters and oversize shirts. Her bump is a noticeable bulge now, and her tits have doubled in size since I saw them last.

"Told you I look different."

I hear the vulnerability beneath the bravado, so I press closer so she can feel my hard dick again.

My head dips, and I trace the ridge of her exposed collarbone with my tongue. "Yeah. Sexier," I say right next to her ear.

She trembles.

My hand slides up the inside of her thigh. She's fucking soaked, cunt fluttering from the first brush of my fingers.

"My room or yours?" I ask, something I never thought I'd have to ask a woman in *my* house.

I moved most of my stuff to a guest room upstairs so Collins could have the primary suite closest to the nursery. Although I'm really fucking hoping this development means separate bedrooms won't be a permanent arrangement.

Collins doesn't reply. I'm not sure she heard me, honestly, over the moans she's emitting.

She spins suddenly, gripping the edge of the counter. "Here."

"Here?"

"Yeah. I'm so—I'm so close. I just need you inside of me. *Please.*

Please, Kit. Please fuck me."

Her voice is breathy and desperate as she begs me.

She doesn't need to. Even if her entire family was in the next room, I'm not sure I'd be able to stop this time. I want this just as much as she does.

But I do tease her a little, admiring the view of her bent over the counter with her legs spread. She's so wet that I can see it. Smell it.

"*Now*," Collins whimpers. Her ass bumps back against my crotch, shamelessly searching for my cock.

"You weren't this bossy the last time we hooked up," I tell her.

"Are you complaining?"

I smirk. "No, ma'am."

"*Don't* call me ma'am. It makes me feel old."

"You're the one who insisted on referring to me as Lili's *little* brother." I grip the base of my dick, rubbing the head against her clit and around the swollen entrance of her pussy.

She moans loudly, arching her back.

"Did last time feel like fucking an *overgrown teenager*, Collins? Did you have to teach me how to get you off?"

She gasps before spitting out a series of gibberish, most of which is swears.

"Do you want to set another timer?" I tease. "I bet you'll come faster on my cock than you did on my fingers."

I indulge an inch, letting the head sink into heaven. Another gasp as her inner muscles contract. Her pussy tightens, trying to draw me deeper.

"You want more?" I ask.

"*Yes.*"

"You feel how hard I am for you? How fucking desperate I am to fuck you again?"

"More," she pleads.

It's obscene, watching the flared tip disappear inside of her. I've never—

I still.

"Should-should I get a condom?"

Collins glances over her shoulder. "You *can't* knock me up twice, Kit."

I roll my eyes. I might have majored in chemistry, but I have a basic understanding of biology too. "I know that."

"Then, what? Did you forget how to have sex during your dry spell?"

I swat her ass, admiring the pink that blooms across her pale skin. "No."

"Then … what's the problem?"

"I've never had sex without a condom before," I admit.

"Never? Wow. You *really* wanted to avoid an unplanned pregnancy, huh?"

She's turned her head so she's staring at the stove instead of me, and I mentally curse. That's not what I meant, and I hate it's the first place her head went.

"There's a difference between unplanned and unwanted, Monty. I told you, I want this. And pregnancy wasn't the only reason I always wore protection. I just … I wanted to make sure you were good with it. I'm asking … permission, I guess? It feels presumptuous to fuck you without one."

She doesn't reply right away, and I'm worried I completely ruined the mood.

"One must have broken last time. So, technically, you already did."

Her cheeks flush an adorable pink.

"So, you're good with my cum dripping out of you after?" I ask casually.

Collins sucks in a startled breath, the pink darkening to scarlet.

I'm *trying* to shock her. This isn't going to last long. And I want Collins to know, once it's over, there's not going to be any sneaking out. That this isn't happening because I'm horny or because she's pregnant.

I grip her jaw so I can kiss her, inhaling her little gasp. My left hand slides into her hair, adjusting her head to the perfect position. My right hand ends up back between her legs, grinding the heel against her swollen clit. She's *so* wet. I can feel her arousal soaking my fingers, the slickness so erotic that I can hardly think straight.

I kiss a line along her jaw and down the side of her neck. Collins tilts her head back. My tongue swipes across her pulse point, pounding wildly.

"*Please*, Kit." Her voice teeters on the edge of torment.

I suck on her sensitive skin, making her hiss. "Answer my question, Monty."

"Yes," she blurts. "I'm good with it."

I smile. "Good with what?"

"With your cum dripping out of me."

I raise an eyebrow. Surprised. Impressed. Horny as hell. "Good girl."

I thrust.

This time, I don't stop after one inch. I *can't*. She's tight and slippery and hot, clutching my cock like she was meant to take me.

The sensation is indescribable. If I were religious, I'd call the clasp of her pussy heaven, here on earth.

I can hear the slurp of wet friction and slap of our skin together.

Feel her muscles tighten and quiver as she takes me over and over again. I clench my ass and tighten my grip on her waist, determined not to come first.

"You feel *so* good," she moans. "It's so good and—*oh*."

I pinch her nipple, enjoying the way she arches her back and presses against me, seeking more friction.

"Kit. Please." She's unraveling, tatters of lust pulling her voice apart.

"I know. You want to come. You want it so, *so* badly." I trail the line of her shoulder with my tongue. She tastes like sweat and sin. "But you need me to get there. Come on my cock, Monty. Let me fill you up and … *fuck*."

She's coming. Squeezing so tight that it's a struggle for me to continue thrusting.

"Do it," she gasps. "Fill me."

I pump into her twice more, then let go. My hips jerk, and my abs tense, and the pressure explodes. It rips through me, like a storm devastating everything in its path. It steals my ability to think, to move, to even breathe. My dick swells and jerks as I ejaculate, pouring so much cum into her that it starts to spill out in a sticky mess.

I'm breathing harder than I was after my run this morning, the rush of euphoria making my muscles tremble. I have to steady myself with a hand on the counter, right next to Collins's. And then I decide *fuck it* and slide closer, squeezing her wrist once.

She lets out a contented hum.

My cock slips out of her reluctantly. I'm still half hard, already aching for a repeat.

I reach for the drawer that holds the clean dish towels, conveniently located right next to her left hip. I pull one out, savoring the sight of my semen on her skin for a few more seconds before gently wiping between her legs.

"You're really good in bed," she mumbles, leaning heavily against the counter.

I laugh. "We didn't make it to a bed, Monty."

"I just meant—" She blinks a few times, her expression dazed. "I kinda thought last time was a fluke."

"A fluke?" I smirk.

"The whole bet thing? I was *sure* I'd win. I don't usually come that hard. Or … at all."

"Like I said, you *had* terrible taste in men."

She shakes her head. Then bites her lower lip. "That wasn't how—I didn't mean to, uh, sort of jump you."

I grin. "You can jump me anytime you want."

"I had more of a plan to seduce you. But then you walked in, and I got … distracted."

"What was your plan?"

"You're going to laugh."

"Probably," I agree. "I'm in a *really* good mood right now."

"Do you want your dinner?"

I shake my head. "Don't try to distract me. I want to hear the plan."

Collins flushes. "You'd have to sit down for it."

I arch an eyebrow, even more intrigued.

"Since all the strip clubs in Vegas were closed … I was going to give you a lap dance." Her gaze drops deliberately. "Let me know when you've recovered."

I grin. My slacks are still unzipped. She can see I'm still hard. Getting harder by the second, since she's naked and suggesting she rub all over me.

Guess I need to remind Collins she came four times the last night we hooked up.

So, I scoop her up and carry her down the hall to *our* bedroom.

CHAPTER 40
Collins

Plink. Plink. Plop.

I make a face as I hit the notes in rapid succession. I haven't set up my keyboard, despite there being plenty of space in the penthouse. Playing it seems silly when *this* is available. But the Steinway that sits in the corner of Kit's living room, overlooking Central Park, deserves much better than this lackluster performance.

I haven't played piano—just *played*, not to practice for a performance or to get paid—in a long, long time. So far, it's going terribly.

I rest my elbows on the music stand and groan.

"You're improving."

I groan again, then turn to face Kit.

He's leaning one shoulder against the doorway that connects the living room to the front hall. And he's wearing a tuxedo.

Panic spikes in my chest as soon as that detail registers.

I push the bench back and stand, scowling at him. "Is this a joke?"

"What?" he asks innocently.

"You're not actually wearing *that* tonight, are you?"

He glances down, then nods. "I was planning on it, yeah. This is my favorite tux."

"Kit!" I exclaim, exasperated. "I've been asking you all day—all *week*—what we were doing tonight. Precisely so I could figure out what to wear, and you …"

He twirls the tie he just pulled out of his pocket around like a lasso. "Maybe I *should've* been a cowboy instead of Indiana Jones," he muses.

"I'm not wearing these"—I gesture to my striped pajamas—"on our date if you're wearing a tux. I don't care if you blindfold me so I can't see. *I'll* still know what I'm wearing."

He chuckles as he walks closer. "That's not what the blindfold is for, Monty."

"Then what's it for?"

"You'll see," he says, spinning me around, then knotting the tie behind my head.

I tense when my vision disappears. "I *can't* actually."

His hands land on my hips. "Trust me."

Then we're moving. My steps forward are tentative, but the solid heat of Kit behind me is reassuring.

We cross a rug, which I think means we cut through the dining room. But then we're back on hardwood, and I'm lost. Are we in the kitchen? Is he cooking me dinner? Or maybe this is a surprise for the baby and he's bringing me to the nursery? But I can't think of anything that would be a surprise in there. We've discussed every detail of what to order and how to arrange it. Plus, I was in there this morning, and nothing appeared out of place. We've both been home all day, so I don't know when or how Kit would've changed things around.

"Almost there … okay."

The blindfold falls away. I blink at our bedroom, still confused. Because it looks the same as it did when I woke up this morning.

"You, uh, cleaned?" I guess.

He snorts, then grabs my shoulders and steers me to the left.

"*Oh*," I realize.

A dress is hanging on the back of the closet door. And not just any dress. It's silvery and silky and familiar.

It's the dress I was wearing *that* night in the Hamptons. Except this version doesn't have an Aperol spritz stain on the front, like the one I haven't been able to bring myself to get rid of.

"Oh," I whisper again, lifting a hand to finger the flawless fabric.

I still love this dress. Even more now because I'll forever associate it with my first night with Kit.

I tear my eyes away from it to look at him. "How did you find this?"

I never told him the brand or where I bought it. It wouldn't have been that easy to find.

He grins. "I've got connections, Monty. I spent a lot of time staring at you that night. I remembered the style and that the color was called pewter. My mom tracked down the rest. You said the original was ruined, so I thought you might like a replacement."

"I would. I mean, I do. Thank you, Kit. This is …" I shake my head. "I can't believe you did this."

I mean, I can. It's thoughtful and considerate and extravagant, something he knew I'd appreciate.

I just can't believe he did this for *me*. That he's *mine*.

He plants a swift kiss on my forehead. "Get dressed and meet me in the front hall."

I snag his sleeve before he can step away. "I'm about to get naked, and you're *leaving*?"

"If I stay in here, we're going to be late for dinner."

"So?" I fist his tie. "We can stay in. Eat mac and cheese on the floor."

"That's not a *mac and cheese on the floor* dress, Monty. This is a *date*, and I'm buying you dinner." He kisses me again. "I'll fuck you later, as many times as you want. Deal?"

I pretend to consider the offer before I happily capitulate. "Fine. Deal."

Kit grins before leaving the bedroom.

I strip out of my pajamas, then unzip the dress and pull it off the hanger.

It occurs to me halfway through pulling it on that my body is a different shape now than it was in August, but the zipper slides back up with no issue. The bodice isn't tight, the silk flowing freely to the hem. It drapes over the bulge of my bump like it was meant to be a maternity dress, the fabric chafing my skin a lot less than some of my other clothes have been.

There's a massive mirror in the walk-in closet.

I stand in front of it, smiling as I survey my appearance. The further I've gotten into my pregnancy, the less confident I've felt. The stranger my own skin has seemed. I know it's a natural, normal, *incredible* part of pregnancy—that the changes are to accommodate the life growing inside of me—but it's still an adjustment. An ongoing adjustment because I keep getting *bigger*.

Right now? I do feel confident. Sexy even.

And it's not the dress. Not *only* the dress at least. It's Kit, who's said—and shown—how much he appreciates my body like this.

I hurry into the bathroom, applying a light layer of makeup. I pull my hair out of its bun and run a brush through it. And then, after pulling on the black wrap coat I wear to work, I make the reckless decision to wear heels. They tap rhythmically against the hardwood as I walk down the hallway. If Kit hadn't indicated we were in a rush, I'd stop in the living room to sit at the piano and pretend I was performing at Carnegie Hall.

Kit's leaning a shoulder against one of the entryway walls when I turn the corner. He straightens at the sound of my approaching footsteps, eyes skimming over the silk swishing around my calves and journeying upward until they land on my face. The appreciative expression on his makes the pinch in my toes worth it.

I attempted to dress up on New Year's Eve, but aside from that he's mostly seen me in baggy clothes meant to disguise-slash-accommodate my growing bump. And I like that I felt comfortable enough around Kit to lounge around in my pajamas and no makeup most of today, but he's also who I want to admire my effort to appear a little more glamorous. And who I want to ruin that effort later.

"You look beautiful," Kit tells me, pressing a soft kiss against my mouth before we head into the hallway and then inside the elevator.

"So, where are we going?" I ask as it starts to descend.

"You'll see," he replies cryptically.

I huff, but I'm not really annoyed. Mostly giddy. This is already the best date I've ever been on.

The elevator stops a few seconds later, only a few floors down.

I stiffen when the blonde who visited Kit at work walks in. Sadie … something.

I know there were other women before August. Since she visited him at work and apparently lives in his building, I'm guessing Sadie's on that list. And I can trust him and love him and feel secure in our relationship and *also* be jealous. I was jealous the last time I met Sadie, too, I just refused to admit it.

"Hey, Kit," she greets sunnily.

"Hi, Sadie," he replies.

Her eyes jump to me next. I'm expecting aloofness, maybe even rudeness, but she startles me by laughing. "*Oh.* Okay. You were right."

I glance at Kit, but he says nothing. One corner of his mouth is curved up though, like he's restraining a smile. Inside joke, I guess?

"Hi. I'm Collins," I say, not sure what else to contribute to the strange interaction.

Kit hasn't mentioned Sadie since the day she visited, but they seem … close.

"Oh, I know," she replies. "We met at Kensington Consolidated, remember? You're Kit's assistant."

"I remember. But I don't, uh … I'm not his assistant anymore."

Sadie nods. "Good for you. It seemed like a stressful job."

I'm not sure how to respond to that, and we stop in the lobby a few seconds later.

"Have a great night," Sadie says, stepping off. "Nice to see you again, Collins."

"You too," I respond, my smile slipping as soon as the doors close.

Kit makes an amused sound in the back of his throat.

I glance at him. "What?"

He shrugs. "Nothing. Just a tickle."

I press my lips tightly together as the doors open again, this time in the garage.

I have no real reason to feel jealous. But it's the same irrational surge I experienced when I saw him sitting alone out on the patio with that brunette. I'd walked in on Isaac actively screwing someone else, and I was hurt and pissed, but I wasn't jealous. I never handed my ex the power to truly hurt me. Kit holds that ability.

"Which one do you want to take?" Kit asks, nodding to the line of vehicles parked ahead.

"What do you mean?" I scan them, looking for the sports car. "Which one is yours?"

His grin is boyish and a little sheepish. "All of them."

"All of—" I study the row more carefully, counting eight and only recognizing two. I figured the car we drove to New Haven was a rental or something. I didn't know he owned two cars. Along with *six* others.

The penthouse has started to feel like home, not a *really* nice hotel I won a stay in. But I still haven't grasped the enormity of how much money Kit has. I'm not sure I ever will.

"You pick."

He nods, walking toward a sleek black car. He pauses to grab something off the tire. Keys, I realize, when the lights flash.

"This car must be worth a lot, and you leave the keys on the tire?" I ask incredulously.

Kit shrugs. "It's convenient. The garage is locked and monitored. Never had an issue."

I really hope our kid inherits Kit's lack of cynicism and pessimism.

I climb inside the fancy car, buckling my seat belt and relaxing against the buttery leather.

Kit starts the engine, but he doesn't begin driving.

"I thought we were in a rush?" I ask.

"Were you jealous?"

I glance out the window, pretending there's something more interesting to stare at than concrete walls. "A little."

When I look at Kit again, he's smiling.

I sniff, miffed. "Glad that amuses you."

"Do you have any clue how many guys I've wanted to punch for talking to or touching you, Monty?"

"How many?"

"All of them," he answers softly.

I smile. "Sadie seems nice," I admit. "I know it's silly. I'll get over it."

"There's nothing to get over, Collins. Nothing's ever happened between me and Sadie."

"Really? You guys seemed … friendly. And she came to the office that time."

"She came to the office to ask me for a gym recommendation. We'd worked out here at the same time before, but she wanted to take classes someplace."

"A gym recommendation," I repeat. "No, you're right; she's definitely not interested."

He grins. "I didn't say she wasn't. *I* wasn't, and I told her why. Told her about you, and she said I should just ask you out. I told her it was complicated, and she just figured out that meant you were my assistant *and* pregnant."

Oh.

I like that he told Sadie about me. I like it a lot.

"Your *Indiana Jones* costume? I called it a cowboy one because the guy I went to that Halloween party with said I should've gone with the cowboy I was staring at all night."

A slow smile spreads across Kit's face in response to my admission. "So, I wasn't only *gorgeous* freshman year?"

Of course, he memorized the compliment I'd accidentally let slip.

"You're incorrigible," I sigh.

Kit chuckles as he reverses out of the spot. "You love it."

I love you.

The words pop into my head, which they've been doing regularly.

Kit starts driving before I can decide if this is the right moment to say them.

Our dinner reservation is at one of the fanciest restaurants in the city. Not the steak house we ate at before, but it has a similar ambiance. Cloth napkins and flickering candles and soft jazz playing in the background.

The biggest difference? Unlike the last time we went out to dinner, I feel relaxed. Happy. An involuntary smile stretches across my face as we get settled at our table for no reason except that I'm excited about this evening.

"What?" Kit asks.

"I was just thinking about the last time we went out to dinner together, at the steak house."

"Yeah." He chuckles at the memory. "About time we did it again, huh?"

Our waiter appears, delivering water glasses and rattling off specials. Kit declines ordering a beverage, and I do the same. I've noticed he avoids drinking alcohol around me, which seems like the exact sort of considerate choice Kit would make.

I'm dunking a square of focaccia in olive oil when my phone buzzes with a call. I check it, then slide it back into my coat pocket. "My mom, checking in," I tell Kit. "I'll call her back tomorrow."

He nods. "Have you talked to your dad lately?"

I shake my head. "No. But that's normal."

Kit sets down his menu and exhales. "I think you should talk to him, Collins. For real. Ask for an explanation about what you saw."

"He's had years to explain."

"He doesn't know you're waiting for him to, Collins."

"I'm not. I mean, what could he *possibly* say that would make it better?"

"I don't know. But wouldn't him saying *something* be better than never knowing? Staying stuck in the same place with it? You want our kid growing up, wondering why you're acting strange around your dad?"

I dunk my bread again. "You're playing dirty."

He shrugs. "Maybe. But I'm right. And I think you know that, that you wanted a push to talk to him, or you wouldn't have told me about it."

"It's just so strange to think of my dad … having an affair. He wears tweed suits. He always smells like coffee. And he's a *scientist*. They're supposed to deal with logic and reason, not secrets."

"Chemistry isn't logical or reasonable, Monty. It's filled with all sorts of mysteries. Are there any undiscovered elements? What is the composition of dark matter? How did nonliving matter transition into the first living organism?"

He says all *that*, then casually sips some water.

I stare at him for a few seconds. "You're kind of a nerd, Kit Kensington."

He grins. "Thanks."

"Will you do me a favor?" I ask.

"*Another* one? I already contributed my nerdy genes to our kid. If Eggplant wins a Nobel Prize one day, it'll be 'cause of me."

I roll my eyes. "Just … don't act any differently around my dad, okay? He likes you, and I like that you guys get along. I don't want my issues with him to affect that. Okay?"

Kit hesitates before nodding, but he does nod. "Okay. But for the record, I still think you should talk to him."

"I'll think about it," I allow.

The waiter returns to take our orders, and then our entrées are delivered in record time.

"This doesn't look as good as yours," Kit comments, picking up the knife and cutting into his chicken.

He's lying—when I made chicken this past week, it turned out dry and bland—but he says it with such conviction that I *almost* believe him.

My response? "I love you."

The words slip out easily, naturally, like I've said them to him a hundred times before. But I haven't. In my head, I've said them a lot. Counting a few seconds ago, I've said them aloud exactly … once.

And I *did* say them aloud.

Kit's blue eyes are wide and surprised as he looks up from his plate.

Did I freak him out? I think I freaked him out. Technically, this is our first date. First date to four-letter word is a big leap.

Even embarrassed, I don't regret saying it. I want him to know how

I feel, even if he's not there yet. Even if he never gets there.

I pick up my fork, attempting nonchalance. Pretending I *have* said those three words to him a hundred times before. "My chicken was dry. I saw a recipe for chicken parmesan that I was thinking I'd try to make next week. The tomato sauce should help with the consistency. Do you know if there's a meat mallet anywhere in your gigantic kitchen? Because I tried looking for one and I—"

"Collins."

"I'll just buy one," I decide.

"*Collins.*"

I reach for my water. "You don't have to say anything. We can talk about—"

"I've been in love with you ever since I saw you, Collins Tate." He pauses, letting that sentence sink in. "Maybe it started as a crush, but it was never a game to me. I was a goner from the start. You thought arguing about whether a hot dog was a sandwich or bringing up Monaco was going to deter me?" He grins. "I just fell harder. I was trying to give you some time to catch up to where I've been for a while."

Tears fill my eyes, making my vision blur. "I'm really hormonal," I whisper.

"Damn it." He reaches across the candles to brush his thumb against my cheek. "I was hoping it might have been because of my romantic streak."

"You factored."

Kit laughs under his breath, brushing my cheek once more before withdrawing his hand.

He doesn't say it again, and neither do I. But it lingers as an invisible, shimmering awareness through the rest of dinner.

"A bar?" I ask dubiously.

After dinner, Kit drove us to a bar. And it's not even a *nice* bar, like the one I was supposed to meet Perry at months ago. It's a dive, with a flickering neon light and a boarded window and no line for entry. The kind of place I'd go for cheap beer in college.

"You'll see." He tugs me toward the entrance by our joined hands. Reluctantly, I follow.

The interior is about what I expected. Vintage sports memorabilia decorate the walls. The bartender is a grizzled older man with a toothpick sticking out of the corner of his mouth. And my heels stick to the floor with each step, like the wooden boards haven't been washed in this century.

The size of the crowd inside is the only surprise. The booths and the stools lining the bar are all full.

I stare at Kit until he looks at me. He smirks at my confused expression, pulling me deeper into the bar.

"… on? Is this on? Oh great, it's working."

I track the sound to the raised stage that sits at the very back of the bar. *Stage* is a generous term for the platform raised a few inches higher than the rest of the floor, but the microphone, chair, and piano add to the effect. A middle-aged man is standing at the microphone, fiddling with the wire wrapped around the stand.

"They do an open mic night on Saturdays," Kit whispers in my ear. "All musical acts welcome."

The realization of why we're here hits a second later. "What? No!"

"Yes." He steers me toward one of the open tables closest to the stage.

No one wanted to sit right in front, and I don't either. But Kit isn't asking. His grip on my hand is sure and firm as he leads me over to the central spot.

"Want anything to drink?" he asks once we're seated.

"What I *want* to drink isn't an option until May." If there was *any* chance of me getting on that platform, it'd be higher with alcohol involved.

Kit leans closer. "C'mon, Collins. Play for me."

"And"—I tabulate a rough estimate of the room—"fifty other people?"

"You've played for a larger crowd."

I have. Recitals at Yale were attended by hundreds.

But that was different. I was one of dozens of students performing. And it was a piece I'd practiced for weeks or even months. I don't even have sheet music with me. I'd have to play from memory, and who knows how that will sound?

Aside from Kit, everyone here is a stranger. People I'm unlikely to ever see again. It's silly that I'm preoccupied by what they'll think. But I'm a perfectionist by nature. Making mistakes or messing up never feels natural.

"What's the worst that could happen?" Kit asks, like he's reading my thoughts.

Maybe he is. He knows I'm not impulsive or reckless. Jumping onstage to perform in front of strangers is something he would do, but I wouldn't.

"I mess up, everyone laughs, and we can never come back here."

"Then we go home. When you can drink again, we'll head to one of the other thousand bars in this city instead of this one and its humiliating memories."

I roll my eyes. "You're making fun of me."

"I'm *encouraging* you, Monty. You don't want to play professionally again? That's fine. It's your decision, and I'll respect it. But I know you love playing. So, play."

I gnaw on my lower lip, glancing at the stage. The man is still up there. Now, he's kneeling in front of an amp. I watch as he stands and returns to the microphone.

"All righty, we're open for business, folks. You know the drill. If you're new here and you don't, first come, first serve. Five-minute max per performance. Second shifts if the stage sits empty, but not before. Happy Saturday." He hops off the platform and heads for the bar.

No one rushes toward the stage. It sits, empty and waiting, right in front of me.

I feel Kit's eyes on me, but he says nothing else. If I stood up and walked out of here, he'd drive me home. But I'm suddenly sick of playing it safe. I want to be worthy of his faith in me. What *is* the worst that will happen? Nothing I can't recover from.

I stand and start toward the stage.

I take a seat in front of the studio. It's brown, not black, the wood surface scarred with years of use instead of flawless. I'm too proud to bang out the series of single notes I played in Kit's living room earlier. Sitting here, I know I'm going to commit to a full piece.

I glance at Kit. He's reclined in his chair, relaxed and smiling as he stares at me. A few other patrons are glancing this way, but their attention is fleeting, not focused. Passing interest, not intent.

There was a time when I dreamed that performing in New York would mean playing at a famous venue, like Carnegie Hall. But watching Kit wink at me, a confident grin on his handsome face? I decide that who's in the crowd matters a lot more than its size or location.

And then I start to play.

CHAPTER 41
Kit

"**S**top stressing."

"I'm not stressing," Collins insists, tucking a piece of hair behind her ear.

I glance pointedly at her raised hand, and she flushes before dropping it back to her lap.

"I get flyaways when I'm telling the truth too," she informs me. "But, fine, I'm a *little* nervous about tonight."

"You've met them before, Monty. And Lili will be there."

Collins exhales. "She said you and your dad were yelling at each

other. About … the NDA."

Nice of my sister to mind her own damn business.

I park on my parents' street and shut the car off. "I was pissed he'd asked you to sign one. But we talked it out. Everything's good."

I was very clear with my parents that dinner tonight would only take place if it was completely informal. I didn't want them grilling Monty about the pregnancy or any discussion of Kensington Consolidated. This is simply for them to get to know her better, but I'm not sure exactly what that will look like, even setting aside the extraordinary circumstances.

I've never introduced a girl to my parents before.

"Let's go," Collins declares, opening the car door and climbing out. "We'll be late."

I smirk as I step out too.

We're five minutes early. My family will be floored.

Sure enough, there's a look of obvious surprise on my mom's face when she opens the door. "Kit! You're early!"

I nod toward Collins as I tug her inside by our joined hands. "She runs a tight ship."

I've never showed up late to anything that involved Collins, but it has nothing to do with her being bossy. I'm just eager to be around her. That's a higher priority than anything else that might be happening.

"Mom, you remember Collins," I say, helping her out of her coat.

"I—yes. Of course." My mom's flustered, her gaze focused on Collins's round stomach.

She peppered me with questions about the pregnancy—after chastising me for the secrecy—but she's uncharacteristically silent now. I'd imagine she's experiencing the same surreal sensation I did at the first ultrasound. A moment where knowledge becomes reality.

"You have a beautiful home, Mrs. Kensington," Collins says politely.

"Thank you. And please, call me Scarlett. Would it be okay—can I give you a hug?"

Collins smiles. "As long as you don't mind the bump."

"I don't mind at all," my mom replies, giving Collins a quick embrace.

I hang up the coats and then flash Collins a thumbs-up.

She rolls her eyes at me, then refocuses on my mom. "If you want to touch too …" Collins shyly gestures toward her stomach.

Mom nods eagerly, then presses her palm against the bump under Collins's sweater. "Wow. Are you—have you been feeling okay?"

"I'm tired a lot," Collins replies. "But no more nausea, thankfully."

"Well, come sit down. Kit, show her into the living room."

I feign shock. "You remembered I'm here too?"

Mom sighs before hugging me too. "You've always had an unforgettable presence, Christopher."

Collins snickers, then pretends to cough to cover it.

Convincing, I mouth at her, grabbing Collins's hand again and towing her toward the living room.

Dad, Lili, Charlie, and Bash stand in unison when we enter the room.

"Finally, the respectful welcome I deserve," I state.

Lili literally shoves me out of the way to reach Collins. "You're an idiot, Kit."

"Something we can *all* agree on," Bash declares.

"No one looks back on their life and wishes they'd studied more, bro," I retort, flicking the back of his head as I walk toward the couch.

"People who flunk out of school do."

"Scotch, Kit?" Dad asks.

I take a seat on the couch. "I'm good, thanks," I answer, glancing at Collins.

She's whispering with Lili.

Bash raises an eyebrow. "You sick or something?"

"I'm driving," I retort. "And"—I glance at Collins—"being supportive."

Bash rolls his eyes, but Dad looks proud. He's made a real effort this past week to make up for his initial reaction.

I apologized too. Because if I'd heard about the facts of the situation, with no personal investment, I'd probably have done more than suggest an NDA. And because I should have told my dad sooner so he didn't have to find out from a box.

Which reminds me, I really need to assemble the crib. I fell asleep reading the instructions last night.

Collins takes a seat next to me as I'm fixing a plate of the hors d'oeuvres set out on the coffee table.

I add a couple more cubes of cheese and hold it out to her. "Hungry?"

"Thanks," she says, taking it.

I give her knee a quick squeeze before picking up a second plate for myself.

Drinks get served—Collins and I both opt for water—and then a brief pause falls.

Maybe I was *too* firm about the off-limits topics. I didn't want my family to stress or overwhelm Collins, so I was overinclusive on the list.

"How's the law firm going?" Lili asks between sips of wine, breaking the silence.

I decide I won't berate my sister later for telling Collins about my fight with Dad over the NDA.

"It's good," Collins replies. "My first deposition is in a couple of weeks. And I have my own office."

"It's a nice office," Dad comments.

Collins smiles at him.

"Well, *anything* has to be better than being camped outside of Kit's," Lili says.

Bash laughs.

"How are your parents doing, Collins?" Mom asks.

"They're good, thanks. Both still teaching. My sister's about to graduate in the spring."

"That's wonderful."

"What does your father teach?" Dad questions.

"Chemistry," Collins answers. "He had Kit in a couple of classes actually. First thing my dad said when he heard I was working for him was, 'Smart kid.' "

I glance at her, taken aback by the revelation. She never mentioned that to me.

My family saw my degree in chemistry as a lark. A classic Kit choice to pick a random avenue. But there's some unshakable pride in knowing that I pursued something entirely outside of my comfort zone. That I could have succeeded on a different path if I'd chosen it.

"Crew mentioned you've purchased a crib," Mom states.

Both of my siblings smile, suggesting Bash told Lili how Dad found out about the baby.

"And Kit indicated you've already gotten all the other necessities," she continues. "Sounds like you're very prepared. But I"—she glances at Dad—"*we* would love to host a gathering this spring. Or over the summer. Not a baby shower necessarily, but some type of celebration for the newest member of our family."

I glance at Collins. Her lips are pressed together, and she's blinking rapidly.

I hear a quiet sniff before she says, "That sounds really nice, Scarlett. Thank you."

"Summer would probably be best," I say. "Amanda and Gerald will have more open schedules. And that way, the guest of honor"—I pat Collins's bump—"can be there."

Mom beams. "Perfect. I'll start planning."

"So, where did you two meet?" Dad asks.

"You know where we met, Dad," I reply. "Lili's move-in. You were there."

"I think he meant, where was your child conceived?" Bash comments, then takes a sip of scotch.

"Sebastian!" Mom exclaims. "I'm sure that wasn't what your father meant."

"It wasn't," Dad confirms, but his eyes are twinkling as he sips some scotch.

"How about we show Collins the clothes before dinner, Mom?" Lili suggests.

Mom brightens even more. "Great idea."

"What clothes?" Collins asks.

"Well"—Lili claps her hands together—"I had a feeling you didn't have much in the way of maternity clothes, based on what you were wearing last week, so Mom sourced some options. They're upstairs in one of the guest rooms. And then we also might have bought a *few* things for the baby."

"There are, like, fifty bags up there," Bash contributes.

Collins's eyes are wide. "Lili!"

"Bash is exaggerating," she replies. "A little. Just come look. Anything you don't like, we'll return."

Collins glances at me, and I give her an encouraging smile.

"Okay." She stands, disappearing upstairs with my mom and sister.

"You ever played pool, Charlie?" Bash asks. "There's a table in the library."

"Sounds great," Charlie replies, standing.

He and Bash head down the hallway in the direction of the library a few seconds later, conspicuously not bothering to invite me or Dad to join them.

A minute later, we're alone.

I glance at my father. "We sure can clear a room, huh?"

We've both apologized. But there's a tentativeness between us that's never existed before. A cut that's scabbed over, but hasn't fully healed yet.

Dad exhales. "Do you want me to leave the company, Kit?"

I stare at him, stunned. "What? No. You just came back."

"And I never asked you before I did. Your mother wanted to make a change professionally, so I decided to do the same. Decided without asking you and maybe without thinking it through."

"Is this about Collins?"

"It's about you. I realized … you've grown up, Christopher. You've become the man I always hoped you would. You were right; I'll never be CEO of Kensington Consolidated. There's a lot of history there, and I thought enough time had passed that it wouldn't matter. Maybe I was wrong."

I exhale. "If you want to leave Kensington Consolidated because you want to leave, leave. Don't leave because you think it's what *I* want." I clear my throat. "I wasn't sure what working at the company together would be like. Now that I do … I'd miss it. So, if you're asking me what I think you should do? I think you should stay. And I know we've never really discussed that part of the past, but I don't think you're the only one who wants to rewrite the past. Grandpa came to visit me last month. At the office."

"He did?" Dad looks stunned.

I nod. "I wasn't sure if I should mention it to you. I know you and Grandpa … it's complicated. But he showed up, and we talked for at least twenty minutes. I swear he looked sentimental, seeing me in your old office. And you and me—it's *not* complicated. If you're worried that's changed because of the company or because of what happened with Collins, don't."

Dad studies me for a few seconds before he says, "I'm really proud of you, son."

I smile wryly. "Despite the whole baby thing?"

He and Mom might have moved past the shock-and-anger stage to start planning parties, but this wasn't how they would have *chosen* for me to become a parent.

"*Including* the whole baby thing," he tells me. "I wish you'd felt like you could tell me sooner. If nothing else, so I could have supported you. But as far as I can tell, you've handled everything remarkably well on your own. Hell of a lot better than I did. You're going to be an incredible father, Christopher."

"Thanks, Dad," I croak, then clear my throat.

He does the same a second later.

We're both silent. But it's not the humming quiet from earlier as we both deliberated what to say. It's the comfortable, relaxed kind we've shared many times before.

"Is Collins interested in fashion?" my dad asks a few minutes later.

I frown as I reach for a cracker, confused by the question. "Uh, no. Not especially."

Dad smiles. "Then you might want to head upstairs and rescue her because Bash *wasn't* exaggerating about the number of bags Lili and your mother had stashed up there."

CHAPTER 42
Collins

When I wake up, the room is dark and quiet. I extend my left arm, finding nothing except cool cotton.

I'm alone in bed.

I slip out from under the covers, padding silently into the bathroom to pee. The tiled floor is heated, warm instead of harsh under my feet. I yawn at my reflection in the mirror, combing a couple of snarls out of my hair with my fingers.

Halfway back to bed, I hesitate. In the weeks I've been living here, Kit's had to take several calls in the middle of the night. Kensington

Consolidated does business with companies all over the world. Three a.m. in New York is normal business hours in other countries. He's probably on a conference call.

But when I head down the hallway, there's a strip of light shining underneath the nursery's door, not the office's.

I shove the door open a few inches, inhaling a quick breath once I can see inside.

That's what draws Kit's attention my way. Because everything in his penthouse is brand-new. Nothing squeaks or creaks or makes *any* unexpected noise at all.

I rest my head against the doorway, surveying the mess on the floor. "Want some help?"

He grins, shaking his head. "Nah, I got it. You build the baby; I'll build the crib."

I smile. "Deal."

"I would take some company though." Kit leans over, grabbing a screwdriver, squints at the directions, then twists a bolt into place. He's shirtless, sitting in the center of the rug with pieces of the crib spread around him.

"It looks good," I encourage.

He snorts. "It looks like a lumberyard."

"Are there supposed to be this many pieces?"

"I have no idea. But I'm going to figure it out." He picks up the instructions, flipping to a new page with fresh determination.

I shove away from the doorway and walk toward him. Sitting on the floor is harder than it used to be since my center of gravity shifted, but I manage. I also have to nudge a slat over to recline on my palms.

"What are you doing up? Did you have a work call?"

"Nah. I just couldn't sleep."

"This rug is surprisingly comfortable." My wrists are starting to hurt, so I relax flat on my back, staring up at the white plaster ceiling. "We should add some stars up there," I suggest. "For the baby to look at."

We agreed on an outer-space theme for the nursery's mural. It covers the largest wall, a scattering of planets and moons and stars and one meteor shower painted on a midnight-blue background.

"I like that idea."

I rest a hand on my stomach, rubbing slow circles and listening to the sound of wood being fitted together.

"I heard you playing after dinner," Kit comments a few minutes later.

"It's a new piece. It needs a lot of work still."

"Didn't sound that way to me."

I smile. "I think you might be the tiniest bit biased."

"Or I have really, *really* good instincts about pianists."

"On par with your carpentry skills?" I tease, glancing at the crib that hasn't gained any more pieces since I entered the room.

Kit sighs and sets the screwdriver down. "I don't think working on it in the middle of the night is helping much."

"Probably not the most practical time," I agree.

He crawls over, lying down on the rug next to me and mirroring my position. "Wow. What a boring ceiling. I promised our kid it was going to be exciting on the outside, so we should definitely add some stars. Do they make glow-in-the-dark paint? If so, we should use that."

"Probably," I say absently.

Of course, that's something Kit would think of. The closer I get to having a kid, the more often it's occurring to me that Kit will be an incredible parent. He's fun and adventurous. By comparison—maybe not even by comparison—I'm pretty boring.

Kit sails; I stay onshore.

"Five thousand for your thoughts," he says.

I huff a laugh. "They're not worth that much."

"I can't accurately assess their value unless you tell me."

I suck on my lower lip. "Do you think I'm too … practical?"

"No," he answers. "I think you're the perfect amount of practical."

I sigh. "I'm serious."

"So am I. I need someone to tell me that eight cars are unreasonable. Although I am considering getting a minivan for the kid, and I don't think that should count."

"A car is a car, Kit. It counts."

"A minivan is *practical* for kids though."

"We don't need a minivan."

Silence.

"You already bought one, didn't you?"

"I don't think a car seat is meant to fit in an Aston Martin. And we're not taking the subway home from the hospital. I don't love the idea of taking the train to Connecticut with a newborn, and I'm sure you'll want to visit your parents. So, yeah, I bought a minivan."

"I don't take a lot of risks," I state. "Performing at that open mic night was the craziest thing I'd done in a while, and I never would have done it solo. I played it safe for my entire life, and now I'm about to become a mom. And I'm not saying having kids ends your life, but it does *change* it. I've never wanted to go skydiving. The thought of voluntarily jumping out of a plane gives me nightmares. But I thought I'd have more time to definitely decide against it or other risks before being responsible for someone else. I'm lame. I'll be a lame mom."

"You're not lame. You're the coolest person I know, Collins."

I blow out a long breath, until it feels like there's no air left in my lungs. What else is he supposed to say? Agree?

"You're just saying that."

"No, I'm not." His thumb skims the length of my jaw, gripping my chin and turning my face toward him. "I've never lied to you. I *will* never lie to you. You want to know what I think? Ask me something. And I'll tell you the truth, even if it's not what you want to hear. So, *hear* me when I say that you're fierce and brave and brilliant. Our kid is not going to fall asleep in this room, staring at the stars you suggested we paint on the ceiling, and think, *My mom is so lame.* Not until he or she is fifteen and a bratty teenager at least."

I let out a watery laugh. Trust Kit to make me laugh and cry at the same time.

"And I'll go skydiving with you," he adds. "If you change your mind."

I sniffle. "I love you so much."

There's no mental tally to add to anymore. I've lost track of how many times I've said that to Kit, which makes me almost as happy as hearing him whisper them back to me.

He captures my palm in his, rubbing small circles around my knuckles with his thumb. "Papaya isn't going to come out requesting a résumé, Monty. We've got some time to get our stories straight about our skydiving adventure."

I laugh. "I don't think lying to your child is great parenting."

"My parents kept up a farce of an old man sneaking down our chimney to deliver gifts for *years*, and I turned out fine. I don't think one fictional trip is going to ruin our kid."

I'm still laughing. I'm so *happy*, lying on the floor with Kit. A moment I want to memorize.

He's smiling, watching me laugh. "It wasn't *that* funny."

I shift carefully so I'm on my side, facing him. "We're going to have to discuss names soon. Non-food-related names."

"Personally, I think Papaya Tate Kensington has a nice ring to it."

My chest squeezes tight when I realize he purposefully included my last name too. "I'm voting against Papaya," I state firmly. "But I'm good with the rest."

Kit tucks an arm behind his head. "Did you know Lili's named after my grandmother? My dad's mom. She died when he was pretty young. One theory about my grandfather's attitude … he never really got over it."

"No, I didn't know that," I say softly.

"I was thinking …" Kit clears his throat. "I was thinking it might be nice, if it's a boy, to honor my dad in some way. Use Crew as a middle name or something." He slants a glance my way. "It was just a thought. It's totally fine if you—"

"I think it's a great idea."

"You do?"

"Yeah." I reach out, resting a hand on the center of his chest. It rises with a sudden inhale. "I think it would mean a lot to him."

Every time I've been around Kit and his dad, their close bond has been obvious. It makes me miss mine more.

He twirls a strand of my hair around one finger, tugging gently, and I'm certain he knows what I'm thinking. But he doesn't push. Kit made it clear what he thinks I should do about the situation, and now he's leaving the choice up to me.

I snuggle closer, sliding my palm lower and pressing my lips to the spot where my hand just was.

"I'm not going to get any more work done on the crib tonight, am I?"

My fingertips slowly, teasingly trail back and forth along the strip of hot, firm skin right above his waistband. "Do you *want* to work on the crib?" I question innocently.

Kit adjusts us with an agility I doubt I was capable of pre-pregnancy, hovering over me just high enough that his abs brush my bump. His head dips, tongue tracing the outline of my lips.

My heart beats wildly, banging against my rib cage like it's trying to escape my chest. My hips lift, desperately seeking some friction. A frustrated whimper escapes my mouth when I don't find any.

"Here?" he teases, mouth ghosting over mine.

"Please," I breathe, nails digging into the bunched muscles of his back with wanton urgency.

This room is one of the few we haven't christened yet. It's not that I *want* to have sex on a rug next to a stack of wood. It's that I want him so urgently that I don't care where we are. It doesn't seem to matter how many times we have sex. My body reacts like it's a novelty each time.

"How do you want me?" He shifts back a few inches, giving me space to reposition.

I don't reply right away. I'm focused on his crotch. He's so hard that I can see the outline of his erection trying to break free from the cotton.

Warmth pools low in my pelvis, anticipating the sensation of that stiff length sliding inside of me.

"Behind," I finally answer, moving onto my hands and knees.

The only downside of this position is that I can't watch Kit. There's something deeply erotic though, about feeling him touch me but not being able to see it. The suspense is a powerful aphrodisiac.

"This fucking view." His deep voice is a gritty rasp as his fingers trail up the inside of my thigh.

I spread my knees wider as shivers sprint down my spine. Warm air hits wetness, making my inner muscles clench around aching emptiness.

Kit groans, and I know he can see it.

Soft fibers abrade my elbows as I lean forward, lifting my ass higher in the air.

He chuckles, but it's not an amused sound. It's throaty and husky and cocky. His hand moves higher, stimulating my clit and coating his palm with my arousal. He pulls away, and I hear the unmistakable sound of him stroking himself.

"Kit," I whimper.

I'm so turned on it feels like he could blow on me and I'd unravel.

"I know, baby."

I've barely registered the blunt pressure of his cock finding my entrance before he's filling me, the stretch an immediate relief and an insatiable encouragement. I want—need—more. I can't get enough.

Kit grunts as I spasm. *"Fuck."*

Sin. That's what his voice sounds like. Dark and intoxicating.

His hands skate up my sides, pulling my—well, his—T-shirt up. I moan loudly, arching my back as his hands cup my heavy, sensitive breasts.

"Pretty sure lame people wear underwear to bed, Monty." He thrusts again, the slick, delicious drag an addictive drug. "And they don't have sex on the floor when there are five beds available."

I gasp, racing toward my release.

"Or beg to be eaten out on the piano." His hands are exploring every inch of my body, calloused palms sliding over sensitive skin. "Or talk police out of pressing charges—"

The first wave of bliss hits, and I'm no longer listening to a word Kit's saying.

Kit

Midway through tackling my usual mountain of morning emails, there's a knock on my door.

"Come in," I call out.

My new assistant, April, appears a minute later. Indy recommended I hire her—they had worked together before Indy started at Kensington Consolidated—and so far, April has been as capable as Indy said. It's still strange, seeing someone other than Collins sitting at that desk. But at least now, we can ask each other how our day was and not already know the answer.

"Mr. Kensington is here to see you," April states.

I frown, quickly glancing at my calendar to make sure I didn't overlook a meeting. I didn't.

"Which one?" I clarify.

My grandfather showing up once was shocking. Twice would be even more so.

But I doubt it's Dad; he would knock himself without sending in my assistant first. Most of the ease that defined our former relationship has returned. The parts that haven't—like him simply showing up, instead now texting me about a good time to come by—are a recognition of some necessary boundaries.

"Oliver," April responds.

"Oh." I straighten, reaching for the jacket I slung on the back of my chair when I arrived an hour ago.

A formal way to greet your uncle. But he's not just my uncle; he's also Kensington Consolidated's current CEO. And I haven't seen or spoken to Oliver since my family found out about Collins. I know Oliver knows, and I should've been the one to tell him.

"Send him in," I add.

April nods.

A few seconds later, my uncle enters my office. Oliver's smiling, which is a relief. And a rare sight, especially at work. He's always acted more stoic and serious than Dad. A little like Bash and me.

"Hey, Kit. Do you have a minute?"

"Of course. Have a seat." I reach for my mug of coffee, swallowing a hasty sip to get some more caffeine in my system. Collins and I didn't get much sleep last night. "Is everything okay?"

"Everything's fine." He settles in one of the chairs and smiles. "More than fine. I hear congratulations are in order. You're going to be a dad."

I relax in response to his warm tone. "Yeah, thanks. I am."

"I thought I'd let things … settle a little," Oliver adds tactfully. "And to be clear, I'm here as your uncle, not your boss."

"Dad and I could've used that disclosure at the start of a few more conversations," I state dryly.

Oliver laughs. "Yeah. It's a tricky balance. If Rory were coming here instead of heading to law school, I'm not sure how I would handle it."

"She got in?"

My uncle beams, nodding. "Yesterday." His expression shifts to serious. "But you didn't hear that from me. Act surprised when she tells you."

"I will. But I already told her I was certain she'd get in."

His smile grows. "Fine. Act like you knew all along."

"Where did Wren end up applying?"

"Where?" Oliver's smile turns wry. "That is an excellent question."

I grin. "Right."

Wren has always been a wild card. She and I were designated the family troublemakers decades ago. My title might be in jeopardy, thanks to a recent series of responsible decisions, but it sounds like Wren is still earning her label.

"I won't keep you," Oliver says, standing. "Just wanted to check in."

I stand, too, buttoning my jacket. "As your nephew—and your employee—I *am* sorry for not disclosing everything sooner. I planned for you to hear the news from me; I was just waiting for the right time. Trying to juggle my responsibilities to this company with the new ones outside of it. But I want you to know that I take my role here seriously.

I would never intentionally jeopardize it."

Oliver nods. "I *do* know that, Kit, but thank you for saying it. And I'm not saying your father acted unreasonably, but I think shock played a role." He smiles. "Me calling him Gramps probably didn't help the situation either. I don't think grandfather was a title Crew expected to take on so soon. You're a lot like him, and he's so proud of that. I also think it makes it hard for him to separate his choices from yours sometimes. A lot of factors went into his decision to come back here, but most of it was you. He wanted to see this"—he gestures to my office—"in person. Wanted the relationship with you that we'd both hoped for with our dad. Finding out you had kept a big secret from him—as your dad *and* your boss—rattled Crew a bit. Made him feel like a failure in both roles. It's a hard moment as a parent, feeling like your child doesn't need you anymore, no matter how proud you are."

I pick up a pen on my desk and spin it around one finger. "You're still my uncle right now, right?"

This might be business-related, but it's not something I'd ordinarily ask my boss.

"Right," he says slowly, glancing at the couch. "Should I sit back down for this?"

I smile. "No. It's not bad. I just … Dad brought me this cosmetics company as a possible acquisition right when I started working here. Things started out strong. We made a solid pitch, and they seemed interested. And then I got … distracted, and things went quiet for a while. They've met with other companies; we're not the only ones interested. I had my team set up a meeting next week, so I know they're still considering us. But it's very possible, maybe even likely, that this deal won't get over the finish line. I could go higher with our offer, but that's a bigger risk. I'm not even sure this company is worth what we're offering now. So, I—what?"

"Sorry." Oliver coughs, but it doesn't totally disguise his laugh. "Sorry, I just …" More laughter. "I can't believe he Brock'd you and didn't tell me."

I frown. "Brock'd? What does that mean?"

Oliver chuckles a few more times before answering, "My first week at Kensington Consolidated, your grandfather gave me a company to look into. Brock Pharmaceuticals. They had decent earnings, solid financials, no red flags anywhere. So, I acquired them. Took us ten years to see any profit."

"So, my dad gave me this company to *not* acquire them?"

Oliver chuckles again. "He wants to see what decision *you* make. A deal might be the right call. Or it might not be. It's *your* call. Crew gave you that company because he expects you to be the next CEO of Kensington Consolidated, Kit. So do I. Trust your instincts, and you'll be fine."

I nod. "I will."

He turns to leave, then glances back. "Your grandfather knows about the, er, situation, by the way."

"Which one?" I ask warily.

"Knowing Hanson, they probably both do. But Arthur, definitely."

"Dad told him?" I'm a little relieved that I won't have to. But I'm guessing Grandpa will make me pay for not being the one to inform him by making our first conversation about the topic especially uncomfortable.

Oliver barks a laugh. "No, Crew was definitely intending to have you be the one to handle that discussion with Dad. Dad was the one who told *me*."

"Then how did Grandpa find out?"

"My guess? He worked in this building for forty-three years. He hired half the people who have offices on this floor, and all of them are gossips."

I groan. "Wonderful."

I knew it was inevitable the news would spread through the company, but I didn't realize it was already circulating.

"He asked if it's a girl or a boy."

"Oh." Not the question I would have guessed my grandfather asked. "We're, uh, waiting to find out."

Oliver smiles. "We waited too. I'm looking forward to meeting him or her, even if it does make me feel *extremely* old to have a nephew with a kid of his own."

I smile back. "Thanks, *Great-Uncle.*"

"I'm back to being your boss, Kit," he says, then walks out of my office.

CHAPTER 44
Collins

I count the binders one final time, releasing a relieved exhale when I confirm they're all accounted for. Printing the exhibits for the deposition, sorting them, and then organizing them in these binders took me most of last week. If one magically went missing, I'd no longer have time to procure a replacement.

I place a binder at each attorney's spot, then stack the extra legal pads and pens at the end of the table so those are available if necessary. Everything's arranged and accounted for; plus, I'm running ten minutes ahead of schedule. I release a relieved exhale, turn toward the

conference room door, and freeze.

Isaac appears equally stunned to see me, abolishing any possibility that he intentionally tracked me down. He's wearing a wool coat, his face ruddy from cold, like he just walked in off the street.

We stare at each other. His hair is shorter, and he has a trimmed beard.

"Hi, Collins." He speaks first, adjusting his already-straight tie as he does.

"Hello, Isaac."

More staring.

I'm surprised to see him, but it's a dulled shock. The energy necessary to sustain it is already dissipating. I don't care that he's here. And I don't care that I don't care.

"You-you work here?" He glances around the empty conference room.

"Yes."

Isaac expected me to elaborate more. Watching him flounder for something else to say is entertaining.

"I'm here for the Handler deposition," he finally states.

I nod.

I didn't pay close attention to the name of the firm representing the defendant. But even if I had recognized Isaac's employer, I'm not sure it would have occurred to me he was one of the lawyers they were sending, even knowing he's working in New York now. His firm is as large as Bradford, Nash, & Monroe is. The chances of us crossing paths were minuscule.

It's strange, seeing him. At all, but especially in New York. This city has changed me. I'm a different person than I was when I left Chicago. Stronger maybe, but not in the obvious ways. I'm more secure in myself, confident in my choices. I don't worry about picking right.

"I was looking for the restroom, walked past, and saw you in here," he explains. "I wasn't, uh … wasn't expecting to see you." Isaac yanks his tie again. He's nervous and uncomfortable, and I'm unbothered. "I'm sorry, Collins. You never really gave me a chance to say that—"

I snort, letting a little snark slip out. "Well, you were busy getting dressed in my boss's office. It didn't seem like the right time for a lengthy explanation."

Isaac scratches his beard. "Right. Yeah. I am sorry though."

"I've got work to do." I start toward the doorway he's blocking, not realizing one of the chairs was concealing my bump until Isaac's eyes fall and widen.

I'm wearing one of the cute maternity dresses Scarlett and Lili bought me, which highlights my new curves rather than hides them.

"Wow. I—wow. You moved on fast."

The words are offensive. But his tone is defeated. A flat tire in vocal form.

"You made it easy."

Even if he hadn't cheated, I don't think it would have been hard. I liked Isaac, but I never loved him. I know that for sure now, having experienced the real thing.

Isaac sighs. "I know."

I wait, but he doesn't move.

"You're blocking the doorway," I state.

"Oh. Right. Sorry." He steps to the left, clearing the exit. "For whatever it's worth, I regret it, Collins. I really, really regret it."

I glance at him, ensuring he sees my sincerity. "I don't."

Then walk away.

I'm midway through a sonata when I hear the front door open and close. My heart leaps as my hands stay steady. My fingers keep finding the right keys, but I press the pedal a second too late. Then I hear his steps approaching the living room and rush through the final lines on the page so I can turn around and see him.

His suit jacket is tossed on the back of the couch, and he's rolling up the sleeves of his button-down.

"Hey," I say, my voice high and embarrassingly breathless. "You're home."

"I'm home," he confirms, finishing one sleeve and starting on the other. "Top or bottom?"

"Top," I decide. "I was bottom last night."

" 'Kay." He presses a kiss to the top of my head, then leans over me to reach the keys. He cycles through the opening chords of "Heart and Soul" twice before I chime in with the accompaniment in the higher octave.

Our rendition lasts a few minutes longer than it did during yesterday's session. When Kit asked me to teach him a song on the piano, I thought we'd attempt a couple of lessons, and he'd eventually lose interest. But it's our routine now. As soon as he comes home, we play something together. My favorite part of the day now.

"Way to carry the team," he tells me, setting an elbow on the stand and covering a yawn with his hand.

"You didn't mess up a single note," I reply as I lean closer, resting my head against his shoulder. "You're home late."

"I know, sorry. I was going over reports and lost track of time."

"It's fine. I just missed you."

"I missed you too. April hasn't figured out the right sorting system for my reports yet."

I roll my eyes. "How sad for you."

He chuckles, tucking a piece of hair behind my ear. "How did the deposition go?"

I tense a little. "It was, uh, fine."

"Fine? That's it? You've been talking about those binders for the past two weeks."

"The binders were perfect. It was—Isaac was there."

"Isaac? Your *ex*, Isaac?"

"Yeah. He was one of the attorneys on the other side. I ran into him in the conference room beforehand."

"He came all the way to New York for a deposition?" Kit asks.

"No. He lives here now. He transferred offices from his firm's Chicago location to New York back in the fall."

"You guys really caught up, huh?" Kit's tone is careful, measured, and I can't tell what he's thinking at all.

I straighten so I can see his expression. Also controlled. "Actually, I knew about the transfer already. His friend's girlfriend texted me months ago about it."

"Months ago?"

I nod. "Halloween."

He hesitates before asking, "Is that why you were really upset that night?"

"No. I—*no*. Maybe I should have mentioned it, but that's not why I was upset. I wasn't thrilled, knowing he was moving here, but I figured the chances of us ever running into each other were … slim."

Kit rubs a thumb along his jaw. "Not *that* slim, apparently."

"I'm only telling you because you asked about my day and he was part of my day. No other reason."

"What did you guys talk about?"

"Not much. He wasn't expecting to see me either. He apologized. Said he regretted how things ended."

Kit scoffs.

"I told him I didn't because I don't. I don't think we would've worked out in the long term, even if he hadn't cheated. But I'm not sure I would have moved to New York if he hadn't cheated—at least not when I did, and I'm *really* glad I moved to New York when I did."

"You mean that?"

I stare at Kit, taken aback by the uncharacteristic uncertainty in his voice. "Yes. Of course I do."

"You wouldn't change *anything,* even if you could?" he presses.

"Well, I'd probably change how I acted on New Year's Eve. And tell you about the paternity test differently and also the—"

"I meant the big stuff, Collins. Moving here. Changing jobs. The pregnancy. It's just me. You can be honest. *Be* honest."

"I wouldn't change any of it, Kit," I tell him sincerely. "I chose to stay pregnant, and I've never regretted it. I love living here, with you, and I'm especially fond of your piano and shower. I feel good about work, and if that changes, I'll figure something else out. And I'm so sorry if I've made you feel like—"

Kit presses a finger to my lips, cutting me off. "Don't apologize. You haven't. But we were talking about your life in Chicago, and I was thinking about what you said at that dinner, about all the ways my life was going to change if I was involved." He exhales. "Yours has—*will*—too, and I want to make sure you … I just … I want to *give* you things, Monty. Not take options away. Not have you stuck, making the best out of a situation you didn't want."

"I want it," I assure him. "I want all of it." I reach for his hand, threading our fingers together. "You've given me everything I could ever want."

He squeezes my hand.

"How was *your* day?" I ask.

Kit groans. "Well … it turns out, Beauté was some sort of test. That's why I'm home so late. I went over all their files again to see if I'd missed anything."

I frown. "A test? What does that mean?"

"That my dad has a twisted sense of humor. Apparently, my grandfather did the same thing to Oliver. Float a questionable company, then leave it to him to decide whether to make a deal or not."

"What did Oliver do?"

"He made the deal."

"And was that the right call?"

Kit hesitates before responding, "It wasn't the wrong call. But I think he'd pick differently now if he could."

"Do you know what you're going to do?"

"Not yet. Levi set up a meeting with Beauté for next week. I'll see how that goes before making a final call."

I nod. A second later, my stomach growls.

"You haven't eaten yet?"

"I was waiting for you," I admit.

"Come on." He stands, steadying me as I move as gracefully as I can maneuver at seven months pregnant.

Even once we're walking toward the kitchen, he doesn't drop my hand.

CHAPTER 45
Kit

Flynn's standing between the elevator bank and Maya's desk, laughing with Asher, when I leave for the day.

"Hey, Kit," Asher greets, his standard smile still in place. Asher Cotes has been my dad's best friend for as long as I can remember. For longer than I've been alive. He's my dad's Flynn, I guess. Asher and his family were at the Thanksgiving gathering my parents hosted, but I haven't seen him around the office as much as I expected to. His role at the company is focused on Kensington Consolidated's international interests and involves a fair amount of

travel as a result.

"Hey, Asher," I reply, accepting his offered hand and slap on the back. "Haven't seen you around much."

Asher nods somberly. "I try to remain a man of mystery. Although not as much as you, from what I hear."

"You mean, the secret baby?" Flynn asks. "How did you find out? Because my best friend waited five months to casually tell me at a bar, 'I'll have a kid pretty soon, so we won't get to do this as often.' "

I grimace. I blew baby announcements all around.

Asher laughs. "I found out from *my* best friend at six a.m.—I was in Shanghai—freaking the fuck out about a box he had seen."

I sigh. "I was *going* to tell him."

"If it makes you feel any better, I'm not sure anything was going to cushion that surprise," Asher says. "Nice talking to you, Flynn. I'm home for the next couple of weeks, so I'll stop by your office soon, Kit. Catch up more."

"Sounds great," I reply. "See you then."

"Good talking to you too, Asher," Flynn says.

Asher heads for his office.

I continue toward the elevators, Flynn falling into step beside me.

"I was on time," I tell my best friend.

Flynn's lips quirk. "I noticed."

"I thought we were meeting at the bar."

We reach the elevators, so I press the Down button.

"We were," he agrees. "But I wanted to see if your new assistant is as hot as your old one."

I scowl as we step inside the elevator and start to descend.

"Relax. I'm kidding. Well, not about Collins being hot. That part is—"

"Are you *trying* to piss me off?"

Flynn blows out a long breath. "I'm bored, okay? All I had to do today was meet you, so I was early."

We're both silent for a minute. A silence exacerbated by the enclosed space.

"I'm really sorry, Flynn," I say. "I know I've been a shitty friend lately. There's just been … I've had a lot going on."

I'm sure Flynn expected this year to be a continuation of the summer. Us living in the city, partying on the weekends, and taking trips whenever we felt like it. We were each other's wingman, sidekick, and comrade … until I got a new partner. And I've been so preoccupied with everything else that I haven't taken the time to look at things from Flynn's perspective. This is only the second time we've hung out since I told him about Collins and the baby.

"It's fine. Don't apologize. I get it."

"I *am* apologizing, man. Seriously. I've sucked lately as a friend, and I'm sorry."

"We're cool, Kit," he insists.

"Should I text Camden?" I ask. "Or did you drive?"

"I walked," Flynn tells me.

I stare at him. "For real?"

Flynn lives on the Upper West Side. About thirty blocks from here.

He shrugs a shoulder. "I told you, I had some free time."

I pull out my phone to text Camden. "We need to get drinks somewhere with decent food. I worked through lunch, so I'm starving."

In a very nonchalant, very non-Flynn manner, he tells me, "I'm good with whatever."

"Rino's?" I suggest, referring to his favorite hole-in-the-wall pizza place.

"That's for takeout. Nowhere to sit and eat."

"We can get takeout and bring it back to my place?" I suggest. "I've got plenty of booze there."

"Isn't that a non–bachelor pad now?"

"Doesn't mean we can't eat pizza and drink scotch. Plus, Collins is going out to dinner with Lili and some other friends tonight. She won't be home until later."

"Okay," Flynn agrees, but it's still lacking his usual enthusiasm.

This is more than me being absent lately. Something else is going on, but I don't get the chance to press him on it before the town car appears to pick us up.

Thanks to some construction and a pizza detour, it takes twice as long as usual to get home. I thank Camden once we're finally in the garage, letting him know I'm planning to drive in to work tomorrow.

When I glance back at Flynn, he's entirely still, staring at the bay where my cars are parked.

"What is *that*?"

I sigh, immediately knowing what he's spotted. "They're really practical for kids."

"Kid*s*, plural? I thought you were only having the one."

"We are. But I figured, eventually, we'll probably have another. And even for one, they're great. Do you have any idea how much stuff babies need? Car seats and strollers and diapers and wipes and—"

Flynn is staring at me, slowly shaking his head.

"You can watch movies in the back," I say, which is probably the only feature he'll appreciate.

Sure enough, he gives the silver minivan a second glance. "Glad it has *something* going for it."

I press the button for the elevator with my elbow, balancing the pizza boxes.

"Seen your sweary neighbor lady lately?" Flynn asks.

"I saw Edna this morning actually," I reply. "She'll be bummed she missed you."

He chuckles as we step on the elevator. The smell of oregano, garlic, and cheese fills the confined space immediately, making my stomach rumble.

"Can you hold these?" I ask, passing the pizzas to Flynn once we're in the hallway of the top floor.

I locate my keys, unlock the door, and hold it open for him.

"Huh," Flynn says, glancing around the entryway. "It looks the same."

I laugh. "What did you expect? She'd paint the whole place pink, then toss around some glitter?"

"I dunno. I've never lived with a chick before."

"Here. I got those." I take the boxes back from Flynn and carry them into the kitchen. "What do you want to drink?"

"Whatever you're having," he calls back.

I drop the pizzas on the island and continue to the bar cart in the living room, fixing two glasses of scotch.

When I walk back into the kitchen, Flynn's standing in front of the fridge. He's staring either at the playing card that's still taped to the front or the sonogram hanging next to it.

"Kid looks just like you," he says, glancing over his shoulder as I approach. "Gray and fuzzy."

"I've gotten that a few times." I hand him his drink. "Cheers."

We clink glasses.

I take a sip.

Flynn chugs the contents in one go.

I lift an eyebrow. "Are you going to tell me what's bugging you now or wait till we've had a few of these?" I ask.

He reaches for one of the pizza boxes, flipping it open and pulling a slice out.

"I got into Harvard Law."

"Congrat—"

"And construction on the new Parks Student Center starts in Cambridge this spring."

"Oh," I mutter.

His father's ultimatum might have been the only reason he applied, but I know how badly Flynn wanted to get into law school on his own merit. Or at least feel like he did.

A donation large enough to fund a new student center? Wipes that out completely.

"I'm sorry, man."

"It's fine. I should've fucking seen it coming." He takes a large bite of pizza, chews, and swallows. "Did Rory get in?"

I clear my throat. "Yeah, she did."

"Figures."

"You don't have to go to Harvard, Flynn. Or go to law school at all. Train for a marathon. Go parasailing. Write a book. Do something *you* want to do."

Flynn scoffs. "He'll cut me off."

"Let him."

"Easy for you to say. You're a Kensington. My dad might not be a billionaire, but he has enough to miss. I'm used to being rich. I *like* being rich, Kit."

I laugh, and he rolls his eyes.

"Yeah, yeah. My life's one big joke."

"I hate to state the obvious, but you could get a job and support yourself."

"Doing *what*? You know me. I'm good at …"

"Partying and getting laid?"

He tosses his crust toward me. He used to pitch, so it bounces off my chest. "I feel *much* better now. Thanks for the awesome pep talk."

"Okay." I rest my elbows on the marble counter, turning serious. "So, you go to Harvard Law, keep your trust fund, and everyone knows your dad bought your way in. Is that really so bad? Same result."

"No one's going to question Rory's credentials. Or say she's only there because of her last name." He glances at me. *"Don't* tell her I said that."

"You have seriously got to be the only person who doesn't get along with her."

"She's annoying."

"She's *nice*. Try it sometime."

Flynn rolls his eyes. "You really think I should go?"

"Do you *want* to go? Setting aside all the shit with your dad?"

He's silent for a minute, then sighs. "Yeah, I think I do. It's what I always figured I *would* do, like you and Kensington Consolidated."

I smile. "I'll miss you when you move to Boston."

"We'll probably see each other the same amount." He sighs. "Sorry. That was a shitty thing to say. I had a bad day, and my dad isn't answering any of my calls, so I can't take it out on him. I think it's cool that you're doing the dad thing, and I'm going to be more supportive about it, starting … right now."

I grin. "Great. Wanna see the nursery?"

Flynn rubs the back of his neck. "Uh, sure?"

When we walk inside, his enthusiasm turns genuine. "Holy shit.

This is awesome."

I glance around proudly. "Nice, right?"

The stars above the crib were added last week. The outer-space mural behind it is perfect. And the rocking chair my dad brought over is in the corner, by the window.

Flynn sprawls out on the rug, studying the ceiling. "I thought you didn't know what you guys were having."

I take a seat next to him, tilting my head back and resting on my palms. "We don't."

"Doesn't space seem boy-themed?"

"No. Girls can be astronauts too."

"I know they can. I just thought maybe you secretly knew what you were having and just weren't telling anyone."

"Collins wants it to be a surprise."

"And you don't?"

"I'd probably find out," I allow. "Just because I'm impatient to know. But it's her call."

"It's your kid too."

"Yeah, but she's the one who's having to grow it for nine months and then push it out. She gets final say."

Flynn considers that. Then agrees, "Yeah, that seems fair."

"Should I buy a cosmetics company just because I can?" I ask.

"Absolutely," Flynn replies.

"Damn." I exhale. "I shouldn't."

"Because I said it was a good idea?"

"Pretty much."

And we both start cracking up, staring up at the ceiling of my kid's room.

CHAPTER 46
Collins

"Y"ou're *sure* you don't want me to come?" Kit stretches the word *sure* so long that it sounds longer than the rest of the sentence combined.

"I'm sure," I confirm. "I need to do this on my own. And if it goes poorly, I probably won't spend the night. You won't even notice I'm gone."

He snorts at that. "Impossible."

"It's not that far. I'll be fine."

"Exactly. It's not that far. Which is why Camden should drive you."

"But then I can't spend the night."

He clicks his tongue, subtly calling me out on being difficult. "We could invite your parents here next weekend."

"I don't want to have *this* conversation with my dad here. My mom said he'll be on campus most of the weekend as part of this lecture series. It's the perfect opportunity to talk to him without her overhearing and wondering what's going on."

"Perfect opportunity, *except* you're eight months pregnant," Kit counters.

"Do you not still think I should ask him about it?"

He sighs. "No, I do."

"Then let me do this. I promise if I wasn't feeling up to it, I wouldn't go. Pregnant women have driven themselves to the hospital in labor."

"Well, let's avoid *that*."

I smile. "My point is, I can handle driving two hours three weeks before my due date."

He studies me, then nods. "Okay. Call or text me when you get there. And after you talk to him."

"I promise." I rise up on my tiptoes to kiss him. "I love you."

"I love you too. And, Collins?"

"Yeah?" I pause with the minivan door open.

I still think it's entirely ridiculous that he bought one, but it feels a lot more manageable to drive than his other fancier cars.

"Be careful," he tells me. "You have my whole world in that car."

My nose starts to sting. I sniff, managing a smile. "I will be."

I spend the drive to New Haven rehearsing what I'm going to say to my dad. I only have one question really.

Why?

I want to know *why*. *Why* has eaten away at me for three years. *Why* reduced my relationship with my dad to rare correspondence. Maybe that would have happened anyway as I grew older and my life naturally separated from my childhood.

But I resent how that separation wasn't entirely natural. That I forced it because I was mad and disappointed and didn't know how else to process seeing my dad kiss a stranger.

I have control over what I say during this conversation. But I've honestly never given much thought to what my dad's answer to that question would be. And I'm trying to prepare for every possibility now. Was it a mistake? A full-blown affair?

Does my mom know?

Did he ever wonder if I knew?

I guess I have more than one question. But his answer to *why* will determine if I ask any others.

Today isn't very warm, but there are signs of spring appearing all over Yale's campus. Flowers blooming. Birds chirping. Grass growing.

I park in the closest spot to the science building I can find, letting out a happy sigh when I can finally unbuckle the seat belt that's been chafing at my belly.

I should have done this sooner. But I've been putting it off and putting it off, waiting for one day when I magically felt ready to confront my father. And it wasn't until I realized I was running out of time to do so before becoming a mom that I finally found the courage to come here.

I want this new chapter of my life to include my dad. I'm sick of holding this barrier between us, but I can't remove it without acknowledging why it was there in the first place.

I text Kit, letting him know I made it safely. He replies immediately, even though he's hanging out with Flynn today.

Walking across campus feels strange. I haven't been back since my graduation, and I wasn't expecting my next visit to be until Jane's ceremony.

I'm breathing heavily by the time I reach the main doors leading into the science building. I remember coming here as a kid, pointing up at the molecules models hanging from the ceiling in the atrium. They don't look so big now.

I opt for the elevator over the stairs, even though it's only two floors.

The walls of the hallway are papered with research papers and presentations. I don't have to read any of the nameplates to know which office to stop outside. My dad's never moved, even when larger offices with "better" locations opened up.

I suck in two deep breaths before knocking.

"Come in."

I'm hit with a heady mixture of relief and panic when I realize he's here. Coming all this way to find an empty office wouldn't have felt like a success. But realizing this conversation is actually about to take place is … scary.

My dad's focused on the papers on his desk. When he glances up, he does a double take, then straightens his glasses. He stands suddenly, alarm stamped on his face. "Collins. Is everything—what are you doing here?"

"I came to talk to you," I state, closing the door and walking— waddling—over to one of the chairs facing his desk.

"Oh, I—let me get that for you." My dad hustles around his desk, clearing the stack of papers off the chair. "I wasn't expecting guests."

"You need a better organizational system," I huff, lowering myself slowly into the chair.

My dad frowns as he sits back down behind his desk. The leather squeaks in protest. "Are you—is Kit with you?"

"No. I wanted to come alone."

"Did you come to visit Jane?"

"I'm here to see you, Dad." I inhale another deep breath, deliberating how to broach the awkward topic.

"Did something happen? Is something wrong?"

I exhale. "Isaac cheated on me."

My dad blinks rapidly. "What?"

"That's why we broke up. It wasn't mutual, like I told you and Mom. He cheated on me, so I left Chicago and moved to New York."

"I'm sorry—"

"I don't want you to be sorry about Isaac, Dad. I want to know why you did the same thing to Mom."

Understanding finally breaks across his face. He clears his throat, taking his glasses off and setting them on his cluttered desk.

My fingers curl, clenching into fists. There's a sharp pain in my chest, my breaths becoming more labored as I realize maybe he's not going to offer any explanation. That I'll have to continue *knowing* this with no resolution, except my dad knowing I know.

"I saw you. Senior year, I saw you. I was going to the library, and I came by here to see you, and you were … kissing some woman in the lab across the hall."

Even after a Connecticut winter and with Irish ancestry, my dad manages to grow paler. "Collins—"

"*Why* would you do that, Dad? *How* could you do that?"

He exhales. "It was a mistake."

I snort. "No shit."

"It was a weak moment, Collins. I have failings and regrets, and I've made mistakes. I wish I didn't. I wish I *hadn't*."

"Does Mom know?"

He exhales. "Yes. I told her … a few months after it … ended."

I swallow hard, deliberating how many details I want to know. "Who was she?"

"A visiting professor. She was only here for a semester. We had a connection, and there were a few times it crossed a line. I told your mother, and we moved past it."

"You sleep in separate bedrooms."

"Collins, I love your mother very much. That doesn't mean that there aren't rough patches. Times when I've hurt her. Times when she's hurt me. Marriage isn't—*relationships* aren't only about who you want to spend the happy moments with. Birthdays and holidays and vacations are usually easy. You can get through those with just about anyone. It's about who you want next to you in the hard times. At funerals and in hospitals. Who you're willing to stick it out with when things get messy and painful and confusing."

I chew on my lower lip. "I didn't think Mom knew. I've been carrying this around, scared if I said anything, it would ruin everything."

"Honey." He rubs at his eyes. It takes me a few seconds to realize that my father is crying. "I'm *so* sorry, Collins. I had no idea that you knew. If there's anyone you hope will think you're infallible, that you don't make mistakes, it's your children. I never wanted you or Jane to know anything about this."

I release a shaky breath. "Did you think Isaac would cheat? Is that why you didn't like him?"

"No. If I'd thought that, I would have been more vocal in my objections. I found Isaac … condescending, among other things."

"But you like Kit."

"Yes." Dad smiles. "I like Kit a lot."

"Because …"

"Because I have a feeling he's the reason you're here."

"He encouraged me to talk to you," I admit. "But I'm really here because I … because I miss you. You didn't just hurt Mom. You hurt me. You'd hurt Jane if she knew about it. And I never understood how you could do that. Especially *now*." I rest a hand on my bump.

"It was a mistake," he tells me again. "I know that's an awful explanation, and I'm not trying to make excuses. I've tried my best to make amends, and if I'd known you—I wish you'd told me sooner. But I'm glad you did now. And I hope—" His voice catches. "I hope, one day, you'll find a way to forgive me."

I stare down at my lap. Or what used to be my lap. All I can really see these days is my stomach. "Are you … busy right now?"

"No," he answers quickly.

"I need to use the restroom. But after, maybe we could go get lunch?"

He nods. "I'd love that, Collins."

"Okay." I hoist myself up, wincing when my abdomen cramps. Still protesting the drive here, I guess. Standing helps some. "I'll be right back."

I leave my bag in my dad's office, heading down the hall to where I remember the restroom being. All three stalls are empty. I pee quickly. When I walk back toward the sink, another cramp hits.

I cross the last couple of feet, gripping the sink counter and forcing myself to take deep breaths as I stare down at linoleum. The tightening ends, and I relax. I wash my hands, reaching for a paper towel at the same moment my abdomen contracts again.

I bite down on the inside of my cheek until I taste the copper tang of blood in my mouth.

Fuck, this *hurts.* Panic claws at the inside of my chest when I have to grip the counter again. These must be Braxton-Hicks, right? May 18 isn't for three more weeks. The pain increases instead of decreasing. There's no clock in here, and I'm too stressed to remember what the different intervals mean.

I'm two hours from home. From my doctor. From Kit.

I'm two hours from Kit.

My chest feels too tight, like it's shrinking while my lungs are expanding. If I'm not in labor, I'm certainly having a panic attack.

The door swings open, and a girl texting walks into the restroom. She looks young, probably a freshman or a sophomore, and blanches when she sees me panting next to the sink.

"Professor Tate," I gasp. "Can you get Professor Gerald Tate? His office is just …" A groan interrupts me. "Down the hall."

The girl nods and flees.

Another contraction hits, and I double over. I shouldn't be this in labor, this fast, right? It takes some women hours—days—to give birth. I *really* don't want to be one of those human-interest pieces—woman gives birth in an elevator or a restaurant or a parking lot. I want a normal birth that makes a boring story. In a hospital bed, surrounded by sterile equipment and trained medical professionals. And Kit. I really, *really* want Kit.

The bathroom door opens again.

"Collins?" My dad appears.

There's no sign of the girl. I don't blame her for fleeing. I wish *I* could flee.

"I think I'm in labor," I blurt.

I wait for my dad to tell me that's not the case. That it's too early and too soon and nothing's happening today.

He doesn't.

He says, "I'll drive you to the hospital," instead.

CHAPTER 47

Kit

"She's in labor." I say it as soon as my dad picks up. Before he has a chance to say *hi* or *how are you* or *happy Saturday.*

This is a *terrifying* Saturday.

"What?"

"She's. In. Labor." I switch lanes, ignoring the obnoxious honk as the person behind me protests.

"Now? At Manhattan General? Is the doctor there? What are they saying?" My dad fires the questions off rapidly.

"She's in Connecticut. She went to visit her dad, and I'm—" More honking. "I'm getting there as fast as I can."

I don't think there's a single traffic law I haven't broken in the ten minutes since I left Flynn's in a panic. Thank fuck I rarely have Camden drive me on the weekends because there's no way I could handle his version of *getting there fast*. And the town car's a lot slower than my Ferrari.

"Are you—fuck. Scarlett! What's the hospital in Connecticut? Do you need us to bring anything? Should we drive? Is there—"

"I don't need you to bring anything, Dad. I need you to tell me what the fuck to *do* once I'm there."

Silence follows. I think the call's dropped for a second.

"You called me for advice?"

"Yes! I'm freaking the fuck out, and I need to not be freaking out when I get there, so tell me it's going to be fine."

"It's going to be fine, son." There's a wobble to my dad's voice, but it grows steadier as he continues talking. "Just be there for Collins. You'll be able to tell what she needs. If you can't, ask. Focus on her. Focus on the moment, on what's about to happen. You won't want to forget what it's like, meeting your child for the first time."

"What if something goes wrong?"

"It won't," my dad says confidently. "Kid's a Kensington. It'll come out sturdy. And Collins is tough too."

"What is it? What's going on?" My mom's voice has joined my dad's, in the background.

"Do you want us to come to the hospital?" my dad asks.

Mom gasps. "Collins is in labor?"

"I'll let you guys know," I say. "Collins's parents are there with her. I'm not sure how big of a crowd …"

"Understood," Dad replies. "Just keep us posted, okay?"

"I will."

"I love you, son."

"I love you too, Dad."

I hang up, then press the accelerator harder. I make the remaining drive in just under an hour. Parking is an excruciating process as I force myself to drive slowly and scan for an open spot.

The New Haven hospital has countless entrances, and I have no clue which one is closest to the delivery room. I ask the first person I see wearing scrubs where to go for labor and delivery, and she directs me to the third floor. I give up on waiting for the elevator after a few torturous seconds, opting to sprint up the stairwell instead.

"Collins Tate," I say as soon as I reach the nurses' station. "Which room is she in?"

"Kit!"

I turn. Collins's mom is halfway down the hallway, waving at me.

I run in her direction.

"Thank goodness you're here," Amanda says. "She's been asking for you nonstop."

"Is she okay? What—"

"She's fine," Amanda says soothingly "But things are progressing quickly, and she was worried you wouldn't make it on time. I don't know what possessed her to come all the way here so close to her due date. Gerald and I would have been happy to visit New York ..." Amanda's voice trails off as Gerald steps out of one of the closed doors ahead.

His eyebrows are pinched tight together with worry, but it relaxes some when he sees me.

"You're here. Phew. I was getting worried." He holds out a hand, which I quickly shake. "That room." He points toward the door he exited.

I nod and rush toward it.

Collins covers her face with her hands and starts sobbing when I enter the room. She's alone, no sign of any doctors or nurses. She's also wearing a hospital gown, which freaks me out even though I know it's normal.

"I thought you'd be *happy* to see me," I tease, walking over to the chair pulled up by her bedside and kissing the top of her head.

"I-I am." She hiccups, reaching for my hand. "But aren't you"—sniffle—"mad at me?"

"Why would I be mad at you?" I ask.

"Because you told me not to come here, and I did, and now—"

"Did you talk to your dad?"

"Yeah," she whispers.

"Was it a good talk?"

Collins nods.

"Then I'm glad you came. A hospital room is just a hospital room, Monty. Here, in New York—doesn't really matter."

Her hand tightens around mine as she breathes heavily through a contraction. "I'm not ready, Kit."

"Yeah, you are."

"No, I'm not. I'm *really* not." She shakes her head rapidly, then winces, pressing her free hand against her swollen stomach. "I was supposed to have *three* more weeks. Twenty-one days. I needed that time. I'm supposed to *work* on Monday."

"You don't think you'll be able to?" I ask innocently.

She huffs, "Kit."

"You weren't going to magically feel ready in three weeks, Monty.

This part was always going to be extra scary. But you get through this, and we'll get to meet our kid. Focus on that part. This is the home stretch. You're so close to the finish line. Mile three, with only one-tenth to go."

"How did you know I ran cross-country?"

This time, I tell her the real answer. "You had some photos from your high school meets in your dorm room. I snooped around a little. I liked the short shorts."

She laughs, then flinches. "*Fuck*, this hurts. It hurts a lot. And I'm scared."

"I know. I am too." My thumb finds her pulse point beneath her wrist, the steady rhythm reassuring. "But you can do this."

She shakes her head wildly. "I can't. I can't. What if I really can't?"

"You *can*, Collins. You're the strongest person I know." I comb the sweaty strands away from her face. "This is it, okay? You just have to get through this last part, and then we get to meet our baby."

Another contraction hits. Collins's grip crushes my fingers.

"I should have listened to you. Dr. Bailey was supposed to be here, and I shouldn't have—"

"Hey, hey." I lean closer so our foreheads are almost touching. "None of that. Watermelon decided to come a little early, is all."

She starts crying again. "Watermelons are *huge*. I can't push a *watermelon* out. You've seen my vagina. It's not big enough!"

I focus on the bones breaking in my hand so I don't laugh. "It's a miracle, Monty. The miracle of life."

She snorts. "The inspiration crap is not helping."

I recall my dad's advice. "Tell me what will help."

"Nothing," she groans. "But try to distract me."

"Okay. Do you want my parents to come? They asked, but I wasn't sure."

"Your idea of distracting me is asking if your parents should come see me like *this*?"

"Right." I pull my phone out of my pocket. "I'll tell them not—"

"Do you want them here?"

"You're carrying the team here. I want to do whatever makes your load lightest."

She deliberates, then nods. "Tell them they're welcome to come. But you and my mom are the only ones allowed in the room."

My dad replies to my text approximately two seconds after I send it.

> **Dad:** On our way!

The door to the hospital room opens a minute later, and a doctor walks in.

"Hi, Collins. I'm Dr. Peach. Let's see how things are progressing, okay?"

Collins glances at me, and I'm already looking at her. We both laugh.

Dr. Peach looks confused.

"Sorry," I tell her. "Uh, inside joke."

"I don't see many couples laughing in the delivery room," she says. "It's nice to see."

I squeeze Collins's hand. She tries to break mine as another contraction hits. Dr. Peach jumps into motion, calling to a nurse with a request for certain supplies.

Two hours later, Dylan Crew Tate Kensington enters the world.

CHAPTER 48

Collins

"A nd this is where Mom and Dad met."

Dylan blinks at the brick exterior of Montgomery Hall, appearing suitably unimpressed by Kit's tour of campus.

"The disrespect." Kit shakes his head. "How could he not care about his family history?"

"He's three weeks old. His interests are pretty limited."

"Oh, look. A squirrel! Dylan, do you see the squirrel? Dyl—seriously?" Kit glances from the baby carrier to me. "He fell asleep."

"Good. Hopefully, he'll sleep through most of the ceremony. Speaking of which, we should get back to the tent."

"One more stop." Kit grabs my hand and pulls me over toward one of the benches that lines the path.

Jane's graduation is a perfect spring day, clear and warm and sunny. I tilt my head back and glance up at the canopy of green leaves overhead.

I take a seat on the bench, but Kit doesn't sit next to me. He starts to sink down on one knee, very slowly, and I *feel* my face freeze with shock.

Kit bursts out laughing, then spins and takes a seat. "Your face." He chortles.

I bang his knee with my own. "That was *not* funny. At all."

He's still laughing quietly, one hand cradling Dylan so he isn't disturbed by the shaking motion. "Sorry," he says, not sounding apologetic at all. "It's not a ring."

I take the black jewelry box he pulled out of his blazer pocket. Kit has used my first Mother's Day as an excuse for an endless parade of presents. "You didn't have to—"

"Shut up and open it, Monty."

I give him a look.

"*Please.*"

I do.

The bright sunshine reflects off the diamond earrings, creating rainbow prisms.

"I asked Lili, and she agreed they looked like you. Elegant and beautiful."

"I love them," I say sincerely, running a finger along the flawless surface.

"My mom said studs were more *practical* with the baby."

I smile at the way he emphasizes *practical*. I can't remember anything that's made me smile more than Kit's thoughtful teasing.

"Thank you." I turn my head to kiss him.

Kit groans, tangling his fingers in my hair to tug at the strands.

I'm exhausted. Tired down to my marrow from all the recent sleepless nights and still recovering from giving birth a few weeks ago. But I feel utterly content, at peace and at ease in a way I've never experienced before. I don't have everything figured out. And right now, I don't feel like I need to. I can just sit in this moment, on a bench in the sunshine, and appreciate the warm press of Kit's lips against mine.

He smiles when we separate, the corners of his eyes crinkling in a way that makes me wonder what Kit will look like in twenty years. Fifty.

"I would have said yes," I whisper impulsively, "if you'd asked."

Impossibly, Kit's grin stretches wider. "Don't ruin the surprise, Monty." He pulls another box out of his pocket, this one long and narrow. "This one's from Dylan."

I glance at our son, still fast asleep. "*Really?*" I drawl.

"Uh-huh. One of his limited interests is jewelry shopping."

I snort before opening the second box. It's a necklace with a simple chain and one round charm hanging from it. There's a tiny *D* impressed into the surface, formed from more diamonds.

"It's perfect," I tell him, rubbing the surface of the charm with my thumb. The metal is smooth, the gemstones slightly textured. "You add more charms for each kid?"

"That's the idea, I think. But it can be complete with just one."

"I think I'd like two," I say, studying it. "One looks a little lonely. But not for a couple of years. Or maybe longer."

"We can wait as long as you want," he tells me. "My hand could use some time to recover."

"Yeah, *your* body was really the one that suffered during labor," I say, lifting my hair and turning my head so he can clasp the necklace.

We stand and start to head back toward the tent where the graduation ceremony is taking place. Dylan wakes up halfway there, his adorable face scrunching as he fusses.

"Shh, it's okay," Kit tells him. "What are you complaining about? I wish *I* were getting carried around in this cool contraption. And it's way better than being stuck in Mom's belly, right? Did you want to watch Aunt Jane graduate? You won't get to if you keep crying. They'll kick us out of the tent. Maybe off this campus because you have a crazy pair of lungs on you, Dyl."

I'm smiling, listening to Kit talk when I hear my name called.

I turn, watching Professor Aldridge approach. She was my adviser for my music major. We kept in touch via email for several months after I graduated, but I haven't spoken to her in a couple of years now. And the last time we talked, I was a full-time pianist. I'm sure she'll be disappointed to hear that I'm no longer playing anything except lullabies.

"Hi, Professor Aldridge," I greet.

It feels strange to call her Leslie now that we're on much less familiar terms.

"It's wonderful to see you, Collins," she says, smiling.

"You too," I reply.

"Are you back for graduation?"

I nod. "My sister's."

"That's wonderful. How's everything else? Are you still in Chicago?"

"I moved to New York last summer," I tell her. "I needed a change."

"In cities? Or jobs?"

"Both," I admit. "I'm a paralegal at a law firm right now. Or I was. I'm on maternity leave at the moment." I glance toward Kit. He's paused with Dylan in the shade under a tree a little ways ahead, letting me have a moment. Mostly because Dylan is still crying and he's having to bounce him around.

"Oh my," Professor Aldridge says. "Your little one is adorable."

I smile. "Thank you. We think so too."

"Are you still playing?" she finally asks.

"Only for fun."

"Well, I'm not sure if this would be too much with everything else you have going on. But I have a friend in New York who's casting for a Broadway musical next spring. They'll have a full orchestral accompaniment, and I happen to know she's looking for a pianist. If you're interested, I can pass along your name and number. See if it might be a good fit?"

I glance at Kit again. I'm not sure he's standing close enough to overhear our conversation, but I know what he'd say if I asked him.

"That sounds great," I tell Professor Aldridge. "Please do."

She beams. "Wonderful. I will. It was lovely to see you, Collins."

"You too, Professor Aldridge."

"Leslie, please." One final smile, and she continues along the pathway.

I head for Kit.

"You booked a gig?" he asks, a wide, proud smile on his face.

"I maybe got an audition," I correct.

His smile doesn't falter. "That's amazing, Monty. I'm proud of you."

I rise up on my tiptoes, giving him a kiss—a *real* kiss, with tongue and everything—despite the fact that my parents are twenty feet away, waiting for us so we can all head to our seats.

Kit grins against my mouth as Dylan gurgles between us.

It's a perfect moment. Not one of the hard ones my dad alluded to. But I know Kit's who I want to stick those out with too.

CHAPTER 49
Kit

I'm pouring coffee into my mug when Collins stumbles into the kitchen.

I smile. "How's my baby?"

She yawns. "He's fast asleep. Must be nice."

"I meant *you*, Monty."

Lili pretends to gag, stabbing a piece of waffle. "I'm eating here. Can you not with the pet names?"

I hand Collins the mug, then fill a second one for myself, ignoring my sister. "You hungry?"

"Yeah." She yawns again, so I steer her over to the table by her shoulders and into a chair.

"Did you decide what you're wearing tomorrow?" I hear Lili ask Collins as I start to fix her a plate.

"No. But Dylan has these really cute striped overalls."

"Okay, then we're going shopping after breakfast," Lili says. "Blue will look best with your hair."

We're in the Hamptons for the Fourth of July. Tomorrow is my grandmother's annual Red, White, and Blue party.

"Can we go this afternoon?" Collins suggests as I set a plate down in front of her. "I was going to see if Kit wanted to go sailing this morning."

"Really?" I glance at her, startled.

Last I knew, her feelings about the ocean hadn't changed.

"Yeah." She bites her bottom lip, holding my gaze. "Your mom said she'd watch Dylan. But we don't have to if you don't—"

"Of course I want to. You're just … sure?"

I don't want her doing this for me.

Lili glances between us with open curiosity, but doesn't ask as Collins nods in confirmation.

"Where's Charlie?" Collins wonders.

"He's by the pool, talking to his grandmother," Lili replies.

"Has she warmed up to you yet?" I ask.

"We had tea last week, and she smiled a tiny bit when I said I was moving to Buckleby, so … progress?"

"You're moving to England?" Collins glances at me after asking the question, but I'm just as stunned.

Lili's smile is a little sheepish. "I wasn't sure how to tell you guys. It's going to *kill* me, being away from my nephew—"

"And your brother," I interject.

"But it's what makes the most sense right now. There's a museum in France that's looking for a landscape architect to redo their grounds, and it's a much shorter commute to England than it is back to New York. I'll keep my place here, of course, but won't be using it much." She half smiles. "I told Bash he could use it on his school breaks since Kit kicked him back to Mom and Dad's."

"Yeah, poor guy," I say sarcastically. "Slumming it in a six-story townhouse."

Lili laughs. "You guys will have to come visit. The estate is this cool old castle, and there's a pub in town and an ice cream shop—"

"*How* do you guys sleep through that crying every night?" Bash questions, entering the kitchen. His T-shirt is on inside out, and his hair is sticking out from every possible angle.

"We don't," I state.

Bash makes a face. "And that's … *normal*?" He sounds aghast.

"Yeah, for the first few months." At least, I *hope* it's only going to be the first few months.

"Sorry he kept you up," Collins says apologetically.

"It wasn't that bad," Bash replies. "But now that I know it's a recurring thing … I might have to buy earplugs for tonight."

"You can always go sleep at Gigi and Grandfather's," Lili suggests.

Bash groans. "Pass."

This is the first year we've stayed at our parents' house instead of our grandparents'. It's the first year our immediate family has expanded, me bringing Collins and Dylan, and Lili coming with Charlie.

We finish breakfast. Bash leaves to meet up with friends. Lili heads out to the pool. Collins and I get dressed in suits, which I assure her is entirely unnecessary because there's no chance we'll unintentionally end up in the water.

Collins transfers a sleeping Dylan into the carrier that doubles as a car seat, we pack up the endless array of baby necessities, and then I drive us to my grandparents' down the road. A parade of vehicles is headed in and out of the gates, party preparations already in full swing.

My parents are both waiting outside.

My mom literally bounces when I park.

My dad opens the back seat door before I have a chance to.

They're *obsessed* with their grandson. If my mom isn't dropping off dozens of new outfits for Dylan, my dad is stopping by to take "Crew Jr." for a stroller trip through the park.

I'll never forget the look on his face when I told him one of Dylan's middle names. He and Mom named Lili after the grandmother who never got to meet any of her grandchildren. I'm glad my dad got a chance to appreciate the tribute.

"Everything should be in there," I tell my mom, who's grabbed the diaper bag out of the trunk. "Pacifiers, toys, change of clothes—"

"We know; we know," she tells me, leaning over the car seat Dad's pulled out of the car to smile at Dylan. "We remember everything."

"He's gotten bigger, Red," Dad says. "Don't you think so? Look at those hands. He's going to be tall. And strong. Maybe a soccer player."

I exchange an amused look with Collins. My parents saw Dylan last night. He's growing fast, but not overnight.

"Okay, well, *great* to see you guys," I state. "Good talk. Really glad we had this quality time together."

Mom smiles. "You two have fun. He's in good hands."

Collins and I climb back into the minivan, and then we're continuing toward the marina.

It's warm out, but not as sweltering as it'll get later in the day. I turn the air-conditioning off and roll the windows down instead, letting the salty breeze sweep through the car. Collins sticks her right hand out the window, having her fingers surf the wind.

Unsurprisingly, the marina is packed. This weekend is undoubtedly one of the busiest of the summer. The busiest maybe.

I find a spot in the crowded lot. Collins glances around, wide-eyed, as we walk down the ramp and onto the floating docks. Her grip tightens on my hand as they shift under our feet, rocking with the currents of the water.

"Hey, isn't that Wren?" she says.

I follow her gaze, squinting through my sunglasses. Sure enough, my cousin is standing next to a Boston Whaler, arms crossed as she scowls at a guy whose back is turned to us. He's wearing the same polo shirt as all the marina employees, suggesting he works here.

"Yeah, it is."

"Should we go say hi?"

Wren's talking now, her ponytail swishing back and forth as she speaks passionately.

"Uh … doesn't look like a great time," I state. "She'll be at the party tomorrow. We can talk to her then."

Collins nods. "Okay."

We walk down to the end of the dock, where the dinghies are tied.

"What—*this* is the boat we're going out on?" she asks incredulously.

I smirk as I squat to untie it. "This is the boat we're taking to the boat we're going out on. Unless you want to swim?"

Collins chews on her lower lip, studying the small boat.

"We don't have to go out," I assure her. "We can go to the beach.

Or the restaurant here has really good lobster—"

"No, no. I want to." She takes a deep breath, then white-knuckles her way onto the rowboat.

I toss her a life jacket from the bag I brought. "Put that on."

She doesn't argue before slipping the straps over her shoulders and buckling it. She's more nervous than she's letting on, and nothing has ever felt more precious than that earned trust.

I toss the bag with the other life jacket on the scratched fiberglass, then climb in the back and pick up the oars.

Collins smiles as she watches me row out to the mooring.

I smile back. "What?"

"This is nice."

It *is* nice. It's also one of the few moments we've had alone together since Dylan was born. The weather, bright and sunny, matches my mood.

I jerk my chin to the left since both hands are occupied. "*That's* the boat we're taking out."

She turns to look at it. "We, as in just the two of us?"

"There's no crew waiting aboard, if that's what you mean."

"It's *huge*, Kit."

"Stop saying that to me, Monty. You're supposed to keep my ego in check, remember?"

I can't tell behind her sunglasses, but I'm positive she's rolling her eyes at me. I *can* tell she's blushing, and I love that I still have that effect on her.

"I can't sail," she tells me.

"Yeah, I figured. I promise your participation won't have to extend past holding a couple of ropes. Just relax and let me do all the hard work." I wink. "That was a sex joke."

"Thanks for clarifying."

I laugh as I work the left oar harder, drawing us even with the stern and folding the ladder down. "Up you go."

"What about you?"

"I'll meet you up there. I've got to untie the sailboat from the mooring and tie up the dinghy so we have a way to get back to shore."

"Okay."

Collins stands carefully, stepping over the bag and placing a foot on the lowest rung. She scrambles up quickly, the lines on her forehead relaxing when she's safely aboard. The sailboat is forty feet, roughly five times the size of the vessel we rowed out in.

I pass her the bag, then maneuver closer to the mooring ball, quickly sorting through the ropes so that the right boat is attached and the right one is untethered. I hoist myself up, using the metal railing, grinning at Collins. She's stretched out on the seat, watching me.

"Give me a sec, and we'll get moving," I tell her.

I started taking sailing lessons when I was five. Checking the bilge, stowing the swim ladder, taking the mainsail cover off, and raising the anchor are all second nature. I can focus on the feel of Collins's eyes on me instead.

"Wanna steer?" I call to her once the sails are straight and lines are taut.

Her reply gets lost in the wind, but she stands and makes her way over to me. Watching her walk *toward* me will never get old.

I move to the left so she can take my place at the wheel, guiding her hands to the proper position. "Don't hit anything."

She laughs, the happy sound only lasting for a few seconds before another gust of wind whips it away.

The marina is a distant dot behind us, nothing except sparkling blue ocean spreads ahead of us.

Collins rests her head against my shoulder, keeping her eyes on the water. My little rule follower, taking my warning seriously.

And then she arches her back, very deliberately pressing her ass directly across my crotch. "Does someone *have* to steer the boat?"

"Not if you want to stay straight."

She lets go of the wheel, turning around in my arms so she's facing me. " 'Kay. Let's stay straight."

Her hands find the hem of my shirt, pulling it up and over my head. It falls, hopefully on the deck rather than into the sea, but I don't bother to check. I'm too distracted by Collins's fingers, tugging on the laces holding my trunks together and then curling tight around my cock.

I grunt as her hand works, dizzy from the sudden burst of sensation.

And then, as if this day couldn't get any fucking better, she sinks to her knees and sucks me into the warm, wet heaven of her mouth.

My fingers thread through the strands that have escaped from her ponytail, glinting copper in the sunshine. The view surrounding us has nothing on the one below me.

Collins swirls her tongue around the head of my dick, swiping the slit at the tip before swallowing it slowly into her mouth again. I groan loudly when I hit the back of her throat.

"I'm going to come fast, Collins," I warn.

She withdraws, and I'm careful to keep the disappointment off my face when her hand doesn't replace her mouth. I don't want her to swallow, not if she doesn't want to. But I was craving the intimacy of her touching me when I came.

And then, after a quick scan of the clear horizon, she steps out of her shorts. Her bikini bottoms go next.

"Monty, we don't have to—"

"I want to," she assures me.

This isn't the first time we've had sex since Dylan was born. But it's *one* of the first times. Between sleep deprivation, attempting to get Dylan on a normal schedule, work, and the general chaos of life, there haven't been many opportunities that have felt right since Dr. Bailey gave Collins the all clear. We're more likely to fall asleep snuggling mid-show these days.

But if Collins *wants* to have sex? That's another story.

I scoop her up with one arm, swearing when she wraps her legs around my waist. I can feel how wet she is, the evidence of her arousal streaking against my stomach.

She giggles as I lay her on one of the bench seats, the rest of her hair escaping its elastic. I yank her tank top up, grimacing when I hear a *rip*.

"Kit!" she protests, but she's still laughing.

"You can wear mine," I promise, fumbling for the tie of her top next. It gives way more easily, freeing her breasts.

Collins moans loudly when I lick a line down the center of her chest. I focus on her left breast first, blowing on the damp stripe. She shivers and lifts her hips, seeking more contact.

"So impatient," I tease, moving to her right boob next.

"Fuck patience," she pants. "I want you to fuck *me*."

"I'm trying to be romantic, baby."

"Sex *is* romantic." Collins squirms again, trying to create more friction between our bodies.

I kiss her hard, memorizing the sound of her sexy whimpers when I suck on her tongue. Then I sit up, spreading her knees wide so I can stare at her swollen, glistening pussy.

She swipes her tongue across her lower lip, watching me look at her, and that shreds the remnants of my self-control. I fist my erection and line it up with her entrance. I only press a little at first, partly as a tease, partly to make sure she's really ready for me. I push in an inch, and she gasps, her cunt squeezing like she's trying to take more.

"You good?" I check.

"Yeah," she breathes. "It feels good. Really good."

I shove in and withdraw a few more times, fucking her with stilted thrusts to ensure she's really ready for more than just the crown.

"Kit, I swear to—"

The rest of her threat gets lost in a loud cry as I finally fill her the rest of the way.

I breathe deeply through my nose, trying desperately not to come instantly. The teasing wasn't only excruciating for her. Her pussy grasps me in a tight, hot, slick fist, pulsing and clenching.

"Still good?" I ask through gritted teeth.

The *sight* of her spread around me … fuck.

"Yeah. C'mere."

I settle over her, careful to keep most of my weight on my elbows. Her hands run up my arms and over my biceps, settling on my shoulders.

"I won't break. I need you to *fuck* me, Kit. Not like I'm a mom or someone you have soft, gooey feelings for. Pretend it's that night in your hotel room again, when we slept together the first time."

I grin. "I had soft, gooey feelings for you then, Collins. Did you seriously think I shared dry-cleaning tips with just anyone? Or made them a drink? Or—"

She digs her nails into my shoulders. "Stop talking."

My grin stays in place as my hand runs down her rib cage. I stretch even lower, finding her knee and settling it over my hip. "So, you don't want me to tell you how tight you are? How fucking incredible you feel?"

"That's allowed," Collins pants.

She's fluttering around me like crazy now, her thighs trembling. All her tells that she's close to coming.

I want to savor this, but I'm rapidly reaching a point where lasting isn't an option.

I imprint it all in my memory. The smell of the salt air. The white vinyl we're lying on, warm from the sun. Collins spread out under me, wild hair and pink lips and heaving chest.

I fuck her hard and fast, just like she asked for. A rapid rhythm that's edging into recklessness. A total loss of control.

I can still be rash. Immature and impulsive. All those traits Collins used to walk away from. But I think she needs them. I think they're the reason she's on this boat, trusting me to take care of her.

She comes with a sudden cry, calling out my name. The wind whisks that away, too, but not until I've heard how much she loves coming on my cock loud and clear.

I fuck her through her orgasm, then finally allow myself to let go.

We lie still and sated, both breathing heavily. I need to get up, check the sails and rigging and get Collins something to clean up with, but my body has no interest in moving yet.

"Isn't sailing fun?" I kiss her chest before pulling out and sitting up.

Collins sits up, too, a serious look on her flushed face. "I want to jump in."

I raise an eyebrow, reaching for the compartment where the clean towels get stored. "Now?"

"Now," she confirms. "You can slow the boat, right? Or stop it?"

"I mean, yeah …" I'm torn on how to react. Part of me is as thrilled as when she suggested sailing. But that felt like a first step toward getting her comfortable on the ocean. I wasn't anticipating it going so well that she'd decide to fully conquer her fear mid-trip. "Scale of one to ten, how much do you want to do this? Because you could wade in at the shore or something, and we could come out here again—"

"Ten," Collins states confidently.

"Okay." I pull out a towel and toss it toward her. Although, if she's swimming, that's not really necessary.

I yank my trunks on and walk over to the main boom, adjusting it so it's pushed against the wind and we're backwinding. Water laps against the sides, audible over the dwindling breeze.

Collins is peering over the edge, her bikini back on.

"Come back to the stern. That way, you'll be close to the ladder."

"Okay," she says, following me.

I glance at her. "Want a life jacket?"

Collins shakes her head. "I'm a good swimmer," she promises. "It's just been a while since I swam in the ocean."

When we reach the rear of the boat, she reaches out and grabs my hand. "You'll jump in with me, right?"

"Of course. If the boat drifts away, we'll just swim back to shore."

She casts me a half-exasperated, half-concerned look. "It's barely moving."

"I know. Boat will be here. You ready?"

Collins glances at the wavy surface, then to me. She's wearing the necklace and earrings I gave her, the diamonds glinting almost as brightly as the red in her hair. "I love you, Kit."

I tug her to me, planting a firm kiss on her lips. "I love you too."
She jumps first. But I'm right beside her.
Exactly where I always want to be.

The End

Acknowledgments

Kit's story is one I've looked forward to writing since I decided to continue the Kensingtons series into a second generation. He was the most fun I've had writing a character, ever, and I especially loved getting to craft his interactions with other Kensingtons and set up the remaining books in this series. (Hint, hint. :) And Collins was a uniquely special character to create. I unintentionally funneled a lot of myself into her, especially regarding career decisions and the uncertain post-college phase a lot of people experience. Their story turned out exactly how I hoped it would.

Megan, I feel so fortunate to have gotten your feedback on this book. Your insight was invaluable and improved this story so much! Thank you for your time and thoughts. I appreciate you so very much.

Sierra, your enthusiasm for this project was *exactly* what it needed. I was nervous about my first attempt at this trope, and this manuscript couldn't have been in better hands. Thank you so much for your input.

Sahara, I'm so happy *Fake Empire* brought us together. Your perspective on this story was so helpful and unique and the elevator scene was all for you. I'm so grateful for all you've done to support me and my books and feel lucky to have you in my corner!

Jovana, you never fail to deliver a thorough and thoughtful edit and I absolutely love working with you. Thank you!

Judy, thank you for being so delightful and considerate. It's always a pleasure working with you and I hope to do so on many more books!

Alison, thank you for another meticulous proof.

Books and Moods, for delivering the gorgeous green cover of my dreams. It's perfect for this story and I can't wait to collaborate on the rest of the series.

Katie and the entire team at Lyric Audiobooks, for all your hard work on the audiobook. Stephen Dexter and Vanessa Edwin, for voicing the perfect Kit and Collins.

All the readers who shared and supported and reviewed this story to help it reach as many people as possible, thank you so very much.

My family, for their endless love, support, and encouragement.

And last, but certainly not least, thank YOU for reading.

About The Author

C.W. Farnsworth is the author of numerous adult and young adult romance novels featuring sports, strong female leads, and happy endings.

Charlotte lives in Rhode Island and when she isn't writing spends her free time reading, at the beach, or snuggling with her Australian Shepherd.

Find her on Facebook (@cwfarnsworth), TikTok (@ authorcwfarnsworth), Instagram (@authorcwfarnsworth) and check out her website www.authorcwfarnsworth.com for news about upcoming releases!

Also by C.W. Farnsworth

Standalones
Four Months, Three Words
Come Break My Heart Again
Winning Mr. Wrong
Back Where We Began
Like I Never Said
Fly Bye
Serve
Heartbreak for Two
Pretty Ugly Promises
Six Summers to Fall
King of Country
Left Field Love

Rival Love
Kiss Now, Lie Later
For Now, Not Forever

The Kensingtons Duet
Fake Empire
Real Regrets

Kensingtons: The Second Generation
False God
Anti-Hero

Truth & Lies

Friday Night Lies
Tuesday Night Truths

Kluvberg

First Flight, Final Fall
All The Wrong Plays

Holt Hockey

Famous Last Words
Against All Odds
From Now On